MW00964937

FINDING HOME

Debra Mitchell

May 27/62

Dear Mary,

Thanks for your interest.

Enjoy,
Debbie Bellas Rubin

AmErica House
Baltimore

Copyright © 2001 by Deborah Bullas-Rubini.

All rights reserved. No part of this book may be reproduced in any form without written permission from the publishers, except by a reviewer who may quote brief passages in a review to be printed in a newspaper or magazine.

First printing

ISBN: 1-58851-088-3
PUBLISHED BY AMERICA HOUSE BOOK PUBLISHERS
www.publishamerica.com
Baltimore

Printed in the United States of America

For my Halloween baby

ACKNOWLEDGEMENTS

Stories have run around my head from my earliest memory. It only took about thirty years and a great man to dare me to write them down. To my husband Frank, who gamely endures living with me, putting up with the moods, and my constant distraction.

To my children,

Adam, who worried over me selling this book because he imagined there being only one copy and that I would miss having it.

Kyle and Julia, who while too young to really understand this process beyond the fact that it is time spent apart, miraculously love me anyway.

There are little bits of the three of you peppered through everything I do.

For Jim, the inspiration behind Charlie. Memories of you warm my heart everyday. When we meet again, I'll be sure and bring a copy.

This particular story, the emotion beyond the romance, was inspired by a journey I once took. One I wanted no part of but like so many other mothers had little choice in. Though there are no names, my heart felt thanks to the many women, with whom I have been privileged to sit with after the loss of their babies.

The story may originate in my mind alone but a book, I discovered, is made better by others. The generosity of my friends and colleagues to *willingly* read my first drafts and those beyond both stuns and humbles me. What you find in the story makes me glad I didn't keep it to myself.

Lastly to Helen, my mother and stalwart cheerleader, who gave me the most wonderful compliment when she read *Finding Home*. She was sorry that she had reached the end because she was going to miss the friends she had found in the book. There is little more an author can hope to hear!

PROLOGUE

He tunneled one hand through tousled dark hair as a smile quirked about his lips. Despite making a bona fide effort to smother his amusement, it was a slippery battle. Warm hazel eyes were filled with adoration as he gazed down at his naked wife. Full breasts showed the first hints common to her condition and he couldn't resist leisurely tracing one of the bluish trails with a fingertip. It was entrancing to watch her embarrassed flush color dewy cheeks.

Her tongue flicked over her upper lip before she worked up the courage to speak. "You don't think anyone heard?" She paused, drew an unsteady breath. "Do you?"

God, she was incredible. It was all he could do not to clasp her to his chest and shout with laughter at the self-conscious fretting. He could hardly believe someone like his young bride existed. There were absolutely no pretenses about her. Every response was so perfectly natural, unpracticed and blissfully foreign to his upbringing. He knew without a doubt that she was all he would ever need.

If he allowed it, fear could clutch at him mercilessly that today hadn't really happened. Worse still, that all the tomorrow's he dreamt for them might not happen either.

A sweeping glance about the attic bedroom steadied his pulse. Shadows still danced prettily against the faded rosebud papered walls as the multitude of mismatched candle stubs flickered erotically in the night. Bridal apparel was strewn everywhere. A testament to his feverish haste to get her out of all that finery. One white silken stocking lay draped over the dresser handle but his eye was drawn to the blue frilly garter that dangled foolishly from the spindle of the antique mirror. Working it down a shapely thigh with his teeth amid her nervous giggles would be a moment he long remembered.

The exquisite gown, that had him awestruck when she had appeared on the arm of his father earlier today, was now carelessly discarded in a heap with his suit pants pooled nearby. His lips curved. There indeed had been a wedding and even better, this was the honeymoon.

Her bottom lip started to quiver and huge brown eyes that never failed to captivate him gistened with the first sheen of tears. "You haven't answered. You do think someone heard? Don't you?" She pressed her face, heated with embarrassment, into his neck and clung. "I didn't mean to call out. God, did I really shout?" A sigh shuttered out. "You make me forget everything when

7

you touch me."

He had always believed himself suave with women but this one could humble him with a few mere words. He framed her face so their eyes were level. "Sweetheart, everyone knows what we are doing. Tonight of all nights." Woeful eyes searched his and he could swear that she possessed the ability to peer into his soul. He vehemently hoped that she liked what she saw there. After all she knew where he came from. Deliberately he sought to lighten the moment knowing that a great deal of her distress could be put down to hormones but a wise man never said that out loud. "And Sweetheart, every other married couple wants to be having this much fun at it!"

Compelling dark eyes flew wide as she swatted his chest. "Stop it! Having a man in my bedroom is new to me…"

A slow pleased grin spread across his lips because he did know just that. "Glad to hear it," he drawled lazily.

Rallying, she cast him an admonishing glance. "You know better than anyone that no other man has been in this bed!"

His smile turned smug. "I know, Darlin," he acknowledged huskily, sweeping her hair aside to nuzzle her neck. "Do you know that you make me beyond happy?"

Her smile was sweet. "Just what is *beyond happy* exactly?"

"*Everything!*" he promised hoarsely.

"I *love* everything," she breathed.

His eyes, dilated with desire, burned into hers. He planned on introducing her to everything in every way possible during their life together, starting now. His lips dipped to her breast and a sultry sigh escaped her. Growling his satisfaction that her inhibitions were so naturally dispensed of, he covered her more delicate body with his lean powerful frame in one careful movement.

One long fingered hand roughened from hard work reached between their bodies and splayed across her lower abdomen. It lingered there as emotion swamped him imagining what would be their reality in less than a year's time. His heart felt so full, it was near bursting. He smothered a laugh as it registered that other parts of his anatomy had similar aspirations. Urgent ones. He hastened to appease those primal desires as well as his gorgeous young wife. Beyond happy was a damned fine reality, he concluded, kissing her parted lips.

Once again, they were destined to give the rest of this household something to hear but he truly believed that no one in this welcoming house would be callous enough to listen.

The water glass slipped from her sweaty palm to roll unnoticed across the floor of the unfinished storage room as the reed thin figure of a woman crumpled weakly onto the rough planks. She clutched mindlessly at the wall stud in a pathetic bid for support. She simply couldn't listen to any more. This was a vile end to what had been an abysmal day.

Her almost bloodless upper lip twitched as the simpering twit's words reverberated unmercifully in her skull. "*'You don't think anyone heard? Do you?'*" She covered her ears with quaking hands in an attempt to obliterate the memory, rocking on her knees like a victim of torture.

The enormity of life's cruelty was mind-boggling. The undeserving bitch in the next room had everything she longed for and had been cheated of. Born from a tremendous sense of being wronged, she had pretended to embody the young bride and vicariously enjoy the sexual fulfillment her God-like groom had bestowed on the little witch a short while ago and was likely repeating now.

Unable to resist, she fumbled for the discarded water glass and positioned it once again next to the unfinished attic wall. Low moans and thready sighs tilted her senses on end. With her free hand, she touched her breast fantasizing larger smooth male hands were caressing there. She surrendered to the throbbing she felt between her thighs and saw him in her mind above her...reaching for her...wanting her...begging *her.*

A little throaty gasp escaped her lips as her panties grew damp. The ragged breathing intensified both through the glass and from her tight mouth as her own fingers pleasured in his stead. This would suffice for now. It had to. But eventually the pendulum would swing to its rightful position. She had been assured of it. And then she would have what should have been hers in the first place. A demented smile played on her thin lips as she silently vowed to do whatever it took to accomplish the deed.

CHAPTER ONE

Of all days, it seemed like today God was trying to fit forty days and forty nights worth of a deluge into one. Desperate, Sidney flicked the windshield wipers into their highest setting only to lower them once again when the hyper frenzy proved more distracting.

The torrential rain drummed relentlessly on the glass obscuring her view beyond the immediate few yards past the car. The storm was unrepentant and at another time she might have turned back. That was not an option today even though darkness was descending worsening what was already precarious. The drive had always been long but today's trip was tedious and something more Sidney was reluctant to put a name to.

Her other travels home during the past decade were always painstakingly planned holiday obligations or vacations. Today was no holiday and certainly no vacation. Besides, she reminded herself sardonically, in order to take a vacation, theoretically one ought to be gainfully employed. No, this trip was definitely set apart from all others. Sidney knew and accepted there would be little chance to carefully plan who she saw, where she went and most terrifying of all when she would actually be going home again.

Home. Sidney rolled the word uncomfortably around in her mind. Where exactly was that? Somehow New York didn't seem to fit even though she had lived there for years. Home couldn't really be Barren's Creek anymore given how she avoided the town of her youth like the proverbial plague other than for obligatory appearances. Until now. One brief phone call from Aunt Vera had changed that.

Sidney drew a deep breath ordering herself not to give into despair. Today it would be altogether too easy. She was leaving strife in New York, only to head off to Barren's Creek, a place that made her on-going bones of contentions with Reg look like child's play. She smiled wistfully as her mind drifted to the lovable cop she shared an apartment and a life with. He had probably received her note by now. It was amazing she couldn't hear his bellow from here. Their eventual phone call would likely be deafening, she decided morosely.

Sidney valiantly shook off all her misgivings about having to leave him knowing she literally had no choice. She had obligations to fulfill and chastised herself before that thought was even complete. Nicole and Zachary were so much more than that. In times of greatest despair, her sister's children felt like the closest thing she would ever have to her own. It was an honor to be their guardian. She had not even hesitated when Kathleen asked her years before to accept the responsibility knowing the probability that she might someday be called upon as she was today.

Her nephew, Zachary was just over eight, smart as a whip, adventuresome and quite a jokester. Nicole was eleven, a willowy blond just on the threshold of young womanhood, who badly needed her mother around. Enter Aunt Sidney, she thought ruefully, skeptical she was up to the challenge.

Kathleen sure wasn't right now and acknowledging that made Sidney's spirits plummet. Reg's reaction to her going to Barren's Creek alone in this weather paled in comparison. According to Aunt Vera's phone call, Kathleen's hospitalization was essential. Sidney knew it just by the way her aunt's voice hitched during their brief conversation. They had kept it short. Vera, a woman known to be at ease with words, simply wasn't up to talking.

Sidney sighed wearily. It wasn't that she hadn't known that this was always a possibility, indeed a probability, with graphic clarity for years. Surely her adolescence had taught her that. Sidney found herself grateful now that she and Kathleen had discussed in detail how a situation like this would be handled. Now was the moment they had planned for and vainly hoped would never come. Tears smarted the backs of expressive doe eyes as her attention wandered ….

Sidney lurched upright as a stone hit the glass in front of her with a startling smack. The transport smattered it's final insult of muddy water as it whizzed by at speeds that made her vehicle appear to be crawling. The star shaped crack in the windshield the stone left at eye level eloquently summed up her recent run of luck.

Duly shaken, Sidney reigned in her errant thoughts to focus on driving. The rain wasn't letting up one drop, rather it was worsening. She almost considered pulling over as she had earlier but dismissed the notion just as quickly. Parked on the shoulder of the road her car would shudder violently with every passing vehicle and only made her more vulnerable. Instead, Sidney concentrated all energies toward driving safely. After all, it would be preferable to tell Reg truthfully that she had been cautious.

Her mind flitted traitorously to another time…another life…another man who would have been just as concerned. Sidney derailed that thought on a sigh. After all, it was the mother of all dead ends. Fate had seen to that.

With abject relief, Sidney took the turn off for Barren's Creek. She was hungry, tired and if she were honest, frightened of what this trip with no end date might bring. Her surroundings became familiar even in the blurred watery world that existed outside of her compact car. Sidney felt a little nervous shudder run through her driving down streets she could have found blindfolded she knew them so well. Of course that would tick off the local Sheriff, she thought mischievously, an affectionate smile ghosting about her lips.

A large institutional building with its foreboding presence loomed on her right and something tugged at her to go straight there. Reason dictated otherwise.

She had placated her worried aunt, who had raised from a small child, telling Vera she would wait out the spring storm and travel tomorrow. The possibility of Reg calling before she arrived could only reek havoc. Her foot punched the gas.

Sidney smiled reflexively driving down the street where their large family home presided on a huge lot swathed with gardens of unruly perennials like a grand lady holding court. This part of coming back was always appealing. The cheerful sight of the old Victorian with the glow of lighted windows just beyond the huge wrap around verandah and smoke curling up from one of several chimneys beckoned her in. She pulled in the wide horseshoe lane hearing the familiar crunch of crushed stone under her tires and felt some of her tension ebb.

Gauging the downpour, Sidney opted for a mad dash to the door with only her purse. She had decided to make a run for it instead of trying to dig out her umbrella, which in all probability given her luck, was pinned under luggage. The willful rain seemed to combat her from all angles instantly drenching Sidney to the skin.

She stood gasping for a few seconds on the wide porch as little rivers ran down her wet face dripping from matted hair. Woolen pants clung uncomfortably fueling fantasies of being rid of them and sinking into a warm fragrant bath. All in good time, Sidney promised herself, beckoning patience she hardly felt. Her hip pinned open the gingerbread screen door, while her fingers trembling with the chill touched the ornate antique knob.

Sidney jerked violently as the door was ruthlessly torn from her grasp. There was no time to react before her arms were seized in a steely grasp and she was yanked into his lean snarling face. The *last* face she had expected to see tonight. She hadn't been this close to him in almost a decade and though her trembling intensified it was no longer caused by the cold.

"*You little fool!*" he savagely bit out between clenched white teeth that were too easily likened to a wolf's.

He was going to eat her alive, Sidney decided frantically. Her breathing grew ragged as darkening brown eyes bulged. Suddenly as abruptly as she had been seized, she was dropped. Sagging weakly against the wall, palms flattened against it for support, Sidney barely squelched the temptation to bolt from the house back to her car.

"What on earth is all the commotion...."

Sidney exhaled in a rush hearing her aunt's soothing voice.

"Sidney!" Vera cried, dashing to gather her close. Just as quickly, the older woman stepped backward out of the soggy embrace. "You are positively soaked to the bone!" she exclaimed with undisguised dismay, leading her niece toward the cheerful fire in the front parlor, where an older man sat silently taking in the scene. Sidney gazed up helplessly at the woman who had raised her, fully anticipating what was coming next. "You promised me to wait until tomorrow! You said you would wait out the storm! That you wouldn't take any unnecessary risks..."

Her expression was steeped in apology. "I didn't, Auntie... not really... the roads were better when I started out... the rain had let up in the city..."

"Funny, the weather reports don't support that claim," a cutting masculine voice accused from behind.

Sidney closed her eyes wearily. A decade had not been near long enough to make her unsure of what was coming next. She could envision his index finger stabbing toward her without turning.

"As usual you decided what you thought was best in a totally singular fashion. Not what the general consensus was of every sensible adult involved in the situation. What on earth did you expect to achieve by arriving a day earlier other than getting yourself killed!" he railed at the top of his lungs.

Another male, more seasoned by the years, cleared his throat. "I think that just about does it," Charlie Ryan said meaningfully.

Luke Ryan shot Charlie a scathing glance but remained grudgingly silent. He stood ramrod stiff, glaring at Sidney, unnerving what was left of her battered bravado.

An old black housekeeper with hips that spanned the doorway, negotiated it like a pro, to wrap a blanket around Sidney's shivering shoulders. Sidney murmured her thanks to Delta whom she had known since childhood. The woman touched her cheek affectionately before pressing a teacup into her hand. "My pleasure, Miss Sidney. It is a blessing to have you home."

"And a miracle she's here in one piece," a deep voice muttered. "We have all been witness to your driving..."

"Lucas!" her aunt admonished but not before the thin thread of Sidney's restraint snapped.

"*That's it!*" Sidney yelled, setting her cup down with a clatter, standing so quickly the blanket slipped from her shoulders. "If you want to have a fight, let's get it over with. However, don't expect me just to sit and take it. I don't do that anymore. I stick up for myself. I knew exactly what I was doing today. I was coming home to Kathleen as quickly...."

"And recklessly...."

A sneer curved the lips Luke could still remember kissing. "Safely as possible. If I had wanted to be reckless, I wouldn't have pulled off the road for two hours...."

Fury burgeoned as Luke stepped toward her to lean menacingly into her face. "*And what!* You sat on the shoulder of the road just waiting for a careless transport to pick you off and crush you like a bug!"

Sidney gnashed her teeth together. "You are being utterly ridiculous!" Yet that same thought had crossed her mind.

"Am I? Am I really? Now if we took a vote of the people in this room just who.... *who* do you think they would agree with?" Luke challenged looming over her, deliberately exercising the same kind of purposeful intimidation he had perfected over the years on a multitude of suspects.

Sidney gritted her teeth and was about to snap out a scathing reply when the phone intruded. Delta snatched it up before the second ring. The occupants of the room collectively held their breath suspecting that at this late hour it would only be the hospital. Delta flinched as a deep male voice blasted out of the receiver and reluctantly held out the phone. "I believe it's for you, Miss Sidney."

Sidney's brow furrowed knowingly, irritably flicking damp tresses from her shoulder to trail down her back. She ignored the blistering stare of the tall muscular man standing with his arms akimbo only a few feet away. *Saved by the bell*, Sidney thought sardonically. In seconds, she reconsidered.

"Sid, what the hell were you thinking!!" A familiar voice bellowed through the receiver.

"Ahhh..." she stammered excruciatingly aware of the eyes trained upon her. One hazel pair in particular.

"You have pulled some impulsive crazy stunts in the past but this...*this...*" His voice was escalating and she hastened to soothe.

"Reg...Honey..." The endearment clogged her throat as one man's stare bore a hole through her. "I drove with meticulous care...."

A loud telling snort cut her off. "Sid... I have seen you drive!"

Sidney frowned deeply at the stinging remark, chose the high road and ignored it. "I took twice as long getting here I was so careful."

"Was that the reason or was it because the conditions were just that tricky?" Reg countered stubbornly. "If you had waited two more days, we could have come together. You know I have been negotiating a few days off..."

"I know but..." Her voice trailed off in uncertainty.

A labored sigh came over the line. "You doubted I could really pull it off so you went ahead without me," he filled in irritably.

"Reg, I know if you could be here, you would. That's enough for now," she revealed wearily having turned her back on her audience but still vividly aware of their presence.

"Sounds like the beginning for a huge discussion," Reg decreed.

She pressed fingers against her eyes. "Maybe but not tonight. OK?"

One man stalked from the room, slamming the front door behind him.

"What the hell was that?" Reg yelled into the receiver. "Thunder? Sid, is it an electrical storm too?"

She shook her head forgetting the man on the other end of the line couldn't see it. "No. Only rain. No big deal."

"Funny that's not what the forecast says," Reg challenged.

Sidney cringed inwardly as it registered how similar the two men's arguments were. It was downright creepy.

The front door burst open bringing a gust of wind and a furious dripping male loaded down with her luggage. Small streams ran down his fiercely angular features from his rain drenched dark hair. She gulped as an inexplicable jolt shot through her. In another life, she would have rushed to towel him off. Instead she stood gaping.

"Over there is fine," Sidney choked out as he slowly turned to regard her blandly. "Just put them down. I'll take them up."

Their eyes met and his clearly did not concur. Instead Luke brushed past her toward the stairs stirring nerve endings she had long forgotten.

"What's fine, Sid? I don't think we have come to any mutual decisions…"

Sidney desperately tried to tune into Reg's voice but her eyes were glued to the rigid back and long legs loping up the staircase. Dear God, he couldn't possibly be intending…

"Wait…" Sidney yelled oblivious to the cordless phone next to her ear as she galloped up the first staircase after him. She glanced around frantically. Luke was already headed up the second sending her mind reeling. "Just set them down!"

Suddenly the powerful figure stilled completely. With an eerie sense of calm, he turned to her silently. Penetrating hazel eyes swept her languidly from head to toe as an involuntary shiver shot through her. God, this was not how she intended to see him for the first time. She was a sodden mess.

"What the hell's happening there, Sid?" came Reg's reply, alarm creeping into his tone.

"Nothing," she stammered. "I told you my Aunt Vera's household is large. She employs several staff to help her run it."

"You are having a run in with the hired help?"

Sidney's expression became shuttered. "Something like that. He hasn't yet been familiarized with the house rules." Two black eye brows jutted upward.

"Rules? Sid, those aren't generally your style," Reg remarked with keen interest.

"Sometimes they are necessary," she stated with more emotion than seemed warranted.

"Just who is this guy anyway?"

"The *door man* apparently. He *greeted* me upon my arrival," Sidney stated icily, skewering Luke with a glance.

His lips curved upward as if enjoying some private joke while he made a grandiose show of setting her luggage down. Sidney barely managed to bank her enormous relief when a deep chuckle came from the man, whose gaze didn't waver from hers. Squinting his eyes mockingly, Luke hoisted his burdens again and swiftly pivoted to saunter down the hallway toward the door at the end.

Oh Lord, she gulped. He was really going into that room. *Her* room. Once upon a time... her guts clenched in sudden turmoil. "No! Don't! Stop!"

The man ignored her like he was stone deaf as Reg's agitated voice flooded her ear. "What the hell is that stupid doorman doing for Christ's sake?"

Sidney barely heard him. What was about to occur was too damaging to her fragile peace of mind. "Don't go in there!"

With a backward glance, Luke arrogantly swept through the doorway. Panic stricken, she streaked after him half expecting to see tiny rosebuds instead of the pale sage stripes that had adorned the walls for the past several years.

"Where the hell is he going?" Reg ground out peevishly.

"My room," she responded absently.

Reg's response was thunderous. "Damned right he doesn't go in there. Put him on, Sid!"

Luke dropped her bags with a careless thud and straightened to lift his amused eyes to hers, expectantly. It was as if he knew that the man on the other end of the line wanted a word with him.

Anxiety of new proportions seized Sidney. "That won't be necessary, Reg. The *doorman* and I can work out some agreeable solution," she hedged. Suddenly her eyes narrowed at his smug expression spurring a calculated comment. "Honey, are you at home?'

"Yeah. Why?" Reg grumbled, disgusted with himself that he had so recklessly abandoned his cover when he couldn't reach her by phone.

"Have you been in the kitchen yet?"

"Only to rip your note off the frig."

"I baked before I left," she cooed and watched Luke's eyes become hooded. "Fudge brownies. Thick frosting. With pecans not walnuts."

"That's great, Sid," Reg replied with lame gratitude. He liked walnuts. "Frankly I would rather have you."

Her voice turned soft and sultry, uncontrived. "Me too."

"Listen, I have to check in with Don about the case. I left in kind of a God damned hurry. Call me tomorrow to let me know how Kathleen is and when you are coming home. We have our project to work on," he reminded her strategically.

"Tomorrow," she reassured him with an expression that had grown wistful.

"Love ya, Sid."

Her heart slammed in her chest. She loved the words. Loved the man. He was her best friend. Hated having an audience. "Ditto."

"Cute, Sid," Reg teased, chuckling. "Worried the doorman will be jealous?"

Her heart froze. "I'll call tomorrow."

"Bye Babe."

Luke didn't budge as he sullenly observed Sidney click off the line and set the phone down on a nearby dresser. She purposefully returned her gaze to his. It was time to set down the lay of the land or life would be intolerable.

"Luke…"

At the sound of his name from her lips for the first time in almost a decade, his pulse surged. He moved to stand directly in front of her pleased to see her quiver at his nearness.

His smile was slow and entirely too satisfied for her liking.

"Yes, Sidney," Luke returned in the closest rendition to a civil voice she had heard since her arrival.

"We need to establish some ground rules we can both abide by."

"Tomorrow," he declared casually lifting tangled tresses off her shoulder. "Right now you need a hot bath and a dry nightgown."

Sidney stared upward into the seemingly bottomless depths of his hazel eyes. They were still filled with gleaming topaz flecks and she felt herself slipping helplessly back to another era. It didn't seem prudent to mention she no longer wore nightgowns when she half expected him to go run the tub.

His lips tugged upward at her confused reaction. She *had* memories. "Go get warm and dry, Sid. We'll talk tomorrow." Luke lowered his face strategically within mere inches of hers until their breath mingled, gratified that it took a visible effort for her to stay in place. " And Sidney…"

"Yes," she replied in a bare whisper afraid to move, fearful her knees might fold.

"I'll work on my greeting," Luke drawled smoothly.

Her jaw fell aghast at his words as she shoved at shoulders ropey with muscle. His amused chuckle was drowned out as the door burst open.

"Aunt Sidney! Aunt Sid! You're here!" Two voices yelled boisterously as Nicole and Zachary skidded to a halt before her. Sidney forgot Luke and rushed forward to hug her niece and nephew, who had obviously been awakened by the commotion.

"You're soaked!" Nicole blurted out, drawing out of her aunt's damp embrace.

"Your Aunt Sidney was in such a rush to get to you two, she couldn't help herself and drove into the night," Luke informed them with a casualness Sidney hadn't heard until now. "She obviously thinks you are both pretty special."

The two kids fell like a heap into her arms once again as Sidney regarded Luke with amazement over their shoulders. He had deliberately gone out of his way to avoid the kids knowing that there was any dispute between them and instead put her in a positive light.

Two other voices came from the doorway. "Has Reginald calmed down, Dear?" her aunt inquired.

"Reg is fine," Sidney assured her economically.

Charlie caught Luke's eye. "We thought we had better rescue one of you from the other up here but for the life of us, we weren't entirely sure who that would be," he shrugged affably. "Maybe time will tell."

"Sidney needs a hot bath," Luke stated flatly and her eyes widened in stunned amazement as the lot of them turned without further comment to file from the room, shouting a combination of welcome and good night.

Alone again, Luke leaned against the doorframe and regarded her leisurely once more. "I like your hair like that. It was short for too long. Make sure you dry it before you go to sleep or you might catch a chill." He turned to leave. "I'm going to go work on that greeting," he revealed in slow husky tones, closing the door softly behind him.

Sidney woodenly made her way to the bed and weakly sank down upon it. She propped her chin in one hand, her elbow braced on a knee, her mouth remained parted in shell shock. What the hell was she doing here? Her eyes drifted and involuntarily caught on a small photo of her and Kathleen, smiling with arms draped companionably around one another. Gazing at it,

Sidney knew precisely why she had come. Great love. *Lord help her*, Sidney thought pleadingly. She was going to need it.

CHAPTER TWO

Sidney's lips curved with smug satisfaction as she gave her reflection a final sweeping perusal. A shocked hand flew to her chest when she glimpsed another figure in the floor length mirror, jarring loose a sensation she had thought had been long since exorcised.

"Nicole!" she choked out. "Where did you come from?"

One brow rose insolently. "I live here." The young girl cocked her head and green cat eyes lit. "Aunt Sidney... you look hot!"

Her startle forgotten, Sidney faced her niece with a bright smile. "Do I?"

"Oh yeah," her niece reiterated convincingly.

Having dressed with great care this morning desperate to undo her rain soaked image of last night, the compliment was disturbingly pleasing. Sable hair flowed softly over her shoulders, trailing halfway down her back in smooth silky waves. As always, Sidney used cosmetics sparingly but with an expert hand to accent her pretty features while leaving a natural look. The cardinal red sweater displayed her curves, accenting her tiny waist while fawn colored pants hugged her hips to taper attractively over shapely legs.

"Uncle Luke will like it," Nicole stated pointedly.

Sidney couldn't decide whether she was more stunned by the declaration or hearing Luke addressed as uncle, striking her momentarily speechless.

"Don't worry about it, Aunt Sidney," Nicole told her flippantly unceremoniously leaving the room.

"Worry? Who's worried?" Sidney postured sprinting after the girl.

Nicole merely rolled her shoulders with a bland look and continued on her way.

Sidney frowned and walked faster, gamely trouping down three sets of stairs after her. "There's nothing to be worried about."

Nicole's smile held all the arrogance of youth. "Guess not."

"Nicole..." Mild panic was setting in knowing she had lost control of the situation before ever possessing it.

"Nic, you're going to be late for the bus again and Mom isn't here to drive you," Zachary taunted in a singsong voice from the foot of the stairs.

Sidney suddenly felt the tug of concern mothers never quite shed. "Nicole, have you had breakfast?"

"I don't eat breakfast," the lanky blond replied sullenly.

Sidney raced down the final flight of stairs. "Everyone should eat breakfast... it's the first meal of the day. You can't learn..."

Nicole slanted her a bored glance. "Aunt Sid, you sound like a cereal commercial."

Sidney stood on the third step from the bottom scrambling for a come back that didn't sound lame or condescending when the bus honked impatiently from the curb.

Nicole slung her backpack over her shoulder with bland indifference, heading for the door. Her loss of control complete, Sidney stared open mouthed.

"Hey Nic, why don't you take this along for the ride?" Luke suggested affably from the front hall. He offered a small bag and a paper cup with a lid with his outstretched arm. Her niece took it with a flirtatious smile while Sidney seethed.

"Thanks, Uncle Luke. See ya." Almost as an afterthought, she turned back to her aunt. "Mom needs her hair washed and no one can…"

Sidney suddenly felt on firm ground again. Kathleen she knew how to deal with. "I'll take care of it. Have a good day."

"Yeah," her niece responded reticently and the screen door banged behind her.

Sidney glanced over at Zachary, who stood unaffected at the base of the stairs. "Is she always like this?"

The young boy wrinkled his nose as he shoved his ball glove into his school bag. "Naw, this is a good day," he replied affably and raced up the two stairs to throw his arms around her nearly knocking her off balance as his bus honked. "Tell Mom I love her and to take her lithium," Zach whispered, pulling away again to jam a baseball cap on his head and scoop up his bag. "See ya, Uncle Luke." Exchanging high fives, he ducked his head into the front parlor. "You, too, Charlie, Auntie Vera. Bye Delta!" he yelled in a pitch that would make Tarzan envious and tore toward the door.

It banged against its frame again before Sidney could move. When she did, Luke stood at the base of the stairs with his hand extended. Her eyes drank him in with a glance and clung. She had been juggling too many balls last night to really get a good look. Now it was disarming to realize Luke was as devastating to her appeal as always. His raven colored hair was thick and neatly styled. Too neat. It beckoned to her fingers. The lines of his face were still rugged and angular with only the ones bracketing his mouth looking any deeper despite the decade they had been apart. Hazel eyes ringed by halos of topaz held her foolishly spell bound.

"Is it improved?" he asked in deep throaty tones that jerked her from revelry.

"What?" Sidney stammered, mortified she had been caught looking.

One side of his mouth lifted in the cocky grin she remembered from another lifetime. "My greeting," he drawled silkily. "I've been working on it."

With an exasperated gasp, she swatted away his hand. He was mocking her, the son of a ...

"Sidney?" a soft lilting voice called from the other room.

"Right here, Aunt Vera," she replied and crisply walked around his lean frame in an eloquent gesture.

"Good. Charlie's here too. Lucas, Darling, come sit."

Sidney peered at her aunt quizzically as she watched Luke settle into a chair across from her as if he did it every day of his life. It slowly began to register that *Uncle Luke* seemed incredibly comfortable in this home. It was as if time had changed nothing. As Delta poured his coffee, Sidney realized that half the foods on the breakfast table were his favorites unless his tastes had radically changed. A horrifying image of finding his jockeys in a drawer next to hers upstairs had her pulse skittering.

Sidney lifted her eyes to find him watching her studiously as if expecting a reaction. She carefully averted her eyes to discover her aunt regarding her cautiously as well. Charlie Ryan remained as enigmatic as ever sipping his coffee, plucking a cinnamon Danish off a platter.

"It's time we discuss Kathleen, Dear," Vera told her gently.

Sidney pursed her lips thoughtfully, jerking her head toward Luke. "Why is he here?"

Vera's gaze held steady. "Lucas is here for the very same reason you are. He is Nicole and Zachary's guardian."

"What!?" Sidney's mouth gaped open before she could think better of it. "Aunt Vera that is ridiculous. Kathleen and I have discussed this scenario a dozen times at length. He was never a part of it."

Vera's smile was placid. "She wrote you a letter, Dear."

Sidney snatched it and rose to go the window to read it more for privacy than the light.

Dear Sidney,
If you are reading this, I will undoubtedly make more sense in print than in person at the present time. First, I appreciate you coming so fast. Don't bother denying it, I know you did and can only hope you were careful. I've seen you drive, Sid.

Kiss my kids please... I know you have already done it...but do it again. I hope whatever happened I didn't scare them. They have never seen me...well you know...probably better than anyone. Help them to love me anyway. I will need it. Just like I will need you.

Honey, you alone aren't enough. Sometimes you need to let others help. Please try to understand my stand on this. Luke knows the kids. He has been living here in the same town everyday of their lives. We have never confided this before because we didn't want you to feel...well self-conscious but Luke is still very much a member of the family. The kids will need and want you desperately...but they will also need him.

I do know what I am asking and I suppose that is why I am doing it in a letter rather than to your face. I can't bear to think of you turning me down and I know in my heart of hearts, you won't. Luke knows the town, the people...you know the system and me. Together you make a terrific team. Still. I need you both...so do Nicole and Zachary.

Please Sidney, I am begging you...

Sidney crumpled the letter in her fist, closed her eyes and shook her head. She hadn't finished, didn't have to. As if she had any choice. Kathleen had always been her greatest Achilles' heel. Sidney gazed blindly out of the window knowing she would do absolutely anything for her...even this.

"It's workable," she finally acknowledged in deliberate business like tones turning back to the three at the table. "Surely we can divide responsibilities and in actual fact spend little time together..."

"No."

Her head jerked up. No amount of time apart could make her forget that tone. "*What?*"

"We make all of our decisions together in unanimous agreement. And the kids spend time with both of us together."

She goggled at him as if he were an imbecile and rounded the table to take a closer look. "Why on earth..."

His eyes pinned hers with unmistakable gravity. "Because those two kids have just lost the stabilizing factor in their life for an undetermined period. They need to see a united front..."

"Why? They never have before. Grant left when Nicole was barely five and Zach was a toddler...."

"We are not Kathleen and Grant," Luke bit out savagely, rising so they stood toe to toe. "We were different..."

She thrust a freshly manicured finger at him as fury inflected her eyes. "Don't...go...there."

"Children..." Vera began to intercede.

"*We are not children!*" Two voices shouted and then stared at one another in shock at their united response.

Charlie cast them a dubious glance. "Sound like a couple of kids to me," he muttered, taking a bite of his sweet roll. "Cranky ones."

Sidney spun away to hide the sudden pang of pain. *Those days are long gone.*

Delta bustled back into the room. "Now don't forget Miss Kathleen's nurse wanted to speak with Mr. Luke and Miss Sidney just as soon as they could both get there…"

Sidney whirled back so fast her hair fanned out in a circle around her. "Why would the nurse want to see you?"

Luke cast glances at both the elders, who hastily studied their plates. "We also share Kathleen's power of attorney…"

Sidney blinked as the pastel pattern of the carpet blurred. This was harder. Much harder to accept. The kids were one thing but Kathleen was *her* sister. It was clear now how long she had been gone and the cost was steep. The breath she drew was shaky as Sidney lifted her gaze. "I see."

It was clear she did see and Luke knew instantly he would prefer her fury to the wounded look in those huge brown doe eyes. "Sidney."

She held up one conciliatory palm. "Let's just go. I want to see Kathleen." His arrogance was much easier to deal with than the quiet compassion she glimpsed in his face now.

Luke carefully showed no reaction. "We can go…."

"I'll meet you there."

The words were more effective than a slap but he took it and still hoped to find some middle ground. Laying a gentle hand on her shoulder, enjoying the silk of her hair under his hand, "Sidney, why don't you let me drive and you can relax…"

"Did Kathleen stipulate that too?"

The glint in her eye as she jerked from his touch was almost a relief after the emotion he had seen touched off moments before. Luke chuckled and let himself enjoy the sparing. "I'll have to scan the fine print."

"Until you have written verification of it, I drive alone," she snarled, snatching up her purse and slamming out the screen door. Luke watched coolly from the porch steps as she gunned the engine and sped away.

The older pair sat in pensive silence as Luke made a disgruntled exit from the breakfast nook. Charlie finally spoke. "Did you…."

Vera was already shaking her head sending red rinsed curls bouncing. "Sidney was sound asleep when I checked on her. Besides, Kathleen would be furious with us."

Charlie grunted an incoherent response.

"Does Luke know?"

Charlie snorted out an incredulous laugh. "I'm still alive, aren't I?"

Vera stretched one hand across the table with a faint smile. "Good. I enjoy your company better that way."

He remained silent but his eyes glowed eloquently. "You know I am Lara Lovelorn's biggest fan...."

A horrified expression transformed her barely lined face that bore more rouge and foundation than was prudent. Vibrant curls flounced when Vera jumped up as if she had been burnt. "Oh gracious I forgot..." She was already scurrying for the door.

"What is it this time?" Charlie called after her knowingly, easing back into his chair, speculatively eyeing his jigsaw puzzle half completed on a nearby table.

"Drake is dangling in a car on the edge of a cliff...."

Like the cop that he was, he had to ask. "Foul play?"

"Of course, a good plot is full of...."

"Conflict, conflict, conflict," they chimed together making her eyes dance from a room away.

"It was tampered with by that rogue Kenneth."

"The bastard," Charlie commiserated.

Revved now, color crept up her neck and mingled with the poorly applied make-up. "Vanessa has just discovered she has feelings for him... Drake, not Kenneth."

Charlie spread his hands, grinning. "Of course not. Our girl's too smart to fall for the wrong guy."

Vera frowned, her forehead wrinkling. "Well she did once but he forgave her." Charlie merely tipped his head letting her ramble. "And despite Drake's involvement with her sister who is perilously ill, she still wants his children but now she may never get a chance to admit it...." Her excited voice trailed off as she hurried toward her coveted study.

Charlie chuckled and his eyes caught Delta's as she refilled his mug. "What tragedy has befallen our doomed couple now?" the rotund housekeeper asked dryly.

"We're likely better off not knowing, Delta."

The old woman snorted her agreement. "She made me late for canasta last week over some ridiculous poison business. Wanted to know how I kill varmints."

Charlie chuckled into his mug. "There's a whole lot of tall tales tucked in her pretty head."

The housekeeper sighed but her dark eyes danced. "You would swear the way she talks about those people, they are real somebody's that live just a piece down the road."

Charlie nodded with his mouth set in firm lines. "To her they surely are. Why just last week it took me twenty minutes to calm her down enough to find out that Vanessa was in dire need of a bone marrow transplant and there was no match...."

Delta clucked with glee as she balanced teacups. "Did it take two or three?"

"A four hankie actually. What makes the whole thing funny is Vera tells me later she ditched the entire bit. Deep-sixed the whole chapter." Delta's heavily lined face wrinkled more with her gust of mirth. "She claims there is enough heart ache already for her young lovers," Charlie told her, dabbing absently at his chin thinking it might be wise to stop by Tanner's cleaners and renew his supply. There's no telling when the next crisis would occur.

Sidney gracefully got out her car like a princess might alight from her carriage as Luke pulled into the spot beside her. Satisfaction snaked through her as she glimpsed his dark scowl.

"Girl, who the hell ever gave you a license?" If she were going to have his heart racing, he decided, there really ought to be more enjoyment involved.

Sidney stood her ground as he stalked toward her obviously far from finished. She had seen his variety of intimidation too regularly to be affected by it. "I am no girl. You and I may not have seen each other for years but believe me..." Deliberately pausing for effect. "*I am all woman.*"

Luke's lips softened into a lazy smile as his gaze leisurely traveled the length of her, enjoying the view. "I stand corrected. So *Woman*, who the hell ever gave you a license?" he reiterated savagely.

"Does it matter? I have one." She shot him a saucy glance, patting her purse. "You have a problem with my driving, sick the Sheriff on me," Sidney retorted and thought smugly of Charlie.

Luke gave her an odd look as his blood began to warm. "I may just have to consider that." He put his hand to the small of her back urging her toward the hospital entrance.

Sidney batted him away irritably and strode on ahead. She kept a meaningful step ahead the entire way and was stoically silent until the elevator. "Always put psychiatry on the top floor," She muttered pretending to focus on the numbers overhead. "Like they need more incentive to jump." Suddenly Luke's presence faded from rankling as her reason for coming home became painfully real.

Warm fingers threaded through hers and she stared at the long tanned strong digits intertwined with hers. The fit was still there. Her delicately shaped brows furrowed in confusion and she slowly lifted her eyes to his. It was mildly disturbing to see the empathy infused there. She gave him a weak smile and took advantage of the elevator doors sliding open to slip her hand away.

Past memories flitted through her mind as she barreled toward the nurses' station ordering herself to stay in the present. Sidney caught the eye of a woman who was busily charting behind the desk.

"I'm here to see Kathleen Stuart."

The woman tucked a stray strand of auburn hair behind her ear as she carefully measured the slightly younger woman before her and flipped the file closed. "You must be Sidney Ryan, Kathleen's sister."

"Yes."

She stuck out a hand. "I'm Fiona Cummings. I've been assigned to your sister's care during the day shift since her admission," the nurse explained coming out from behind the desk to lead them down the hall. "The Sheriff and I have spoken before," she added gesturing toward Luke.

Sidney froze as her challenge from the parking lot ricocheted foolishly through her mind once more.

Luke winked. "Charlie retired 6 months ago. I got his job." He flipped opened his jacket revealing the cheap tin star identifying him as Town Sheriff.

If he was looking for congratulations, he had delusions that could land him in this ward, she decided crankily. "Guess Town Counsel wanted to keep the job in the family. Effective job searches are known to be costly."

Luke's smile stayed in place, his voice easy, though it won't have killed her to say a kind word. Just one the way she used to. Of all the congratulations he had received since taking the promotion, hers was the one he missed. "Mayor Pincombe does like to pinch her pennies," he agreed smoothly.

Fiona bit back a chuckle, seeing the nerves, barely escaping the vibrating energy that sparked between this couple, and knowing what Kathleen expected of them. Sensing a diversion was called for, "I understand you are in Social Work at St. Mark's in New York."

Sidney turned, surprised the other woman was so informed.

A psych nurse to the bone, Fiona touched her arm. "Kathleen told me." Brows shot up making the RN smile. "She told me during one of her regular appointments with Dr. Dixon."

"Oh."

"She's quite proud of you. Talked endlessly about you getting your Master's, starting work on your Ph.D."

Sidney shifted uncomfortably. Those thoughts certainly weren't on Kathleen's mind now as she took note of their direction. "She isn't out of seclusion yet."

The little sister knew her way around the psych ward, Fiona observed sadly and just a little relieved that Sidney was up to this. Family rarely came down to these rooms but Sidney's professional background and a quiet conversation with the Sheriff yesterday had reassured her otherwise. "No but restarting her lithium has already brought some changes."

Sidney stepped cautiously up to the high window of a door she had peered in more times than she cared to count and her heart fell to her knees. Her sister, a stunning blond known to turn every male head as she walked past, lay curled in a fetal position like an unkept waif on a bare mattress that was the only thing in the small room with dingy gray unadorned walls. Stringy hair, that needed washing more than Nicole ever needed to know, obscured her face. A faded blue hospital gown covered her back and was obviously tied in the front. Some things don't change, Sidney noted wryly

"Thanks for keeping her decent with the second gown," Sidney murmured certain that the caring nurse beside her had added the other gown wore the right way around to preserve Kathleen's modesty.

"No problem. She'll do it herself in a day or so."

Sorrowful brown eyes meant to seek Fiona's but stalled at Luke instead, finding the steadiness there she had always known she could count on. "She's depressed."

Neither Luke nor Fiona answered, as it wasn't a question and Sidney was precisely right.

"She was high when she came in?"

"Yes," Fiona concurred as a flash of Kathleen jumping atop the nurse's desk nearly nude claiming she was going to be the first female president sprang to mind.

The cycle was the same, Sidney considered privately and perhaps there was some comfort in that familiarity. First came the mania with its outrageous behavior that kept those privy to it gossiping for weeks and then in the quiet and seclusion of the psych floor came the crashing low that immobilized her sister, making menial tasks like brushing her teeth seem all but impossible.

"I'd like to go in."

"Don't expect too much, Sidney," Luke murmured lifting a hand to run over her hair. He had gone in yesterday and received no response.

Her lips curved. "Of course not." The smile widened with pure bravado. "It's just like old times."

Luke watched as she slipped soundlessly into the quiet room Fiona unlocked for her. Though he doubted anything would happen he was prepared to lunge in after her. "Sidney's very good for Kathleen," Luke murmured.

Fiona met his eyes, saw the respect and pride reflected there. "I imagine she is." Just the same, she planned on watching closely.

Sidney stood just inside the door watching dust particles float on the sunlight streaming through the grated window. She intended to give Kathleen plenty of time to notice her presence not that she was counting on it. At this stage of the game, she knew better than to count on anything.

With painstaking slowness, she made her way around the mattress where her sister lay tightly curled like an animal intent on self-preservation. She sat down a couple of feet in front of her cross-legged on the floor. Her gaze flickered to the door and she met Luke's eyes through the observation window for a mere second. Strangely, the brief contact was bolstering. They had walked this path together in another time…another life.

"Kathleen…" she began softly. "It's me. It's Sid." She paused deliberately. "I came as soon as I heard." Eyelids fluttered open after several tries. "I love you." Blue eyes stared unfocused. "Kat, it is going to be all right."

"Yeah?"

Sidney stifled a gasp and leaned forward instead. Had she really heard a response or just imagined it? "Kathleen?"

"Sid." Kathleen's fingers moved in the barest of movements.

Tears smarted as Sidney reached out desperate to take the gesture as an invitation and covered her sister's limp hand with her own. "I love you, Kathleen."

"Knew you would come." Counted on it.

Sidney sniffed as a lone tear fell. "Where else would I be?"

"My kids…" Kathleen started weakly but the thought was too hard, the emotions too potent, to complete.

"Luke and I will take care of them."

"He loves them."

"Yes," Sidney admitted without any pang of resentment.

"And you," her sister added weakly.

"Yes, I love the kids too," Sidney rushed to reassure.

Kathleen tried to reach through the quagmire thwarting her thoughts. That wasn't what she meant but she couldn't seem to get her mouth around the words. Not today anyway. She let herself sink back into nothingness. It was all right to do that now. Sidney was here and some things Kathleen knew Luke could take care of himself. He merely needed the opportunity. She had provided that. The rest was up to him.

CHAPTER THREE

"Are you all right?" Luke said amid the clatter of the coffee shop, regretting that he hadn't bullied her into going to his home where it was quieter.

"Hmmm."

"Sidney?" Luke asked with concern at her remoteness, barely resisting the urge to reach for her hand.

She looked up at him bleakly. "Fine. I'm...." she shook her head forlornly and expelled a shuttering breath. "How did this happen? We spoke on the phone just a week and a half ago. She seemed fine. Really OK. Looking back I can't pick out anything that would have tipped me off."

"I don't know what happened, Sidney." Truly, he was just as mystified. He and Kathleen saw each other or spoke almost everyday. She was his solace and connection to all he had lost when Sidney left him years before. He had only been out of town for a little over a week at a conference and Kathleen had seemed very much herself when she had seen him off. It made utterly no sense. "But we will get Kathleen back on her feet," he vowed as she gazed at him with woeful eyes. He caved in and reached for her hand that rested on the table near her teacup. "Sweetheart...."

"Well... isn't this a real walk down memory lane," a sultry voice cooed.

Sidney's spirit shriveled as she self-consciously slid her hand from his and onto her lap. Even after this many years, she still cringed at the mere whiff of this woman's pungent perfume. Her eyes flickered upward to see that Vivian Filmont's honey blond hair was fashionably coifed dramatically framing a face that barely showed the passage of time. Even if it, did her figure almost looked improved upon. Sidney's eyes narrowed. Shit! It *was* improved upon. The plastics bills must have been hefty but if customer satisfaction counted for anything, Vivian likely paid them with a coy smile.

"You look fabulous Vivian," she remarked meekly.

The other woman gave her a calculated languid perusal. "And you haven't changed a bit, Sidney. Why I thought living in the big city, you might have become sophisticated but not our Sidney. You look just as *wholesome* as ever," Vivian declared haughtily.

"I would say that's quite a compliment, Sid, to still be just as beautiful ten years later," Luke expressed meaningfully.

Vivian sniffed. "Well, beautiful might be filling her head with..."

"The truth," Luke stated with finality in his tone and an uncharacteristic icy edge to his voice.

Vivian faltered for an entire second. "Oh there's Miriam Jennings. I really must talk to her about that business at the high school. Scandal is a difficult matter." She slid a baneful glance at Sidney. "One that must be dealt with expediently."

Sidney mentally impaled an imaginary sharp object in the woman's departing back. "Shouldn't her chosen profession get her attention from your office?"

Luke chuckled. "I don't think anyone has to pay for what Vivian is offering," he drawled.

"If they did, they would likely demand their money back. I can't imagine she is a good fuck," Sidney remarked dryly.

Luke sputtered his coffee, barely managing not to spew the hot liquid across the table.

"Problem?" Sidney asked sweetly.

"Your mouth. What happened to it?" he remarked cynically.

She looked him straight in the eye. "I grew up."

"Is that what you call it!" he retorted sarcastically.

Sidney barely hid a secret smile and Luke's hazel eyes narrowed suspiciously. She had cursed purposely. Evidently, there was something she wanted to prove; perhaps that she had changed, or that she couldn't be easily predicted, that their years apart really had resulted in differences between them.

Sidney wallowed in a smidgen of conceit. It felt triumphant to shock her former husband. Luke had been entirely too confident last night...too cocky... like he was certain he could pick up where they had left off. The rules had changed. She had changed. This woman didn't *need* a man any longer. If she was with one, it was because she chose to be and Sidney wasn't choosing him.

Luke decided a change of topic was in order and unfortunately necessary. "Do you know what Vivian meant by the scandal at the high school?"

Sidney shook her head wearily and suddenly jerked upright with renewed attention. "Not Kathleen?"

Luke gave her a steady sympathetic gaze. "Sidney, you know this is the time of year when Kathleen begins to organize the annual drama production?"

"Oh right...do we need to assist temporarily?"

Luke was grateful he had finished with his coffee. "Ahhh, no. It's a safe bet that the production is canceled."

Sidney's face fell. "That bad?"

"Kat planned on tackling Man of La Mancha..."

Sidney's eyes widened with the possibilities that presented.

"Kathleen's mania was escalating the day of final auditions…"

"Oh no…"

"She interrupted the students who were trying out for the female lead…"

"Dulcinea…"

"Aldonza…"

"Same character…"

"Right."

"She was a prostitute."

"Yes," he confirmed knowing she was already presuming the worst.

"She didn't…" Sidney laid her head down on arms that were crossed on the table in front of her. She opened one eye to squint up at Luke.

He nodded reluctantly. "Kathleen thought the girls needed to be more seductive…"

Sidney closed her eyes in pure dread. "Please tell me she didn't demonstrate…"

"Sidney, Kathleen was out of control. No one realized until it was too late. I was just arriving back in town or I might have seen it coming," he told her trying to soften the blow.

"So she came on to students…"

He would have nodded once more but her eyes remained closed as if she wanted to shut out reality. "And some staff…"

Her eyes flew open. "Which staff?"

"Wilmont."

"Noooo!" she moaned in utter horror. Gerry Wilmont had been the principal at the local high school since the days she had attended. He had been judgmental and condescending then. Little had changed. She vividly recalled the hard time he had given Kathleen when she had begun her teaching career having been privy to her mental health diagnosis. However, he had also hypocritically jumped at the attention Kathleen created with the lavish dramatic productions she was capable of bringing together every year. Those feats had made their professional relationship tolerable. Undoubtedly that was history now.

"Sidney, Kathleen can deal with that when she is well again. We both know that she is capable of taking responsibility for her actions when her moods are stabilized," Luke reminded her staunchly.

Sidney nodded though it hardly lessened the anxiety she felt for her sister.

A beeper went off and Sidney automatically reached for her belt loop from well-formed habit. Luke spied the movement and smiled. "It's me. You're off duty, Sweetheart."

Sidney smiled plastically. He had no idea how off duty she was. She watched him get up and head toward the phone at the counter. He used it without asking and Sidney knew that this was obviously an established custom. The staff here treated him with a casual familiarity that was a rarity in New York.

Luke strode back toward her with deliberate intent. "Sidney, the school just called. Zach took off…"

Grabbing her purse, Sidney was half way to the door before he could finish. She was just opening her car door when his larger hand closed over hers. The contact sizzled nerves, defied logic.

"We'll take my car," Luke told her in authoritative tones needed to cover the unexpected passion rattling his senses. Good God, it was only her hand.

Sidney looked up at him with something akin to annoyance to mask the disturbing stirring swirling in her middle. "Sure. A cop car will be less threatening when we find him."

"He hasn't felt threatened the other hundred times he's been in it and besides we won't be driving anything when we find him," Luke replied confidently.

"Oh yeah?"

"Yeah." He gave her a nudge toward the passenger seat though it suddenly seemed more advisable to stuff her into the back where he wouldn't be tempted to touch. "We're wasting time."

She grudgingly gave in because time was being wasted. All that mattered right now was finding Zach and getting to the heart of the matter. She frowned as she fastened her seat belt. That was the critical issue. Zachary's heart. He had never really been apart from his mother until now. Grant, not known to exorcise his parental rights, had rarely if ever requested over night visitation. This separation from Kathleen, given its circumstances, was obviously more frightening than Zach let on.

She sat scowling as Luke drove decisively. He obviously had a strong hunch where their nephew might be. It was lowering to have to admit that without him, she wouldn't have had a clue.

Within minutes, they were out of city limits on a dusty rural road. Sidney knew every curve and rut though she hadn't seen it in more years than she cared to count. Unease racked her body while she swallowed hard, struggling to appear indifferent.

Luke pulled off the road without comment though the silence between them was humming. He was out of the car when he realized she hadn't joined him. He opened the passenger door, "Coming?"

She could only stare. "Why here?"

"The creek is his thinking place."

Like his mother. She always came here too, Sidney thought, even when her moods didn't allow for any rational thought whatsoever. Sighing, she morosely climbed out of the car and gamely trouped after Luke. She stumbled over an exposed tree root and cursed it ripely, causing him to glance over. "You still walk too fast."

It cheered him that she remembered their long running joke about his legs being too long as much as seeing her rally. Bringing her here was a tough call. "I'm out of practice." He rolled a shoulder letting her catch up though she batted his offer of a hand aside. "Have to work on it."

"Along with your greeting."

"Uh huh," he drawled and gestured ahead. "Zach ought to be just over there."

Sidney froze as her heart lurched into her voice box. The narrow rope bridge that joined the walking trails and spanned the creek was dead ahead. As if time had warped, the rickety structure did not appear any different from the way it was preserved in her memory. "On the other side?!"

Ah, some things didn't change. "That would be over there."

Damned bridge. Damned bridge. Damned bridge. And damn Luke as she watched him measuring her carefully. Well if he expected to see her crumble like the young girl she once was, he was mistaken.

Look straight ahead, she implored herself adamantly, pokering her spine. Never look down. Of course odds were that she would. Sidney stood at the edge, steadied her nerves and took a step.

"You could stay here and I'll bring him back," Luke offered chivalrously. She was as pale as water.

"You said yourself the kids need to see a united front. Come on." Sidney squared her shoulders, bolstered her courage and led the way with feigned bravado. She calculated going first meant avoiding the humiliating probability of Luke turning around to check on her.

Sidney stepped out on to the bridge hearing the gurgle of the wide creek below, swollen with spring. She licked her dry lips and stepped onto a plank that looked better suited to a fireplace. The bridge swayed ever so slightly and her gut clenched. She could sense Luke looming just behind her. In another lifetime that would have been comforting. Now it was horribly intimidating. The bridge seemed endless though logic told her it was probably only about twenty-five feet across.

Look straight ahead. Focus on the trees just getting their leaves on the far bank and remember why you are doing this....Zachary. Zachary. Zachary. He's over there and needs you...and Luke. Both of us, she reminded herself and took another forced step. Determined to get the dreaded journey over with, Sidney single-mindedly made a beeline to the center of the bridge. The swaying of the structure intensified and her stomach lurched to bump against her pounding heart. She smiled out of sheer relief when a dot of red on the other side became more recognizable as her nephew's ball cap.

"Hey Zach! Over here!" Sidney called clutching both sides of the bridge in a fierce white knuckled grip. Maybe he would come to them and this horrendous moment could be over, she prayed in earnest.

The small figure of a boy rose from where he had been sitting against a tree. Spotting the two familiar adults on the bridge, Zachary bolted toward them. Sidney's smile widened only to flip flop by the daunting realization that Zachary was barreling toward the bridge.

Luke's voice was a low warning near her ear. "Sid…" but Zach's feet had already hit the planks of the narrow wooden platform with vigor sending the entire structure swinging, the prettily budding trees on the bank tilting. Sidney was paralyzed with terror when Zach's lanky body catapulted into hers. He clutched her waist throwing off her balance. She staggered to one side as both hands grappled for purchase while the suspended bridge bounced and swayed.

Doe-eyes bulged as she stared helplessly down at the creek envisioning herself rushing down to meet it. When suddenly, two strong hands gripped her shoulders to gently right her body until she stood again, Luke at her back. His scent filled her nostrils, her heart tattooed a jittery beat while his low whisper tickled her ear. "Easy, Sweetheart. I'm right behind you."

"Aunt Sid, you OK? You look a little weird," Zach asked peering up quizzically with his arms still wrapped around her narrow waist.

"Fine," she squeaked out.

"Why don't the three of us get off this bridge and find ourselves some lunch. I'm buying," Luke casually invited.

"A double cheese burger and chocolate shake?" Zach asked hopefully.

"Sounds good. Should we make it three, Sidney?" he said doubting she could choke anything down.

"Sure. Three," she gasped out knowing she would agree to almost anything if it meant getting off this bridge.

"Better go grab my backpack," her nephew yelled exuberantly, shoving away from her to run back across the bridge. It began to mimic the pendulum of a grandfather clock as it swung side to side.

"Oh God…" Sidney gulped as she gripped Luke's arms bringing his chest hard against her back.

"Take a deep breath, Sid. Look straight ahead. Take my hand…"

Dignity worked itself free. After ten years apart, she must look like a weak idiot. Rallying, she straightened her spine and turned to face him with dogged determination. "I'm all right. I would just like to get off of here. I'm…" She met his inquiring gaze straight on. *"Hungry."*

Sidney was instantly rewarded by the warmth and approval that invaded his hazel eyes. Bolstered, she navigated around his taller body intent on escape. Their hips nudged one another and his hand found her elbow. Sidney felt the floodgates threaten to open. There was so much to remember. So much to forget…

The bridge shuddered once more and she knew without turning that Zach was gaining on them. "Hey buddy…" Luke called out behind her in baritone tones that echoed through the woods. "Take it easy. The bridge hasn't been checked yet this season."

The tidal wave of memories vanished like smoke as Sidney's breath expelled in a gust while she scrambled to the bank. Her feet rooted to muddy ground she could have been easily convinced to kiss while she fought to breathe normally again.

"Oh Uncle Luke," Zach returned laughingly as he sauntered nonplused across the merrily swinging bridge. "Someone was out just last week checking the ropes. I told you. Remember?"

A deep chuckle rumbled in his chest. "Oh right. Forgot, Zach. I've been *distracted* lately," he told the young boy walking beside him but his gaze was on the impossibly large brown eyes snapping at him. A devilish glint in his eyes, Luke leaned toward her. "Wouldn't have killed you to take my hand. It still fits," he murmured into her ear.

"Says you!" Sidney retorted. "Hey Zach, race you to the car. First one there, turns on the siren and lights!" she claimed snatching the keys from Luke's jacket. He suddenly wished he had the forethought to ensconce them in his hip pocket. Her retrieval would have been intriguing.

"You're on!" Their nephew yelled, taking off like a shot.

Luke made no attempt to join in, preferring to watch, enthralled. If Sidney was trying to annoy him, it wouldn't work. He didn't care if she was infuriating, ridiculous, frivolous or just plain exasperating. It only mattered that she was back. Better she was in his face and with no end date in sight.

The chaos was comforting, Sidney told herself, trying to shut out her niece and nephew's bickering as she shredded romaine into the bowl Delta had shoved at her. Hearing from Reg would not hurt either. She frowned ripping the leaves with undue gusto as she mulled over the multitude of messages she had left scattered among their friends and the precinct for him. It was a useless emotional reaction to the day's events to do so, and she knew better.

Reg was presently so deep undercover his own mother wouldn't recognize him let alone be able to nab him for a chat. She tore ruthlessly at the lettuce capturing Delta's attention when she sent the stainless steel bowl flying with a reckless hand.

An arm, ropy with muscle and sharp reflexes despite retirement, shot out to rescue the salad as it skidded to the end of the counter.

"Taking tossing a little too seriously, Miss Sidney," Delta clucked as Charlie handed the bowl back without comment and turned back to his crossword.

"Mmmm," Sidney muttered, hurt that Charlie barely spoke two words to her in the past hour other than to ask for the chair she was planning on sitting in so he could prop up his feet. Glancing through to the family room she could see that Nicole and Zach were finding common ground blasting targets with their Nintendo. "So Delta, ever give any thought to retiring?"

The old black woman cackled as she bent over the oven to baste her roast. "Now Miss Sidney, what would become of me with nothing to do but sit around all day?"

Sidney shrugged innocently. "I don't know. Some people take up puzzles. All kinds of them. Jig saw, word jumbles, cross words..." Charlie didn't spare her a glance but his brows knit together. "And they do them until their ass is asleep," she growled carrying her bowl across the kitchen and knocking Charlie's feet down in the process.

"Sidney Ryan, pull that stunt again and..."

"Why, you remembered my name!" she exclaimed, fluttering a hand to her face conjuring up the image of southern innocence. Probably helped that their surnames were one and the same, she grumbled.

"Might be easier if you had come home more often," the broad shouldered man with silvering temples snarled.

"I had a job..." she contended and hastily amended. "I have commitments..."

Charlie nodded coldly. "And here, you only had family. People who love you. An aunt who raised you from a little thing..."

Defensive and guilty as her conscience was tweaked, Sidney's voice rose drawing the children's attention from the violence of their video game to what promised to be real blood letting. "I know who Aunt Vera is, thank you and what she's been to me...."

"Of course you do," Vera cooed soothingly breezing into the room, her frothy tiered skirt fluttering. She laid a comforting arm about Sidney's shoulders with a tender smile, turning aside momentarily to shoot Charlie a meaningful look.

"Good Christ Vera. The girl doesn't need you coddling her. She knows you would have liked to have her home more."

"Charlie." Vera's voice trilled but Charlie knew precisely where he was treading and was long past caring. This was no holiday so he didn't plan on tiptoeing around sticky topics.

"What? She can't up and leave if I piss her off with Kathleen in the hospital," he contended with gleaming eyes. "It's time we straighten a few things out."

Vera opened her mouth but Sidney spoke first. "Maybe it is," the young woman she thought of as a daughter agreed, making her stomach jump. Sidney flattened her palms on the kitchen table directly across from Charlie. "Let's start with folks who retire and don't say a damn thing about it," Sidney spat settling her hands on her hips. "Most people have a party when they retire." Particularly those in long time public service like a sheriff of over thirty years, she stewed, hurt at being left out. "I bet it was lovely."

Vera cocked her head thoughtfully, seeing the hurt feelings in both of them that they so often tried to foist off on her. "It certainly would have been if Charlie had agreed to one."

"What do I need with a God damned party? A bunch of blow-hards making up nice things to say. Embarrassing shit," Charlie huffed intent on returning his attention back to his puzzle, miffed when the point of his pencil broke. How was he going to look busy now? He looked up annoyed to see Vera cocking her head, clearing her throat. His eyes slid to where Zach and Nicole had crept close drawn by the heated words. "Hell Vera, the kids have heard me say shit before."

"Lots of times," Zach agreed, his head bobbing.

Vera rolled her eyes disapprovingly but was glad that it made Sidney smile.

"Sides, one party would have been bad enough but two dog and pony shows…"

"Two? Why would you need to have two?" Sidney frowned.

Charlie swiveled leveling her with a look. "We do everything in twos."

Brown eyes darted about the room as Sidney noted that the others seemed to know exactly what he was talking about. "What do you mean?"

"Charlie, this isn't the time."

"It's never the time, Vera," he challenged sorry for the hurt that flickered across her pretty face but not enough to back down.

"What do you do twice?" Sidney asked in a subdued tone fearful of the answer.

"Holidays. At least the ones you decide to grace us with your presence for. Fewer all the time though. Easter, Thanksgiving, Christmas..." Charlie stabbed the air with his pencil to accentuate his point. "Do you know how much shopping a man has to do to give the same people presents twice and try and act like he didn't just do that same fool thing the day before?"

Sidney bit down on her lip. "You have two Christmases?" A conclusion, hastily drawn, smacked her right between the eyes.

"Yeah, it's great, Aunt Sid," Zach babbled slapping at his sister's elbow when it jabbed his ribs. "One day we spend with Uncle Luke and I get a ton of stuff and then you come..." His sister's hand clamped over his mouth and despite a valiant struggle he couldn't shake her free.

"I didn't know."

"Of course you didn't," Charlie lectured. The words were pumping like a geyser now probably, he supposed, because it was a relief to get them off his chest. "You come. We're grateful for the few days we get and shove the rest under the carpet. Well it's spring and I think we need to do some cleaning." He thumped his fist on the table making Sidney jump. She had only seen him this mad at one other woman. One she never wanted to be paired with.

"This from a man who thinks dust bunnies should be kept for pets!" Delta scolded, riled that her little girl was being dressed down just a day of being home. If that ornery goat wasn't careful Miss Sidney might just get in her car and drive back to the city to that man she lived in sin with.

"What else don't you say?" Sidney asked thinking she might as well catch all the hell at one time.

Brooding eyes peered into hers. "Not what, who. We pretend that Luke doesn't exist when you're here and that stops as of now!" he shouted and then lowered his voice. "You are both members of this family and dammit neither of you are children."

"I never asked anyone not to talk about Luke. But no one ever did and it seemed more comfortable all around so I didn't..." It wasn't like she had never been tempted.

"Well let's get uncomfortable and see how it fits," Charlie recommended cantankerously, rising out of his chair fearful he might be seeing the first sheen of tears. He could hold his own in an armed hold up but he would rather be shot than see Sidney cry. He glanced over his shoulder just before passing through the archway to the dining room. "Maybe I didn't have a retirement party because I didn't think you'd come."

Sidney closed her eyes, pressing fingertips to her forehead where the promise of a nasty headache was brewing. She felt her aunt's hand on her shoulder but moved away.

"Sidney."

She shook her head swiping at her nose with the back of her hand. "No. He's right about most of it. I need some air." The wind felt good on her hot cheeks as Sidney pushed open the gingerbread door and stepped out onto the back porch. She leaned forward on the railing unmindful of the cold raising bumps on her skin.

"Sidney."

She whirled around, eyes bulging as indignant tears welled. From the pitying look on his face, she didn't need to ask how much he'd heard.

Luke gentled his voice the way a smart horseman would to calm a startled mare. "Sidney, he didn't mean to make you cry."

Her mouth twitched as she looked away knowing he was reaching for her. She planned on batting him away but when his hands closed around her shoulders, drawing her close, she humiliated herself and burrowed. "He yelled at me Luke. The only person I have ever heard him yell at other than one of his men was..." Her voice trailed off as she realized her blunder.

Luke tipped up her chin. "Was my mother, who deserved it far more often than he indulged in."

Sidney chewed her lip, being lumped with Virginia Ryan was a bitter pill to swallow.

"It's not the same thing, Sid. He yelled at you because he misses you. He's gotten used to it over the years, maybe even resigned but when he heard you were coming for Kat...." Luke inhaled deeply, pondering.

"He's barely said a civil word to me since I arrived," she huffed. "At least you yell..." She stopped herself before she dug a deeper hole but he was already chuckling.

He took advantage of her nearness to stroke a hand over her hair, sure it had never felt softer. "See it runs in the family."

Sidney rolled her eyes and groaned, ordering herself to move out of his arms, startled that it took an effort. "Lucky me." When she judged they were a safe few feet apart, she turned. "Did he celebrate his retirement at all?"

It was hard he found to know what to say. Honesty could hurt. "We had a house party."

Sidney nodded accepting that as her own just desserts. "Here?"

Luke shifted his weight. "At my place."

"A party's a lot of work."

He sighed hearing the question, wishing he didn't. "Kat and Rebecca helped."

Her sister and best childhood friend. Together they were known as the three musketeers. Without them, she was merely alone. "They would be wonderful hostesses."

Her demure acceptance irked him. "Dammit, Sid, if I had thought for an instant you would come I'd have invited you." He looked away and fought back a stinging curse. "You could have even brought…" Luke dragged a hand over his face.

"Reg?" she finished blinking her shock.

"Yes," he ground out, annoyed that she was so stunned he could be civil. "Well…"

"Well what?" he snapped. She wasn't the only one who was making adjustments.

"That's very kind."

"It's not kind," he bit out, holding up a hand like the traffic cop he occasionally still had to be. "And it's not generous. It's just middle ground. Dammit, Sid, after all this time, we need to find some. We used to share something." His tone softened. "Someone." She squeezed her eyes shut and turned away but he couldn't let it go. Not any more. "Well, we lost Natalie." His index finger was waving dramatically toward the house, a barometer of the pain he locked inside. "But those people we still share. They are your family but they are mine too."

"I know." In the brief day she had been back she had seen that, more so than in years of visits. "We'll fix it Luke." It was a rare day when anyone could surprise this man and yet she knew she had. His baffled stare was so gratifying, she decided to top it. She stepped forward and brushed his cheek with a kiss before going in the house leaving him gawking.

Charlie stroked his chin with one hand as the other held the drape so he could watch them on the back porch discreetly. She hadn't spoken but he had known Vera was behind him for some time.

He hadn't acknowledged her in the off chance some extraordinary thought might spring into his head to save his sorry butt. He pretty much guessed that not only was he uninvited to the dinner that his stomach was making noises over but he was also going to find himself sleeping at that cold heartless excuse for a house his bitchy wife had coveted. The one he avoided other than to pay the taxes and pick up his pension check.

Sidney's impromptu kiss to Luke had his jaw falling to his chest. "I did that!" He turned swiftly, fearful Vera would miss the moment and practically fell on her.

"Looks like Sidney's did it, Charlie. After all, your lips are right here," Vera countered with the dry wit she only displayed privately.

His eyes narrowed until he heard her sigh wistfully.

"They do look good together."

Taking a chance, Charlie draped an arm around her shoulders. "Darlin' they always looked good together, even as children."

True enough. "Charlie, about your spring cleaning."

His eyes shifted to hers warily. There would be no cozy quilt and soft woman for him tonight.

"Cleaning can be done a lot of different ways."

If there was a point, he didn't see it. Delta was for cleaning. He was for relaxing.

Vera saw his confusion and smiled maternally. "You can clean with a broom and beat the dirt out of your rugs. And you're right, some things do need tidying." She laid a hand on his rough cheek. "Try a feather duster, Charlie. I want Sidney to stay."

Sidney leapt on the warbling phone with the same energy a lioness takes down its kill. She clutched the receiver to her chest feeling foolish, glancing around grateful when the others looked away. They were likely embarrassed for her. An hour ago, it had been the druggist saying Delta's rheumatism medicine was ready for pick up.

"Babe? Babe, are you there?"

"Reg!" Her face lit. "I'm here and have been for hours. Where have you been?"

He heard the worry there and felt a stab of guilt over it. How much more would she put up with? Considering that, Reg thought of the vulgar language, the pimp who had tried slap and tickle with one of his girls until being taught some manners and the stink of the cesspool he had been loitering in for the past twenty hours. "No where, Babe. Just no where."

Sidney smiled sadly knowing what he meant and wishing she was there to ease some of the strain. "Are you eating? Getting some sleep?"

He clucked his tongue. "Right back at you, Babe."

Sidney made a face she knew he would appreciate. "I will if you will."

"Deal, Sid. Nothing to do after work without you anyhow," he grumbled.

She giggled like a schoolgirl knowing better. "Reg Buckman, you led a very active social life before I was your main squeeze."

Reg put his tongue to his cheek remembering fondly. He'd have to be dead to forget. "Well, you know, Babe, they do say a man has to sow his wild oats before making that enormous commitment…"

Sidney had played enough poker to know a bluff when she heard it. "Staying in with Rauja again, Reg."

Reg kneaded the huge mongrel feline, which was draped over him like a rug, purring as loud as a transport. "Yeah Babe. Just us fellas watching Letterman and me dreaming of snuggling up with you instead of this flea bag."

"Think of it from Rauja's point of view." Knowing she had hit her mark when he snorted.

"God, I miss you."

Feeling guilt. "It's only been a day."

Yearning. "Thirty two hours since we kissed goodbye."

"You remember the time of our last kiss?" Sidney asked, incredibly touched.

Luke leaned on the wall knowing that just on the other side of it, she didn't have a clue he was there. Eavesdropping was an activity he had never contemplated until today and after one brief experience wouldn't recommend it. He wasn't the least bit surprised the man in Sidney's life remembered their last kiss. God knows, he hadn't forgotten.

CHAPTER FOUR

Something was wrong, she had felt for a couple days. The dinner in front of her was delicious but she could barely touch it, her stomach was too jumpy. Sidney let the easy conversation float around her hearing it like it was muted.

"So can I go?" Zach frowned and tugged on his aunt's sleeve to get her attention.

She turned blankly to him. "What?"

"Can I go?" Zach asked again, impatience in his eyes.

Her eyes darted around the table in a feeble plea for help.

"I think Todd Fitzgerald's birthday party at the bowling alley sounds great, Zach," Luke answered easily. "Maybe Nic could go with you tomorrow after school to find a gift."

"I don't want to look for some geeky little kid's present," Nicole complained.

"Too bad," Luke shrugged. "My secretary said there's a big sale on at the mall."

Vera glowed her approval. "Yes Lucas that's right. All the spring fashions. Carlene has talked endlessly about it." When she would have preferred her assistant to be working, she grumbled privately.

"All right Zach but if we run into anyone I know," Nicole aimed a carrot stick at her brother like a weapon. "You have to pretend not to be with me."

Sidney felt indignant for her nephew but a sidelong glance said he couldn't have cared less. Zach jumped up to pluck the money Luke was holding in his hand. "Thanks Uncle Luke. If there's any left over, we'll bring it by the station," the little boy pledged throwing his arms about his uncle's neck.

Luke ruffled Zach's shaggy blond hair affectionately. "If there's any left, just put it in your bank."

Nicole rose from the table with the grace of a gymnast eyeing Luke strategically, who held up a bill in two fingers. She smiled sweetly, moving forward to collect, frowning when he held the money just out of reach.

"Not so fast Nic."

The willowy blond sighed, angling her hips stubbornly. "Ahhh, Uncle Luke."

"Who's my best girl?" he asked in tones that were known to make grown women melt.

She rolled her eyes, gave into giggles and leaned over to peck him on the cheek knowing it was what he wanted. The only thing he ever truly asked for despite all the things he did for them. Their hands met as the money pressed into her palm. "Thanks Uncle Luke."

He waited until she was almost to the hall, away from the press of so many adults. "And Nic?"

"Uh huh."

"Try and be nice to the little dude. He misses your Mom."

She turned slowly around, her expression clearly showing Zach wasn't alone. It had been over a week. "Sure Uncle Luke."

Charlie glanced around and saw potential. "Hey Vera. Why don't we see if the kids want to go the movies with us and then for ice cream?"

Sidney was stunned by the speed her aunt said her farewells and went off to collect the kids. "That was subtle."

Luke quirked a lop sided grin, making a mental note to treat his Dad to a beer at Smitty's. "Dad has never been known for being particularly refined."

She snorted before thinking better of it. "Yes, your mother reminded him of it often enough." She winced with regret instantly. "Shit, Luke. I'm sorry. I have no right…."

He lifted a brow. "You have more right than most. After my Dad, my mother saved up her nastiness for you."

Sidney frowned contemplating that. Somehow thanks sounded both appropriate and stupid. Another thought dawned. "I tried to write to you after she died. I could never seem to get the words right."

He rolled his shoulders appreciating the gesture but hating the memories it conjured up. "It's OK, Sid. I can't imagine it was easy for you to feel badly over her death. She gave you little to love about her."

Sidney shook her head gritting her teeth, feeling the sudden urge to slam her fist on the table the way Charlie had the other day. "Dammit, Luke, don't do that."

At a genuine loss, he stared at the sparks of anger he had touched off. Funny, he had been trying to let her off the hook. "Do what? I just meant I understand you not feeling any remorse…"

"Remorse had little to do with it," she countered. "I wasn't writing to Virginia. I was writing to you. I was worried about you. Whatever she was, whatever she did, she *was* your mother."

That had him gawking. Lord, of all women, this one knew best how to tie him in knots. "You worried about me in New York?"

Now she mirrored his expression. What did he take her for? She angled her face away from him under the pretense of fiddling with the daffodils on the buffet. "Of course I did." For several years, it was almost a full time preoccupation, she lamented.

He narrowed his eyes on her slender back. What the hell was so interesting about the damned flowers? "Sidney, turn around..."

"In a minute." Wanting to swear when her voice hitched.

"Are you crying?"

"No dammit!" she ground out through a clenched jaw.

He was beside her in an unnerving instant. Two fingers under her chin turned her face gently to his. "Sweetheart..."

He could move her face but she didn't have to look. Her eyes stayed stubbornly focused on the weave of his shirt. "You thought so little of me that I wouldn't have cared about you losing your mother!?"

Luke inhaled wearily. This was a hard call. How much could he say without risking her running? Sure Kathleen remained very ill but he still sensed if he pushed the wrong buttons she might be in New York before he could stop her. "Sidney, I'm a lousy mind reader. I learned that about a decade ago." She put a hand over her mouth and fought back the rush of tears. "After you left, I questioned just about everything that could be questioned."

She wanted to resist but couldn't. "And what did you come up with?"

"Not a whole hell of a lot." It didn't help that after leaving their marriage and this town, she refused to speak with him other than through lawyers. "Care to help me out?"

She was peering into Pandora's box and knowing once open, there would be no closing it. "Luke..."

He cursed when the phone rang cutting her off. It seemed like after an eternity of looking for answers she might be prepared to give him some. "Don't answer it."

"I have to."

The expression in her eyes said it all. She thought it might be *him*. He knew she had been waiting for the call. Luke moved to the window as she flew to pick it up, concluding grimly that jealousy was a lowering emotion he would prefer not to have first hand knowledge of.

"Don?" The quiver in her voice was immediate. "Where's Reg? I haven't been able to reach him for..." Luke watched the anxiety transform into fury. "Well get him the hell out! Screw that Don." She held her silence albeit hostile. "How long? Don't pussyfoot around for chrissake! This is me you're talking to." She nodded grimly forcing herself to listen. "Yeah, Don. My head understands that but it doesn't make it easier." She combed a hand restlessly through her hair. "I hate this. Really hate this," she sighed again pressing fingers to her eyes. "Don...do me a favor? Go to Marino's on 32nd

Street and buy him one of those fudge tortes." She nodded blinking back tears. "That's sweet Don. I'll make a double batch when I get back." She laughed shortly and then hung up.

Luke watched as she pursed her lips miserably and wandered out into the kitchen. It took every ounce of his considerable control not to go after her but it didn't seem his place. He groaned, not that he knew what the hell was his place in her life. All he knew was he wanted one.

He edged toward the doorway to see her sitting at the kitchen table digging into a carton of Hagan Das. "Is it overstepping to ask what happened?"

She sighed glumly, looking up to see him leaning against the doorjamb and envied the strength she saw. "Reg is in jail."

Luke gave his head a mental shake that could knock his teeth loose. "I thought he was a cop."

His shock made her laugh. "He is."

Luke rubbed his temple and grabbed a spoon to sit across from her. "What's a cop doing in jail?"

"Not blowing his cover." Sidney shrugged lamely. "It's part of the gig. There was a murder in the area that Reg has been infiltrating. If he weren't a cop, he would be a priority suspect. If they don't haul his ass in like the others for questioning, it will be too conspicuous."

Luke decided, small town life with all its pitfalls and bureaucratic bullshit was looking better than it had this morning when the mayor was hassling him. "So how long will they hold him?"

"Twenty four hours maybe forty eight." Sidney spread her hands. "It varies."

This obviously wasn't a first but rather a chronic hazard to Reg's work. "He's good at what he does. Right?" Her brows knit together. "Carl has said a few things."

She nodded a little uncomfortable with Luke's best friend and fellow cop being brought between them. "Carl and Rebecca have been down for a couple visits."

He knew that and still had trouble sorting out how he felt about it. "My point is Reg can take care of himself so he'll be fine."

"Yeah," she agreed and noticing his spoon for the first time tipped the carton of Caramel Cone Explosion toward him. "I just hate to think of him there. He hates cages." She surprised him then with a brave smile though the tears didn't seem far off. "The kids are taken care of so I'm going to go up to bed."

Luke watched her go and with her his plans to whisk her off for a quiet drink at his place. It was growing disturbingly important to him to take her there, show her the home that he had always hoped to build for her and their family.

She turned, one hand curled around the polished banister of the back staircase. "Thanks for listening, Luke. I appreciate it."

"Get some sleep, Sid, and try not to worry." An odd strategy suddenly struck him. "Reg would feel better if he thought you were fine."

Her wistful gaze grew distant. "Problem is that Reg only believes I'm fine when I'm with him."

Luke listened to her feet pad softly up the stairs he could remember chasing her up in days gone by to wrestle her out of her clothes and dug deeper into the ice cream. It was a strange and growing concern that this man she lived with was beginning to sound like someone he could learn to like.

"Are you asleep?" a soft lilting voice whispered, soft lips nuzzling his ear.

"Hmmm." Luke murmured groggily because he was and partly because the slender hand that was leisurely caressing the length of his thigh was distracting. Her nails lightly skimmed his hip and traveled the over the hard plane of his belly. He sucked in his breath quivering at her tantalizing touch.

"You are awake!" she cooed softly.

He growled huskily while her hand made large fleeting circles around parts of him that called out to her digits. He was responding like lightening to her teasing. An involuntary shutter rippled through him as he waited impatiently for her to touch where he needed her most.

His eyelids at half-mast, Luke saw his wife kneeling beside his hips with only moonlight streaking across her features. Her other hand joined the sensual torment that its counterpart was engaged in. Cool fingertips barely lifted from his thigh when her other hand began to trace from his shoulder trailing over his chest creating the illusion that a single hand was quicker than the speed of light. Both hands continued the feather light stroking his body within bare inches of pure intimacy. He trembled in the effort to remain still.

"Touch me, Sidney," he commanded huskily

"Oh I am. Can't you feel me?" she replied silkily.

"Feel you? I want to swallow you whole." Luke contended hoarsely.

She smiled beguilingly in the shadows. "Promises... promises."

"Sid... just a little over to the..."

"Here?" Her fingers moved with in a fraction of his preferred destination pleased when his breathing became ragged.

"Closer..."

"Here?" she asked with feigned innocence.

"I can't take much more…"

"A big strong fella like you… a cop," she teased relentlessly.

"Sid!" he cried catching her fingers in his larger hand.

She stilled completely and leaned over his face. He was momentarily distracted by the outline of her nipple in the moonlight. His mouth never felt so dry. Luke knew how exotic she would taste. How incredibly mind numbing it would be when she joined with him…and he also knew with absolute conceit that he had taught her most of what she knew. It wás part of the allure. His wife was an eager student who constantly embellished his tutelage with her own guileless experimentation.

He directed her hand to close over the searing length of himself and watched her smile beguilingly in the night at what she found. Her hand began to move in a mesmerizing rhythm until his breathing became more rapid and shallow. Long arms stole around her, urging her downward until their mouth's melded together in an explorative kiss.

A child's lusty cry rent the air demanding immediate gratification.

Her mouth moved just a scant inch above his so she spoke into his mouth. "I need to…"

"*Yes you do*….but first go see to the baby…." He baited her shamelessly.

She giggled and scampered off the bed with a last smacking kiss to his cheek. "I won't be long."

"Promise?"

"Promise," her lilting voice reaffirmed.

He sat up like a thunderbolt in his bed and searched the cloaked night for signs of her return. But there were none. Just like there were no sounds of their child. Her side of the bed was cold to the touch and there was no indentation on the pillow. A crib did not occupy a corner of this bedroom. It never had. Both the woman and the child were figments of his imagination. As Luke eased back onto the mattress, his despair sunk to new depths.

Sidney dashed up the stairs clutching shopping bags in both hands. She stopped at one landing to call out the window as Luke pulled out of the drive, his long arm waved out of the cruiser. She giggled when he flipped the lights on. God, he looked good in uniform, she sighed dreamily.

Her heart felt as light as the airy spring breeze that fluttered the lace curtains. They had shared a wonderful lunch alone for the first time in months, feeding each other forkfuls of pie and then shopped for Nat's birthday presents. Some silly woman had the nerve to remark that one year olds don't even remember their birthdays so why bother making a fuss. They ignored her. It promised to be quite a day with Winnie the Pooh plates and napkins, silly party favors and the gift of a wooden rocking horse, they could neither afford or resist.

Delta had told her Natalie was still napping but she planned on waking her up. Still out of sheer habit, Sidney lightened her tread on the last set of stairs. She stowed her packages in the little frilly bedroom that was almost ready for the baby to move into. She rolled her eyes knowing it could have been ready months ago but she liked having Natalie near. Besides the crib hardly took up any space in the huge attic bedroom and though she had read some fathers become jealous of their own babies, Luke didn't seem to mind, and it was handy with Natalie still nursing. A lot of mothers with babies the same age had quit by now but her daughter had a real preference for her and Sidney saw it as a compliment. Just the other night, she had brought her into bed and when Luke watched the baby nurse, Sidney swore she had seen pride glow in his gaze.

Being a good mother and wife were everything to her. People were quick to point out her age and expect her to fail but she was tough. Tougher than a lot of folks knew Luke teased her often enough. Natalie would be one in only three short weeks and they were making out just fine. So fine, the urge to think of more babies had started to sneak in. A wistful smile curved her lips as her hand touched the doorknob. Maybe she and Luke should take a long walk one evening soon and talk about it.

"Hey sleepy girl! What are you dreaming about? Must be good if you would rather snooze than go for a walk with Mommy? It's beautiful outside. We might even spot a robin red breast." Sidney chattered cheerfully as she neared the white crib tucked in the far corner of their bedroom away from drafts.

She smiled anticipating the beauty of her sleeping child, who lay stretched out on her back as she typically preferred. The patchwork quilt Aunt Vera had given her at birth was pulled up to her shoulders as if Natalie had just been put to bed making Sidney frown. It was usually kicked to the end of the crib by now. Sidney felt the first licks of alarm seeing her daughter's treasured blanky crushed into the crib rails rather than clutched in a chubby fist.

"Hey Nat!" she called breathlessly, dashing toward the crib. "You and your blanky have a fight, Sweetie Pie? I'll have to tell Daddy…"

Sidney stopped mid sentence frozen with dread. Her baby was chalk white, pouty lips tinged with blue. The scent of urine and stool struck her nostrils with the force of a brick wall. She shuttered violently. Natalie never pooped during naptime.

It was wrong. Sidney sensed that even as the horrible shaking started turning her movements awkward. She stumbled against the crib, sobbing out her daughter's name, looked into the little face that she had given life to and felt her heart fracture.

Her feet flew down the stairs, shallow breaths puffing out rapidly. She should knock, knew it was only polite but her hands just threw open the door, relieved to see a lamp on and the person she needed most.

Vera's head snapped up from her book. Her arms were opening and the smile Sidney always could count on was tender. "Oh Honey." Sidney fell sobbing into her arms heedless of an explanation, knowing one wasn't needed. Undignified hiccupping sobs escaped as tears fell unchecked. Vera rocked her gently without speaking, only sliding a dainty hand over the loose tumble of hair. Finally Sidney drew away to peer into her aunt's face with large sorrowful eyes.

"It's been a long time since we've done this." Vera murmured softly lifting tousled hair off the younger woman's slight shoulder.

Sidney nodded with a hollow stare.

"Was it the dream again?"

Sidney nodded, her eyes welling with fresh tears.

Soft knuckles stroked her cheek. "Sidney, it's only natural that you are thinking more of the baby right now."

A shuttered breath escaped her and she slid wordlessly into the comfort of her aunt's embrace again. A few minutes later, Vera gently disengaged the young woman in her arms to gaze into her shattered face. "Sidney, it isn't just the baby you dream about, is it?"

Sidney sniffed softly, giving a tiny shake of her head. It was so easy to admit things in this room she couldn't anywhere else. They sat together for a long time in a gentle hold that they had both known and found solace in for over two decades. For being so outwardly different, they shared a strong bond that they publicly allowed few people to witness.

Though it wouldn't have taken much to talk her into curling up there for the rest of the night, Sidney eased back to give her aunt a small smile that they both knew was all false bravado. "Thanks Auntie. I'm fine now. I'll let you go back to your book."

"You are always more important than a book," Vera reminded her firmly. "Any book."

Sidney's smile softened. "I know. You are always the biggest perk of coming back."

Vera's eyes flooded with emotion as she shooed her out with a sentimental smile. "We'll talk more in the morning."

Sidney's lips curved thoughtfully as she wandered down the hall once more. They would talk in the morning. Of that she was certain, but she also knew that the Vera she saw in the light of day was never quite the woman who held her in the night. Vera, she had learned years before, had both a public persona as well as a private one. Sidney loved the woman who was her eccentric literary aunt but when the chips were down, she always went to the woman of the night.

The bathroom door adjoining Vera's frilly lavender bedroom creaked open. The man with the pensive expression went directly over to the bed and settled himself on the edge of it to face the woman who sat in quiet reflection.

"That hasn't happened for awhile," he remarked.

"No and it was fortunate thing that you were where you were."

The man gave a small shout of laughter. "Says you woman! I have a ring around a part of my anatomy that one doesn't belong."

Vera let out a peal of laughter. "You are deliberately trying to make me laugh," she accused.

"That would be one hundred per cent on the money, Darlin," he agreed with a sneaky grin. "I know how worried you are about her. Everyone has been concentrating on Kathleen but in many respects our more worrisome patient is the younger of the two."

Vera smiled at his perceptiveness. "It has been a grueling year for Sidney."

"She needed to come back here for more than a holiday she couldn't wheedle out of. This whole business has been left too long."

"I suppose."

"It has Vera," he declared staunchly. "For both of them. If they don't look this straight in the eye and deal with it, they can't move on."

Vera's eyes narrowed suspiciously. "I thought you didn't want her to move on."

The man stroked his chin and sighed. "I want her to get married...."

"Well ...."

One authoritative hand shot up. "Don't go there, Vera. I refuse to be a party in that matter. You and my son will have to deal with that one day." *God help you when that day comes.* "I would like to see Sidney have some babies and laugh more."

"She laughs in New York."

He frowned deeply at what that implied. "If she goes back, I want her to be at peace enough to come home more and really want to be here."

"I would like that as well." Vera said wearily.

He gave her a pointed look. "Maybe you should have her read that book you are working on."

"Not tonight. She isn't up to it yet." Vera hedged though for the life of her she had no idea how to actually get Sidney to read her work any longer.

The man edged forward on the bed and let his gaze rove over the woman in the lace nightgown that afforded him a view he had appreciated for decades. "I'm up for something tonight, Vera." His gaze lingered meaningfully. "If you are interested."

Her smile was as old as woman. "With you Charlie, I am always interested."

He gave her a calculated leer. He not only knew that, he counted on it.

CHAPTER FIVE

Her hand blindly reached across the bed, fumbling over the covers. Sidney growled low as her arm stretched and still couldn't find him. Strange. The man was typically hard to miss. She moved her foot under the covers across the bed seeking the familiar weight, causing her forehead to furrow. The cat was gone too.

Her eyes flicked open and shut again to blink out the strong sunlight. Why weren't the blinds down? Reg always pulled them before bed. She sat straight up in stunned shock. Because she wasn't in New York.

Her eyes flew to the clock on the bed stand. Shit! She had overslept again. Sidney sprang from the bed grabbing the clothes closest to her and wrestled them on. Her feet were still bare and her hair tumbled in a tangle down her back as she raced down the back stairway skidding to a halt in the kitchen.

"Lordy, Miss Sidney. Where is the fire?"

Glancing about, Sidney ignored Delta to focus on her nephew who sat calmly spooning up his Frosted Flakes. "Zach, did you put your creative writing assignment in your book bag?"

"Yup." A little dribble of milk trailed down his chin.

Sidney snapped her fingers together, willing thought. "And your library book, the overdue one that we got a notice about."

He screwed up his face defensively. "That wasn't my fault. It got put in Auntie's study on her bookshelf by accident. And I couldn'a done it. I'm not allowed in there."

"That's because Mom doesn't want you reading smut," Nicole put in drolly.

Sidney reined in her impatience. "Auntie Vera does not collect smut on her bookshelves."

Nicole laughed. "No, Aunt Sid, she writes it."

Blowing hot, Sidney tapped a foot. "Nicole, Auntie Vera writes love stories."

The pretty blond cocked her head to one side enjoying her aunt's reaction to the hilt. "How would you know? Mom says you haven't read one of Auntie's novels in years. You just pretend and read enough to be able to say *something* to her."

Sidney realized she was holding her breath and let it out in shuttering rush, "I would say that is a matter between Kat and I." She paused. "And Auntie and I. But I don't want to hear you talking that way about Auntie

Vera's work."

The screen door banged and Charlie's heavy tread could be heard coming down the center hall. "Why? It's the truth." Charlie muttered from the doorway having overheard their exchange.

Gifting the older man with a pointed glare, it occurred to her that he appeared very at home, dressed only in an undershirt so worn you could see through it and pants where his belt lay open. "Charlie."

He quirked a rakish grin, settled at the table and winked at Nicole. "But it's great smut and it keeps you kids living in high style," he added gesturing to the large gracious home with his rolled paper.

Sidney waved that aside, ran her tongue over her teeth longing for her toothbrush, and turned back to Zach. "Just hand in the book and pay the fine."

"I don't have the money."

"I gave you the money yesterday."

Zach tapped his fingers to no particular rhythm. "Sure but I couldn't find the book then."

"Well you have it now."

"So I need more money."

Considering she had almost completed her doctorate, Sidney could only blame her inability to follow this conversation to having just woke up. "Zach, what did you do with the money I gave you yesterday?"

"Well I couldn't give it to the librarian without the book so it was just going to waste…" She leaned forward expectantly. "I spent it on some cards," he admitted sheepishly.

"Baseball cards?" she asked trying to squelch her growing irritation.

"Oh no, Aunt Sid. Way better than that." He dug into his knap sack to withdraw a wad of cards with ghoulish figures on them. "See."

"You bought all those?"

His look easily conveyed that she was a novice. "No just four."

Sidney did a double take as Delta cackled by the stove. "Four? My money only bought four?"

Obviously offended, Zach spread them out for her perusal. "One is a hologram and another is classed as rare!"

Sidney's lips flattened into a thin line. "OK. Fine. You need more money."

"Uh huh."

"How much, Zach?"

Sidney jolted unnerved that she hadn't even noticed Luke sitting on a stool at the kitchen island behind her. His legs were crossed casually at the ankle as he sat sipping coffee where he had obviously finished off a plate of eggs. Money was exchanged with his nephew but his eyes roamed over her. It seemed to Sidney, he was taking his time about it.

"The one end of the paper is wet again," Charlie complained sourly. "Delta, you tell that damned paper boy he isn't getting paid unless my paper comes dry for an entire week."

"Do you live here?" The impulsive words were out before Sidney could snatch them back.

Charlie stilled completely and stared while Nicole snickered. "He has to. Auntie told Mom Charlie is good research material."

Luke choked on his coffee while Sidney looked cautiously away glad when a timid knock at the door distracted her.

"That'll be Carlene." Zach mumbled through a mouthful of soggy cereal.

Sidney stretched to absently pull open the door not particularly interested. She had known Carlene, her aunt's long time research assistant, since childhood but had little in common then with the mousy girl and she presumed even less now. "Zach, hurry up. The bus will be here any..." Sidney's head swung back around blinking. "Carlene? Carlene Joselyn?"

"I heard you were back, Sidney."

Well, the voice was the same. Quiet and slightly nasal but that was where the similarity ended. Her drab brown hair was highlighted to a lustrous gold, flashy clothes showed off curves Sidney never would have guessed were hidden under the unflattering fashions the girl once favored and makeup transformed her once plain Jane features to someone who would get a second glance from a man who had bothered to look. "Carlene, you look incredible!"

Flushing from her toes up, the young woman couldn't have been more pleased though she had taken three tedious hours to make herself up before coming over. "Thanks. I had a little make over last Christmas."

Money had never been better spent, Sidney mused. Suddenly self-conscious over having just rolled out of bed, she smoothed a hand over her hair.

"Sit and eat, Sidney," Luke encouraged pulling out a chair where Delta had just placed a full plate. He would take her sexy rumpled look over Carlene's artificial one any day.

Sidney sat across from Charlie whose was strategically hidden by his paper. She thrust out a hand to lower the newsprint so she could see her niece. "Nicole have you eaten?"

"I don't eat breakfast. I thought we covered that."

"Nic..." It was time to lay down the law.

"Did you wash Mom's hair when you saw her yesterday?"

That brought Sidney up short. "No. Maybe today or at the latest tomorrow."

"That's what you said yesterday and the day before that!" Nicole shouted with sea green eyes blazing.

Sidney barely stifled a sigh. Accepting mental illness was difficult enough for adults, teenagers were at a severe disadvantage to even begin to understand its complexities. "Nicole, your Mom has been deeply depressed...

"Aunt Sid, she *needs* her hair washed. You said that you would take care of it!" Nicole's accusatory voice heightened to a shrill pitch as she stood defiantly before her.

Sidney blinked at her niece aware that every eye in the room was riveted to them now. "Nicole, your mom can hardly get off the mattress..."

"A mattress! You mean like on the floor!" Nicole's eyes widened in horror. "Like an animal!"

Sidney cringed. Major blunder. Too much reality. "The less there is in the room the safer your Mom is right now," she hastily explained rising to draw her niece toward a chair. "Let's sit down..."

Nicole shook off her aunt's hand. "I don't want to sit down! I want to know why you didn't do what you said you would do!" Hurt and anger were fused in her tone as she pivoted to stomp from the room.

Sidney dogged her heels. "Nicole, wait!"

The teen whirled, battle-ready, her blunt cut blond hair flying about slim shoulders. "It wasn't such a big thing to ask. I just wanted you to do her hair...."

"And I will," Sidney persisted. "But yesterday that was not what she truly needed. Nicole, your Mom just needs some time..."

Nicole stopped so abruptly that Sidney bumped into her slight frame. Her niece spun about with the agility of an Olympic gymnast. Angry sparks flying from her aqua eyes. "You just don't get it, *Aunt Sid!* Maybe it's OK to be a freak in New York but this is little Barren's Creek. Everyone is talking like Mom is some moron...some nut case...if she can't act normal, at least she can look it!" she raged, anguished tears coursing down pale cheeks.

Sidney stared, vaguely aware of her aunt's presence just beyond them. The scene was so familiar though some of the players had changed. Years had passed since she was the young girl enduring the agony of watching Kathleen fight her demons. Now Nicole stood before her just as bewildered and lost.

Willing to risk the probable rejection, Sidney drummed up a tender smile and reached out to run a hand over her niece's hair. "Nicole, your Mom has

60

a mental illness, a mood disorder, but no matter what anyone says....she is not a nut case! Kathleen is an intelligent woman who lives with manic depressive disorder and most of the time, quite admirably." Nicole studied her with luminous aqua eyes, devoid of the fight now, merely resigned to misery. "When she gets readjusted to her medication, your Mom will be the same person you remember. As soon as possible, I will get her hair washed along with anything else she needs. *I promise!*"

"How do you know, really know, all that for certain?" Nicole asked, her voice strained and quivering.

Sidney slipped her arm around her distressed niece. "Because I have seen this before. Not for years mind you...but I have seen your Mom like this and she always gets better."

"Really?" Nicole squeaked out as fat tears began to fall.

"Yes. She wants to get better... to come home. And what better motivation han you and Zach, the best damn kids on the planet." Sidney told her tenderly and tugged Nicole close, grateful she didn't resist.

"I don't want her to look some bag lady," her niece mumbled against Sidney's chest.

Sidney couldn't help but crack a small smile. For the first time since she had come back, tears and shouting aside, she had actually reached Nicole. Sidney lifted her gaze to spot Zachary wide-eyed and woeful in the doorway. She lifted one arm inviting him close. The young boy flew to her side and anchored himself there. Sidney closed her eyes as she held her sister's kids tight, desperate to be what they needed and wondering how parents knew if they were getting it right. Her eyes flickered open and found the hazel ones of the man, who had once been her universe. There was something warm and approving there. Sidney closed her eyes again....for a split second she thought she saw something more.

"Eat now." Luke ordered briskly, shoving another plate in front of her after the kids had gotten onto their bus..

Sidney toyed with the eggs. "I still think they should have stayed home."

"No. They wanted to go to school and keeping things as close to normal is good for them."

"I agree with Lucas, Dear." Vera chimed in pouring her a glass of juice.

The fork was halfway to her mouth when the phone rang. With a swiftness that had Luke's head swiveling in admiration, Sidney grabbed the receiver. When her face fell, he knew it wasn't Reg. When she grew irritated and paced into the dining room replying curtly, he knew it was worse.

Five frustrating minutes later, Sidney flopped back into her chair and took a vicious stab at her eggs.

"So who was it?"

She glanced up. "Trust me, you don't want to know."

Those words tweaked his temper like a charm. Shutting him out had been her specialty for a decade. Luke's hand closed over hers as the fork touched her lips. "I think I do."

Her eyes swept the room meaningfully. Delta was rinsing dishes at the sink as Carlene fixed herself a cup of tea while Vera glanced through the research materials she had brought. Charlie folded his paper neatly and picked up a new section. "Later."

"Now." Luke insisted with an insincere smile.

She drew a hostile breath. "A disgruntled shop keeper in Ridgetown."

"Another one, Miss Sidney? How many can there be?" Delta sighed. "That makes the fourth one in the past three days."

Sidney smiled wryly. "Who can bother to count, Delta?"

"Depends what we're counting." Charlie muttered, lowering his paper.

Sidney cut the air with her hand. "Nothing to worry about. It's all taken care of."

"The guy on the phone didn't seem to think so." Luke challenged.

"He'll have to wait his turn." Sidney grumbled realizing her food was cold.

"For what?" Luke demanded, annoyed that it seemed so difficult for her to confide in him.

Vera smiled over her teacup knowingly. "Kathleen do a little shopping, Dear?"

Brown eyes twinkled and met as the two women burst into giggles. In times like this, they had learned that laughing beat crying. "Do we have room in the foyer for a suit of armor, Auntie?"

"Oh my!" Vera exclaimed. "Would there be a knight to go with that?"

Sidney broke into a grin. "Auntie, what would you need with a knight when you have Charlie here?" She fluttered her lashes innocently. "Do you know that *his* paper is mysteriously delivered to *your* door?"

Delta's shoulders shook with silent laughter. "Well that is convenient seeing as he parks his slippers upstairs." She bustled past the table to pluck some fresh basil from the window planter. "Now if he could just keep his jig saw pieces off my parlor floor. They stop up my vacuum."

Bushy brows shot up and narrowed ominously. "That's why I can't finish my puzzle! Dammit Delta!"

She snorted. "You can't finish that puzzle because it's the Titanic sinking at night and 950 of those 1000 confounded pieces are navy blue!"

Living alone with Reg and Rauja was so much easier to follow, Sidney decided, though this was entertaining.

"Eat!"

"It's cold." She scowled at Luke, mimicking Charlie, going for the same effect.

"Delta can make you something else." Luke insisted.

Sidney gaped at his audacity. "Delta is not my servant!"

"Why yes I am, Honey! It's what I do!" The old woman chortled cheerfully heading for the fridge for fresh eggs.

"See Vera. The girl's been away so long, she doesn't know Delta's place!"

She ran her tongue over her teeth, seething. "Delta's *place*?!"

Delta, who regarded herself as part of the family she had worked for since Vera was a girl, merely laughed. "Don't take any offense, Miss Sidney. I don't. When he really gets on my nerves, I just chase Charlie here out of my kitchen." She leaned over with a gleaming smile. "With my broom!"

Stepping between them, Vera smiled placidly, long used to their bickering. "Of course it never comes to that."

Luke couldn't resist. "Unless you count the time Charlie gutted his fish in the kitchen sink."

"Thought the garborater would be handy."

Delta narrowed her eyes at the mumbling man. "Took the repair man four hours and a lot of cussing to get those fish heads out of the pipes. Miss Sidney you have never seen anything like it. I swear every cat in the neighborhood was fighting for space on the back porch."

Luke chuckled. "Now Delta, Dad dispersed the cats." He had caught the tail end of that squirmish and wouldn't soon forget it.

Vera put a hand over her heart. "Yes with his silly starter pistol. Took several years off of poor Carlene's life." It took an effort to fight back a smile. "It was so peculiar, ironic really. We working on a quite a delicious murder and off went the gun." Carlene blanched at the memory. "There, there, Dear. We're upsetting you all over again."

Carlene swallowed nervously. "Maybe I'll go wait in the study."

"Certainly Dear." Vera agreed soothingly and watched her hapless assistant depart. "Poor thing. Violence jars her delicate system."

Luke could comment but politely held back and saw his father was doing the same. "So everything's fine, Sidney. Just tell Delta what you want."

"Delta, I would greatly appreciate it if you would tell the Sheriff to," The voice Sidney had forced herself to keep easy became a shout. "Mind his own God damned business."

"Now Miss Sidney, don't get me in trouble with the law. Cooking's my thing. Jail time doesn't appeal to me in the least ways."

"I'd mind my own business if I thought you were taking care of yourself."

"The point is Luke, I can take care of myself just fine. I am used to living in a quiet apartment doing my own cooking and cleaning."

"Well then…" His hand made a sweeping gesture as he shouted at her. "It should be easier here with Delta to help!"

"Maybe!" Sidney shouted back storming toward the side door. "If this place weren't such a zoo!"

"Where are you going!?"

"To get some air."

Air might be good, he silently agreed, following her out. He wasn't accustomed to losing his temper so easily. The breeze was lifting her hair over her shoulders and away from her face. She was a photo he wanted to frame. "You are getting cold. You should have a jacket."

"Sheriff I'm sure there are a whole force of men waiting for your leadership. I hate to think we're depriving them."

"You are as stubborn as your niece."

She spun about. "You are comparing me to an unreasonable adolescent?"

Luke smiled with too many teeth. "Of course not, it wouldn't be fair to Nicole."

"Don't you have a job, *Sheriff?* She asked in biting tones.

"Don't you?" Luke retorted as his nerves frayed.

She stared at him unblinking as her pulse raced. It was clearly time to evacuate the premises. "Later Luke," she told him flatly, stomping down the interlocking brick path to the garden gate.

"Where do you think you are going?" he yelled.

"Away from you!" she retorted without looking back.

"Like that?"

"Like what?!" Her eyes followed his gaze and flickered over her cropped T-shirt that barely covered her mid drift, snug jeans and bare feet.

"You aren't wearing a bra."

"There are worse things," she retorted glibly, spinning on her heels before her color rose. "Later."

"Much later," he grumbled and flung open the kitchen door to stalk back into the house where he noticed a sudden spurt of activity. Charlie was buried in his newspaper. Vera was jotting down notes in the margin of her current work in progress. Delta bent over the sink humming with annoying cheerfulness. Only Carlene stood wide eyed frozen in the doorway drawn back down the hall by the shouting.

Vera quickly rose and put a reassuring arm around her assistant's shoulders. "Carlene, why don't we take our tea in the other room and take a look at what you have found out about car engines. If we are going to tamper with one in Chapter Six, we ought to do it properly."

Luke propelled through the kitchen toward the front of the house.

"Headed out, Son?" Charlie called affably.

"I have a job to do." The younger man ground out.

Charlie shrugged casually but one side of his mouth quirked upward before it disappeared behind the funnies.

Delta refilled his coffee cup with a blinding grin. "It sure is good to have Miss Sidney home. Isn't it, Mister Charlie?"

Charlie raised his gaze to her wrinkled smiling face, enjoying her company more than he would ever let on. "Livens the place up with Kathleen in the hospital."

"That's for darn certain and it has every sign of getting darn right more lively everyday," she clucked approvingly.

"That it does Delta," he agreed happily. "That it does."

Sidney walked quickly down the tree-lined street, somewhat shocked by the chill but knew she would rather endure frostbite than return home for a coat. She flung open another garden gate and hurried down the path to the back of a large white clapboard home with attractive shutters, woodwork and well tended gardens. She opened the kitchen door without knocking and began spooning up left over eggs with hardly a hello to the startled attractive redhead clearing breakfast dishes. Her husband entered the kitchen hip hopping toward his wife as he tied up his shoes intent on collecting a kiss. He cocked a little grin at the sight that greeted him.

His wife's childhood friend was silently stuffing anything handy into her mouth. Chewing with her cheeks stuffed like a chipmunk, Sidney opened the refrigerator, scouring it intently. She pulled out anything that struck her fancy and set it on the kitchen island behind her.

He studied her behind for a minute, enjoying the view, before shifting his gaze to the excited expression of his wife. Rebecca was obviously thrilled to have Sidney rudely raiding their kitchen. "Hey Sid...."

Sidney stopped to poke her head out of the frig with slightly raised eyebrows. Her jaw still moving.

"Try the counter near the stove," he recommended affably. "The OJ is fresh squeezed."

Sidney gulped down whatever was still in her mouth. "Thanks," she murmured and made a beeline for the juice jug as Rebecca thrust a small glass into her palm. In light speed, she was chugging down several glasses before wiping her mouth with the back of one hand.

"Jeez Sid, did Delta quit without giving notice?" her friend asked laughing.

"Naw. Delta's still there." Sidney slid into a chair, satiated for the moment.

"So what's the deal?" Rebecca asked.

Sidney regarded the couple that obviously was amused by her ravenous appetite. "Every time I got some food on my plate, something ruined my appetite."

Carl gave a shout of laughter. "Something, Sidney... or someone?"

"I plead the fifth, Carl."

"Because I'm a cop?" he asked with light in his eyes.

"Because you're his friend."

"He's also my boss."

"My condolence card is in the mail," Sidney retorted dryly.

"He's good at it," Carl told her knowing she wondered but wouldn't ask. "He's a terrific leader."

Sidney shrugged with contrived indifference. "Well I wish he would save it for the office."

Rebecca giggled and glanced her husband's way purposefully. "Speaking of that place, shouldn't you be..."

Carl nodded hurriedly. "Right! Kiss me, darling." He headed Sidney's way with out stretched arms in order to reach his wife, and leered when the brunette puckered mischievously.

"Choose the right woman, Carl," his wife warned from behind Sidney. "Or you may find yourself playing poker tonight with a bunch of belching men..."

"I like poker..." he confided smoothly.

"Better than dancing toe to toe with me," his wife asked in silky suggestive tones.

Carl skirted around Sidney, who was scooping fruit salad into a bowl, to sweep his wife into a dramatic dip. "It's a close second."

"Go to work, Carl. I have been waiting for days for Sidney to make an appearance."

Carl gave her a smacking kiss and turned to go. Sidney's voice stopped him. "You said he is a good leader...."

Carl turned back to study at her face. "Yes."

"Is he well liked?" she asked softly.

Carl smiled warmly. "Yes, Sid. Very well liked." *Even by you although you will hardly admit it,* he wanted to add but wisely refrained in deference to his own personal well being.

"Have a good day, Carl. Sorry about barging in. My manners are in the toilet this morning. Your boss told me so." Sidney added saucily.

He laughed and kissed her cheek. "Anytime Sidney. You know that. See you, Ladies." He hastened out then. Being late was not normally a bugbear but something niggled at him that the sheriff might be surly this morning. He bit back a grin thinking of it. If there was this much emotion between the two of them perhaps Kathleen's suspicions were not totally unfounded. It was something to consider. Seriously.

Rebecca heard the front door close and put down her tea towel. "Are you done eating me out of house and home yet?" she teased as Sidney slurped up the syrup at the bottom of her fruit cup.

Sidney nodded with a guilty smile.

"Good." Rebecca stated, grabbing her hand to lead her into the nearby sunroom. She tugged Sidney down beside her on the settee. "Do tell, Sid."

"What?" Sidney asked innocently.

"*What?!*" Rebecca expounded incredulous. "You haven't been in the same room with the man for how many years…"

"Close to eleven.."

"And…." Rebecca asked eagerly.

Sidney shrugged. "We haven't killed each other yet but there have been moments."

"Just moments of potential violence…." her childhood friend hedged.

Sidney laughed with a glint in her dark brown eyes. "Afraid so, Becca."

Rebecca eyed her somewhat dubiously. "Sidney, have you taken a good long look at that man since you have been home?"

Sidney stared off into space before giving in to a dramatic groan. "All right. I've looked."

"And…"

My insides still melt at the mere sound of his voice. "He doesn't look like a cop with a desk job."

Rebecca's eyes bulged. "That's it?! Are you blind, Sidney? Most of the females in this town, young, old, attached or otherwise salivate at the sight of him."

Sidney remained prudently silent for a space of time. "Anyone in particular?"

Rebecca laughed triumphantly. "You do care!"

Sidney looked pained. "I have no right to care."

Rebecca smiled sadly at her friend's distress and put a hand over hers. "In all these years, you have never asked…"

Sidney expelled an exasperated breath. "No I haven't. After all, it sounds pretty stupid, doesn't it? I left town. Ended our marriage. I live with another man and have for years…."

Rebecca decided to throw all caution to the wind. Someone had to. "He plays poker every Thursday night with the guys. Hangs out at Smitty's most Friday nights till closing and works a fair number of Saturdays to let others spend it with their families but Sundays are his day with the kids."

Sidney's head jerked up. "Nicole and Zach?"

"Uh huh."

Sidney stared in shock though she should have seen enough to have known. "He's like a father to them."

Rebecca hid a smile. "For someone with such advanced education, it takes you a while to catch on."

Sidney sighed, her brow still furrowed in confusion. It shamed her to ask. "Does Kathleen spend Sunday with them?" Like a family.

"Sometimes. More now that the kids are older. When they were little she need the break. After all Grant never took responsibility…"

Sidney was nodding but all she could think was, *neither did I.* She certainly worried about her sister being a very single parent after Grant dropped out of her and the children's life. Guilt riddled her to realize that while she merely fretted over her sister's situation from afar, Luke stayed and did something about it.

"Don't, Sidney!"

The sharp edge to Rebecca's voice made her glance up.

"Don't start flaying yourself alive because you left here looking for a new life and found one. Kathleen never expected you to sacrifice yourself for her."

"I could have come home more…"

"Maybe in a perfect world. But you know better than anyone, nothing is perfect…."

Tears glistened in her eyes; ones she wished had all been shed. "It was damned close," she sniffed.

Rebecca's heart clenched to see the pain in her friend's face, even after all these years. She stroked a hand over her loose hair. "I know, Honey. I was there." Sidney nodded tearfully. "I have missed you so much. I knew you got here days ago but I stayed away to give you a chance to get… adjusted."

Sidney laughed ruefully. "It took about ten seconds for my *adjustment* as you call it. Luke met me at the threshold and proceeded to…."

"Carry you over it?" Rebecca put in impishly.

Sidney chortled. "Yank would be more accurate. Yes, yank and yell would sum up the greeting I received." *I'm going to work on my greeting.* Luke's husky promise echoed in her ears and caused an alarming ripple in her middle.

"Carl said you arrived in the middle of that storm the other night."

"Uh huh."

The alluring young woman with curly red shoulder length hair and sparkling green eyes chuckled. "Bet you got it with both barrels."

"Yes even with his gun holstered."

Rebecca's smile spread. "Does he know Reg taught you how to use one?"

"Not from me."

Her ally giggled. "Then he was lucky the other night."

Sidney sighed. "I was pretty strung out when I arrived. The drive was really horrendous but..." She leaned forward and thrust out her index finger in a feigned gesture of a threat. "If that is ever repeated I will deny ever uttering it."

"Understood."

"But leaving New York, wondering how Kathleen was, what had happened, leaving Reg right now..."

Rebecca's eyes narrowed. "What does that mean, Sid?" she asked with concern at her friend's tone.

Sidney was instantly regretful for her lack of discretion. She wasn't up to discussing this with anyone yet. She could hardly manage to with Reg. "Nothing really," she lied expertly. "Reg is just in the middle of this case and I worry about him."

"It's tough being a cop's wife..."

"I'm not Reg's wife," she stated simply.

Rebecca met her friend's steadfast gaze. *And just why is that?* She longed to ask but refrained. It seemed to cross some imaginary line of taboo topics so she remained silent and nodded in a conciliatory fashion instead. "I bet Reg misses you. Do you talk often?"

"We been missing each other the past couple days." Sidney cleared her throat. "Reg has been somewhat detained."

Becca raised her brows. "God you make sound like he's in..." Her hand flew to her mouth. "No!"

Sidney spread her hands. "It's part of the cover. It isn't like he hasn't been on the inside before during other cases but..." She looked away giving herself a moment.

The pretty redhead knew how to comfort another cop's wife. She slid her arm around Sidney's shoulders and eased her close. "Reg's partner looks out for him, Sid. Don will have him out..."

"He's likely out now but Don is afraid to call me."

"Why wouldn't Reg call?"

"Because he will have to go back to the streets for a day or so for it to look convincing."

Rebecca nodded slowly. "If he disappears for 24 hours, goes home, showers, rests..."

"It could be hazardous to his cover and his health," Sidney divulged wearily.

Rebecca studied her friend's remote worried gaze and knew that for all the times Carl had arrived home late and found her worried, it was paltry in comparison. "Do you think Reg will ever transfer out of narcotics?"

Sidney laughed surprising her friend. "He was in vice before that and it wasn't much better. Who knows?" Though they had some serious discussions about it.

"If the case wraps up can he take some time off? Come stay for awhile?" Seeing her friend's shoulders droop, Rebecca wished she hadn't asked. "I'm sorry Sid. It's none of my business."

The brunette smiled with chagrin. "Sure it is. I'm surprised you haven't asked before now why I haven't brought Reg here?"

God knows, she had wanted to and had bite marks on her tongue to prove it. "Well, it has crossed my mind."

Sidney remained elusive. "Why bother? We're not married. This way he could go to his family on holidays and I can come here. Separate and simple."

"Is that how you see it?"

"That's how I need to see it. I have had the other... the let's try to be one big happy fucking family. It didn't work." Her tone grew savage as she spoke.

Rebecca felt guilty dredging this up. "I'm sorry, Sid. This obviously upsets you..."

Sidney sighed at her lack of control and hastened to wave away her friend's apology. "No, Becca. I'm sorry. I have been tied up in emotional knots these past few days and truthfully I am not used to being separated from Reg..."

"Uh hmmm."

Sidney averted her eyes for a second. "And then to discover what a part of the family Luke is..."

"Kathleen and Vera thought being discreet when you visited was best. They didn't want you to feel any pressure."

"And Luke agreed?"

The other woman swallowed. It was hard to know how much she should confide. Typically Sidney was home for such short duration's. "I believe it was Luke's idea."

Sidney looked away. "He didn't want to be anywhere near me…"

"No! Sidney…that is not true. In fact I happen to know exactly the opposite."

"Oh really? How?"

"Because every Christmas while you were with Kathleen, Vera, Charlie and the kids, Luke was here with us staring out that window toward your house."

Sidney's eyes widened with disbelief. "Every Christmas?"

"Every Christmas," she confirmed.

Sidney frowned and looked away slightly. "Are you telling me that in the last ten years, there hasn't been one Christmas that Luke has been in a relationship that…"

"Luke hasn't been in a relationship."

Sidney jerked around to gawk at her long time friend. *What?!* In over a decade, Luke has not had one relationship! Rebecca, do really expect me to buy that?!"

Rebecca gave her a level look. "There have been women, Sidney. Luke is no eunuch. In fact in the first few years, there were a fair number of women. Carl used to joke never to call them by name until you could see the color of their eyes. "But no relationships, at least not the kind you mean. None that last more than a few weeks or involve any kind of a commitment. He is Barren's Creek most eligible bachelor but only the most tenacious females dare take him on. He sends out pretty clear signals."

Sidney continued to shake her head in utter disbelief, flabbergasted by this news. "This is so hard to believe Rebecca because over the past few days whether we have been fighting, driving together, refereeing the kids or at the hospital seeing Kathleen, the blatant sexuality that man emits is…"

"Only for you."

Sidney groaned. *What the hell was she going to do with that!*

Rebecca pulled her distressed friend into her embrace once more. "Sidney, just take it one day at a time and things will sort themselves out."

"Yeah?" she said in a small voice.

"Yeah. But do me a favor, will you?"

"Sure."

"Wear a bra next time you come over to clean out my frig," Rebecca stated wryly.

Sidney withdrew from their hug as her cheeks grew hot. "You don't think Carl noticed, do you?"

Her friend made a small scoffing sound. "Oh, he noticed all right. Sidney, it is a cool spring morning."

Sidney moaned at the implication. "You couldn't…"

"Like two buttons, Honey. Don't worry though, Carl is welcome to look at the menu. That man knows he is on the best diet in town."

Sidney burst into rippling laughter at her friend's self-assurance. "I think I had better start setting an alarm clock. This getting kids off on the school bus is…" She shook her head at a loss the other woman understood.

"Peach of a job, isn't it," Rebecca commented dryly. "I don't want any breakfast… where's my geography book… Mom, I hate egg salad…"

"I have been getting all that and more, minus the Mom part of course," Sidney related with a tinge of sadness she couldn't completely hide.

Rebecca smiled empathetically. "Sid, anytime I can give you a hand…"

"I'll call," she promised getting up. "I have to go change and head up to the hospital. I'm going to try and get Kat into the shower."

Rebecca's expression turned anxious. "We haven't even had a chance to talk about Kathleen…."

"We will. I'll call you later and give you an update."

"Promise. I want to know as soon as I can see her."

"You are a good friend Rebecca."

"We were once the three musketeers," Rebecca reminded her wistfully.

"No Becca. We *are* the three musketeers. Thanks for breakfast. Best meal I've had since coming home," she called from halfway down the walk.

Rebecca watched her go with a lump in her throat, liking what she had heard. Sidney had referred to Barren's Creek as home for the first time in recent memory, called them the three musketeers-present tense and when she said Luke's name, whether she knew it or not, her eyes sparkled. She desperately hoped Kathleen were stable enough to notice. It might make her present suffering feel worthwhile.

CHAPTER SIX

Her moan was low and throaty. "God...that feels good."

Sidney beamed though she was almost as wet as her sister and not dressed for it. "How's the water, Kat? Too hot? Too cold?"

The reply was slow but Sidney understood the wait. Nothing happened fast when you were depressed. "Fine. It's fine."

"The shampoo is almost out." She pooled something fragrant in her hand and thrust it under her sister's nose. "Time for some conditioner." Flared nostrils attested to Kathleen's approval. "I brought some of mine." She didn't add that she couldn't find much of anything in the chaos of her sister's room. Though Kathleen was never scrupulously neat, when she was cycling high, the results were eye popping. For once, she was glad to have Delta as reinforcement in setting the bedroom to rights.

Twenty minutes later Sidney was brushing out her sister's hair thinking how pleased Nicole would be when she told her. However, the satisfaction was dulled by the lack of conversation. Kathleen stared off out of the window, her eyes remote and dull. "Hey Kat! Look at you sitting in a chair all dressed. You look..."

"Like hell, Sid," her sister said in flat soft tones.

Sidney smiled tenderly and dragged a chair to sit directly across from her older sibling. She picked up her hand and warmed it between both of hers. "No Honey. That was last week. Things are looking up."

Kathleen raised skeptical blue eyes to Sidney's dark brown luminous ones. They were still overly large for her oval face and framed by long sooty lashes. A smile tugged at Kathleen's mouth in her mind at the beauty of her sister but the action never made the journey to her actual lips. Instead, she looked blankly at Sidney.

"Aunt Vera said she had a good visit with you last night."

"She talks... a lot," Kathleen reported with little inflection in her voice. "Something about a new book."

Sidney rolled her eyes. "Oh yes, the ongoing saga of Drake and Vanessa."

"It pays the bills," Kathleen said without a trace of humor.

Amen, Sidney added within the realm of her own mind. Somebody has to keep working in this family. "Yeah it does and it keeps our lovable but flaky Auntie out of trouble."

"So that just leaves me."

Sidney frowned. "Leaves you what?"

"In trouble."

Sidney shook her head slowly. "No Kathleen. I'm right here and you are fighting your way back. The trouble is behind you."

"Liar."

"I love you."

"Good."

"The kids love you."

"I miss them."

Sidney paused for a second considering. "Can I bring them up? Tonight? For just a few minutes."

Kathleen took her time before reacting at all. "I... yes." She yearned for one of Zach's hugs. "Better ask Dr..."

"I did. Dr. Dixon is pleased with your progress. He thought it was a good idea as long as you agreed," Sidney explained.

"Luke..."

Sidney's eyes narrowed. "What about him?"

"Bring him too."

"Oh," was all she could think to say.

"I mean it, Sid." Kathleen paused to swallow past her dry throat. "I want to see Luke."

Sidney met her sister's eyes and saw the truth in them. "I'll bring Luke."

The babies' bassinets were lined up for admirers in front of the viewing window. Sidney's mouth curved slightly but not quite into a true smile. She sensed rather than saw the familiar figure behind her. They had not seen one another for some time but her signature perfume was still a little too liberally applied.

"They're beautiful, aren't they?" the older woman observed. "Whenever my work gets a little too intense I come down to maternity and just stand here to watch for a bit. The babes are always different of course but the wonder they inspire is the same."

"Yes," Sidney agreed. She turned slowly to smile warmly into the middle-aged woman's round face, framed by curly brown hair. "It's nice to see you."

The woman smiled in return. "I heard about Kathleen's manic episode and wondered how long it would be before you arrived."

Sidney brows knit in bemusement. "You were that certain I would come?"

"Absolutely. Your devotion to Kathleen was always readily apparent. I understand you are taking care of her children."

Sidney's smile turned wry. "I have help."

"Your Aunt?"

"Oh, Vera is involved of course but I was referring to Luke."

The other woman's eyes widened with something Sidney suspected was amusement before she closed it off. Still it took her a few seconds to formulate a reply. "That was Kathleen's doing."

Sidney made a scoffing sound. "Yes and I am wondering what her lithium levels were at the time."

The older lady's eyes showed both empathy mingled with now undisguised humor. "I suspect Kathleen had her reasons…"

"Meddling is my guess but at the present time I won't take her to task for it. That discussion can wait. We need to get her stable."

"If there is anything I can do to help…"

Sidney smiled immediately. "I may take you up on that. You are the reason I went into social work you know."

Surprise flashed across Sally Jacobson's pale complexion. "I am shocked that I made such an impression. After all…"

"You are a compassionate social worker who brought me a lot of comfort when very few people were able to. I never expected you to solve all of my problems. Some things are just too wrong to fix."

Sally regarded the young woman in front of her sadly, not particularly sharing her perspective but knew that a debate would not be productive. Perhaps coming here…coming home would help her put a part of the heartache to rest. Maybe Kathleen's naming of joint guardianship had been anything but arbitrary. Indeed, the more the seasoned social worker considered it, given what she knew of the bond between these sisters and the man involved, Kathleen's actions seemed almost calculated. Her brow furrowed together. That did not quite fit with her sudden manic episode after years of stability. Or did it?

Carl stretched his legs out in front of the chair he had occupied during the meeting as his colleagues filed from the room. He watched them go. He stayed. The man at the desk in front of him continued to work on the report he was processing so Carl made himself comfortable and waited.

Luke laid down his pen and lifted his eyes without moving his head. His gaze was intent and unyielding. It made most people he settled it on, squirm. The sheer talent of it had saved his butt in a number of precarious situations. It was likely the one trait of real worth he had inherited from his mother. One of the few people it did not work on however sat before him and from the expression on his face Carl was enjoying himself to the hilt.

"Don't you have somewhere to go?" he finally said in the stillness of the room.

Carl gave him a toothy smirk. "You do."

Irritation piqued. He never missed anything scheduled. "What?" He flipped through his day-timer with agitation.

It was hard not to laugh but in deference to his health Carl managed, "A lovely woman raided my kitchen this morning. She was ravenous. And sexy as hell."

Luke intensified his stare to bore a hole through this man's eyes. "And your point is?"

"Feed her. Take her out for dinner."

"Go back to work, Carl."

Carl shifted to lean stubbornly forward in his chair. "I am working." He stabbed his finger forward, not at his boss but rather at his best friend, knowing that was understood. "And this may be the most important work I ever do, you stubborn son of a bitch."

Luke sighed fiddling with his pen. "I took her out the other day."

Carl lifted a hand. "Oh yeah. Where?"

"The Tin Box."

Carl rolled his eyes. "The diner and arcade? Next you're going to say you took the kids…"

Luke averted his gaze.

"Oh Christ!" Carl expounded.

"We had Zach with us. He ditched school…."

One large hand flew up. "Save it. We'll solve the small fry's problems later. Right now you are all I can handle."

Luke groaned inwardly. For someone who was touted as a leader, his skills were going straight to hell. He couldn't even effectively get rid of Carl.

Carl scrutinized his long time friend from narrowed eyes. It was time to take the gloves off. "Now that you have seen Sidney, spent some time with her after all these years, what do you think?"

Luke's countenance hardened instantly and a muscle began to tick in his lean cheek.

Carl saw it, ignored it. "Do you love her still?"

"Get out of my office, Swanson." Teeth were bared. "Now!"

Carl rose but didn't move. "Well that pretty much sums it up. Now you need to decide what you intend to do about it." He headed for the door, paused. "Kathleen doesn't have manic episodes very often. This is likely your best shot."

"There is the small matter of the man she lives with," Luke bit out between clenched teeth.

Carl leaned against the doorframe knowing there was nothing small about

Reg. "I didn't see a ring on her finger."

Luke rubbed his temple as if it ached. "What the hell is the matter with that asshole anyway? Why hasn't he done that yet? Sid's lived with him for almost a decade."

Carl sat back down with a pleased smiled. Now they were getting somewhere. "Are you sure it has been that long?" he asked innocently.

"Yeah, it will be ten years in September," Luke replied absently. "Don't you remember when I found out? We went out and I pickled my liver so well..."

"You could barely walk upright for three days without holding your head," Carl confirmed.

"You bastard." Luke squinted one eye ominously at him. "You didn't forget."

"No," he admitted frankly. "And I haven't forgotten all of the holidays you have spent alone even though you have been with us, the children you wanted to fill that house of yours with, the home you made from dreams you shared with her or that room next to your bedroom that no one but you ever goes in..."

Surprise flickered across his face for an instant before he could carefully bank it. "What do you know about that room?" he demanded in a low voice.

"That you keep your heart in it. Christ Luke, do something about it! Don't wait until Reg gets off his ass and puts a ring on her finger because if he does she'll be lost to you forever."

Luke gave a little huff. "Marriage doesn't always last forever," he said wearily.

Carl gave him a sympathetic look. "Luke, what happened between you and Sid was...."

Luke stood up in one lithe lethal movement. "Get out of my office, Carl. I heard what you said. I don't want to hear it again."

Carl got up shaking his head. He stopped at the door with the frosted glass pane and spoke without turning around. "I care about both of you. I know Reg. He is a decent man and is devoted to her but she hasn't married him. There's a reason. I have seen the way he looks at her. It isn't him. I would wager, it's you. Do something about it or get on with your life. Your status quo is not living, Luke." He opened the door and exited without a backward glance.

Sidney sat in the parking lot for a long time feeling foolish. The idea of actually going in was horribly unnerving. It by far would be the most public place she would have to face down and one she had avoided fastidiously during visits. It was irrefutably his territory. More so now than ever.

Though the police station had always been neat as a pin under Charlie's long time command, even from her vantage point in the parking lot Sidney could see touches she knew where Luke's. Shiny new bike racks and park benches were close to the entrance. Spring flowers were a burst of color in large planters. A sign on the door proclaimed the building smoke free and there was a can for butts near one for litter. The walk looked freshly swept.

She toyed nervously with the ring on her finger. She had put it on out of habit. Kathleen hadn't even noticed. Part of her missed seeing it on her hand. Part of her felt traitorous to wear it at all. She whipped it off in one impulsive movement, shoving it deep into her pant pocket. Sidney drew a fortifying breath and got out of the car.

She walked through the two sets of clear double doors toward the front desk. There was one young constable and a clerk on duty. Sidney didn't know either one, which helped ease some of the strain. "I'm here to see the Sheriff," she announced quietly.

The woman glanced up from her filing, largely unaffected. The young constable with hair so closely cropped his scalp shone through, gave her an over bright smile as he rushed to the counter.

"Do you have an appointment?" the woman stated from behind him in a shrill voice prompting the constable to glare at her over his shoulder.

An appointment? It had never even occurred to her and she was mortified. "Ahhh no. I didn't think…" Sidney stammered longing to dash for the door now. "I just didn't think…"

"Rita. This woman never has and never will need an appointment to see the Sheriff," a deep gruff voice rumbled happily from an open doorway. He saw her nerves, understood them and sought to soothe. A broadly built man of medium height with thick brown hair and an ear spitting grin rounded the corner to come into Sidney's view.

The smile was automatic and wide. "Hey Jack," she said extending her hand knowing if he noticed the tremble there, he was kind enough not to say so.

He eyed her proffered hand dubiously. "You think that is going to satisfy me. Get over here, girl," Jack ordered and wrapped her up in his massive embrace. The rookie constable behind the desk looked on woefully.

Luke stood for a second, strangely warmed to see them together. It had been a long time and of course things were different then. "Look out Jack. The last man who called Sid a girl got read the riot act."

Sidney felt a flush creep up her neck though she couldn't say whether the cause was Luke's remark or merely his arrival. "Some men can get away with more than others when they are charming enough."

"Ahhh… I'll have to work on may charm along with my greeting," Luke stated philosophically. "Wanna step into my office?" he asked with the gaze of a shark who is eyeing a guppy.

Sidney ordered herself to remain outwardly indifferent even as her blood began to hum. "Yes, if you have a moment. There's a couple things we need to discuss that couldn't wait."

"I'm glad you came," he told her in deep warm tones that loosened the anxiety crowding her chest. "Hand her over Jack."

The older officer released her with an affectionate squeeze. "Don't be a stranger, Sidney."

He watched the pair disappear around the corner and down the corridor that led to Luke's office. When they were out of sight Jack turned back to the young constable who was still gaping. "For God's sake, Dennison, close your mouth and forget you ever saw her. She's taken."

"I didn't see a ring on her finger. " He had made a point of looking.

Jack gave him a lop sided grin. "Dennison, it would be lousy career move for you to even consider anything with that woman."

"Jeez, it's not like they are married or anything." Dennison frowned while Jack howled as he sauntered back to the evidence room.

Luke sat in the chair opposite her. His legs were so long their knees touched. There was a certain appeal in not sitting behind his desk, he decided. "So Sidney what's up?" *Besides me.*

In the days of old, she thought privately, *it would have been you.* Shocked that such a thing would spring to mind, she hastily looked away, cleared her throat. "Are you busy tonight?"

He fought the urge to blink. She was reading his mind. "Not after seven."

She gave a pleased nod. "That'll work. Kathleen is up to seeing the kids briefly and when we go up I would like you to come along. Is that OK?"

A staggering sense of disappointment choked him of free speech so he nodded.

"Kathleen asked for you," she added.

His ego couldn't have deflated faster if it were a balloon popped by a meat cleaver. "I see."

Sidney fidgeted for a minute. He seemed hurt but she couldn't really fathom why. "I would feel better if you were there as well. You know the kids better than I do. You are so natural with them. I always feel so inept."

"You?" he sputtered. "Nic and Zachary can't say enough about you. You were wonderful the other day at the diner with Zach explaining the rumors he had heard at school and again this morning with Nicole. Sid, Kathleen knew what she was doing when she chose guardians."

Sidney regarded him with silent astonishment. He had no idea how much it meant to hear not just those words but particularly from him.

"Are you all right?"

She nodded, gave a weak smile and rose to go stand by the window, needing to put some distance between them.

Luke moved to stand just behind her but was careful to not touch. "You are not all right. Tell me, Sidney."

She bit her lip. It was stupid. She couldn't possibly tell him though it was doubtful she could get out of this room without doing so. "It means a lot to me to hear *you* say that. Sometimes I think that maybe *it* happened for a reason..." Her voice cracked with the onslaught of her emotion. "That I won't have been a good enough..."

Suddenly two strong hands settled on her slim shoulders in a firm grip and spun her about with startling speed. The look on his face was stark and grounding. "Never. Never say that Sidney. You were a great..."

The door burst open abruptly. "Sheriff..."

Luke didn't move, didn't look. "Not now."

The Deputy stood riveted in the doorway. He had known his Sheriff, as an officer, for years and had never seen him touch a woman with this kind of familiarity in a bar much less in his office during working hours. "Ahh... but Sheriff..."

"I said..."

Carl strode past the stupefied officer. "Luke, you'll want to know about this." He stopped for a second taking in Sidney's presence and her proximity to Luke. After all these years of wanting to bridge the space between this couple, both his friends, it was briefly stunning to see them together. "Sidney, you need to hear this too."

Sidney jerked around at his words filled with sudden dread. "Kathleen... the kids?"

· Carl looked disconcerted. "It's the PTA at the high school."

Sidney drew a ragged breath and glanced at Luke who was listening intently. "They're protesting because of what happened the last day Kathleen was teaching..."

Carl nodded. "They are conducting a march. A big one." Sidney's eyes instantly reflected pain. "It is to start at the high school, go down the main street and end in a rally at the hospital on the lawn that the psych ward overlooks."

"No!" Sidney cried. "Luke, you have to stop them!"

He met her eyes with difficulty. "We can monitor them but unless they break a law..."

Horror gripped her. "So if they are peaceful, you can't do a thing?"

"I can't do anything until they break a law..."

"Trespassing! The land at the hospital is private property. They will be breaking a law," she exclaimed feeling hopeful.

Luke sighed in frustration. "Other than the strip just adjacent to the building, that land is actually a park which makes it public property. So they won't be trespassing unless they are within fifteen feet of the hospital wall."

Sidney ran her tongue over her lips. "So they can be cruel, judgmental and harass Kathleen from the grass below her window and all you can do is stand by and let it happen."

"Yes," Luke confirmed dismally hating that he couldn't change those facts. Once again he was letting her down. Some things time couldn't even change.

Sidney nodded and then pursed her lips thoughtfully. "All right. Good day Gentlemen. It seems I have somewhere I have to be." She strode purposefully toward the door and Carl politely cleared a path.

Both astounded and concerned, Luke followed on her heels. "Sidney, just what the hell do you think you can do!" he demanded hotly.

She spun around neatly in the middle of the large open squad room. "More than you apparently. Don't look so worried, Luke. I'm not eighteen anymore."

CHAPTER SEVEN

Sidney scanned the crowd on the hospital grounds. Dread licked at her like a pack of dogs on the hunt. The gathering was large, growing and showing their fangs. There were a great many familiar faces in the group that Sidney had successfully managed to dodge for years. If she were to protect Kathleen's interests, that was not going to be possible today. She knew Luke was somewhere in the crush though they hadn't come together. It didn't matter, they were clearly here on different business. His official; hers family. The two had no common ground. She had not felt this alone in a long time. She conjured up Reg's reassuring voice in her head. Comforting her, encouraging her, bolstering her....

An elbow caught her in the ribs earning a grunt just as a chant was gaining momentum. "Speech! Speech! Speech!" A podium of sorts had been quickly erected from some discarded crates and a microphone was hastily set up. A bottled-blond in a fur trimmed jacket was being assisted up by some burly men, introducing herself as the reigning president of the PTA. Vivian Filmont flanked her other side looking elegantly superior. Her surgically augmented nose even seemed to tilt slightly upward from where Sidney watched.

Sidney felt her spirits plummet as the intent of the speech began to register. The president of the PTA was droning on about the weighty responsibility society had to all children to ensure the mental stability of their educators.....and how the good citizens in the crowd needed to safe guard innocent students from the slanderous and immoral behavior of individuals who could not be counted upon to conform to acceptable moral codes. She heard her sister's name hissed behind the hands of people in the crowd.

Sidney's heart shriveled seeing this gullible crowd lap up Miriam Jenning's rhetoric and salivating for more. Pointing in the crowd drew Sidney's attention away from the podium and upward to the hospital building. On the top floor, which if the entire town hadn't realized before was psychiatry, they did now, and the windows were crowded. Sidney silently prayed that her sister was not among them.

A clipboard was thrust into her hands and she stared down at it miserably. It was a petition to have Kathleen fired. "Hurry up and sign it lady. I don't have all day to spend on this nonsense," someone was complaining by her elbow.

Her thin thread of restraint snapped unleashing a rage that propelled her forward clutching the petition. She began to pick her way through the mob intent on reaching the podium where Vivian had taken the mike and was purring venomous slander about her sister that dated back to childhood. She was so close to the bitches now she could all but feel their perfumed necks under her hands, when a furtive movement caught her eye.

Luke was threading his way through the throng toward her with an expression she knew well. She veered in the other direction only to see Carl head and shoulders above the mostly female crowd closing in on her. Sidney glanced between them for a frantic second before bolting for the platform. As she cleared the front of the crowd, her recognition was instantaneous. What were whispers became catcalls. Coming forward was the *sister,* the crowd was hissing the word like a slur.

Fueled by strong personal conviction, professional training and most of all great love, she made a lunge for the podium.

A steely band encircled her wrist, his voice hoarse in her ear. "Sidney, don't. You can't accomplish anything other than inciting this small-minded crowd. They are not representative of all of Barren's Creek."

Sidney swung about to gape at him like he was brain damaged. "Luke, these people certainly are representative of the Barren's Creek I remember." *The town that spread malicious rumors after my baby's death.* "Besides you can't argue with these numbers. The county fair can't count on this kind of turn out for chrissake. I can't allow Kathleen not to be represented. Think of the kids! They have to live in this town. It doesn't matter how they treat me. I am going back to New York when this is all over."

Luke gnashed his teeth knowing he could physically over power her and how easy it would be to give in to that macho impulse. God dammit, so much of what she said was true. Except the last part. He had quite a lot to say before she headed off to the city again and if he had to put her in lock up to get the job done, so be it.

"You're sure about this, Sid?"

Sidney turned in the direction of Carl's voice and saw an ally. "Yes."

"I'll give you a boost up and stand by if you need a quick getaway," Carl promised soberly.

She gave Luke a last pleading glance but his face was carefully expressionless. Before she could speak again, Sidney found herself propelled onto the platform by hands she knew by heart. An irresistible backward glance confirmed Luke's strong hands were on her waist. Carl stood off to one side talking into a walkie-talkie. Her eyes collided with Luke's for a split second. "Thanks."

His eyes questioned her wisdom again but otherwise he remained stoically silent. Rising to stand, she brushed against the purchased curves of Vivian Filmont, who sneered petulantly into Sidney's face. "Coming to lend your support?"

"I wouldn't miss it," Sidney retorted.

Miriam continued her demented babble but was throwing anxious glances their way. Sidney broke apart from one viper to confront the other. The one that had the more important implement. The microphone.

"Is this a private party or can anyone join?" she asked Miriam sardonically.

Horrified by the prospects, Miriam covered the mike causing a screeching that had the crowd covering their ears. "You weren't invited," she spat piously.

Sidney smiled cagily. "The other side never is."

Miriam haughtily snubbed her, turning aside to uncover the microphone. "That concludes today's rally. Please make your name count on the circulating petition to protect our children from another such intolerable occurrence that could result in permanent scars to their well being," she added righteously.

Sidney growled and snatched the microphone in a stunningly swift maneuver that left a stupefied Miriam grabbing pitifully at air. "There are several problems with that plan, Madam PTA President. First, the *sister* has the petition," Sidney snapped, holding the clipboard up like a trophy. Both women jumped at it like foolish puppies after a stick. Easily out maneuvering them, Sidney kept the object just out of their reach privately vowing when the game became too tedious she would smack one of them over their lacquered hairdos with it.

"The next big problem with your clever plan is only one party has been heard from. As many of you have already concluded, I am Kathleen Stuart's sister, Sidney. Like Kathleen, I spent most of my youth in this town. I have been living in New York for some time but I have kept in close contact with my sister. Kathleen was diagnosed with bipolar disorder or what many of you know as manic-depressive disorder when she was twenty. I came here as soon as I learned Kathleen had experienced a manic episode. She hasn't had one for over ten years. Of course, by now all of you have heard the tantalizing details of her out of control behavior at the high school where Kathleen has been a dedicated and well-liked teacher for over nine years. Unfortunately mental illness isn't choosy. A breakdown can occur anywhere. If Kathleen could have planned it, I can tell you without a doubt that she would not have been near any of her students."

A loud heckling voice called out from the crowd. "Well, she was and you can't guarantee that it won't happen that way again."

Sidney took a huge breath and squared her shoulders. She could hear Miriam and Vivian snickering behind her, ignoring them she looked directly into the hostile crowd. "You are absolutely right. I can't guarantee that. Neither can Kathleen. Neither can her psychiatrist. No one can." The crowd began to murmur self-congratulations among themselves. Sidney saw it and seethed. "However... I can remind you of Kathleen's teaching career. I can refresh your memories about the countless unpaid hours every winter and spring during which Kathleen plans and produces some incredible stage productions." Her eyes hastily scanned over the petition and lit on several names. "I believe Mrs. Poweress's son David was in Oklahoma two years ago and Mr. Singleton, wasn't your pretty daughter Melissa in Annie Get Your Gun. Haven't most of your kids been involved in many of these shows and benefited from the experience? Shows all of you have enjoyed seeing your kids perform in and bragged about. They were possible because of Kathleen's driving force. Can anyone deny that?" A guilty hush fell over the crowd. "Also it seems only fair to remember that in all of Kathleen's years of teaching, this is the first time her mental illness has affected her work. I would like to think that almost a decade of dedication to her students, *your* children, counts for something." Sidney was pleased to see the reflective faces on the people before her. Some of the tide seemed to be shifting. "But probably the most important issue today has less to do with Kathleen personally and everything to do with the philosophy all of you hold as parents and role models to our town's youth. There will be times in everyone's life that things do not go as planned. By treating Kathleen as a pariah to be duly disposed of, what message do you send to your children? It seems to me that we are saying if you screw up, that's it. It is unforgivable. You can't fix it. Do you really want your children to believe that? Adolescence is a time of conflict and frequently crisis. Teenagers are often working out huge problems. Make them believe that is possible. That they can right any wrongs they make. If you turn your back on Kathleen, in some small way you are turning your backs on own your kids. Think about that before you put your name on this petition." She indulged herself by shoving the clipboard into Vivian's belly.

Sidney stared for a long pensive moment at the stunned crowd before her and swallowed hard. She could see much of their animosity deflating. Whether she had changed anyone's mind was debatable.

She suddenly wished Reg was among the faces. She ached to show him that professionally she wasn't completely washed up and instantly smiled in chagrin. Idiot, Reg knew that. She was the person who needed to believe it.

From behind her, she heard the mutterings of two disgruntled women whose best-laid plans had been thwarted. As she turned to step down, Vivian bestowed a haughty glower upon her. "Tough words about parenthood from a woman who isn't anyone's mother," she hissed in low guttural tones that came naturally.

Sidney stopped cold, paling as if she had been sucker punched. Suddenly strong hands were lifting her down. Several people came forward pledging to support Kathleen in her recovery. She numbly replied and followed where she was being led. Several officers she recognized seemed to be forming a protective wall insulating them from the crowd as Luke guided her to his waiting car. He tucked her in it and sped away.

They drove in relative silence for a few minutes before she remembered they hadn't come together. "My car..."

"Jack's bringing it. I fished the keys out of your coat pocket." It was concerning that she hadn't noticed. Something was wrong.

"Where are we going?" she asked dully.

"Home," he said simply.

"Oh." Sidney absently glanced out the window. She recognized the neighborhood but it wasn't Vera's. Luke pulled into a driveway of an attractive sprawling home of field stone and natural wood nestled in lush gardens. She blinked dumbly at it as Luke got out of the car and came around to tug her out.

Her brows gathered in a deep frown. "You said you were taking me home..."

"My home," he said succinctly and took her arm to lead her to the house. She walked along side of him vaguely taking in her surroundings. They seemed oddly familiar although she knew without a doubt she had never been here before.

Once inside she found herself settled in a comfortable corner of the sofa while Luke went to make some tea. Sidney absently dragged her fingers through her long hair when the clatter of china being set down gained her attention. Luke settled his long lean frame beside her on the plaid over stuffed sofa and proceeded to pour her tea. He added some liquid honey, a slice of lemon and stirred it gently. She smiled wistfully at the peculiar sight of a virile man doing such a delicate task with such innate ease.

A memory flitted from the deep recesses of her mind before she could squelch it. A man balancing a tiny baby on his thighs, tenderly dressing her in a little sweater and bonnet to tie it beneath a small dimpled chin. Tears brimmed in her eyes.

"Sidney?"

She smiled self-consciously and hastily averted her face. Long fingers caught her chin and gently tilted it toward him. Sidney met his concerned hazel eyes and two tears fell despite her valiant efforts to stem them.

He smiled warmly and framed her oval face with his hands. His thumbs rubbed away her tears while she became lost in the depths of those eyes that seemed to look too closely for comfort. "You really aren't eighteen anymore," he stated with unmistakable pride. "What you said to that crowd was very compelling. Vivian and Miriam were fit to be tied by the time you were through."

"I noticed," she said wryly.

His gaze was penetrating as he spoke. "What did she say, Sid?"

She began shaking her head almost immediately as if anticipating his question.

He leaned forward so that their breath mingled. "Tell me."

She pursed her lips for a second and then lifted desolate eyes to his. "She reminded me I wasn't anyone's mother."

Luke's face hardened like granite. A muscle she had once stroked, ticked in his cheek. His words came out slowly between clenched teeth. "You most certainly are someone's mother."

"Not anymore," she said in a soft emotion laden voice.

"Forever Sidney. Some things can't be changed," he stated with finality.

"But they were." Her shoulders slumped and she felt so weary she could drop. Luke saw it and took the risk of pulling her into his arms. He felt her stiffen as she came in contact with his chest. He whispered hoarsely in her ear. "Sid, let me dammit.....just let me. You don't always have to go it alone. I'm right here."

He felt a shuddering breath rack her slender frame and then the glorious sensation of her relaxing in his arms. She gave in and let her body mold intimately with his and he luxuriated in the contact. He had longed to do this for more years than he could count. He had almost given up on it ever occurring and had even confided that to Kathleen not so very long ago.

Sidney allowed herself to sink into the comfort that was solidly him. She still dreamt of this. This feeling of absolute safety. She was enveloped in a blanket of security and something more…

She straightened, struggling within his hold, needing to break the spell that had begun weaving. "The kids… they must have heard… I have to go…" she was trying to rise and Luke was willing to let her but only with his hand tucked firmly in hers. She glanced down at their entwined fingers and slowly lifted her questioning gaze to his.

"I told you we still fit," he told her without a trace of humor.

She gave him a thin smile. "Can you take me back to the house?"

Luke nodded with a sense of satisfaction that since coming here she didn't call Vera's house home. It was likely an over sight given the stress of the day but he would choose to take encouragement where he could find it.

Hero worship was foolhardy, Sidney lamented, as she sank further into the foamy bath. For the next half hour, she planned on doing nothing more than lay her head against the rim of the old claw foot tub and contemplate just that.

She and Luke had been swept into the house amid a hero's welcome befitting Superbowl winners. Zach squeezed her so tight her circulation was likely compromised and Nicole had given her a rare but very sweet peck on the cheek. Charlie held her chair out at dinner like he was seating the queen. During the meal, Vera made Luke painstakingly recount the entire incident not once but three times while she scrupulously took notes saying the scene would be perfect for a future novel. Delta strut into the dining room after dinner brandishing a triple layer chocolate cake ablaze with enough sparklers to get the fire chief's attention. They were overplaying the situation shamelessly.

It was embarrassing.

Who was she kidding, Sidney thought, closing her eyes. She loved every minute of it.

Every keyed up muscle in her body loosened in the fragrant warm water and as the tension eased, her heavy eyelids drooped. Just for a second, she told herself. They were not due up at the hospital for well over an hour.

Water sloshed wildly over the tub rim as she jerked upright sputtering bubbles and obscenities. Sidney pushed dripping hair out of her eyes only to narrow them as her lip curled in a snarl. "Luke, what the hell are you doing?"

Good question, he asked himself bewildered, standing foolishly in a combat position in her bathroom doorway. First, it was likely going to take both hands to pick up his jaw that had fallen to his chest at the sight of her. Christ, was it some trick of the eye or had she grown more beautiful?

"It was getting late so I came up to see if you had fallen asleep. Your door was open....."

She had mistaken his kicking in the door initially for gunfire and instinctively plunged under the water. Her voice rose shrill as she jabbed the air with a sudsy arm. "The bathroom door was *not* open!"

Luke shifted his eyes sheepishly. The way it sagged on its abused hinges irrefutably proved that. "I was worried. I knocked several times. You didn't answer..."

She flounced back under the water totally unaware of the provocative vision she was, enticing bubbles clinging to every curve. His hazel eyes dilated with desire as she tipped her head back and closed her eyes on a growl.

He stood rooted to the spot feeling incredibly stupid and remarkably drawn to her. One of her nipples peeked out of the frothy foam and seemed to be begging him to…He groaned at his lack of self-control. He was acting like the randy adolescents he hustled along after high school dances.

Luke raised his eyes reluctantly to hers expecting to see fury. His ego recouped when he glimpsed confusion and uncertainty instead. His upper lip curled into a sly grin suddenly enjoying himself. "I knocked repeatedly. It's getting late. I thought something was wrong."

Savage annoyance rapidly overrode her jangled nerves. "Something's wrong all right. You are trespassing…"

"Now that's a crime," Luke drawled smoothly leaning back against the open door in a decidedly casual stance. "You ought to take it up with the Sheriff." He waited a beat. "Oh wait… that's me," he acknowledged cockily and moved forward with the predatory grace of a wolf stalking its prey. Luke placed a hand on either side of the tub and leaned down while Sidney sank beneath the water past her chin. His eyes touched her through the thin cover of the dissipating suds and she shivered involuntarily.

"The water's getting cold…" she stammered awkwardly. Her fingers closed over the bar of soap that had slipped to the bottom of the tub.

"I could help you out…" he offered silkily, gallantly extending a hand.

Water flying into his face had him stumbling backward with his face dripping, to realize his shirt was half soaked by her handiwork. He grabbed a hand towel and headed toward the door. The mood was effectively broken but still progress seemed to have been made. He paused in the door way reflectively and turned back to see that she was glowering at him from the depths of the tub.

"Sidney….the years have only brought improvements," he declared rakishly, tempting fate without a care.

He sidestepped past the doorway at the first hint of her snarl, attesting to the kind of instincts that had often kept him safe in the line of duty. A bar of soap ricocheted off the doorjamb where his head had been only a second before. He smiled cagily. At least it was a reaction.

All four of them stood in the elevator, heads tilted in the predictable security of studying the floor numbers.

Zachary was so excited at the prospect of seeing his mother he was in constant motion.

Nicole absently twirled a sheath of pale blond hair around her finger as if she were bored. It was a bluff, Sidney decided and smiled tenderly feeling for her niece. If you looked closer, into Nic's startlingly clear sea green eyes, the nerves were there and with them, the fear.

Sidney knew she was embarrassed to visit her mother on the psychiatric floor of the hospital. It was so much more acceptable to have cancer than it was to be mentally ill. She gave her niece's shoulder an affectionate squeeze and when Nicole raised her gaze, sent her a reassuring smile. Luke caught Sidney's eyes over Nicole's fair head and she swallowed self-consciously at the approval she saw there.

The elevator door opened like a curtain to the premier of a play it seemed to Sidney. Butterflies knocked in her chest as she wondered whether anyone might just break a leg in this production. It was strange to feel so fiercely protective of both the kids and her sister simultaneously knowing that she could scarcely keep them all safe from any potential emotional trauma.

Her nerves smoothed out as she caught sight of her sister sitting serenely in an armchair a short distance away. Sidney knew she would be clean and dressed because she had seen to it herself but now Kathleen had her hair styled and some make up on.

"Mom!" Zach cried excitedly and surged forward like a ball out of a cannon.

Kathleen smiled and though Sidney could see it was taking an effort, she was accomplishing it. Zachary hurled himself against his mother visibly knocking the wind out of her.

"Hey Buddy, take it easy. You have been eating a lot of Sid's muffins," Luke teased as he stepped forward to steady Kathleen and give her a companionable wink as he squeezed her shoulder in support. Kathleen's eyes lifted from the top of her son's head to Nicole, who remained standing a few feet away watching.

"Rotten place to visit isn't it, Honey?" she said knowingly. "What will your friends say?"

Nicole swallowed hard and tried to blink away her tears. "They better say nothing if they want to stay my friends," she said in a choked voice.

Kathleen smiled lifting her arm in invitation and Nicole walked into it. She looked up at the pair who remained in place watching and gave them the first genuine smile they had seen since her admission.

Sidney wore a radiant smile as the elevator doors slid shut with Luke, Zachary and Nicole inside heading home. After all, it was a school night, Kathleen had reminded them and they seemed to appreciate hearing her sound like herself.

Sidney wrapped an affectionate arm about her sister's shoulders revved over the success of the visit. "You did great, Kathleen!"

"My room," Kathleen stated in flat tones. "Can we go there?"

Sidney swung around to look at her sister's face. It was disturbingly blank and her shoulders were suddenly slumped. Her heart sank to her knees as the realization struck home that the half hour visit had been a carefully contrived act. After all, Kathleen had the dramatic flair in the family.

Numbly she steered them back down the hall toward the private room that the success of Lara Lovelorn's novels could purchase. Thank God for small miracles and all the bored housewives that depended on Aunt Vera's torrid romances to get them through the day, Sidney miserably mused.

"My mouth's dry," Kathleen said starkly as she sat on the edge of the bed.

"Water or gum," Sidney automatically offered.

"Water... no... gum." Kathleen stared bleakly at her sister as if she were terrified of making a wrong choice.

Sidney saw the raw fear and took both of Kathleen's hands in hers. "You did terrific with the kids, Kat. Now it is just you and I. I don't expect anything from you. I'll get you whatever you want." She reached over to the bedside table, poured some water and handed it to her.

Kathleen took it silently and sipped. When she put the glass down, she reached out for the stick of gum Sidney was unwrapping. "I hate the drugs I take. They make my mouth feel like a desert... and they make me fat," she said in tones ripe with disgust.

It was the first show of emotion since Luke and the kids had left. "What else?" There was more, Sidney knew.

"I like being high," Kathleen admitted bluntly like confessing a crime.

Having seen her sister during a manic phase, she had to admit it did look fun from a one sided perspective. "What does it feel like?"

"Fun. Wild. Being free. Nothing... nobody to worry about," Kathleen said dispassionately, her eyes remote. "I hate this part."

"Being low. Depressed."

Kathleen nodded slowly.

Sidney squelched a sigh. The sands of time were reversing themselves. This conversation could have easily taken place a dozen years ago, and had. It was so easy to imagine, she had to stop herself from glancing to the other chair expecting to see Luke in it. The three of them had been through a lot together.

During those tumultuous years, Sidney often figured without Luke's unflagging support she would have ended up sharing a room with her sister on this very floor. Instead she ended up…Sidney exhaled slowly giving herself a mental shake. At this rate, she and Kat might be sharing a room yet.

Sidney got out of the cab absently handing over some bills. She walked woodenly around to the rear of the house and let herself in the kitchen door. The teenager making himself a formidable stack of sandwiches at the kitchen counter, licked mustard from his finger and grinned.

"Hey Sid. Welcome home!" He turned his head in the other direction and hollered. "Mom…"

Rebecca came strolling through just as he let loose. "Jason, keep it down…" She stopped dead as she noticed Sidney standing forlornly just inside the door. "Sidney… What is it? Reg?" Rebecca babbled anxiously, walking forward to wrap her arms around her distraught friend.

Sidney shook her head initially unable to speak, vaguely aware that Jason had fled the room at the first hint of emotion. "It was all an act. Kathleen isn't better…I thought she was…I must be losing all my professional capabilities… I don't seem to have a clue anymore…I thought that maybe in another week we could get her home…than another couple weeks and I could head back to New York…" Tears brimmed in her huge dark eyes as her voice hitched. "What the hell am I going to tell Reg? He doesn't need this now," she wailed softly when suddenly the hairs on the back of her neck felt prickly.

She reluctantly withdrew from the comfort Rebecca offered to swing her head around, knowing he would be there. Luke stood silently regarding her with a stony expression. Carl was just behind him.

She closed her eyes in embarrassed misery. One hand flew to her face and she mumbled into her palm. "I'm sorry. I'm intruding. I didn't think…I shouldn't have come," she babbled in a faltering voice.

"Sidney, don't. I'll go…" Luke's deep voice stated in morbid tones.

She turned around from where she stood with a hand on the screen door. Her heart learned how to ache just a little more as she stared at the ravaged look in his eyes.

Carl strode purposely between them and eyed them both irritably. "Or you could both act like the adults you are and stay. Rebecca and I don't play sides."

Rebecca eyed her husband thoughtfully. "That's right. You either both stay or you both go." She turned to Sidney with pleading eyes. *Please stay.*

Sidney tunneled one hand through her hair. "I could really use a drink. Are you pouring, Carl?"

"What would I be pouring?" he asked, his mouth curved with satisfaction.

"Rye. Three fingers. Yours, not mine. On the rocks. No mix." She gave him a level look. "Don't be stingy."

He chuckled and walked over to where she stood, offering his arm. He guided her past Luke and into the living room. "Come give me those instructions again."

Sidney sat down and took the drink Carl had just poured. She put it to her lips and took a long sip. Within minutes, she had drained it. Luke's eyes were trained on her. She knew it without looking and resolutely planned on ignoring it. She stretched out her arm. "More."

Carl eyed the empty glass and hesitantly refilled it. She drained it only slightly slower, took a long breath and eased back into the cushions.

"Where the hell did you learn to drink like that?" Luke asked caustically.

"Away from here," was her glib reply.

Luke growled under his breath. "Obviously."

"Tea with honey and lemon lacked potency in New York," she reported dryly. Rebecca smothered a giggle that had Sidney glancing up. "Promise not to tell, Becca."

"Promise," Rebecca pledged with amusement that made her green eyes dance.

"Tell who?" Luke asked tersely.

Words slipped from her tongue effortlessly now. "Reg gets pissed when I drink beyond what he deems acceptable."

"And what's acceptable to *Reg*?" Luke volleyed back.

Sidney made a cranky shrug and yawned before answering. "At least a drink ago and a drink away from where I want to be." She held out her drained glass to her host.

Carl eyed the glass and the man shooting him a scathing look. By day Luke was his boss; always he was his friend. The woman who held out the glass was also dear to him. Tonight his loyalties were truly compromised. He took the glass and felt hazel eyes slice into him like a thousand razor blades. "Sidney, I can only guess your limit. Mine is three." He refilled the crystal tumbler with her beverage of choice and handed it back. "So drink up, Kiddo. Tea with lemon and honey is the next offering."

Sidney made a face. "Yuck, Carl. I'll go it alone after this."

"So Reg wouldn't approve of this behavior either?" Luke queried, his curiosity stirred.

Sidney shrugged. "I plead the fifth."

"We aren't in court," he bit out.

"Feels like judgment day to me," she grumbled.

"I could probably learn to tolerate him with those kinds of standards,"

Luke stated sullenly.

Sidney smiled inanely as if amused. "You two would actually like each other once you got over the macho bullshit."

Luke studied her with newfound annoyance. "What makes you think there would be any macho…"

Her body was beginning to feel delightfully limp after a day filled with tension. "Trust me. I've slept with both of you. There would be macho crap so thick no one would be able to see the two of you for the flies…"

Rebecca hurriedly stuck a platter under Sidney's nose and hooded eyes. "Try a pig in a blanket Sid."

Sidney giggled as a comment sprang to mind, saw blazing hazel eyes skewering her and waved the food aside. "Naw Becca, but I am thirsty."

Carl pressed a glass into her hand.

She sipped and stuck out her tongue. "This is Coke. Carl, I am no longer a minor. In fact tonight I feel like a God damned antique…"

Luke found his feet and paced. "Drinking and cursing… very attractive, Sid. Nicole would benefit tremendously from seeing this."

She regarded him sullenly. "Well at least she would see there is a bigger world beyond the stodginess of this bumfuck town."

Highly suspecting the vulgarity was merely for shock value, he overlooked it with an effort. "Is that the only thing you have against Barren's Creek?"

Her brow furrowed as she struggled to follow the conversation. Words were growing fuzzy around the edges. "I don't have anything against Barren's Creek. Some of my best friends live here," she yawned again and didn't bother to hide it.

Luke stared in bafflement as if he was meeting her for the first time. The scrutiny hardly ruffled her demeanor. Her eyes were closed.

"It's been a long day," Carl stated aloud to no one in particular.

Luke considered his options and stood up decisively. "Come on Cinderella. The ball's over." He extended his hand thinking he would tug her out off the sofa. He shook his head ruefully realizing she was asleep and stooped to pick her up in his arms. "Sid, let's get you home before you turn into a pumpkin." Primitive satisfaction rifled through him when she instinctively curled toward his chest.

"I miss our little pumpkin," she murmured sleepily while her eyes remained closed.

Luke stilled completely with her in his arms. *Me too Sweetheart. Me too.* His heart hammered in his chest as he glanced up to see sympathetic expressions on the other couple's faces. Agony flooded his eyes though outwardly he remained stoic, carrying her out of the front door that Carl held open.

Carl helped Luke settle Sidney into the car and then made his way back to where his wife stood on their wide covered porch. Her eyes were incredibly sad, he readily noted as he looped a long arm about her shoulders. They both waved with tight smiles as Luke drove away and turned to go back inside. Rebecca stared up at her husband with wide sorrowful eyes shocked that this pain could still be so sharp. "I want to go kiss our kids."

Carl nodded. "I'm with you, Darlin'." *And then I want to hold you close,* he promised with his eyes.

Rebecca read the signals from lengthy experience and smiled. "I want to do that too," she replied aloud and they walked up the staircase with their arms still entwined.

CHAPTER EIGHT

Sidney's feet pounded the soft ground of the path, ironically matching the rhythm thudding in her head. The run seemed a fitting punishment for drinking straight rye on an empty stomach. The worst ache though was in her chest. She missed Reg. Sidney knew without a doubt that after he gave her a few stern words about imbibing a spirit stronger than wine, he would tenderly minister to her ailments. She missed his burly fussing. His hands massaging her back... his lips nibbling on her ear... and according to Delta, his phone call last night. Or more pointedly, phone *calls* last night.

She stopped on the path bracing her hands on her thighs, panting out breath that puffed out in the cold morning. Self-recrimination had her closing her eyes in misery. Reg had finally been free to call and where was she? Wallowing in self-pity and rye until she passed out. Bravo.

There was no answer at their apartment this morning and she certainly had been in no condition to make any calls last night. She hadn't even spotted Delta's note until this morning though it was right on the bedside table.

Funny, she really couldn't even recall getting back to the house, let alone to bed. She must have done it in a stupor, probably embarrassed herself in front of Charlie and would undoubtedly pay for it in teasing today. Sidney supposed she should likely thank Vera for helping her to bed though she didn't remember it. How else could she explain how neatly her clothes had been laid aside? The fact that she awoke wearing a nightgown. She rarely wore one any more. Indeed the peach and ivory gown she woke up in was in her drawer from years gone by. She shook her head as if to clear the fog. That night gown was so old she had it when...

Sidney choked on the air in her lungs as she reeled in stupefying shock and staggered off the path to lean against the closest tree for support. She dragged a hand over her flaming face as the shocking realization of how she had found her bed and just *who* had put her there, struck. She gulped past what was surely her heart wondering just what else might have happened last night.

Maybe it was cowardly to hide in her room all day but Sidney did it just the same. She heard the comings and goings in the house and chose to ignore them. She was entitled, or at least she told herself she was. After all, she wasn't used to living in the midst of all this hubbub any more. Surely she

97

deserved a little peace and quiet to soothe away the nasty headache that drummed over her forehead with the all the pomp and circumstance of a Macy's parade.

So, she indulged in a bubble bath until the water was stone cold. She thumbed through pages of her doctoral work that had been neglected for weeks. Dutifully she even returned phone calls to the many peeved merchants her sister had paid bizarre visits to in the last couple of days prior to her hospitalization. By the last one, Sidney laid her head wearily down on her arm resting on the dressing table, staring remotely off into a shadowed corner of the bedroom. And she remembered.

"Oh Sidney, the little crib will fit there perfectly." Vera was trilling, hugging Sidney's shoulders affectionately. They seemed the only part of her anyone could reliably wrap their arms around now.

Charlie snorted from where he kneeled on the floor. "It won't be fitting anywhere if we can't get the blasted thing together." His forehead furrowed over the lengthy instruction page, batting it in frustration. "Look here. It claims there is a part G that fits into rail L and goes into slot K. Which would be fine and dandy, if I could just figure out what thing in that pile over there happens to be part G."

Luke smiled without looking up. His father had worked a ten hour day and been puked on by a rookie, who had seen a body for the first time. True it was an old gent found dead on the toilet, but it was death just the same. So, Charlie was cranky and contrary but he was here. Even as he argued with Delta over which side of the end rail faced out, Luke knew he was pleased to be included.

"Mr. Charlie," Delta began turning her head slightly away, wrinkling up her nose. "I'm telling you, you have to read those instructions and get it right or Miss Sidney will have to take that child to bed with her and Mr. Luke every night." She fanned the air with a meaty black hand. "Oooee, you smell like something that needs to be put outside."

Charlie narrowed his eyes, dug through the assorted nuts and bolts and ignored the bossy woman. What a thought! Sidney taking his grandchild to sleep cuddled beside her. Yes, he could see it. Strange. Virginia hadn't even wanted to locate Luke's nursery on the same floor where she slept, instead making a suite for him and the nanny on the third floor. He was fairly certain his son didn't even glimpse his mother's lily-white bedroom until he was school age and then only from the doorway. No big loss, Charlie snickered to himself. He made a practice of avoiding the place himself.

He smiled watching his son fuss over his daughter-in-law, insisting

Sidney prop up her feet, worried over her swollen ankles. Hell he had never cared for Virginia's ankles anymore than the rest of her. He sure as hell had never run his hands over them lovingly the way his son was Sidney's as she grew prettily flustered by all the people in the room. Perhaps he had admired Virginia's feet that one fateful night that changed the course of his life but he could no more recall that than any other details. If he had, Charlie sure hoped he had enjoyed himself because he had been paying for it ever since.

"Charlie, Luke says Pete Mitchell found old Mr. McCallahan dead..."

"In his John is what I heard at the market," Delta put in.

"Oh, poor Pete," Vera lamented thinking of the baby-faced constable barely out of his teens. "It must have put him in a state."

"A state!" Charlie choked. "For Christ's sake, Vera. He's a cop. A green one..."

"Really green today." Kathleen laughed unconcerned when the gruff man slanted her a pointed look. "Heard he puked all over your shoes, Charlie."

"Well that explains the bowling shoes, Mr. Charlie," Delta chortled. She had actually assumed that they were all he could lay his hands on before his bitch of a wife threw him out of the house last evening after reeking havoc at Sidney's baby shower. The one Vera had cheerfully planned and Virginia Ryan had predictably ruined. Delta had watched from her window as the older man eased himself over their wrought iron fence to sneak into the pool house for the night. Of course Charlie hadn't been alone for long.

"What a dreadful day for you Charlie and then to come over and battle this testy crib," Vera soothed fluttering her lashes. "You are welcome to stay for supper."

Charlie sighed, rocking back on his heels pleased that the blasted contraption was starting to look like something those pretty bumper pads could be tied to. He had already smelt dinner. The homey aroma of chicken stew and dumplings tempted his nostrils like a pretty woman standing on the corner of an army barracks. "Can't. Like to." He let his eyes roam to hers meaningfully. "Have to go to the hill and clean up a mess before it begins to smell."

Brown eyes smiled with a patience he didn't understand but was blessed for. "Of course, Charlie. Another time."

Sidney glanced between them, seeing what was there and uncomfortable with it. "I made you some muffins. There are in a bag downstairs in case you wanted to take them to the station."

Bushy brows lifted knowing what that implied. "As if I could wait until tomorrow gal! They'll likely be supper and a great one at that."

Sidney's eyes clouded over in dismay and words tumbled out without caution. "Surely Mother Ryan will let you have some supper!" She struggled to her feet. "I could call and apologize for yesterday. None of what happened was your fault…"

He was looming over her in an instant silently willing the others to bud out. Everything was his fault more than this sweet young woman, his son was fortunate enough to marry, knew. "I can handle my wife, Sidney. If I eat your muffins for supper it's because I want to and that fancy cook of Virginia's gives me gas. You aren't to blame because she came here yesterday and ruined a perfectly fine party."

"But…"

"Good Christ! It moved!" Charlie swore, his hazel eyes blinking wide that something had poked clear out of her rounded belly.

Luke's lips curved at his father's shock and nudged his big hand back to his wife's belly. "Feel that, Dad."

Charlie's mouth worked several times but nothing intelligent came out. He had never felt a baby inside a woman before. Delivered one in the back of a cruiser once and that hadn't been over fast enough for either him or the screaming mother. This child, kicking inside the pretty young girl who reminded him so much of all he had lost, was a wonder.

"Delta dangled a needle over my stomach and says the baby's a boy, Charlie."

Charlie looked up without moving his hand to stare into the innocent beauty of his son's wife. "Bullshit! She's a girl and as pretty as her mama," he retorted gruffly. "Who is the best thing that ever happened to my son." He saw her tears and decided to put them down to hormones. "Makes the best damned baked goods a man ever dreamt of. She does only one thing wrong."

A lip quivered. "What?"

His hand left her womb to graze her cheek. "She doesn't call me Dad."

Tears clung to lashes. "Oh. I can fix that….Dad."

His lips spread into a grin. His whole life he had wanted a daughter like her by the woman he could never truly have. If this was as close as he could get, it was just fine.

Sidney didn't bother to brush the tears away. They had already begun to dry on her face when she impulsively strode out of the room into the hall. She didn't stop, couldn't or she would likely reconsider. Her hand gripped the knob and pulled open the door to the only other room on the attic floor. It smelt musty from being closed up and she could see in the dim light it had gotten crowded with boxes of things the kids had likely out grown. She forced herself to step into the small space and push aside the dusty curtain.

Sunlight streaked into the room bringing the little pastel animals back to life.

"I liked putting up this wall paper. Virginia always hired tradesman for that mausoleum on the hill. No husband of hers was getting his hands dirty."

Sidney spun about blinking, trying to gulp back her shock.

He moved forward to place steadying hands on her shoulders. "I didn't mean to startle you. You have been up here all day. I was getting..." His voice broke off. It was hard to admit worry. Females fretted, he was merely concerned, Charlie decided with dignity.

"I was just looking for something," Sidney said lamely feeling foolish over being caught in this room.

He knew that. She had been looking for the same thing for almost a decade. Yet, no amount of looking could find what she had lost. "I miss Natalie too, Sidney. I miss that we didn't get to watch her grow to be just like her Mama." It was hard to say having never admitted it before. He thought not talking about the baby might make her loss easier but the fact Sidney hardly ever came home shot that theory to hell.

Sidney pressed her lips together to stem the trembling but her eyes still welled. "I can remember you fiddling with that seam in the wallpaper for almost an hour because you wanted it to be perfect. Delta claimed you made her burn dinner over it."

"Delta doesn't need me to burn dinner," he said not because it was true but to make her laugh.

"Charlie..." Sidney giggled lifting a hand to her mouth.

"Now that, a man can really take offense to," he claimed his eyes locking on hers.

"Your name?"

"Not to you it isn't."

"Charlie..." Sidney pleaded more with her eyes than her words.

"Dad," he bit out like a bullet.

She opened her mouth and was stunned to see her aunt standing in the doorway listening intently. Something in her gaze couldn't be denied. "Dad," she whispered back and let his arms wrap around her.

Standing in the little room with frolicking animals on the walls that the baby they were intended for had never seen, one of them found something that had been lost. He smiled. "That's my girl."

Vera spun away as her hand flew to cover her mouth just in time before the little sob escaped.

Sidney rolled over groggily, hearing the noise and smacked the clock radio but that didn't stop the ringing. She lurched upright to grope for the phone knocking it off the nightstand before clutching it to her ear. "Reg!"

He chuckled into the phone as his ego soared. "You gambled right on that one, Babe."

"Are you all right? Where have you been? Who the hell is feeding Rauja these days, he'll be a mere shadow by the time I see him again."

He quirked his mouth to one side in pure amusement at her rapid-fire interrogation. Few cops could do better. "I suppose I ought to answer those in the order in which you asked just so we can keep things straight. Fine. Working. Mrs. Gilpin, the saint, who incidentally has been leaving food for me too. Finally, who are you kidding, Babe? That cat is the size of a small pony. It would take until doomsday for him to waste away."

How was it he could always strip both the anger and the worry away so effortlessly? "God, I miss you."

"Were you missing me last night?" The awful words were out before he could haul them back.

The pause fairly crackled. "I was feeling sorry for myself last night and had a little drink." Her voice hitched. "Several little drinks."

Brows rose. Reg knew she enjoyed liquor now and again, he just hadn't thought that was on the agenda just now. "Sid, could that interfere with our project?"

Her gasp said it all. "God, Reg. I didn't think. I…"

"Sidney, take a breath. It's done. I just wondered whether you knew something I didn't."

Her breathing harsh and spirits forlorn, she hung her head in the shadows. "No. No, I don't. Reg, what if…"

"Babe, it was a one time deal right? Relax." Time for diversion. "I'm going to take the whole thing as a compliment that you are lost without me."

"I am."

"God, women aren't supposed to make you hard over the phone." Particularly when it's long distance, he complained privately.

Sidney giggled. "As a former vice cop, Reg, you know that for some women it's a livelihood."

"Not my woman."

The laughter was loosening the tension now. "Very primitive, Reg. I like it."

"When are you going to like it in person?"

Her sigh reached him first and he steeled himself for what he didn't want to hear. "Kathleen is a long way from well."

Stony silence prevailed. "We're not talking days or a couple of weeks here, are we?"

"No."

"I'm coming to you."

Her eyes closed in the dark. "Reg, you can't. It's a lovely romantic gesture but you couldn't live with yourself leaving the job right now and we both know that's what this would mean. Mark can't just let you take a vacation. You would be handing him your badge."

He sighed deeply. "I hate when you're right."

"Usually I can kiss you back into a good mood."

"Very soon, Babe. Count on it." He was.

She heard his weariness and felt torn. He needed her but had too much moxie to say it out right. Kathleen needed her and didn't have to say it at all because it was so obvious, and as much as she hated to admit it even to herself, she couldn't leave town yet. There was something besides Kathleen and the kids pulling her. Something that needed to be settled. Perhaps part of it was Luke but there was something else too, she felt it. Keenly. She just couldn't put a name to it yet.

CHAPTER NINE

Luke had given her three days.

The first day, he was arrogant filling his time with things he had neglected, and there was quite a pile. While he worked away, he gloated about how she might be missing him.

The second day, he was philosophical. They needed a little space. Let her miss him, it would do her good. The phone could ring any time, he reassured himself, and it would be her.

The third day, he skipped right to hostile. Would it kill her to make the first move, just once?! Did she think he was going to rearrange his life indefinitely to be places she wasn't. Well those days were over. He had ten stinking years of them and it was plenty.

Those were the reasons he had tracked her down today and when he listed them, Luke was confident they sounded quite reasonable. Until he ended up in the restaurant he knew she was having lunch at. Now he felt a little foolish but that emotion quickly transformed itself when he learned she wasn't alone.

Sidney sighed and beseeched herself to keep her tenuous hold on her temper. After all she had promised Reg that much, though the other night she would have promised him anything. This meeting was worst than she had dreaded and it seemed a long way from over.

It had already been a tedious morning following up her sister's path of purchases that bore no ties, not even loose ones, to rationale thought. Indeed the laundry list had never been quite this bizarre. Sidney winced thinking of the amount of compensating cash Vera would pay today bailing Kathleen out. In only a couple cases, Sidney had been able to appeal to the proprietor's sense of empathy and reverse Kathleen's wheeling and dealing. Regardless in each encounter, she was obliged to listen to a lengthy rehashing of her sister's flamboyant behavior. She had dutifully, in the hopes that it would help further her case for leniency but by noon the repeated scenarios were fraying her nerves. She still had one last appointment to keep but first had to endure this horrendous and fated meeting.

Stein had been droning on for the better part of an hour about a settlement she had no intention of taking. It was a wonder he even realized she was still there, which did present certain enticing possibilities, fueling fantasies of going to the ladies room and escaping out the window.

"Ms. Ryan, have you listened to a word I have said?" a condescending voice inquired.

Sidney shot him a disarming smile. "Considering your hourly rate…"

"Which will include the trip here…"

"Of course and the return…"

"Er… no. Reg and I struck a one way deal," the small man, decked out in an outrageously expensive suit, admitted reluctantly.

Sidney carefully hid her smile. She would have killed to be a fly on the wall during that negotiation and winced at her choice of words. They were not ideal.

"Ms. Ryan, I implore you to take this matter more seriously. Must I remind you of your employer's stand…"

"I don't think that's necessary. They made their position quite clear." *I've been hung out on a ledge with my ass hanging over and all they are good for is a little push,* she mused dryly.

"Well then what we need to discuss…."

However, Sidney didn't hear the rest, she was too busy goggling at the tall dark stony-faced man striding toward their table. "Can be handled at another time," she cut in flatly knowing she had to get him out of here.

"Ms. Ryan!" the irate man rebuked in a hiss.

"It's *Mrs.* Ryan actually," a deep unyielding voice informed him with menacing tones wondering at the formality of the other man's address to begin with.

Jeremy Stein's head snapped up to shudder at the tall fierce looking man who scowled at him. The predatory grace with which he carried himself was entirely unnerving. "And you would be…"

"*Mr.* Ryan."

Stein's eyes bugged out of their sockets. His gaze darted to Sidney, who struggled to appear outwardly serene. "Does Reg know about *him*?" he asked bluntly.

"*You're not Reg?*" Luke asked with some readable measure of surprise as his eyes flickered over the man's obviously tailor made suit.

Both diners seated at the table, abruptly gasped in horror born of very different origins. They stared wide-eyed at an equally bemused Luke.

Stein was the first to break his silence with a small hysterical laugh, shooting Sidney a sly glance. "Obviously he hasn't *met* Reg."

"What the hell does that mean?" Luke demanded growing agitated.

Sidney struggled to maintain a calm demeanor. "Mr. Stein and Reg don't resemble each other very closely."

"A masterpiece of understatement," Stein expounded with far too much glee for Sidney's jagged nerves.

"I believe that concludes our meeting, Mr. Stein," she informed him caustically.

"We were not finished."

"Oh, I beg to differ. *We're done*," Sidney informed him with an insincere smile.

Stein reluctantly accepted her stonewalling and began to stow the documents in front of him into his brief case, vowing to charge her for another full hour regardless whether they spent it together or not. He rose from the table with such haste, it jostled making the china jump. The man who stood over him was resting his hand far too close to his holstered gun for his liking. "I'll be in touch, Ms....er...*Mrs.* Ryan."

"There was never a doubt in my mind," she replied sardonically. "Oh and Mr. Stein, be certain and tell Reg that our meeting was successful, I ate all my lunch and look fit as a fiddle," she cooed with feigned sweetness.

Stein gifted her with brittle contempt as his eyes flickered meaningfully to her virtually untouched plate. She knew without a doubt that he wouldn't dare tell Reg. The man was insanely protective of her. It would be highly satisfying to see the meeting of that man and this one. Of course only from a discreet distance.

Luke sank into the chair across from her the second it was vacated pondering the other man's abrupt departure. One would think Sidney had bit him. It aroused his cop's natural sense of curiosity as did the fact she was idly toying with her food now.

"So now I know who he wasn't," Luke leaned forward and lowered his voice. "Who the hell was that, Sid?"

Sidney screwed up her lovely features. "A blight on society," she sighed deeply. "Unfortunately a necessary one at the present time."

He regarded her wearily. This woman like none other, played havoc with his well tuned reflexes. "Could you replay that in English?"

She broke into a large captivating smile. "Nothing to worry about, Luke. Reg and I have it covered."

The reply was far from pleasing. Like any seasoned cop, he knew when to back off. "Something wrong with the food? We could send it back."

She glanced up. "It wasn't the food. It was the company."

"Has the situation improved?" he asked silkily.

She chuckled in spite of herself. "That depends. Am I to presume this meeting is a coincidence?"

His eyes never wavered. "If I thought I could persuade you of that..."

"You can't."

"I thought not. Delta mentioned that you were headed here to clear up some of Kathleen's debts. How did it go?"

She rolled her eyes.

"That good?"

"It ultimately went… satisfactorily." Suddenly it was like a burden lifted, having someone to confide in. Someone who she knew would understand. "But Luke, the things Kat bought were so bizarre even for her, or maybe I've just forgotten. After all it has been years since we've been down this road."

We. The word resonated in his ears and had his pulse scrambling. She saw them in this together. His mind flirted recklessly with the possibilities. "So was this your last stop?"

"No I have one more out on County Road 74. Kathleen, it seems, really got around."

Luke gave her a commiserative smile. "Want company?"

She rolled her shoulders in indecision. "A navigator could come in handy."

"I drive."

"Don't think so," she said impishly.

He growled softly. "When did you get so stubborn?"

"I prefer independent."

"I prefer the truth."

She smiled wryly. "Don't we all? But eventually you learn to take what you can get."

Sidney got out of the car and looked around. Any other day the scene might have been picturesque. The rich green hilly pastures were dotted with grazing cattle tidily sectioned off with wooden fences recently whitewashed. The name on the mailbox matched the one she had written down but the place appeared to be an ordinary dairy farm. What on earth could Kathleen have been doing here?

"If Kat bought cattle, they are headed to an abattoir before they come home with us," Sidney pledged somewhat surprised Luke didn't respond and realized he was still in the car. She expelled an exasperated breath and rounded the vehicle to throw open the passenger door. She stooped to peer in at him. "Are you getting out?"

"Soon," he promised staring straight ahead.

"Why the wait?"

"I'm looking for something."

"What?"

"My teeth. I think I swallowed them back there on that curve you took on two wheels."

She let out a whoop. "Now that is an accomplishment. I rid the wolf of his teeth. An entire contingent of lawmen will line up to thank me."

"Hardly," he retorted deadpan. "I rarely show them my teeth."

"Ohhh. You save it all for me," she chortled.

"You require a nip or two far more often than any of my officers." His eyes took on a strange glow. "Fortunately, you are far more tasty…"

"You must have an excellent memory." Her reply low and breathy.

"Superb," he assured her with persuasive eyes.

It was more than time to abandon this precarious bantering, she concluded swallowing hard. Parts of her body were beginning to respond to the timbre of his voice. She had clearly read one too many of her aunt's novels. "I have a farmer to find. You coming?"

The man in question was predictably in his barn examining a laboring cow in a manner that had Sidney's mouth falling open. However, it was his ruddy complexion that paled when he swung around and saw a lethal looking man in a sheriff's uniform by her side. "Now, Miss Ryan…"

"It's *Mrs.* Ryan actually," Luke corrected enjoying the glare Sidney threw him.

The farmer gulped. "Mrs. Ryan… I hope I didn't give you the wrong impression on the phone. It isn't that I won't consider reversing the deal I made with your sister. It's just that I was so darned excited to think of getting rid of it. Now that may sound ungrateful because it's been here as long as I can remember. My Granddaddy fancied odd things… "

Sidney stared in utter puzzlement. "That's what I am not clear on. What exactly is it that my sister agreed to buy from you?" Already dreading the answer.

The farmer broke out in a wide grin. "Oh…well it is quite a sight. I'm sure you'll be impressed… most everyone is. It just doesn't fit in my plans for the back pasture…"

"*What*!!" Sidney snapped. Every single person she had met today seemed to insist on babbling. "What is it! Just tell me, dammit!"

A warm hand clamped gently on her shoulder while his breath stirred wisps of hair near her ear. "Easy, Sweetheart. This man has a whole herd of heifers at his disposal to trample us. I can only shoot the first six," he teased hoping to ease her tension.

She giggled hysterically and saw that the farmer was not relieved in the least by her amused reaction to Luke's quiet remark. "If I had brought my gun, I could handle the rest. I use a clip."

Luke's heart slammed against his ribs. "Sweetheart, your sense of humor is in the toilet," he scolded.

She laughed louder. "Who was kidding?"

The older man dressed in grimy overalls was uneasily edging toward the rear of the barn, gesturing for them to follow. "Why don't I just show you? You know what they say about a picture being worth a thousand words."

Yeah. Yeah. Yeah. Sidney's mind screamed impatiently but she forced herself to remain outwardly docile. Her compassionate side deduced this poor gentleman was close to the edge and eager to get back to his cow. They dutifully followed him to the back of the building where he and Luke struggled to open a large sliding door.

"Well there it is. It's mighty fine really. Lots of potential. Just needs a little paint...."

The sight greeting them rendered Sidney momentarily speechless. Before Luke could think of any worthy comment, the woman by his side broke into guffaws. She doubled over in hysteria, holding her aching ribs. Luke eyed her dubiously and with a jerk of his head indicated for the farmer to give them a moment.

"Sid?" he asked tenuously.

She lifted twinkling eyes that were teary now from her laughter.

"You OK?"

Though she had calmed her shoulders still shook. "Don't you get it Luke?" she pointed outside. "It's a windmill! A God damned windmill! I didn't get it until now but the rest of it finally makes sense. The suit of armor from the auction house... the thoroughbreds from the race track... the tavern paraphernalia from the restaurant supply place... Kathleen thought she was Don Quijote."

A deep chuckle rose from his chest and within minutes they were holding each other just to stand upright. Her bright eyes gazed up at him. "We have to laugh. Otherwise I'll just cry and I have had enough of that for one lifetime."

"Touché Sweetheart," he called out to the farmer over his shoulder, knowing the man was eyeing them nervously. "How much do you want for that?"

Sidney's eyes widened as she drew away from him in surprise. "Luke, you can't be serious. It has to be twenty feet high."

"My property goes back a fair ways and backs onto the conservation area."

"Why on earth would you want it?"

His gaze was disturbingly warm. "It would make a mighty unusual garden shed. Besides, it makes you laugh. I haven't seen you do much of that. I would consider it money well spent if it accomplishes that." Besides he planned on using the money he inherited from his mother knowing she would despise that windmill. It was perfect all around.

She gave him an uncertain look. "You and Kathleen might be bunking together soon if you keep talking that way."

He dismissed that idea with a flick of his hand. "Not feasible. It would screw up the system."

She blinked. "What system?"

He smiled companionably. "Kathleen gets into hot water. You get Kathleen out of said hot water and I keep you out trouble in the mean time. It's a long-standing tradition with the three of us. We just haven't tried it in years."

Sidney stared blindly at the windmill while Luke strode off to haggle with the old farmer. She could only guess how the resurrection of their so-called system would effect all of their futures.

CHAPTER TEN

Carl leaned casually on the doorframe that led to the Sheriff's private office, and while he had yet to be acknowledged, Carl knew his presence was not undetected. Luke was uncannily perceptive. Years of policing had only heightened his natural ability. The light tick of the muscle in the Sheriff's angular cheek indicated that his friend was not only aware of him but did not relish the interruption.

Carl strategically cleared his throat.

Luke spoke without eye contact. "I'm busy."

"I'll wait," he responded undeterred, sauntering towards one of the armchairs that faced Luke's large functional desk.

"Wait all you want but your ass is going to fall asleep. I have three more reports to complete, a staff conflict to negotiate and a Town Council meeting to attend," Luke rhymed off morosely.

Carl smirked. "You don't sound enthusiastic over your duties today Sheriff. Could it be the bloom is off the rose with being promoted or..."

Luke narrowed his eyes and growled. "I told you I'm busy."

Goading him had always held pleasure. "And you miss her."

Luke stilled and laid his pen down. He folded his large hands in front of him and brought his thumbs together in a light, tapping beat. His eyes sought out the Carl's for the first time during this brief but obviously calculated conversation. "That's not new."

Carl nodded. "But it is harder now because she is right in front of you."

"Not tonight she isn't," Luke stated desolately.

"There's always after the Council meeting."

"That bumbling bunch of bureaucrats takes forever," Luke lamented.

Carl stroked his jaw thoughtfully. "Don't they rotate the chair?"

Luke looked up for the first time and considered his colleague at length. "Hmmm." He suddenly felt the urge to celebrate the spirit of volunteering and began to attack the reports on his desk with renewed vigor.

"Have you been out to dinner yet?"

Luke sighed. "Not the kind you mean."

Carl groaned in exasperation. "Do I need to define *date* for you? The town's most eligible bachelor..."

"I never wanted that distinction," he declared sullenly.

"Oh, don't I know it. Well do something about it would you or I may feel compelled to make more of a nuisance of myself," Carl pledged.

Luke shot him a sardonic look.

"Yes, Luke, it is more than possible. Don't make me do resort to it, Pal."

"I feel duly threatened," Luke promised and picked up the phone.

"Are you calling her?" Carl hedged eagerly.

Luke snarled and stood up making a show of stroking his holstered gun. "I'm calling to make a late reservation for two. Get out of my office!"

Carl broke into a wide grin and vacated the office. His work was done for the day. Now if he could only figure out how to put it down on his time sheet.

Luke took the porch steps two at a time feeling buoyant as he reached for the door. He figured Mayor Pincombe was still picking her double chin off her lap. Never had the council meeting been so streamlined. Those tedious management courses he had taken to fill up his life without his wife had finally served their purpose.

His smile soon faded. Charlie sat studying a section of his puzzle in the front parlor, Vera was curled in a wing chair reading and the TV echoed in the family room where he could hear the kids laughing over the din of a situation comedy. The kitchen was neat as a pin and without Delta in it. However, the sable beauty he wanted to whisk away was conspicuously absent. Odd, he thought to himself, her car was in the driveway.

"Try upstairs, Lucas."

His head whipped around to Vera, who had laid her reading aside to quietly observe him.

"Upstairs?" he asked blankly.

Vera frowned like a parent would at an errant child. "Sidney's upstairs." Luke nodded cordially and turned toward the staircase when she spoke again. "Be nice. She isn't feeling well."

"What's…"

"Ask her."

Her peculiarly brusque manner kept him from inquiring further. Luke bit back his frustration and headed up the first set of stairs. By the end of the third flight, he was slightly winded. To think he had once carried her up these same steps effortlessly. Ah, the elixir of youth and young love, he marveled and wished it back.

Luke rapped softly on the door and was about to knock again when he heard her voice, soft and sleepy, bidding entry. He opened the door to see her curled on the bed just rising up on an elbow. "I woke you."

Sidney waved his apologetic expression away. "It's OK. I needed to get up anyway." She glanced at her watch. *I have a call to make.* "And grab some supper."

"You haven't eaten? Perfect. Throw something pretty on and we'll go out."

Sidney frowned, immediately shaking her head. "Another night maybe but not…"

Luke tensed instantly in no mood for rejection. He had jumped through enough hoops already this evening. "Sid, you said yourself, you have to eat. Well Delta's gone for the night. Wednesday's canasta…."

"Your Dad is planning on taking the kids miniature golfing because Vera is apparently in the throws of some pivotal chapter. She needs absolute quiet and I plan on taking advantage of that…" Sidney started to explain.

"Great! We'll go out too and Vera can write in the front room naked if she likes."

Sidney giggled. "Now there is an image I never thought you would voluntarily conjure up again. I remember the time you ran into Auntie Vera wearing only a skimpy towel. You were a nervous wreck afterward. Vera even installed her en suite to prevent another such occurrence. She told me she didn't want to disrupt the delicate balance of our marriage by being a distraction to you."

Luke's gaze became heated. She had actually said the word *marriage.* He hadn't heard that word from her in over a decade. The last time it was written on legal documents. Ones he had yet to deal with. "Our marriage was not delicate."

Humor fled as her expression turned serious. "No, then it wasn't."

"Not while we lived here. The rest was my…"

Sidney chewed her lip and held up a hand to silence him. "Let's not go there. Not tonight."

"Right." It could wait, he readily agreed. "Tonight we're going to dinner."

"No, we're not, Luke," she replied emphatically. "But thanks for the invite."

Couldn't she ever give in? Just once! He blew out a breath shocked by his own sharp burst of temper. He recklessly strode over to the closet that once held his clothes and threw it open with more momentum than was warranted. Luke knew without turning around he had startled her but was long past caring. Stubbornly he rooted through feminine garments. He glanced over his shoulder to see Sidney had rolled over, pointedly ignoring him.

His fingers suddenly found silky material that reminded him of the feel of her hair. Further investigation confirmed it was a dress, an exquisite one. He became aroused just imagining her in it. He pivoted easily and thrust out his find with one long arm. "Here. Slip into this Sweetheart and I promise it is the most work you'll do all night." *I'll even volunteer to get you out of it later*, he finished privately knowing it was merely a pipe dream.

Sidney rolled over with painstaking slowness, one hand resting on her lower belly. She spoke in halting speech patterns as if addressing someone who either didn't speak the language or was slow mentally. "No thanks. I am not going anywhere. I don't feel well. If there is not an immediate concern with either the kids or Kathleen... and I mean one that involves blood, fire or danger... please *leave*."

Luke let the turquoise silk dress flutter to the floor to pool prettily on the thick floral carpet. His face became an expressionless mask as he moved toward her. "Heaven forbid someone try to do something nice for you Sidney." Hands braced on the edge of the bed, he leaned in. "I *will* leave. Somewhere out there is a lovely female, who will enjoy sharing a quiet dinner and some intelligent conversation with me. After all I am not touted as the town's most eligible for nothing."

Hurt flickered in bottomless brown eyes but she didn't comment. The door slammed shut behind him rattling the panes in the dormer windows.

Vera watched discreetly from the front window as Luke gunned the engine like his lights and siren were warranted. She shook her head sadly. That man was entirely too much like the one who had raised him. It had taken Charlie years to get things right with the woman who lived in his heart too. A small flicker of hope sparked when she conceded that Charlie had finally got it straight. Dread edged in. Someone had to die for that to come to pass and Reginald Buckman was not in the same league as Virginia Ryan. One was a saint and the other had been a righteous bitch.

"Is Carl here?" Luke asked in brittle tones as he flung open the kitchen door he hadn't bothered to knock on.

Rebecca, hand on her chest, had jumped at the brusque intrusion. "God, Luke, you scared the hell out of me. And no, Carl is out bowling." Her eyes narrowed. "He was under the impression you were busy tonight."

· Luke swore under his breath feeling like a heel having rudely invaded her home. What was the matter with him? He rolled his eyes. The answer wasn't tough. Sidney. The longer she was in town the worse his predictability became. He was an emotional time bomb set for repeated detention and she alone seemed to be privy to the schedule. He was vaguely aware of a chair being pulled out and a mug of coffee being set down.

"Sit. Now that you're here, you aren't going anywhere. I have a few things you need to hear," Rebecca ordered in no nonsense tones.

He sat obediently, more out of politeness, than for any other reason. Luke seriously doubted Rebecca could clear up any part of this mess. It seemed an impossible and unenviable task. He picked up the coffee grateful for the distraction it offered.

"Sidney didn't feel well enough to go out, did she?"

"Apparently not."

Rebecca gave him a level look. "So you have forgotten."

His head jerked up. "Forgotten what?"

"How lousy she feels."

Luke frowned irritably. "How she feels when?"

The pretty redhead with striking green eyes shook her head in disgust. "Men."

"What about us?" Luke retorted defensively.

"Think, Luke." Rebecca tapped her forehead. "In the past, when did Sidney retreat to her room and lay in bed during the day curled up in a ball?"

He narrowed his eyes as he scowled. Suddenly his eyes popped wide. "She still has those horribly painful periods?"

"So it seems."

Luke made a disagreeable throaty noise. "That doesn't make sense. After she had Natalie, she went on the pill and it cleared up drastically. So unless she stopped taking…"

"Exactly."

His mouth hung open as the potential possibilities struck him. "She's trying to have a baby?"

"It seems so."

"She's not married to him." He couldn't bring himself to put a name to the man and besides, Rebecca understood who he meant.

"Marriage isn't essential for pregnancy."

Luke groaned feeling foolish. Of all people, he knew that. "But if she is in bed…" A new thought, a grounding one, dawned. "Maybe she is in bed because she is pregnant?" A disturbing vision of Sidney with a hand pressed to her abdomen flitted through his mind.

Rebecca shook her head. "I don't think so. She called earlier looking for some pain relievers and not the variety a pregnant woman would take."

"Oh."

"Yeah oh."

Pensive silence ensued. "Did you have any?"

"Pain relievers? Not the kind she preferred."

Luke nodded and rose to put his empty cup in the sink. "Thanks for straightening me out, Rebecca. Sorry for acting like an ass."

She smiled as he walked toward the door far calmer than when he had come through it. Her voice was soft when she spoke. "Luke…"

He stopped and turned.

"Sidney is likely disappointed. I think she wanted this very much."

Luke heard her voice through the bedroom door from the hallway and presumed Vera had come up to check on her. Seconds later, he realized the conversation was one sided.

"I am too... That's right we just have to be positive. It will happen..." Her voice seemed sad and wistful. "It did and we weren't even trying... I'm fine, really... OK, OK. I feel awful but I will be fine..." A pause grew before she laughed lightly. "Are you free in a couple weeks?... Ditto, Reg. I will. Good night. Kiss Rauja for me."

Luke lingered for a few long minutes in the hall. It seemed like an intrusion to knock immediately after she had hung up and the last thing he wanted to do was discuss *that* phone call. It was all he could do not to scream in frustration. If he was ever going to sway her heart, he needed more time. Never in his wildest imaginings did he think she might be contemplating pregnancy without being married first. He almost snorted at the ludicrously of that thought but times were different. As she had pointed out, she was no longer eighteen any more.

"Who is it?" came her soft reply to his gentle rap on the door.

"The very stupid doorman coming to beg your forgiveness."

The door flung wide and she stood before him garbed in a loosely flowing nightgown with little rose buds embroidered on the collar as her hair rioted in waves over her shoulders. Enormous brown eyes stared up at him with a mixture of frank surprise and shock. She looked years younger and virginal. His heart thudded in his chest.

"You came back?" she breathed with blatant surprise.

"I'll always come back, Sidney," he promised and gently eased past her intent on getting into the room.

Her tongue glided slowly across her upper lip as she watched him place a paper bag on the dresser. "What's that?"

"The usual," he commented evenly.

Her brows furrowed in puzzlement.

"A bottle of something for cramps, heating pad, hot water bottle, some scented stuff for the bath, some..." He smiled delicately. "Well other things."

Her eyes glistened as she glanced between him and the bag. She caught sight of both of them in the pedestal mirror across the room and felt herself transcending time.

She stared at him for so long, Luke was afraid he had embarrassed her beyond the capacity of speech. "Sid..."

"That was very thoughtful," she murmured and turned slightly away.

"I've embarrassed you. I'm sorry, Sidney," he stated dejectedly and started for the door. He no longer belonged here. Tonight was proof of that.

A hand touched his sleeve. He stared at her pretty fingers before lifting his eyes to her face. Her lips curved into a gentle smile but what held him spellbound, was her gaze. Something there reached him in a way she hadn't in over a decade.

Her hand touched his cheek and she rose on tiptoe to kiss his mouth sweetly. She lingered there for just a split second and he froze. Words echoed in his head. The phrase from long ago whenever they had a misunderstanding or one of them had been hurt. In the days of old, he would put a finger to his lips and…

She moved gracefully away though she longed to be held.

God, he wanted to touch her. Should he dare? Idiot, he berated himself. How would he apologize for *that?*

"Sid…."

"Yes," she responded demurely.

He liked that she wasn't searching for a robe to put on. Perhaps she didn't realize how transparent the thin cotton was in the lamplight. "Can I use the bathroom?"

Sidney was momentarily taken aback but gestured for him to go ahead. She called through the door when she heard the water running. "What are you doing?"

"Running your bath." Luke suspected for a brief instant when she opened the door, she might throw him out but she only handed him the bath oil from the bag. He poured in a generous amount until the scent of magnolias drifted upward carried by the steam.

"I love that smell."

"I remember."

"The tree on your front lawn will be gorgeous in a few weeks. The buds are huge."

Surprise flashed across his fiercely chiseled features. "I didn't think you were in any shape to notice that the other day."

"Just barely. But observation comes easily. It has to. For years, before I was promoted to Assistant Director of Social Work at St. Mark's hospital, I did field work most of the time. When you are entering someone else's home you really need to pay attention to even minor details no matter what is running through your mind."

He studied her for a second. "You sound like a cop."

She smiled. "Reg says everyone in New York should think like a cop. It keeps you healthy."

"I like you healthy. Maybe I can thank Reg one day for his guidance."

Sidney gave him an odd look as if trying to decide whether he was sincere. She seemed convinced when she spoke again. "He would thank you in return for this. He worries that there is no one looking after me. I can't seem to convince him that I can take care of myself."

His hand reached out to lift her hair from her shoulder and smooth it down her back. "Maybe he knows it but just can't help himself."

She frowned lightly considering his words.

He smiled with gleaming teeth. "It's a guy thing, Sid. Don't try so hard to figure every little thing out." He glanced down and turned off the taps. The water was dangerously close to the top. A torrid memory of over flowing this tub came back to savagely assault already taunt nerves. He lost the battle and smiled lustily.

"We made a real spectacle of ourselves that day. Thank God, Auntie Vera is a hopeless romantic. Besides I think she used it later in a book."

He jerked his gaze to hers shocked that she was recalling the same event.

"I don't have complete amnesia, Luke. I remember things too."

His breath came out in a relieved rush. "I was afraid that maybe after all that happened the good part just fell away."

She gave him a leveling look. "No one forgets times like those. They only come once a lifetime and that's if you are very lucky. I was."

"You were..." He breathed in awe of what she was revealing.

"Blessed," she filled in knowing that he needed to hear it.

He stood staring into the depths of her dark eyes knowing she was peering into his... searching for something. Mist swirled from the hot water that brimmed the tub. He longed to undress her and join her there and demonstrate that she was still blessed... still his...

Sidney trembled inwardly. This spell was beguiling. It could inspire actions that would be difficult to undo. She knew grudgingly she had to break it or risk hurting him. Again. "I think I would like to get into that." He stared blankly. "The tub, Luke."

"Right," he nodded coming out of his trance. He willed himself to leave the confines of the steamy room. Sweat beaded his brow. The cooler air of the bedroom hit him and cleared his stunned brain to a workable degree. He strode back to the bathroom and eased the door open enough to stick his hand in. "Sidney, did you check the bottom of the bag?" Water splashed and he steeled his willpower knowing she was within arm's length and nude.

"No," was her absent reply as the bag was wrenched out of his grasp and he knew the instant she found it. "Ha! I have been salivating for this all day."

He grinned as smug satisfaction coursed through him. "Most guys have to show up with a dozen roses for that kind of reaction, Sid."

She chortled with delight. "A Hershey bar at just the right moment will win me over anytime."

"I'll keep that in mind," Luke drawled sensually. He could well afford other indulgences then when they were together years ago but those were not the way to her heart. She didn't have the kind of love you could purchase. Indeed that was always her appeal. "Have a nice soak, Sweetheart."

An hour later, he eased open the door without knocking. As he suspected, she was in bed laying on her tummy with the covers pulled up and an electric cord peeking out from the blanket. Same woman. Same scenario. A decade later. Same feelings.

He approached the bed with quiet tread. "Sidney…"

"Mmmmm," she sighed sleepily.

"Sweetheart, you can't fall asleep with the heating pad on. It's dangerous."

"Not with you here. Come to bed, Luke, and rub my tummy. It hurts."

He gulped and stood staring down at her. *How much of the painkiller did she take?*

"Are your clothes off yet?" she murmured drowsily.

He drew a shuttering breath, his mouth uncomfortably dry. She was calling to him like a siren song…..

He sighed and hung his head. This wasn't how he wanted to hold her. He could have the dream tonight but be damned tomorrow and a long time afterward for his deceit. Being honorable, though vastly unappealing, was really the only wise choice.

"Sweetheart, I'm not tired so why don't I rub your back instead."

"OK," she agreed with a cranky shrug.

Luke sat on the edge of the bed and eased the blankets off her expecting to see her nightgown. His jaw fell open to see an expanse of ivory skin.

"Your hands, Luke. Put them on me. It's cold without the covers," she protested weakly.

He took a deep breath and placed his hands on her shoulders trying to visualize himself as her nurse instead of her lover. He began to knead her muscles and ease the tension there. When she gave a low groan of pleasure, hot blood coursed through his veins awakening parts of his body that had never known how to forget her.

"Lower," she murmured sleepily and his eyes rolled into the back of his head.

His hand glided up and down her slender back, kneading and stroking. Her breathing evened out and he suspected she had fallen asleep, deciding glumly it was for the best. His thumbs idly caressed the small of her back reluctant to leave.

"Hmmmm. You are so good at that. If being a cop doesn't work out, you could always do this for a living. Of course, I'm a very jealous wife. I would have to insist on being your only customer."

His eyes narrowed in dazed shock at her light teasing. She believed that he was a rookie and they were a young married couple still. Luke groaned inwardly. He had to get out of here before it was too late and he didn't know how to leave. "Shhh, Sweetheart. You aren't feeling well. You need to get some sleep."

Her head was turned to the side, her hair streaming over the pillow. Her lips curled into a serenely beautiful smile. "I should or I'll be sorry, won't I? Natalie always wakes so early."

His heart clenched in one vicious flash while his face hardened in an attempt to contain his broiling emotions. She had to be dreaming. Large hands continued to stroke up and down her back out of sheer habit from another life.

She sighed and surprised him by rolling over in one easy turn. He greedily drank in the sight of her bare breasts and his mouth grew dryer than he thought possible. Her eyes were closed but she was smiling sweetly. "Thanks Luke. Your hands are magical," she told him softly lifting one hand up to find his face. He was shocked when her hand threaded through his hair to caress his neck and pull him toward her. She had amazing strength when she chose to use it and besides he was limp with shock. Her lips pressed on his and he tensed above her as two pert nipples branded him through the cloth of his shirt.

Fueling his discomfiture, Sidney laughed. "Hey, that wasn't a kiss. I wanna kiss. I have *referral pain*," she complained cheerfully.

Those words once had been commonplace in their life together. During his worst moments, he had never thought to hear them again. Even hearing them now was bittersweet. She wasn't asking *him* for a kiss, she was asking her husband. Still he felt her breath mingling with his and did not honestly know how to deny either of them. She could enjoy it as part of their past and he could have right now what he often dreamt of…was starving for…

His lips brushed hers, shifted, changed the angle and gently caressed them. They hadn't changed. If anything they were sweeter from lengthy deprivation. He cherished the moment not knowing when another like it might possibly come again. He pulled back for an instant and she gave him a glorious smile. "Keep that up and Natalie might get a sister faster than we had planned."

Oh Lord, she had just given him an out and he damn well didn't know if he wanted it any longer, but the miserable reality was he had to. "Right, Sweetheart. Get some sleep and feel better." It took all his restraint not to spring from the bed but to ease off gently. He quickly unplugged the heating pad and mentally chastised himself for not simply doing that in the first place without ever making his presence known.

CHAPTER ELEVEN

Sidney jogged in place and battled her anxiety as she waited for the door to be answered. Maybe this wasn't a good idea after all. She tried to distract herself by admiring the huge buds on the magnolia tree and trying to envision it in full bloom. It was futile; panic streaked through her anyway. She had run alone many times, why today of all days should she choose to invite him, Sidney debated absently.

She strained her ears for some sign that he had heard her knocking. She stiffened when bold footsteps could be heard through the door, and had the insane urge to bolt around the side of the house leaving him to believe that it was a kid playing Nicky Nicky Nine Doors. Sidney groaned, being Sheriff, he might take the matter seriously and follow in hot pursuit, gun drawn.

The door sprang open and if she hadn't steeled her reflexes, she would have jumped. His head jerked up ever so slightly at the sight of her and Sidney quivered as a slow wide grin crossed his features.

"Sidney!"

She smiled hesitantly still rhythmically bouncing in place. "Charlie told me you still run." Her eyes shifted self-consciously. "I still run. Reg and I, we run. I thought maybe you might…"

Luke lazily propped his arm against the doorjamb, enjoying the bounce of breasts as she jogged on the spot. It did his ego good that she seemed so tangled up over being here. "Running is the last activity I thought you would be interested in this morning." She blushed at his words and he felt a little stab of regret for embarrassing her.

"Actually exercise helps the cramps. So, after the first day, which is pretty much the worst, I force myself to get on with things. Besides I feel a responsibility to Nicole not to convey that menstruation is something horrible."

"Yes, but Sid, most women don't experience the variety of discomfort you do."

Some part of her was shattered by his statement. How many women was he intimate enough with to know the nature of their periods? She sighed, what rights did she have to care at all? Their life together was over.

God, he loved how absolutely expressive those fabulous eyes were. "Men know about women's periods, Sweetheart. It doesn't mean it's all by first hand experience," his rich voice explained knowingly, smugly pleased that she cared.

Her face flamed scarlet and she stared at his feet realizing for the first time that they were bare and his shirt hung open. "Maybe this isn't a good idea after all..." she stammered intent on escape.

Luke sensed her inclination and his hand snaked out catching her wrist in a gentle vise. "It's a great idea. You aren't going anywhere except inside while I change." He tugged her inside, closed the door meaningfully and ensconced her in an armchair. She lifted her eyes up to him and was sure her heart stopped. His chest was beautifully sculpted by muscle and lightly furred until the hair tapered to where he had neglected to fasten the button of his jeans. Her invitation was obviously a little early on in his day.

If anything he was more muscular than she recalled and his shoulders more dramatically broad. His nipples begged...

"Sid..." She started with a jerk. He was smiling from ear to ear with gleaming white straight teeth that instantly resurrected her image of him as a sleek wolf. "Can I get you anything while you wait?"

A cool breeze. It's hotter than.... "No...no thanks," she stammered instead.

"All right," he drawled smoothly and sauntered back down the long hall. In a few short moments, he returned and much to Sidney's relief wore a snowy white T-shirt and navy sweat pants. Still even clad simply for the purpose of running, his sexuality was blatant and compelling. She fought to rein in her attraction. It no longer had a place in her life.

"Ready?" he asked companionably.

She shot out of the cozy chair as if she were sitting on bare springs in her eagerness to depart. They ran silently for a few long minutes before the quiet became comfortable. They followed the road until it ended and wound into a path that led through the conservation area. They stayed the course with no discussion.

"Did you like what you saw?" he finally asked in neutral tones.

"What?" Her eyes widened. *God, he knows I noticed his body.*

"My decor, Sid. The living room. Do you like it?" he expanded. What did she think he meant, Luke wondered.

"Oh... yes, it's lovely. Beautifully masculine yet with a few softening touches that ease the harshness." *And there wasn't one bit of pretentious junk there.*

Luke chuckled at her assessment. "Yeah, that was pretty much what I was going for," he joked. "Actually I did it fairly piece meal according to whatever caught my eye, scoured some antique shops and then had Rebecca and Kathleen give me a hand. They helped tie it all together."

Her head angled in consideration. "Now that you say that I can see bits of the two of them in the room. The Westminster clock on the mantel…"

"Rebecca's purchase."

"And the whimsical limited edition print over the sofa…."

"Kathleen."

They jogged again, the sounds of the birds and nearby creek punctuating the quiet.

"There are no pictures," Sidney finally remarked starkly.

Luke frowned but continued to keep pace. "Sid just about every wall has a print or two…"

"Personal pictures," she redefined.

Luke stopped and jogged in place. He remained there until she also stopped and turned to look back at him. "I have personal pictures. Quite a few actually, and you are among them. So is Natalie. I just prefer to keep them in a more private place."

His bedroom, she guessed. "Do you still take pictures?"

"Often. I have my own dark room now." He waggled his brows. "Wanna see it sometime?"

Sidney burst into tinkling laughter. "Now there's a line mothers need to warn their daughters about."

"Did Vera warn you?"

Sidney rolled her eyes. "You know she didn't. Hell, what could potentially happen in a photographer's dark room is something she would love to put in one of her novels."

He agreed with a devilish spark inflecting his eyes as she double backed to pull his arm. "Come on. I'll race you to that huge fallen tree that spans the creek."

"I've got the door," Sidney stated quietly trying to stem disappointment that she certainly had no right to.

Luke stepped through the door with the woman in his arms and the reaction was immediate.

"Carlene! What on earth happened? Are you hurt? Were you run over? Was it a hit and run? We didn't hear…"

"Auntie! There was nothing to hear. Carlene was out jogging near the creek and twisted her ankle," Sidney explained, ordering herself to remain calm. Someone had to. She went to the refrigerator, grabbed a bag of frozen peas and tossed them casually to Luke. He settled a demure Carlene, dressed in designer exercise wear that had never been perspired on, at the window seat. She was one of the few women Sidney knew who wore eyeliner to run.

"Carlene, I had no idea you jogged!" Vera expounded excitedly, frowning as she examined the young woman's foot. "It obviously isn't your sport."

Carlene's face fell instantly, dismayed that the others might share her viewpoint and hastened to dissuade them. "I strayed from the path a little and stumbled into a groundhog hole. It could have happened to anyone. Even Sidney!"

"Well, Sidney wasn't running alone. How long were you stranded down there, Dear?"

Carlene fluttered her lashes. "Only twenty minutes....maybe half an hour."

Vera was shaking her head with matronly disapproval. "Twenty minutes too long, Dear."

"Well, maybe when my ankle gets better I should find a jogging partner..." she hedged nervously, her gaze flitting toward Luke. "Sidney will be going back to the city soon..."

Luke shared a communicative glance with his father, who had kept up the pretense of concentrating on his word jumble. "I think I can likely help you out there, Carlene."

The injured woman holding the frozen vegetables on her ankle, glanced up with transparent hope. "You can?"

"Sure. Constable Peterson jogs every morning and he lives near you. I've seen him glance your way on a couple of occasions. I think he would be thrilled to join you as often as you like. I'll mention it..."

Panic swept her. "No... no, don't." The bag of peas slid to the floor as she scurried to rise without a grimace. "It's OK. Maybe running isn't my ideal pursuit."

"Oh Dear, that's the pain talking." Vera tipped her red curls to angle her head. "You seem to be bearing weight quite well, Carlene. Perhaps your ankle will heal quickly and then you can reconsider Lucas's offer. Think of what might happen..." Vera bubbled as Carlene paled.

Luke's attention strayed to Sidney, who snatched up the two bagged lunches on the counter and vacated the room. He strategically followed her. She definitely had the right idea. Much to his surprise he found her sitting on the front porch digging into one of the bags. She glanced up at him with a sandwich in her hand.

"Swiping the kids' lunches, Sid?" he asked with amusement.

"They didn't need them. It's pizza day at school. Delta made them by mistake," she smiled sheepishly. "I forgot to tell her. Zach and Nicole just left. They said to tell you hello and good-bye. They didn't want to interrupt the drama unfolding in the kitchen."

"They have remarkable instincts," he observed dryly and gestured to the

128

other bag that sat unopened in her lap. "Do you share or did you work up an appetite?"

She made a face and tossed one bag to a nearby wicker chair. "I share."

He retrieved it but sat beside her instead. "I prefer to swing. It relaxes me."

She chuckled. "Running ought to do that."

"Running does do that. Carrying a quaking female batting eyelashes that God didn't give her at me for half a mile doesn't," he grumbled and reminded her of Charlie.

Sidney laughed without a hint of sympathy. "So do something about it."

"Like?"

"Discourage her."

"I do," he groaned. "Or at least I don't encourage her but I can't bring myself to be out and out rude. She seems so…"

"Desperate? Harmless? Pitiful?"

"Yeah," he concurred.

"She might benefit in the long run if you are straight forward. Carlene is sweet although a tad naive. She just needs to readjust her aim."

A dark brow jutted upward. "Jealous?"

She snorted derisively. "Eat your *lunch*, Sheriff."

"Have dinner with me."

Her grin faded and she gave him a wry glance. "You need to concentrate on one meal at a time."

"Yesterday's catch was over two pounds."

Her breath caught as her appetite was fueled. The man forgot nothing, she decided uncomfortably.

"Too late, Sidney! I saw that. You're tempted!" he teased with glee. He wasn't above exploiting her penchant for fresh lobster. Long fingers reached out, caught her chin and gently tugged it toward him. "I'll even buy seconds if they are called for."

She laughed lightly. "I only did that once and paid for it all night long as you ought to recall and then for an entire day afterward because Nat didn't like the flavor of my milk."

His expression grew distant as memories swirled. That night was etched in his mind. It had been their first night out for dinner without the baby. Sidney had overindulged with both the wine and lobster at his urging and instead of pursuing sensual sports that night he had played nursemaid.

"You called me crying at the station the following afternoon. You were so tired and still suffering from indigestion. I could hear Natalie crying nonstop in the background."

She smiled ruefully. "You came home with the lights on and squealing the tires, scaring Delta and Vera half to death."

He gave her a telling look. "I wouldn't have if they had a clue anything was wrong in the first place. Something they could have helped with."

"I purposely stayed in that bathroom with the door shut so they wouldn't hear Natalie. Everyone was already expecting me to fail as a mother being so young. I couldn't bear for people to have more reason," Sidney related with mild chagrin.

He shook his head sadly. "Sid, Vera and Delta would have never judged you. They love you...."

The whole thing seemed so silly now. "I know that but back then I was pretty vulnerable to the things I heard whispered around town..."

"You mean by my mother," Luke said flatly.

Her expression became carefully guarded. "Whatever, Luke. Regardless, you showed up, took Natalie in your arms and she...."

"Let out the kind of enormous burp I had only heard from cops I had been stuck on surveillance with." Luke laughed.

"Your mother would have said it was breeding or the lack of it."

"Pardon?" he commented blankly.

"Your mother once confided to me that I had both the manners and class of a truck driver and should have set my sights on one. Not on you," she admitted with a trace of hurt still infiltrating her tone.

A large palm found her cheek and turned her face so their eyes collided. "Did you set your sights on me or did you just settle because..."

Amazement flooded her features. "You think I married you because I was pregnant?"

"After you left, I admit it occurred to me. I was so desperate for answers." *For you.*

Sidney put her tongue to her lips for a second still peering into the depths of his captivating hazel eyes. "I became your wife, Lucas Ryan, because I had never felt the things you made me feel. I didn't need to be married to have your baby."

His eyes bore into hers and loved the genuineness he saw there that he had never really experienced before or after with anyone else. "Thank you, Sidney. That counts for something. Sometimes late at night all by myself I used to think that I had ruined your life."

Astonishment flickered across earnest pretty features. "Oh no, Luke. Despite how things turned out, I would never trade that time away. Many parts of it were the best moments of my life. It has taken me a long time to accept that nothing will ever equal what once was."

Luke blinked at her acknowledgment. Whatever this Reg meant to her, she obviously didn't believe marriage to him would be the same as theirs. He opened his mouth to try to think of some worthy reply when his father strolled onto the porch with his beeper in the palm of his rough hand.

A shrill noise was relentlessly emanating from it. "This thing is ruining my concentration," he complained.

Luke frowned and took the very device his father once carried religiously to click it off.

This man was born to retire, Sidney smiled. "Was the crossword that difficult, Charlie?"

Charlie gave her a tolerant look. "I'm working on a word jumble about enlightenment and that thing was damned annoying though not as much as that name you insist on calling me," he growled and left them staring after him as he stalked back into the house.

Luke gave her a thoughtful look. "He missed you horribly through the years. Whenever Vera told him you were coming home, he would get all excited and if something came up...well let's just say, I was always glad Vera informed him."

Guilt assailed her. "I felt so much pressure to come home in the first few years and so unable to follow through," she admitted quietly recalling the many times she had canceled plans at the last minute.

"Was it me?"

She shrugged. "Yes. No. Truthfully, it was everything. The disapproval of my moving to New York, the constant interrogation about my living arrangements, worrying about Kathleen coping with two little kids, the possibility of running into people I wasn't prepared to deal with, the push and pull to visit the cemetery...."

The intrusive bleeping of another page shattered the atmosphere and Luke tried to mask his exasperation. This was one of the most meaningful conversations they had shared since she had come back.

"You have to go," she stated and touched his arm. His eyes stayed on hers impressed at her level of understanding and lack of resentment. Many women would shriek at the untimely interruption. "Maybe we could finish this at dinner."

Pleasure surged through him. "Tonight?" A slow pleased smile spread across his face when she nodded. "I'll make the reservation," he promised as he rose to go. Something caught his attention out of the corner of his eye as he trouped down the steps and he turned just in time to catch the sack lunch sailing toward him.

"You might need to eat between now and then," she grinned

131

mischievously from the porch swing.

He laughed and ran down the walk waving as he went. The moment tugged at her heartstrings. It was so similar to send offs during their marriage except the gurgling child in her arms was missing.

Sidney resisted one last glance in the mirror. After all, it wasn't like this was a date. She and Luke were simply sharing dinner away from the chaos of the house. A quiet place to discuss Kathleen and the kids and gorge on lobster. Pleased with her take on the situation, she strolled into the police station toward the Sheriff's office.

His fresh-faced secretary, barely out of high school Sidney deduced, glanced up at her arrival. "May I help you?"

"Yes. I'm here to see Sheriff Ryan."

"He's tied up at the moment. Was he expecting you?" she asked blandly as her eyes indiscreetly traveled over Sidney's peach floral dress. Its simple lines flattered the striking brunette's soft femininity and didn't look a bit like office attire. It wouldn't do her any good with the sheriff though. Julie was fairly certain that despite being dreamy looking, Sheriff Ryan was gay. After all he had never once looked at her as more than staff and she certainly had sent out the signals. And reliable ones at that.

Sidney caught the perusal and for one ludicrous moment felt the urge to ask how many other women showed up in similar circumstances and apparel. "Yes. No. I mean... yes but he was going to pick me up. I... I thought this would be simpler." Though it wasn't turning out that way she was so nervous.

The younger woman's face was screwed up with the concentration of trying to follow Sidney's inane explanation. "Who shall I tell him is here?"

"Sidney."

"Sidney..." the young woman parroted her expectantly.

"Yes,. Sidney." She leaned forward meaningfully. "He'll know who I am."

"Sidney *Ryan*, Julie," Luke's deep voice informed from the open door of his office. One glance confirmed that his novice secretary's eyes were bulging, her mind swirling with heady speculation. "We were married years ago," he declared further as his gaze looked past her. His eyes locked on the beautiful woman he hardly ever hoped to take out to dinner again. His heart started a trip hammer beat. It was going to happen tonight.

Sidney's eyes were mesmerized by both Luke's words as well as his heated perusal. A tinge of sadness flickered over her features. *We aren't married anymore*, her eyes reflected.

I wish we were, hazel eyes conveyed. His eyes drank her in like a starving man gorges at a feast.

Strolling past his secretary's desk he spoke while taking Sidney's arm. "Julie, consider me out for the day. My pager is on my desk. Jack Walken is covering."

His young secretary goggled at him. This Sheriff was always available, day or night. Her eyes followed her boss and his former wife as they walked out side by side. They were casually chatting and she readily noted their easy report. The warmth she saw in her boss's gaze was something Julie had never seen there before. Too bad he was gay or they might still be together.

Sidney pressed her lips together in fierce concentration. Her tongue touched her lips as she gripped the nutcrackers with all her might.

"Sid, I could help...."

"Don't be silly!" she protested with an indignant frown. Suddenly the scarlet claw that had been held in the vice of the crackers she was clenching with white knuckled hands, flew out of the tenuous hold and smacked him squarely in the forehead. Hot liquid dripped over his eyebrow and into his eye leaving him blinking.

"Luke!" Sidney cried immediately dismayed and then barely suppressed a giggle as he mopped his face. "Are you all right?"

He squinted an eye in suspicion of her sincerity and searched for something with his hand. Sidney presumed it was another napkin. Instead he held something out to her in the palm of his large hand. "I believe this is yours."

Sidney eyed the annoyingly intact lobster claw in his hand and lifted starry eyes to his twinkling ones. "Gee, I bet you haven't had a date try to take your eye out in years."

"Not with such an engaging smile," he revealed huskily.

Her beguiling smile widened. "Do I need to beg now?"

He chuckled. "For my forgiveness?"

She snorted. "No. Your help. I really want to get that claw open."

He gave a sharp bark of laughter. "For a price!"

Sidney looked hesitant at his stipulation. "Can I afford it?"

He gave her a disapproving look. "I didn't mean to imply anything near as horrible as your creative mind is conjuring up." His head inclined suggestively to the small dance floor of the dimly lit bistro. "I'll open the last of that ocean beast for one dance."

"Just one?"

He held up an index finger.

"For all the rest?" Her finger circled above her plate.

"The entire thing," Luke confirmed solemnly.

She pursed her lips thoughtfully to one side. "OK," she suddenly agreed cheerfully and shoved her plate toward him. "Get cracking! I'm salivating."

"Ooooh, I love a date that drools."

"Save the chit chat and get to work Sheriff," she implored humorously.

A lazy sensual grin settled on his tanned face as he concentrated on his task. In short order he had unshelled a small pile of succulent seafood. His gaze lifted to see that his dinner guest was indeed riveted to the fruits of his achievement. His lips curved into a devilish smile as he speared some of the tender lobster and leisurely dipped into a pool of drawn butter. His eyes connected with hers as he lifted the fork toward her lips.

"I can do that," she hastened to tell him with nervous undertones.

"I intend on earning my dance."

"You have…"

"Sid, if you want the lobster take it… from me." The fork was within an inch of her lips.

Her brown eyes peered at him as if searching for something. "I want it," she finally stated unequivocally and opened her mouth expectantly.

He grinned and fed her the forkful of seafood. When her tongue flicked out to catch the drip of butter, his mouth went dry watching. She might be feasting but he was starving and nothing on the restaurant menu would satiate him.

"More," Sidney declared, forgetting to feel ill at ease.

He rolled his eyes in his mind. That was the masterpiece of understatement. Without further comment he speared another forkful, putting it to her mouth. She no longer hesitated but took the implement greedily into her mouth and closed her eyes savoring the flavor. His eyes took on a decided glint as he repeated the ritual until there was no more to offer.

"Mmmmm," she murmured in a low growl.

His thumb reached out to rub her bottom lip. Her eyes flickered open. "You have butter on your lip."

"Oh," she breathed in a dazed voice that was hardly louder than a whisper.

He rose out of his chair and stood beside hers. "I believe this is my dance."

She nodded silently. In truth, she didn't trust herself to speak. This evening was too reminiscent of what once had existed between them. The easygoing conversation, the laughter, the sensual teasing. What his compelling eyes suggested could happen….

Sidney closed her eyes as he took her firmly into his embrace. Her head rested lightly on his broad chest delighted by the soft cloth of his shirt under her cheek. Her head could deny it all she wanted but her body remembered this. The song was slow and the intimate hold hardly scandalous, she reassured herself. Couples nearby were dancing just as closely. So she allowed herself to relax within his grasp and felt herself slip back to days when this was her norm...her right.

One hand stroked the silky hair that fell down her back. His other hand was holding hers with their fingers intertwined. His thumb gently caressed hers in slow languid strokes. Their bodies swayed gently and she felt his breath tickle her ear where her hair was pulled back by an antique comb.

A contented smile graced her lips and the hand that was holding hers moved to her jaw to gently tip her chin upward so their eyes met. She blinked almost shyly at him. Her luminous eyes were entranced by his engrossing hazel ones. She stared as his head lowered until his lips were a mere inch from hers. Only a few weeks ago, she would have been outraged by this. Now her lips begged for the contact. All vestiges of reason fled her mind. The only thing that mattered...

A little groan escaped as their lips touched. Sidney wasn't certain whether the noise was hers or his. Without thinking her arms crept around his neck and the fingers of one hand threaded through his hair. It was even sweeter than in memory though their lips were barely brushing. She opened her eyes and stared up at him, dazed.

"It seems the music has stopped," he told her hoarsely. "Our dance is over."

"Is it?" was her stunned reply.

"We could have another."

She swallowed hard and felt reality come flooding back with a brutal snap. She was thirty-one. Not eighteen. They were no longer married. Their daughter was dead. Sadness inflected her expression. "We probably shouldn't." She averted her eyes self-consciously. "We need to get home. It's getting late."

"You don't want dessert, Sid? That isn't like you," he remarked quizzically as he steered her from the dance floor with a possessive hand on her waist.

"Times have changed, Luke," she murmured in flat tones.

Not so much as you would like to think, Sweetheart, he mused with an inward smile. He had enjoyed *his* dessert and knew he had been on a deprivation diet far too long.

CHAPTER TWELVE

Luke highly suspected he shouldn't have come and was growing more certain by the moment. He stirred his coffee absently and realized there was a lull in the conversation. "Nicole and Zach are thrilled about you coming home tomorrow."

Kathleen smiled, she desperately needed to hear this. Interesting too. The remark had absolutely no relevancy to what she had been saying. Just who was the psych patient anyway, she considered wryly. "Are you?"

He stared at her in open confusion. "Am I what, Kathleen?"

"Glad about my discharge?"

He threw her look of reproach. "Of course I am."

"Aren't you worried that Sidney might be headed back to New York?"

Luke gave her a weary glance of the resigned. "That's going to happen eventually."

Kathleen chose to reserve her opinion on that score. It was too early in the game to call as far as she was concerned. "Eventually is at least three months from now."

Surprise flickered across his features. "How do you figure…"

"It's time for a drug holiday and Sid agreed today to stay for the duration." She smiled serenely as he stared at her. It was clear that his thoughts were racing. "Dr. Dixon and I discussed it with her today. I take it she didn't say anything about it at dinner?"

He shot her an annoyed glance. "She really didn't eat dinner. I don't know when the hell she eats." The last time he had seen her really eat was the evening he had taken her out.

"Remember, Sid doesn't eat when she's disturbed about something." *Take it as a positive sign.*

"Well she was waiting for a phone call from what's-his-name and afterward wanted to be alone…."

Kathleen gave Luke a sympathetic glance. "She needs to see Reg. She is going to do that before I go off my meds."

His irritation burgeoned. "It's only been weeks. Can't they stand to be apart…"

Kathleen cut him off deftly. "If the situation were reversed, wouldn't you want to see Sid after…"

His eyes shifted. "Case made, Kathleen."

"Has it helped seeing her?"

He laughed lightly though there was a somewhat hysterical edge to it. "Helped what? Drive me to distraction. Function less well at work. Snipe at the men I am supposed to be leading." His eyebrows jutted up. "It's helped all of that. I'm so unglued your daughter has started giving me advice."

Kathleen giggled. "Nicole?"

"Yeah and for the most part it has been good." He smiled warmly at the woman sitting across from him in the hospital coffee shop. "She's truly her mother's daughter."

Uncertainty flashed across her lovely face. "I don't know whether that's in her best interest or not."

Luke reached for her hand. "I *know*. This has just been a rough time."

Her eyes met his. "It might get rougher…"

"We'll all be there and be prepared this time. It will be different because we know what we're facing."

She took a huge breath. He didn't have a clue what they were facing. "I am worried I might scare the kids. They haven't really been exposed to this before."

He nodded his understanding. "Nic and Zach are expressive kids and they are welcome to hang out at my place or Carl and Rebecca's anytime. We'll make that very clear."

"Don't let me hurt Sidney, Luke," she pleaded, crystal blue eyes welling.

"That only happened once, Kathleen."

"Promise me," she asked beseechingly.

"Sidney will be safe," he pledged confidently and slid onto the bench seat next to her to drape a brotherly arm around her shoulders. Kathleen closed her eyes and hoped he could keep that promise. It suddenly seemed that her best-laid plans were fraught with peril. She vehemently hoped the result would be worth the risk.

Sidney belligerently wished she had her gun in her glove box while she seethed after pulling over to the shoulder of the road. She felt like using it. Nothing life threatening. A flesh wound would do. It would likely make her point and something needed to.

The lights of his cruiser whirled in her rear view mirror. She could see his long legs striding toward her door in the side mirror. His body language emanated barely leashed tension. Her eyes narrowed, he wasn't the only one who was pissed.

"Sidney, for chrissake!"

"Something wrong, Officer," she drawled in deliberately controlled tones.

"Wrong! Dammit, Sid!…"

"You are being terribly forward, Officer. Isn't it standard procedure to ask for my current driver's license?"

He stooped and leaned menacingly on the sill of the open driver's side window. "I think we can dispense with standard procedure..."

"I insist on it," she said as Luke swore under his breath. "I have an appointment to keep so could we get on with it, please."

"Sid..."

"It's Ms. Ryan, actually."

He bit back his irritation at her peevish manner. "Sidney, we don't have to do this..."

She eyed him dubiously and pointedly glanced back at the lights. "Apparently we do."

Reason fled and stubborn annoyance prevailed. "All right. Have it your way. Mrs. Ryan, I need to see your license, insurance and ownership of the vehicle."

Sidney dutifully handed over all three. Luke snatched them in one swipe and stalked back to his cruiser. When he called in the necessary information for verification, a stupefied dispatch clerk stammered back the appropriate replies as they became available. Luke tersely signed off and approached the incensed driver once again.

He leaned down bracing his arms on her door. "It appears Mrs. Ryan..."

"I prefer Ms. actually," she informed him aloofly.

"As I was saying, *Mrs*. Ryan, your license is valid but there appears to be the small matter of an unpaid traffic violation. Shockingly, it is for speeding which of course is also the small matter that brought us together today," he told her snidely.

Sidney continued to stare straight ahead. "Reg told me he took care of that. It must be a mistake," she contended coolly.

Luke snorted in blatant disbelief. "Ahh, well regardless of unkept promises by third parties, the violation remains outstanding..."

Sidney could feel herself losing her tenuous hold on her rampant emotions. She was running late. "Write it up and I'll take care of it," she ground out between clenched teeth.

He shook his head intent on getting her off the road. "I'm afraid that is no longer adequate given how overdue this fine is..."

Sidney drew a shuttering breath and swiveled her head rapidly to pin down his gaze with hers. "Luke, write up the God damned ticket now! I have to get going!"

He gaped at the marked strain he saw etched on her features. "Sidney! I can't let you go like this. You are..."

"*I have to see Reg. Now*," she contended, spacing her words very deliberately.

"You shouldn't drive like this," he stubbornly maintained.

"Unless you arrest me, that is precisely what I intend on doing," she asserted in rigid tones. "So either write up the citation or get out your cuffs. I promise you'll need them."

Confusion swirled in his brain hazing his vision. He obviously did not comprehend her feelings for this other man. She was beside herself to get to him. The realization was grounding. Defeat settled in his gut like food poisoning. "Forget the ticket, Sidney, just drive more carefully."

"Write the fucking ticket, Sheriff!" she insisted in tones fueled by pride.

"Sidney!"

"Do it!" she screamed.

His entire frame was rigid with fury as he rapidly scrawled the violation. The fines were hefty given the outstanding citation but his options were few. She snatched it from his hand without a glance and shoved it in the glove box. He deliberately leaned into the car making her shift to the side in order to preserve some vestiges of personal space. His hazel eyes bore into her dark distraught orbs. "Drive more carefully, Mrs. Ryan, or I may be forced to take more drastic action."

"Like?" she taunted.

Like taking you over my knee. "That remains to be determined." Suddenly another thought struck him. Something he had overheard a few nights ago during a telephone conversation. "Doesn't Reg worry about you when you drive?"

"Yes," Sidney replied grudgingly.

"Then consider driving at a lesser speed for his peace of mind." *And mine.*

She continued to frown but nodded in a gesture of acquiesce.

He felt mild relief soften his stiff joints. "You are free to go then." *Mrs. Ryan.*

Sidney glanced up at him with a shuttered look. "Thanks. I'll be back in a couple days," she murmured and guided the car back onto the road with a conscious effort of restraint.

Luke watched until her car was a mere speck in the distance. If he thought he could get away with it, he would escort her to wherever she was headed but knew that was beyond sensibility. It was a damned fine coincidence that tonight was poker night and they were playing at his house. He didn't care how many hands they played only that the drinks were stiff and uncounted. Knowing where the woman he had married years ago was going to be spending the night, a large amount of alcohol was definitely called for.

The innkeeper was careful to shift his gaze without moving his head. Clever, he congratulated himself. The man had not an inkling he was being watched.

Ted Blanchard considered himself a worldly man but his newest guest had his head spinning. He wasn't prejudiced he reassured himself. He had welcomed all kinds into his gracious and expansive turn of the century manor. He was merely cautious. Perhaps curious. Though it had crossed his mind to collect the room fee up front, but the man had him blinking by offering to pay in advance. He claimed a woman was coming. Seeing her would likely be worth the price of admission, Ted decided privately as he cockily gave the man dwarfing one of his stylish wing back chairs another furtive glance.

Just who did the uptight dude in the beige cardigan think he was fooling, Reg sighed. He was reasonably certain the old gent was going to lunge over his gleaming walnut desk any second if he so much as gave the silver tea service a second take. Hell, he probably wouldn't have been shown into the drawing room at all if he hadn't flashed several dead presidents at the stodgy innkeeper.

His eyes flitted to his watch. She should be here by now. Hell the way Sid drives it was a wonder she hadn't arrived first. That thought had him gripping the arms of the chair in a steely hold. Maybe she had been in an accident, rolled the car, hit a tree, been kidnapped by gypsies. Jesus! Get a grip, Buckman. You are going to need it when she gets here.

Reg almost started to laugh at his own hysterics. He could keep his cool in countless dicey situations but thinking of Sidney in any kind of peril made him crazy. Crazy in love.

His head jerked up and he stared like an idiot as she stood teary eyed in the large archway. The gawking innkeeper behind her faded from significance as he strode forward, arms wide, clasping her against him to bury his face in her hair.

Ted Blanchard sagged onto the high stool behind him. It was preferable to falling down and his knees had gone to jelly. For a man who thought he had seen every pairing, even the odd threesome; this couple rendered him speechless. He leaned forward goggling unabashedly. The man, he had so many misgivings about, was crying.

Reg gently closed the door to their room, his eyes gravitated to where Sidney stood with her back to him. Outwardly serene, but he could see the nerves jumping. Sable waves of hair flowed over her shoulders and halfway down her back. The silky sheen called out to his fingers. His chest felt unnaturally tight knowing what he needed to say and the sooner the better. He crossed the room soundlessly despite his stature, wrapped long arms around her from behind to feel her soften against him with a sigh.

He turned her so that they faced one another. "Sid, I can't stay. Not even the whole night..." His voice dwindled as the whimper escaped before she could stem the emotion. Almost immediately, a brave smile was summoned up and he felt his soul shrivel. "Babe, don't. I would rather you get angry. Break something..."

"Because you are dedicated?" Sidney asked softly.

"Is that what I am?" he asked skeptically. "I feel like the world's biggest heel. You shouldn't be alone tonight...."

Her knuckles grazed the small spot of skin above his beard. "This isn't just about me. You shouldn't be alone tonight either."

I won't, he thought with self-disgust. *I will be surrounded by whores and pushers.*

Her voice suddenly took on strength. "Reg, you are making the world a safer place one small chunk at a time. Lily could only be proud of that."

He closed his eyes in a renewed surge of emotion. "I brought the book."

Sidney smiled tenderly. "I knew you would. Let's look at it. I want to remember. To remember Lily with you."

He led her silently to a floral sofa and settled them both on it. As she lifted the cover of the book, he reached a massive arm past her for the box of tissues he had purposely brought along. He knew without a doubt that in short order they were going to need them.

Reg wasn't sure how long he stood over her, watching. He only knew that it wasn't long enough. She was asleep, curled on her side wearing one of his T-shirts. She put it on earlier claiming it would be cold in the bed without him. Liar, Reg smiled.

When she didn't think he was looking, Reg had seen her put the worn garment to her nostrils and inhale deeply. A glorious smile had graced her beautiful oval face and his heart swelled at the knowledge that he had been blessed to ever stumble across her that afternoon years ago in the projects. A place she had no business being and one that she had barely escaped. He squelched the memory determinedly. In the next few days, he could hardly afford any distractions.

He kissed her brow smiling as she sighed sleepily. He had really meant to leave it at that but yearning got the better of him. His lips moved over hers with thistledown lightness. One slender arm reached upward to clasp the back of his head. "Babe, I didn't mean to wake you..."

"I have sonar when it comes to you leaving. Love you. Be careful."

"Ditto. We have that project…"

"Promise me," she breathed.

"Promise," his baritone voice rumbled in the dark. "I have to go."

"I know."

His thumb brushed her cheek and felt the wetness there. "Love you, Babe." He headed to the door with long strides. If he didn't leave now, Reg doubted he could.

"Love you, Reg," she murmured as the door closed. She rolled over in the large four-poster bed that was meant for lovers. She curled into herself huddling in his huge shirt drinking in his scent. There was little else to comfort her especially tonight. Hot tears fell unheeded and it was hard to resist the urge to dress and return to Barren's Creek. She longed for the sanctuary of her Auntie's room. She would be gone now despite the long drive in the dark if not for knowing how disturbed Reg would be if he ever learned she had done it.

Reg moved quietly down the stairs to the dimly lit foyer of the inn. The owner was still seated behind his desk even at this late hour working on some papers before him. On closer inspection, he was merely doodling. Reg was almost upon him before the older gentleman glanced up. Reg worried that the CPR he may be obliged to perform would make him late.

All color drained from the hotelier as he stared whey faced. Reg steeled himself against a reaction he truly thought he had grown used to over the past year or so. It must be the day that made him so thin skinned, he morosely concluded. Reg was thankful Sidney loved him enough never to see the person the innkeeper obviously saw. Reg had detected strong disapproving vibes earlier when he checked in and heavily suspected if it had not been for the color of his money, he would not have been welcomed at all. His work clothes were obviously mind numbing for the old man. He laid a brawny arm on the front desk and proceeded to conclude his business.

"I have to leave prematurely but I wanted to make some arrangements for my lady first. I scanned your breakfast menu and jotted down her preferences. I would appreciate it being sent up about eight thirty. There should be some flowers arriving just prior to that to be added to her tray. In addition, if there are any additional costs I want to reconcile them now. I don't want her approached to settle any bills…"

The stunned clad owner of the stately home listened attentively to the startling image of the hulking man before him. There was no congruency between the image and the man's attentiveness to his lovely companion.

The next day, the innkeeper followed his directives to the letter personally. This couple, out of countless others, intrigued him. The lovely soft-spoken woman wistfully accepted the flowers visibly touched by the gesture. She chuckled when her breakfast was wheeled in and even asked in jest whether vitamins had been left as well. The innkeeper, long since jaded by some of the extramarital shenanigans he had witnessed, felt some glimmer of sentimentality returning as he considered this oddly endearing couple. As he went to leave the lady to her breakfast, he spied the oddest thing resting on the coffee table. It was a journal similar to the sort new mothers kept. He glanced back at the woman who was gazing idly out the window. She would look enchanting with an infant in her arms. He could bet that the man who left would like nothing better than to put one there. That thought made for striking imagery.

Sidney parked her car on the road. It was barely noon and no one was expecting her for hours and possibly, depending on a phone call she was to have made later this afternoon, not until tomorrow. She headed toward the house where she desperately hoped to find company. The kind she was sorely in need of.

She opened the kitchen door quietly and glanced around when the voice she was seeking most called out cheerfully. "Carl, Honey, you're early...."

Rebecca's vibrant green eyes widened when she spotted Sidney standing forlornly in the kitchen. Her dear friend hadn't seemed this lost for a long while. "Oh Honey, what is it? Where's Reg..."

"He had to go..." Her voice trembled and her meager bravado dissolved in a heartbeat. Sobs shook her as stared woefully into the sympathetic face of her childhood friend. Two feminine arms stole around her quaking shoulders and pulled her close. Sidney found herself sniffling and together they groped for tissue.

"Reg had to go because of the case..." Rebecca hedged a guess.

Sidney nodded. "This cover he has been working under just gets deeper and deeper. I figure that if I were in New York right now, he wouldn't be coming home at all. I think Reg is secretly relieved that I am here out of harm's way."

"I don't know how you stand it," Rebecca admitted frankly.

Sidney made a little scoffing sound. "Right now I am merely faking it. I tried to call Sherry this morning from the inn to see if Don could tell me anything but no one was home. Being here has left me out of the loop so Reg can get away with telling me only what he wants me to know."

Rebecca reached a consoling hand across the kitchen table and clasped her friend's. "He has been fine before, Sidney. He'll be fine now."

Sidney desperately wanted to believe, but there had been too many occasions when Reg hadn't been fine. "Becca, he tried to cover but Reg is as broken up right now as I..." Her voice cracked under the strain of the emotional turmoil and took a deep steadying breath.

The front door banged open with a distant thud as Carl called a greeting. "Hey Hon, I dragged some company home for lunch. Don't worry about having enough food though. He's looking a little green around the gills after last night." A loud chuckle combined with another man's disconcerted grumble could be heard from the hallway. "Maybe I should just offer you some of the hair of the dog that bit..." Carl stopped in his tracks when he caught sight of Sidney. Luke's slightly taller frame slammed into him from behind.

"Jesus, Carl. I have enough trouble staying upright today without trying to make a door out of you!" His eyes widened reflexively as he took in her presence. Her face was chalk white and looked more fragile with her hair pulled away from it and bound at the nape of her neck by a silk scarf.

"Sid, are you all right?" Carl asked quickly with inner alarm.

"Uh huh," she murmured lamely. "Fine, Carl. Just tired."

Something venomous swirled in Luke's gut at the thought of her being fatigued after spending the night with her lover. Any concern that he had felt at the initial sight of her was squelched like a bug under his shoe. "Maybe you should try sleeping more and screwing less then, Sid. It would do wonders for your appearance. You look like hell."

Rebecca gasped at Luke's brutal comment and a quick glance at Sidney's stricken face confirmed it had hit home. Quickly banking her reaction, Sidney coolly assessed Luke from head to toe in a lingering perusal. "You look lousy too, Sheriff. At least I can say I feel inwardly satisfied." Her eyes bore into his with a caustic glare. "*Can you?*"

"Certainly. The company I keep these days is a definite improvement over my past tastes," he informed her with disdain.

"Luke!" Rebecca cried in flagrant disapproval while Sidney hastily averted her gaze. One sidelong glance assured the redhead that her friend's eyes were glistening with unshed tears as she hastily rose from the table.

"Becca, I have to go..."

"Sid, don't..." the other woman began to plead.

Sidney was already halfway to the door. "I *need* to go."

Without further comment, Sidney gave her friend a brave smile and vacated the kitchen like there was a keg of dynamite set to detonate. Rebecca whirled in the direction of the two men. Her green eyes flashed with anger as she sought out the taller of the two. "Lucas Ryan, of all the ignoramus behavior I thought you might be capable of, you just out did my wildest expectations." She was trembling with rage and her husband was tremendously grateful it was aimed elsewhere. Carl had only seen his wife this furious a handful of times and that was plenty. He watched as she squared her shoulders and approached Luke.

"Luke Ryan, get out of my house. *Now!*" she roared.

Luke stood utterly dumbfounded. In all the years he had known Rebecca, he had never heard her speak like this to anyone, let alone to him. He shifted his stunned gaze to Carl, who was coolly regarding him.

"You heard Rebecca. Get out, Luke," he repeated his wife's decree in flat tones and was incensed when Luke's eyes narrowed. *"What?!* You didn't think I'd stand up to you because you are my boss now. Think again. Your treatment of Sidney was despicable." Carl stabbed a finger at Luke's chest. "You don't have a God damned clue what she is going through. All you can think about is your own rampant jealousy for a man you have never met. Well at least that is well founded. Reg is a man deserving of your jealousy. He would never treat Sidney the way you just did." Carl walked briskly back to the front door and threw it open. "See you after lunch, *boss.*"

Luke walked blankly in stupefied shock out of the door, which clicked shut behind him. He glanced down the street in the direction of Vera's gracious Victorian home knowing Sidney was likely there by now. He sighed heavily. He would be no more welcome there than he was here.

"So is this the only way I am going to get to see my son?" Charlie's voice echoed into the foreboding silence of Luke's office. If the atmosphere in the squad room had seemed terse, the stale air in this office was suffocating. "I'm retired. This place makes me edgy." It made him want to do more than crosswords but he knew it was his son's turn.

"I have been busy," Luke informed him barely glancing up. Eye contact, he knew, was never beneficial when one was lying out right.

"Busy making an ass out of yourself from what I understand," his father quipped.

Luke absorbed the accusation with little outward reaction. He had perfected his poker face while growing up in his mother's household. "Did Sidney say that?"

Charlie tipped his face toward the heavens. "You were an ass to her too!?"

Luke narrowed his eyes. "Who did you think I was an ass to?"

"Everyone playing poker at your place the other night. From what I understand you drank yourself into a stupor and said every dumb ass remark that popped into your head."

Luke rubbed his forehead wearily. "That explains the reception I have been getting."

"What did you say to Sidney?" Charlie inquired with a sense of impending doom.

"Whatever I said during poker… what I said to Sidney was worse," Luke suggested drolly.

Charlie groaned. "That explains a lot."

"How is she?"

"It's been a rough couple of days. She's missing…"

"Yeah, yeah. I know. What's-his-name."

"Oh charming son. This benevolent attitude will get you a long way…*off a short pier*!" he yelled in exasperation.

"You aren't exactly the president of Reg's fan club."

"That's different," Charlie muttered. It was a matter of loyalty.

"Does she go to Vera in the middle of the night?"

Charlie rubbed his chin thoughtfully. "Vera goes and sits with her for about an hour before coming to bed. She's afraid Sidney might not come because it might get back to you."

Luke looked grim. "What about Kathleen? I have been calling and she seems fine…"

"Which is damned curious. Sidney comes home for Kathleen and suddenly the worry is more about Sidney."

"Kathleen is putting off her drug holiday…"

Charlie confirmed that with a nod. "For about a week or so."

Luke's forehead wrinkled. There were a number of things that didn't seem to fit. "I am missing a few pieces in this puzzle, aren't I, Dad?"

Charlie bestowed a small smile on his son. "You have excellent instincts, Son. You get that from my side of the family."

Luke rolled his eyes knowing how irrational that was. "Am I ever going to get this straight, Dad?"

Charlie refrained from answering and dropped a small paper bag of aromatic muffins on his desk blotter instead. It was obvious who had baked them. His son lifted his eyes to convey his gratitude. *I'm counting on it, Son… I'm absolutely counting on it.*

Luke glanced back down at the agenda on the table in front of him. They were just about to finish the new business. It was one of the most efficient meetings he had chaired. It even out did the now infamous city council meeting of last month but there was no satisfaction gleaned from today's effort. It was brisk and business like for all the wrong reasons. His staff were cautious and perhaps even intimidated by his recent demeanor with two major exceptions: Jack and Carl. Jack simply wasn't threatened by anyone and Carl was outright pissed.

"So does that clear up any deviations we had regarding policy in the evidence room?" Luke questioned evenly. Heads nodded around the table and chairs were already being scraped across the floor in anticipation of adjournment. Luke saw it and cleared his throat purposefully. "Although the Fourth of July is still weeks away, I would like to take this opportunity to invite all staff and their families to my home for a barbecue." If was an invitation Luke made annually knowing his men had it on their calendars long before he ever announced it.

Pervasive silence greeted his gesture, a huge departure from the reaction he typically received. Luke cringed noting that a couple of the younger constables seemed to be holding their breath. He drew a deep breath. "I thought perhaps we could roast something over a spit." Other than some spontaneous coughing, stoic silence prevailed. Luke's sardonic gaze swept the faces that filled out the table. "Perhaps I should volunteer further."

Jack Walken couldn't resist. "For what, Sheriff?"

Luke flicked him a benign look. "To be the pig that gets roasted."

Carl gave an abrupt shout of laughter, Jack chuckled and a number of the cops Luke had once worked side by side with, joined in. Only the two rookies on the force remained guarded. Luke's lips curved into a sly smile and the novices of the group relaxed, cracking embarrassed smiles.

"I think maybe Jack and I could deal with what goes on the spit," Carl suggested with a cagey smile.

"You did the other day, thanks," Luke acknowledged.

Carl gave him a pleased grin. "Don't mention it."

Luke chuckled with relief that the easygoing atmosphere seemed to be restored and reached forward to press his buzzing intercom. "Julie can you hold whoever it is for just a few more minutes."

"I think you want to take this call, Sheriff," she insisted tightly.

Luke frowned automatically. It was an odd gesture on his secretary's part. Julie was young but she knew what he expected of her. Tension flickered across his face as he listened to the caller. He abruptly ended the call and shoved back his chair.

"Carl, can you finish up here…" Luke asked, already at the door jerking on his jacket.

"Sure, but do you need a hand with whatever…"

Luke turned back for a brief moment. "If I learned anything the other day, I should be able to handle this. Thanks though."

Carl stared after him thoughtfully. Wherever he was headed, it was undoubtedly linked to the only person who ever seemed capable of putting that kind of expression on his face. Sidney.

CHAPTER THIRTEEN

"How long did you say she's been here?" Luke asked, staring past the earnest old man, who nattered in his ear.

The balding caretaker, drew a breath, glanced at his wristwatch. "Almost an hour now, Sheriff. At first, I thought maybe she just needed a private moment but she seemed worse after a piece not better. She hardly ever comes you know. Hates it here." Luke nodded. He knew that and what's more, understood it. "Almost called Vera but then it occurred to me that you and she were once…well you know and back then you were real good at comforting her. I always said to my Caroline if it weren't for your mother's God damned meddling…." Luke glanced over at the old man who had been a fixture at the cemetery since he was a boy.

"I've thought the same thing myself, Mr. Belker."

Dan Belker stared at the younger man's departing back as he strode over to where the woman he had married was, the woman who had given him his only child, the woman who was weeping dejectedly alone….

Luke's features were rigid as he took in the sight of her. She had pulled a striped armchair over to the wall where one of her palms was splayed on cold marble. It was as pathetically close as Sidney could get to what she longed for most. She sat slumped forward and her shoulders shook as she sobbed. Long loose sable brown hair fell in curtains obscuring her face, but Luke had a fair idea the emotions he would see there. He had seen them before. It had been years but obviously, time had not healed her wounds. She just covered them well.

"Sidney," Luke spoke softly as he drew close.

She jerked up at the sound of her name. "Go away." She swiped at her wet cheeks. "I'm fine. I just need a minute."

"You have apparently had a number of them. Let me help."

Her head snapped up to stare at him. "Someone was watching me?" God, the prickle up her spine earlier *was* warranted.

"Mr. Belker saw you and was concerned."

"Damn small town. Nothing can be private," she ground out bitterly.

He knelt beside her chair careful not to touch, at least not yet. "Sidney, this is private. It is just you and I at the grave of our daughter." Luke regretted his choice of words instantly. Her reaction was immediate and caustic as a slender hand smacked the marble.

"*This* is not a grave. It is a God damned drawer in a cold marble wall in a stinking mausoleum." Searing sparks flew from her eyes. "There is no dirt. No place to plant flowers. No sun to shine down. No way to tell the seasons. This..." Her hand swept the carefully measured space in front of her that bore their child's name cutting the air in one viscous swipe. "Is despicable." Tears brimmed in enormous brown eyes as she pursed her lips in a futile attempt to still their trembling.

His eyes shifted to the small space and then back to her desolate expression. His hand smoothed the hair from her cheek in a gentle caress. "I agree, Sidney. I'm so sorry." He saw a flicker of surprise cross her face. "There have been so many times over the years that I have wanted to tell you that. Apologize for letting my mother bully you into agreeing to this when I knew how you felt."

Guilt washed over her sapping the last of her energy. "You didn't know right away. By the time I admitted it, it was too late to change the arrangements..."

"They could have been changed," he maintained staunchly. "It was merely the beginning of extremely poor judgment on my part. At the time of our life when you needed protection the most, I let you down. I left you alone with *her*."

Sidney pressed her fingers to her aching eyes for a second before looking at him. "It's water under the bridge now." Despite her attempt not to, her eyes flitted to the right and she cringed slightly knowing he saw it.

"I hate that too," Luke revealed in low tones.

Her brows knit together. "What?"

Hazel eyes looked directly into hers. "That my bitch of a mother is beside our daughter. They weren't compatible in life. I hate to think of them side by side now," he admitted allowing his gaze to wander to the drawer in the wall that bore his mother's regal name. The cold eyes in her picture seemed to sneer at him even now.

She held his gaze pensively. "I'm..." Her voice trailed off helplessly.

· "You're surprised?"

She gestured lamely. "Well... yes. Mostly about your observation of their relationship. Your mother strove to appear the model grandmother."

Luke snorted. "Babies can't be fooled. Natalie whined constantly around her for good reason."

"I was always sure that your mother held that against me too. That she thought I did something to make Nat dislike her."

He smiled sadly and took her hand. "You always tried so hard. Sid, you were incredibly sweet..."

She laughed with a hysterical edge. "Bull shit, Luke. I was terrified and

152

desperate to make a good impression… oh hell, a passable impression with Virginia." She glanced away for a second sliding her hand from his. "Of course I never could. Very few people in my life have hated me quite so completely as your mother."

Knuckles grazed her cheek still wet from tears. "My mother's specialty was hatred. As hard as it is to believe, it wasn't personal, Sidney."

She was glum. "It sure felt personal. By the time I left, I was convinced that I was the world's biggest failure." *The worst thing that could have ever happened to you. The albatross around your neck. Barren.*

His eyes reflected the torment consuming him at her blunt confession. "I am the one who failed…"

Sidney smiled tearfully and touched him for the first time since he had arrived. Her fingertips rested lightly on his cheek and just stayed there. "Let's not do this. Arguing over who failed most won't change anything. It won't bring Natalie back…" Tears clung to her lashes again as she began to tremble. Her emotions were bubbling so close to the surface. Speaking was far too difficult. The past few days and their significance were finally exacting their toll. She really needed to be in New York but that was impossible right now. Out of desperation, she had come here hoping to feel a connection for her suffocating sense of grief. She did. Her daughters were together. Laid to rest in different places but together in their mother's disabled heart.

He felt her stiffen as his arms reached around her but pulled her into his embrace anyway. "Sidney… Sidney…" he murmured hoarsely into her ear. "Let me. Let me please. I just want to comfort you. I haven't been able to all these years. Let me now."

Shattered eyes searched his pleading ones. Suddenly Luke felt her crash against his chest. She clung to him as sobs racked her smaller body next to his more solid one. He spoke soothingly into her ear and was shocked when she began to speak.

"I was so close… to having the dream again… she was so beautiful… you would have thought so… we loved her… there was nothing we could do… dammit… dammit… I am a lousy cop's wife… whatever made me think I could be anything else… you would think I would learn… but I didn't and my baby paid the price… my beautiful girl…" *My Lily.* Her words disintegrated into incoherent weeping.

Luke held her tenderly, a hand gliding up and down her back pondering what he had heard. Her rambling hadn't made sense. She kept referring to their daughter as hers alone. She had rarely done that before. Even now. Of course, he knew Natalie was gorgeous. She was the spitting image of her mama. Luke frowned as he turned over her garbled speech in his head and finally decided that she was simply distraught. It was unfair to take her words at face value. He luxuriated in the sweet fragrance that was hers alone and felt privileged that she accepted his embrace.

Luke glanced over at her as he drove. Her passivity frightened him. That coupled with the fact that she hadn't put up any argument about leaving her car at the mausoleum and letting him drive her home were grounding.

The static interruption of the radio made her jump but the actual details of what was said was a mere blur. Luke's reply made more of an impression. It was an unusual for him to curse.

"What is it?" she inquired softly.

"There's a problem with a call I need to check on. It's Smith's beat. He's my youngest rookie. This call is out of his league and it's showing. I'll just get you home…"

"Where is the call?"

"On Jefferson Court."

"That's on the way. Go straight there, Luke."

"No." Apprehension seized him unmercifully.

Sidney frowned deeply. "Luke, I'll wait in the car…"

"I could be awhile," he stated with deceptively even tones. *I want you miles away from where I'm going.*

Sidney gave him an insulted glance. "Do you doubt my ability to keep my word and stay out of your way, Lucas Ryan? I am not eighteen any more. I am a full grown woman…"

"You were then too," he murmured softly guiding the car to the address he needed to be. *I remember.* "OK, Sidney. You win this round but stay in the car."

The stress he put on the last four words rang in her head as she watched him stride up the walk of a tidy ranch home in a pretty residential neighborhood. Several other vehicles crowded the drive way and the front of the home. The small home must be crammed with officials. Her eyes narrowed thoughtfully as she studied the house. A stroller sat on the porch, a receiving blanket draped over the handle. Petunias had recently been planted in flower boxes under the windows. A blanket scattered with toys was on the lawn near the front door. The sight made her chest feel tight once more. She recalled days like those with her first daughter and had dreamt of similar times with her second one. Fate had made both mere figments of her imagination.

She was simply too weary to speculate on what could possibly have transpired in this home to bring all of these personnel here today. As time passed, Sidney finally got out of the cruiser to stretch her legs when her gaze traveled once again over the cars. Her guts clenched. She had overlooked one. The coroner's dark long vehicle was parked directly behind theirs. Her eyes locked on the crest that signified his official capacity.

Her gaze wandered again to the house of a family with young children for a second time before she went up the walk.

Luke fought not to close his eyes to shut out the sad scene before him. A pretty woman with short dark hair in a sweater and jeans was clutching her baby and screaming hysterically at the lot of them. Smith may be the rookie, but none of them seemed equipped to deal with Sandra Pensar at the present time. The woman's husband, still in his overcoat from being summoned home in the middle of the afternoon, wasn't faring any better. Jerry Pensar was desperately trying to reason with his wife in a situation that was devoid of logic. Only tragedy existed here.

"Sandra, please, these people want to help us..." the man begged.

"Help us! Don't be an idiot! They want to take my baby! *Our baby!* And you are just going to let them!" she accused him bitterly.

Jerry dragged a hand over his face trying to think of something to tell her. A way to make things better. God, could anything make this better? He drew a haggard breath and opened his mouth to speak when a soft voice came from behind them.

"What's your baby's name?"

The entire group spun around in some oddly choreographed way to stare at Sidney, who stood quietly composed inside the front door. She scanned the ring of men forming a half circle around the frantic mother.

She instantly noted the hard glint in Luke's eyes, that she knew from prior experience, was covering his alarm at her sudden appearance. She purposely bestowed a quick look upon him that she hoped would convey some reassurance that she knew what she was doing. Indeed professionally she did. This was familiar territory for her. A quick speculative perusal told her that the same could not be said for the rest of group before her.

The woman who held her baby crushed against her in a desperate grip studied at her with wide suspicious eyes for a long mute minute. The baby, she held in the crook of her arm and shielded with her other arm as well, had only fuzzy beginnings of blond hair covering her nicely rounded little head and wore an adorable pair of fuchsia overalls with a shirt adorned by little bunnies. Cozy corduroy slippers covered her feet. The baby's eyes were closed and her pretty cherub face was mottled and startlingly pale. The tiny rosebud lips were an disturbing shade of blue. Under any other circumstances, the little child in her mother's arms would have likely protested the tight hold she was clasped in. However, this baby would not do that today. Not ever again. This baby was dead.

"Jennifer," the mother finally choked out.

Sidney maintained steady eye contact as she slowly moved forward into the circle. "It's a beautiful name. You obviously love Jennifer very much."

The woman stared at Sidney like she was the only other sane human being in the room. "I do," she breathed.

Sidney slowly and deliberately shifted her gaze to the baby the woman held. The mother's gaze flickered downward as well. Sidney gave her a long moment of pensive silence before she spoke again. "I am so very sorry, Sandra."

The woman shuttered and her mouth worked in agony. No intelligible words came out only whimpered sobs. When she raised her face again to Sidney's, her face was streaked with the twin rivers of her tears. "I can't let them take her," she said brokenly letting her eyes indicate the men in front of her.

"I understand." Sidney nodded while maintaining her empathetic gaze. "Gentlemen, this is not considered a scene which we need to be concerned about, is it?"

The two officers that had preceded Luke to this address glanced at their boss, who was listening intently to the woman he had once married. All three and the coroner understood her implication. She was asking whether this was a crime scene. Luke glanced at his men and the coroner he had known both professionally and privately for years. He turned back to the woman he was rapidly getting a different view of. "No, it isn't."

"I didn't think so." It was exactly what she presumed it was. Crib death. "So then there really isn't a reason why any of this needs to be rushed, is there, fellows?"

"None at all," Luke quickly supplied vehemently wishing he could go back in time and say those very words to her in another circumstance. He had failed her once. He wouldn't do it again.

Sidney nodded with quiet satisfaction, smiling sympathetically at the young mother who remained shell shocked before them and the traumatized father who stood helplessly watching. "Sandra, do you have a place where you used to rock Jennifer?"

"Her room. The nursery."

"I bet the baby's room is pretty. Would you like to go there with me and we could sit and talk. You could rock Jennifer while we chat."

"Could I?" she asked both relieved and astounded that the baby wasn't going to be wrenched out of her arms.

"Of course. No one will rush you. Saying goodbye takes time," Sidney stated with quiet understanding.

"I don't want to say goodbye," she whispered bleakly.

Tears welled in Sidney's eyes. "I know. I wish I could fix it so you didn't have to... but I can't. No one can."

Sandra stood mesmerized by the other woman. She really did understand. She wasn't offering the magical solution Sandra was prepared to beg for but she cared. She woodenly nodded and slowly moved toward the hallway the led to the nursery trying not to think that it would be the last time she took her baby there.

Sidney let her go ahead and turned toward the men who watched clearly afraid to interrupt. "We're going to be awhile. Why don't all of you get comfortable?" Her gaze shifted to look directly at the man she had once called husband. Sidney gestured for a private word with him after glancing at the slumped figure of Sandra's husband. "Talk to the father, Luke. He is as distraught as she is, merely more subdued." Her eyes peered into his as if looking into his soul. Her hand grazed his tense cheek where a muscle flexed. "You will know what to say. Trust yourself to help him not as a cop but as another father."

Luke stared into the depths of her dark brown eyes and saw the trust there. He nodded buoyed by her confidence in him.

Sidney's throat constricted as she took in the picturesque little nursery done in three shades of rose. Stenciled bows and bunnies edged the room. Flounces of pastel balloon curtains billowed at the windows. Shelves of dolls, stuffed toys and music boxes filled the small cheery space. Sandra was sitting in a white wicker rocker cradling her dead baby girl and humming softly as tears streaked her face in steady streams.

Sidney pulled up a small stool that sat across the room and the young mother glanced up. "Jerry brought that in here to sit on when I was nursing Jennifer so we could talk."

"Jerry sounds like an attentive father."

Sandra nodded bleakly. "He's a wonderful father. Jennifer adores him. She flaps her arms at the sight of him coming through the door at the end of the day." She pressed her free hand over her mouth. "God, she won't be doing that anymore. I don't know how we'll get through this. If we can."

"Sometimes what seems impossible is a little easier if you just look at one day at a time. Sometimes only hours at a time. Take care of today and deal with tomorrow, tomorrow."

Sandra's lip trembled violently as she stared down at the still baby in the crook of her arm. "I'll never see her walk... or ride a tricycle... dry her tears when she falls…"

Sidney silently watched the mother before her grapple with the sheer enormity of her loss. "It's incredibly unfair to know that all the plans you had for your child are never going to happen… both for her… for you… for your husband."

Sandra's face fell and the words blurted out like a purging. "I just put her to bed for her nap. She has been cutting her second tooth and had been fussing." She pressed her lips together. "Oh God, I was glad to put her down." She lifted watery blue eyes and the guilt was swarming there. "I haven't been getting much sleep and…"

"And you're human." Sidney gripped the other woman's hand hard. "Sandra, you need to know… *really know* that no matter what you read, what some well intended or some not so well intended person says, you did nothing… *nothing* to make this happen," Sidney told her adamantly.

Her dark head hung in defeat. "I even read about SIDS. That's what crib death is called, right?"

"Yes. It stands for Sudden Infant Death Syndrome." Such a cold clinical term for a phenomenon that shattered everything that mattered.

"I didn't worry about it because I was doing everything they said to do in the article. We don't smoke. I breast feed Jennifer and put her to sleep on her back." She was shaking her head and staring at the baby in her arms. "How could this happen?"

"I don't know," Sidney admitted. It was an answer she didn't even have for herself.

Sandra's hand gently rubbed her daughter's fluffy hair. "Her hair's so soft. I always wondered what it would look like when she was one. When she would have enough for a pony tail…"

Sidney sat with the other woman while she rocked her baby for the last time and talked about all of the dreams, plans and hopes that would never come to pass now. Sandra did almost of the talking. Sidney knew that all that really mattered was that she was there listening. Really listening and sharing her tears. She was careful not to provide any false reassurance that the days ahead would be better. It would be an enormous lie. And a cruel one. The journey this couple was about to involuntarily embark on would be hellish.

"Why don't I go get Jerry? The two of you could spend some time together with Jennifer," Sidney finally suggested.

Sandra averted her eyes. "I don't know if he'd come. He wanted me to give her to the *doctor,*" She knew what he really was but couldn't bring herself to say it. Coroner was suddenly the most despicable of words. "I couldn't… he's probably mad… disappointed."

Sidney reached to lay her hand on top of the other woman's that rested on her child. "Sandra, it's far more likely that he is heart broken and distraught that he doesn't know how to help. Tell him what you need today and in the days to come. Encourage him to do the same. You both need each other now. Let me go get him," Sidney urged gently.

Tearfully, Sandra nodded but stopped Sidney before she could reach the door. "Is this your job? To come with the police when this happens?"

Sidney smiled sadly over her shoulder. "No. The Sheriff and I, you probably didn't notice who he was. He was one of the last to come in…"

"The tall man with the dark hair. His eyes were sad."

Sidney imagined they were. "He and I were married years ago. Our little girl, Natalie, died of SIDS two weeks before her first birthday."

Sandra's eyes widened and reflexively clutched her dead baby a little tighter. "I didn't know it could happen to babies that old."

"It can happen up to age two but it is far more common in young babies like Jennifer," Sidney informed her and left to go down the hall to find this woman's husband and her baby's father.

It wasn't hard to do. He and Luke were sitting at the kitchen table. A box of tissues between them. Jerry's despondent face snapped up as Sidney entered the room and he stood up expectantly.

"Sandra's still in the nursery with the baby, Jerry. She would like you to go be with her and Jennifer."

His tortured eyes searched hers. "Is she all right…"

Sidney laid a consoling hand on his arm. "She's a long way from all right. Just like you. No one expects that of either of you but she is talking and she needs to be with you. You need it too, Jerry."

He nodded numbly. "Shouldn't we let the coroner take…" his voice hitched. "Take the baby first?"

Sidney peered into his face. "No. You need this time together. Jerry, there is nothing wrong with holding your baby even though she is dead. If you don't know what to say, just sit together. Cry together. Doing this now… spending this time with Jennifer and Sandra will help later."

"I wish I had known these things when we lost Natalie, Jerry," Luke revealed solemnly to the man he had been sitting with while Sidney was down the hall with his wife.

Jerry glanced between this couple, and felt some kind of peculiar bond despite only having set eyes on them a mere hour ago. "I'll go. Will you both…"

"We aren't going anywhere," Sidney knowingly reassured him. She watched the man go down the carpeted hallway. A place he would have been

159

countless times but now the journey was different.

"He's afraid he won't know what to say to her," a masculine voice she would know anywhere told her.

Sidney nodded without turning around. "What did you tell him?"

"Just to say something. That talking and not stopping is the most important thing. And just loving her. It's clear that he does."

"I got the same impression."

"Sidney, are you going to turn around?"

"Eventually."

"What made you get out of the car?"

"Initially stretching my legs. Seeing the coroner's car and the baby things made me come in the house. I just had a feeling," she told him. Two large hands settled on her shoulders. She never even heard him get up.

"I am very proud of you," his deep voice said near her ear.

"I just grew up, Luke. Leaving home has a way of making you do that."

"You did more than leave home," he clarified meaningfully.

"What you saw today is professional training. I do this for a living the same way you do policing."

He turned her gently, pleased that she did not resist. "You may be a social worker but what I saw today was a compassionate caring woman overlooking her own pain to help others with their tragedy."

Her large eyes searched his. "Have you ever told a stranger about Natalie before?"

"No," he admitted.

She smiled with pride reflected in her gaze. "I guess we both have grown up."

Luke was mesmerized with her so close. Their hearts beat only inches from one another. The emotions of the day were swamping his senses and her nearness beckoned to him. He longed to sink into the comfort he knew he could find there. She wouldn't deny him today.

The front door creaking open, admitting his two constables and Frank Barrett, the coroner, had them breaking apart.

Sidney moved to the counter self consciously as she heard the other men approach. A spell had been weaving about them that she had been reluctant to break. She'd felt more at peace in the last few moments than she had been for days. She glanced at the coffee pot and welcomed the distraction.

"Can I get anyone some coffee?" she offered. Within minutes, she was setting steaming cups before the three men, who had joined them in the kitchen. She took the chair that Luke was pulling out for her next to him and sat.

Constable Smith was the first to break the silence. "Mrs. Ryan…"

"Just Sidney is fine," she suggested gently.

The young constable glanced over at his boss, slightly disconcerted until he saw acceptance there. "Sidney, I was never so glad to see a woman in my life as when you showed up."

Sidney gave him a warm smile tweaked with humor at his remark that in any other circumstances would have made him the target of relentless teasing. Today, his colleagues understood precisely what he meant.

Frank Barrett gave Sidney an approving glance and stuck out his hand. "It's been a number of years Sidney. It's a pleasure to see you again but we must find a way to meet under different circumstances."

She smiled professionally, had to keep him on that level for her sanity. "I appreciate you giving this couple some time…"

The coroner waved away her thanks. "I wish I could redo a few other instances such as this one," he told her in sincere tones he knew she understood.

"Our knowledge about healthy grieving has come a long way in the last decade. It still has a long way to go but change only happens one small step at a time," she replied appreciative of his remark.

"Well you made all the difference for this mother…" Smith hastily contended and was taken aback when Sidney resolutely shook her head.

"No. I merely helped her cope a little better in the worst of circumstances but no one can fix this kind of pain. This mother's life changed forever when she walked into her baby's bedroom this afternoon. She and her husband can only begin to imagine how their baby's death will change them. It will change *everything*. The way they see themselves, their marriage, the plans they had, the dreams they dreamt for their child."

"The baby who won't celebrate her birthday, take her first steps, say her first words. She'll never go to school or fight with a brother or sister over a toy. Her parents will always wonder every year on her birthday what she might have been like at that age, what her voice would have sounded like in conversation. Conversations they will never have now. All those tough questions you dread as a parent but now would beg for the opportunity to try to come up with an answer if it meant having her back. However, you know that it is all so futile because you never get your baby back. It was all gone in an instant. In that horrible moment of going to the frilly crib and finding the little person, who was a great deal of what made you get up every morning, not breathing." Sidney sniffed a little as she spoke staring off with an unfocused gaze. Tears stung her eyes and it was useless to try to stem them. A large warm hand covered her smaller one and she blinked as she realigned her gaze to look at him.

"I thought of Natalie that same way the other day. Nicole had come to see me at the station and didn't kiss me when she left. I wondered if our daughter would be doing that very same thing. I decided if she was, I won't like it, but to have her here... here with you and I... almost a teenager now... I would give up anything even her kisses while she was a self conscious adolescent."

"Natalie loved your kisses, Luke. It is hard to summon up an image of her ever turning you down," Sidney told him with a wistful smile. "I remember how she used to wave her arms up and down when you pulled in after a day shift. She had an uncanny sense for knowing when you would arrive. Of course, the fact that you put on the lights and siren for her helped," Sidney added with a mischievous light in her dark eyes to deliberately lighten up the emotionally charged moment. The chuckles from the men around the table and the warm smile Luke gave her, was a telling measure of her success.

The young cops at the table were shocked to hear their Sheriff talk about his daughter so candidly. To their knowledge, he really didn't mention her to anyone. Then again, no one spoke much about his wife until recently either. Lately around the station, a number of old stories of their relationship were resurfacing. Many that gave them a whole new view of their boss. It became harder and harder to believe that the couple who sat before them were a divorced couple that had been apart for over a decade.

The coroner remained pensively silent. He had known Luke Ryan for years in a number of capacities and always liked him. He had only met Sidney Ryan under the most tragic of circumstances. Still when he had heard that their marriage had ended the year after their baby had died, he had felt saddened. Their conversation today gave him pause that they had never found their way back to one another.

CHAPTER FOURTEEN

Luke unlocked his front door and led Sidney in, looping his arm through hers. It felt so incredibly natural. If it had been any other day, he might have been able to convince himself that they were returning home after work. Today's work was highly irregular and the toll it had taken was beginning to show.

Sidney's shoulders had drooped the instant he assisted her into the car. On the way home, she barely said two words. She hadn't even commented when they pulled into his drive instead of Vera's. He watched her slide off her shoes and curl up on the sofa, lay her head on the armrest.

"I'll make a call first thing in the morning and have a resource package sent out that will help Jerry and Sandra."

Luke's brows drew together in curiosity. "There are things out there that help couples if their baby dies?"

"Hmmm. Booklets that give parents ideas about funerals, memorials. They include a lot of quotes from other parents who have been there. Most importantly they make someone, who is despondent, feel a little less alone. There is also a baby book they might appreciate."

"Maybe they already have one," he suggested. "We did."

"Not like this one. It is for babies who have died either at birth or early in their life. It is a place for grieving parents to record what the funeral was like, what they will miss, how they feel... kind of like a journal," Sidney explained softly.

Luke was intrigued. "Would that have helped you?"

"I think so. I did something similar actually. I wrote Natalie letters."

He sank into the armchair opposite her in surprise. "You did?"

"Lots the first year I left. Fewer as time went by. I even wrote a couple last year." Sidney swallowed nervously, lowering her eyes. Suddenly she was revealing more than she ever intended.

"Could I read them sometime?" Luke asked thickly.

She opened her mouth and closed it again. No one had ever read those letters. Reg didn't even know they existed.

Luke felt an immediate stab of regret. He had obviously overstepped. "I'm sorry Sidney. I had no right to..."

"You have every right. You can read them. I don't have them with me but I'll get them for you eventually," she promised.

His heart swelled at the gesture rendering him speechless. Luke wasn't even sure he knew where to look, he so precariously close to erupting. He blindly sought refuge in the kitchen mumbling an excuse about finding them something to eat.

Sidney followed his departure with her eyes thinking it was odd that he left just then. However, it occurred to her she could use a moment to get a better grip on her own emotions.

His first agonized sobs had her head jerking up in shock and on her feet in a heartbeat. When she stood in the doorway of the kitchen, her heart clenched at the sight of him. Luke was leaning against the counter with his back to her. His wide shoulders racked with his weeping.

Without a word, she crossed the spacious kitchen and wrapped herself around him from behind. He stiffened at the contact and tried to muscle her away. With shocking strength, she turned his tense body so that they faced one another. The desolate expression etched on his face made her knees go weak.

"Don't push me away! Earlier today, you asked me to accept your comfort. Now take mine. I, of all people, understand your pain," she implored passionately.

"I'm not sure you can. It is more than losing our daughter." His eyes never wavered from hers. "*I failed you.*"

She was shaking her head before all of his words were out. "Luke…"

He framed her face with shaking hands. "I restrained you while ambulance attendants pulled our dead baby from your arms. You begged them not to take her…to let you say goodbye….to let us say goodbye. I lied to you for the first and only time that day when more than anything, other than a miracle, you needed to be able to trust me. I failed you in the worst way possible."

She struggled to reason with him though the images being conjured up were brutal. "They insisted it would be better just to take her away. I know that now. They told you I would calm down then and accept it. The whole scene was absurd. We were in our bedroom with strangers and I had just discovered the worst reality a mother could know."

"And when you knew they won't listen to your pleas, you turned to me. *Me.* You begged me Sid. You pleaded for me to get Natalie so we could hold her one last time and I denied you."

Hot tears poured from her eyes remembering the savage moment. "Luke, you acted on their advice. People who were supposedly more experienced in these horrendous kinds of situations. What did we know about matters like that?"

Luke shoved away from the comfort of her embrace believing he was undeserving. "A lot apparently! Everything you did today eased that couple's pain. You may claim to have learned it in a college somewhere but what you insisted upon today for Sandra and Jerry were the same requests you were trying to make when Natalie died. The things I could have enforced but instead I held you hysterical in my arms desperate for our baby, who you had just found dead in her crib."

Sidney mentally shook herself to remember that she wasn't eighteen. Her baby… Natalie… had been dead for well over ten years. The anxiety that was consuming her was old… not fresh. It was a by product of the day's events… of the horrible anniversary she was facing…

"Sidney?" his voice called to her softly. The concern in his tone easily heard.

"Right here."

"I don't think so. You are remembering."

She shook her head in a large exaggerated movement. "No. I'm forgetting. To survive you have to forget."

Warm hands cupped her oval face. "To survive you need to let go of the pain."

"You haven't," she accused in a whisper.

"Neither have you."

They stared at each other for a long minute. "Maybe we need to do it together."

His eyes burned intently and it seemed to Sidney that the topaz flecks in them gleamed. "There's a few things we need to do together," he told her huskily and lowered his head.

She gulped and felt her heart rate scramble. Sidney knew she had to leave yet her feet were rooted to the spot. Shallow breathing echoed in her ears. She watched with a mixture of anticipation and hesitation as he leaned down toward her. Finally, let her need out weigh her logic.

"Luke…" The name was barely off her lips when it was swallowed by his, in a searing mating of mouths. Her knees began to fold… like they were no longer capable of supporting her. As if mind reading, Luke slipped an arm beneath them swinging her up against his body and strode from the kitchen. She tried to look past him. He cleverly covered her mouth once more with a dire urgency that stirred and awakened nerve endings.

Curious little shivers rippled through her she hadn't felt in years. Shimmers of delight that she had half convinced herself were embellishments born of their many years of separation. Things she assured herself, that her demented mind conjured up in her sleep to torture her with. Sidney struggled to find her voice before she was past the point of no return. A place she had been before. A time that had resulted in a child...

"Luke... I can't..." she decreed weakly.

He shuttered as he leaned over her settling her in the middle of a large bed with massive walnut columns at each corner. "You can... you should... we need to... *I want to*... I don't know how not to..."

Her eyes clouded in confusion blinking up at him. "How not to?"

"*Love you, Sidney*! I don't know how to stop... don't make me... not tonight..." The rest of his frenzied words were lost as he spread blistering kisses in a searing trail from her ear down the slim column of her neck.

Her chest heaved with the passion he was inspiring... that was overwhelming her sense of reason... her last vestiges of honor. Her present was sliding away as she remembered what was.

"Oh God..." she moaned weakly, feeling his mouth on her breast through the thin layer of silk that was her blouse. Long lean fingers were making short work of the buttons. Suddenly the flimsy material was spread wide and he seemed to be everywhere at once.

Time was suspended. Logic was abandoned as Sidney surrendered helplessly to the sensual assault that was playing havoc with her mind. Her hands joined his passionate pursuit with a will of their own. First timidly and then with feverish haste. She flung his shirt off and to the floor in one wide arc. Her eyes caught his as she turned back toward him. His upper lip curved in a pleased carnal smile as his hazel eyes smoldered with laden promises of what was to come.

Involuntary shivers claimed her. Dear Lord... she knew what was to come... she had never forgotten. She had merely buried it. Deeply. Now waves of pleasures were rifling through her and the ardent treasure she knew him to be was unearthed. For her... by her... and God help her, she wanted it... needed it....

His fingers moved to her waistband and Sidney dragged her hands through the length of her hair that tumbled in disarray over her shoulders. She closed her eyes as she felt her slacks slide off her legs, partly in anticipation, partly in guilt. Delicious sensations swirled in her middle downward where a relentless throbbing was begging for fulfillment.

She could hear his murmuring but knew not what he said. Suddenly, Luke covered her body with his own. Sidney gasped at the shock of his weight upon her. His burning erection, even through his clothing, was a wake up call of the most graphic kind. She pushed his broad shoulders in one spirited shove and sprang from the bed.

Blushing profusely at the extent of her nakedness, Sidney stood quaking by the large bed. Her chest was heaving and her body shook with unfulfilled passion. Luke lay sprawled upon the bed clad only in his pants. His hands were eerily suspended in the air where they had been on her seconds before. They dropped limply to the bed as his eyes squeezed shut in misery.

She hastily began gathering her clothes biting her lower lip in a vain attempt to stem her tidal wave of emotion. Sidney knew she had to be quick or she would never make it to the door. Not that Luke would physically stop her. That would be her own doing. "I have to go."

More of her soul shriveled when she heard the agony in his voice. "Please, Sidney. Don't leave me… not again… not like this… *not* tonight…"

"You are no longer my partner," she told him in a trembling voice.

"I am the only husband you have ever known."

"Reg deserves my loyalty."

Luke sat up in one deft movement to impale her with his gaze. "Is he satisfied with that? Is it enough for him? *Enough for you!?*" His eyes were riveted to her face. She couldn't even look at him. "Sweetheart, you are starving. Starving for *me*! I know it! I *feel* it! Come back to bed!"

"*I can't,*" she cried brokenly with tears dangling on her lashes. Sidney tugged the last of her clothes on carelessly and fled the room unable to resist one last glance at him on the bed. Wishing. Hoping against hope. Knowing soon he would be alone. Again.

"I miss my wife," he said starkly.

Sidney hung her head in dejection, her hand on the door. "I'm not her any more."

"*You're her,*" he insisted knowing she was leaving anyway.

Sidney stood in the hall prepared for flight but something Carl had said recently over coffee rang ruthlessly in her head. *Have you seen his house? All of it? Even the little bedroom next to his… he keeps his heart there.* She shook her dazed head. The words made no sense.

Her eyes darted to the closed door a few feet away. Strange. No other door in this house was closed. Her hand turned the knob aware that she was intruding and yet unable to stop herself.

She gasped upon opening the door. Her mouth remained slack as she stared at the wallpaper. It was tiny rosebuds. Not exactly like those which covered the walls of her bedroom during their marriage, but so very close. Laminated images of photos he had taken were artistically arranged as if hanging in a gallery. The entire family was there. Kathleen and the kids. Carl, Rebecca and their two children. Vera and his father. Jack. There was even a tiny oval of his mother with him as a baby; neither were smiling.

Sidney stood riveted to the portraits. Their beauty was arresting. None of the shots were conventional, which made them the best kind of photos, ones taken when the subject is oblivious to the camera. She was pensive for a long minute. Something tugged at the recesses of her mind. Something Luke had said while they were running… *there are pictures… personal ones… you are among them… so is Natalie…*

Her eyes gleaned the wall before her again eager to view the likeness of the little daughter that was lost to her. She must have misunderstood. She and Natalie weren't there. Disappointment stabbed at her and she turned to go when her breath left her lungs in a rush. Her baby's laughing face was so alive in one large close up in the arrangement dominating the opposite wall, Sidney could almost hear her cheery gurgle. She numbly moved to the picture and laid her hand upon it as if willing the image to life. Helplessly her eyes scanned the other large images amidst the rosebuds. She smiled sentimentally. There were pictures of her and Nat kissing….dancing cheek to cheek, both in nightgowns as they often did after a shared bath….Natalie at breakfast with pabulum clinging to her hair and her hand reaching out to smear the same goo in Sidney's long locks… Luke's deep laughter as he snapped the picture still echoed in her mind.

Her eyes fell upon two pictures side by side she knew first hand. She had taken them. They were of Luke and Natalie. In one, she was sleeping on his chest while he reclined in a large armchair. She recalled wistfully how Luke had been working long hours being new on the force, determined not to receive any preferential treatment because Charlie was Sheriff and volunteered for nights so he could spend his days with them. He was constantly exhausted but he was happy.

The other picture she had taken was a novice photographer's desperate attempt at a family portrait. She had set up the tripod, dressed up Natalie and Luke to both of their chagrin's, and tried to pose them for the benefit of the camera. The end result was hardly perfection. Natalie's fussy dress was flipped inside out at the hem. There was a wet spot on Luke's shirt where Nat had spat up and Sidney had tried to wipe it. Her blouse was improperly buttoned after hurriedly nursing Nat and one of her hair combs had fallen out during the fray of trying to get the shot before the baby howled again. She could still remember her disgust when the photos were developed but Luke had loved them.

He said the picture was perfect because it captured everything a family portrait should: real life, a little bit of craziness, and most important of all, true love. He said when he looked into the faces of the two females in this picture that was all he saw. The love there. It became his undisputed favorite photo. Apparently it still was. Sidney shuttered as she stared at it. It had a prominent place on his wall. The family they had created together…lost together… grieved together… even closing her eyes could no longer shut out the truths that this room held. She walked out of it and back into the room beside it. To him.

He was laying on his side with his back to the door. By all indications, he had not heard her return. She stood staring at the broad expanse of his bare back and then decisively, soundlessly, made her way around to the other side of the bed.

His eyes were open and burned fiercely into hers but he didn't move, didn't speak. Sidney regarded him silently and put her hands to her blouse. She slowly began undoing the buttons. He stared with a heat that reached out licking her with flames that sizzled nerve endings. When the last of the buttons were undone, she slowly pushed the garment off her shoulders letting it flutter to the carpet.

"Tell me what you miss." His voice was a bare whisper in the night. She swallowed hard.

"You wouldn't have come back if you didn't miss something. Tell me, Sidney. I need to know. Is it only Natalie?"

She stared at him wearing only a lacy bra and slacks. "I miss my husband. I don't think I ever said goodbye to him."

"Is that what you are doing now?" he asked quietly.

"What I am feeling, doesn't feel like good bye," she admitted softly.

"What does it feel like?" he asked holding his breath.

"Like being found again when you are very lost." The words tumbled out surprising even herself.

His breath expelled in a gust and he rose in one lithe movement. Before she could blink, Luke stood staring down into her dark eyes with a palpable intensity. "I have missed my wife."

Her tongue traveled slowly over her lips as she stared up at him enraptured. She took his hand in hers and lifted his index finger to her lips. "I have the worst kind of referral pain. It is from a heartache that I can't seem…"

His lips swooped down on her swallowing anything further she might have said. Long lean fingers moved swiftly to the fastening of her bra and flung it away to crush her against him, luxuriating in the feel of her bare skin next to his thudding heart. Two sets of hands worked feverishly at waistbands until nothing stood between them. Their eyes never wavered from one another for fear they might vanish leaving only the unsatisfying remnants of a dream.

"Come here, Sidney. Now. I can't wait any longer." Having already waited years, he held out his hand, drawing them toward the huge bed where he relentlessly dreamt of her.

"I'm here." Slender hands on his body brought reassurance.

"Stay. In my dreams you always leave." As if to guarantee her presence, his hands skimmed over her making bold passes that his mouth followed. His need for her was becoming unbearable. Luke told himself the next time he would savor but now he needing the joining. There was so much he wanted to say, but her name was all that left his lips, as he made their bodies one.

She went completely still beneath him, staring up with wide eyes. Anxiety gripped him as his eyes remained locked on hers. "Sidney? Sweetheart? Are you all right?"

Her smile was sweet as she laced her hands with his. "I am just savoring the moment. One I thought would never come again."

"Ohhh," he half breathed; half groaned. If this was all there was, it was enough.

"Move." Her voice sultry, commanding, urgent. "I want to feel you..."

Their hands fisted together as he moved above her remembering a rhythm that had eluded him with any other woman. His eyes stayed on hers absorbing sensations he saw mirrored in those mesmerizing brown eyes. His groan was low and guttural as her body fisted around him, her fingers clutching his in a merciless grip until she abruptly let go to throw them around his neck, burying her face there.

Knowing he had taken her back to a place he believed to be theirs alone, with one last thrust, he followed.

"I'll move," he pledged hoarsely in her ear, having collapsed heavily upon her. He didn't budge, couldn't for a long moment. She felt too good next to him. Like a wish that had been granted. Even when guilt made him shift his weight, her hands intercepted him with an astonishing grip.

"Stay. I'll let you know if you are crushing me," she vowed. Seconds later a stomach growled and she giggled. "You're hungry."

"That wasn't me. My *appetite* was just satiated." However, he didn't think for long.

"Wasn't me," she insisted stubbornly.

"Sid, it was, Sweetheart. Come on, we'll feed you."

"I don't want to get up," she protested tightening her grip. *I'm afraid to leave this room and have the spell broken.* Tomorrow, she knew, would arrive soon enough.

"Don't then," he asserted, smoothing her hair from her brow, glimpsing the fear. "I'll be right back."

Sidney watched him with twin surges of hesitation and curiosity as he rose from the bed totally uninhibited. His body was similar to the way she remembered him. Lean, muscular and provocatively sensual. He obviously didn't regard his promotion as a desk job and it showed magnificently.

Once alone, she inquisitively took in her surroundings. The furnishings were elegant, beautifully masculine in rich dark wood with clean bold lines. A multitude of candles, varying in size, shape and style, dotted the room. Curiously, none of them had ever been lit. Without thinking, she snapped up a book of matches and began to light them one by one. She was igniting the last wick when he returned.

Sidney whirled at the sound of his footsteps and her hair spun about her causing the tiny flames to dance.

Luke sucked in his breath. Other than the candlelight that bathed her and the silky blanket of her hair partially obscuring her breasts, she was nude.

"Lord, you're beautiful."

She gave him a sad smile. "No, that's, Kathleen. I'm the other sister."

He shook his head once slowly and strode toward her. "I know which sister you are." He caught her chin possessively between two fingers. "The one that is mine."

Anxiety knocked in her chest before she determinedly squashed it. It would be dealt with soon enough. Tonight, she had already promised herself, was theirs.

Suddenly shy, she glanced between the flickering tapers and the matchbook in her hand. "I lit them without thinking."

"I was going to do it when I came back. I never wanted them lit before." He took her hand, kissed it. "I do now."

She felt awkward naked before him after all these years. It took a supreme effort not to cover herself with her hands.

She was nervous, he could see and was hesitant to spook her. He was desperately afraid she might leave and decide what had happened was a mistake. Decisive, Luke took her hand. "Come back to bed, Sweetheart. We'll have a picnic."

She perched prettily on the bed and without asking he began helping her into his shirt that had been tossed to the floor earlier hoping to soothe. "I won't be able to let you eat unless you are covered up. It's been too long since I've had my hands on you."

She giggled feeling more self-assured and savoring the heady scent of him on the cloth. "I'll eat fast."

"I'll feed you fast," he told her wryly popping a juicy bit of melon in her mouth before she could speak again. "And I'm in charge of any drips," he decreed, demonstrating by licking her bottom lip with the rough edge of his tongue catching a drop of dew.

"I want more." Needed it.

"Cheese?"

Sidney shook her head and resolutely moved the tray aside. "You," she breathed and pushed him down onto the bed amid the tangle of sheets.

"Me?" She couldn't possibly know what it meant to have her initiate this. He gazed up at her dazzled by the desire in her expression.

"Now," she stated with an urgency she couldn't explain, didn't dare dwell on. Instead, she straddled his hips, bracing her hands on his chest. "When we're finished, we'll both be hungry," she promised. The tails of the shirt that she wore grazed the hard planes of his stomach and his hand wandered underneath to settle on the curve of her hips.

Luke stared in awe. He knew this woman. He had dreamt of her relentlessly over the past decade. He was experiencing his fondest dream wide-awake.

Sidney was surprised she had slept. She was even more surprised, and somewhat panicked, to find herself alone.

Though the hour was late and the day had been long, they hadn't been able to keep their hands off one another. It wasn't just the sex though that aspect between them had not lost its elemental magic. It was the precious rediscovery of treasured emotions long since denied. His hands upon her had always brought pleasure but tonight they were worshipful. A rekindling of something she never believed could be hers again.

It shouldn't have been. She knew that. She had made commitments and promises to another man. A good man. Her best friend. Hot tears slid from the corners of her eyes to pool in her ears. Shame was a potent drug swarming through her system.

It was only training that kept Luke from stopping in his tracks as he crossed the room to her after realizing she was awake. Worse still, she was crying, silently staring at the ceiling as fat tears leaked out. He had hoped while he ran the water in the sunken tub, added the scent she loved, lit the candles, that he would find her asleep.

He had planned to wake her slowly with soft kisses, quiet words, the ones he had held back for years too long. Her awakening without him was his worst fear because he knew she would think, she would judge. Not him, but herself and she wouldn't be forgiving.

He framed her face with both hands, brushed at a tear with his thumb, kissed her brow. "Don't."

Their eyes caught and held.

"Luke."

"I mean it. Don't." His voice was low but the tone held an edge of desperation. "The line has already been crossed, Sweetheart. Leave it be tonight."

God, she wanted tonight. Wanted the promises she saw in his eyes. The ones that had once been the foundation for her life. Dawn would come soon enough, wouldn't it? After how she had left years ago, didn't he deserve this much, she rationalized unable to fully admit she wanted it for herself as well.

"OK"

Her simple acquiescence was a bare whisper in the night but Luke heard it trumpeted and gathered her close in stark relief. "I ran a bath," he murmured already lifting her from the bed. It seemed the wisest course of action to take control.

She let her head rest against his chest, enjoying the thud of his heart beneath her ear, and smiled. "It smells wonderful…" Her voice trailed off with a sharp intake of breath as he carried her through the door he eased open with his foot.

He set her gently to her feet enjoying her reaction.

She turned back to him gaping with wonder. "We dreamt of this."

They had. It had been a well-enjoyed pastime when they were a young penniless couple to dream of the kind of home they might build together someday. With all dreams, they indulged themselves with great decadence. While the rest of the house was tasteful and earthy, the master bath, easily as large as any of the other bedrooms was lavish.

Subtle shades of taupe were warm and offset by glinting gold facets and shimmering glass. The beautifully textured ceramic floor was toasty warm beneath her feet. As she braced a hand on the ornate marble column that separated the bathing area from the vanity, her eye was drawn to the spectacular stained glass exterior wall that arched elegantly over the sunken bath. Thick ivory towels were neatly stacked in recessed shelving. Several groupings of gold candles flickered erotically as tantalizing steam rose from the foaming bubbles in the bath.

"We used to dream of exactly this," she murmured wondrously, stunned that he had included it in his home.

"After you left, I only dreamt of you."

Uncertainty niggled in as she wondered how many other women had stood in this very spot. A place they had imagined they would enjoy together. One of so many dreams lost.

One hand slipped from hers and touched her chin. "The only other women who have been in this room, have been on a house tour."

Sidney blinked at how transparent she must appear and to her dismay, he chuckled softly. "That, Sweetheart, is always what I love most about you. You are utterly genuine. You can't fake anything. You simply don't know how. It is the essence of your incredible inner beauty." His eyes swept over her curvy figure with undisguised pleasure. "Your outer beauty is also unrivaled."

"Years ago in the shadow of Kathleen's spectacular looks, you alone made me feel exquisite."

One finger strayed from her chin to trace her bottom lip. "You are exquisite, Sidney."

She let out a little rushed breath. "When you say it…"

"Believe it." He pressed his aroused body to hers. "Believe this. No other woman is you and you are all I have ever needed…"

Her hand reached down to cup him and his breath caught.

One side of his mouth lifted rakishly at her forward handling. "Let's get in first."

"In the water?" she asked with widened eyes.

He laughed in unbridled anticipation. "It's quite deep. There's lots of room. It was built for lovers…"

She automatically frowned.

He smiled as he cupped her face. "It was built with you in my mind. I have hardly ever used it because it was tortuous with you only in my head and not my arms."

Her eyes didn't know how to stray from his. "I'm here now."

He was backing them toward the lure of the steamy bath. "Get closer."

Her chest was visibly moving with shallow breaths. "Yes," she agreed with an urgency and nudged him suddenly causing him to lose his balance. Luke tried to release her as he stumbled backward but she clung to him with an unshakable hold.

Sidney let out an excited shriek as they plunged into the slippery tub. Luke's head plummeted into the water in his valiant attempt to keep Sidney out of it. He surged out of the suds sputtering and covered in fluffy foam. Sidney squealed at his fierce features looking positively silly adorned by the white fragrant suds.

"Are you hurt?"

She shook with merriment. "Well I have an ache but I think you have the cure."

He frowned at the scare she had caused and wholly intended to scold her when a delicate hand clasped him in a firm, demanding grip. He sucked in his breath harshly.

"Make my ache go away," she encouraged him in husky tones.

He closed his eyes as he felt his control slipping away. He growled low and pulled her onto his lap. Her smile was welcoming... enticing... entrancing. Her eyes darkened and his mouth lowered as he slipped into her like a wish she had finally granted. "Close enough, Sweetheart?"

Her eyes glistened. "You couldn't be close enough."

He moaned. "I'll consider that a challenge."

"Do that." She swallowed and deliberately clenched her muscles making him shudder. His mouth clamped down on hers as his body began to move until water sloshed wetting the tiles and talking dissolved into broken sighs.

As the world spun away fracturing into brilliant splinters of light, she called his name and he declared his love. His world stopped when she pledged her own. His rebirth was complete.

Sometime later, she lay in the bed again in the space his body made for her. His arm was flung possessively over her body keeping her close. As she remembered, they fit together perfectly.

"What are you thinking about?" It was a dangerous question but he preferred to ask her while he had his hands on her.

"Tonight was so sweet." She shifted to angle her face so he was watching. "Whatever happens..." His mouth opened and she put her hand to his lips. "*Whatever happens* it meant something." She smiled sadly. "Being here like this, it seems so unfair that another couple across town are in such pain."

His heart shifted. She wasn't thinking of Reg. At least not this moment. "We can't change Sandra and Jerry's pain, Sweetheart."

Tears welled. "I hate crib death. Maybe it is an immature stupid reaction but I do. It ends a child's life and changes everyone else's."

He laid a palm on her cheek, velvety soft from the bath. "I would do a lot differently."

Tears fell. The words were so few. They hurt so much. "I would too."

CHAPTER FIFTEEN

It may not have befit his role as law keeper but Luke fully planned on shooting the person drumming on the damned door.

He eased from the bed and hurriedly pulled on a pair of jeans. He glanced over at her and his heart began to thud. She was everything he remembered and more. Don't wake up.

He wanted the pleasure of doing that personally. He felt the need to make an impression in the light of day if he was going to persuade her to confront the things he believed they needed to face together. He certainly did not need some idiot intruder to complicate what was already a tenuous situation.

He opened the door and gave Carl a sly grin as relief poured through him like a torrential rain. This man he could easily handle without Sidney being any the wiser. After all, hadn't Carl been a one-man cheering section since she had come home? However, as Carl swung about as the door opened, his expression was disarming.

"Luke, we need to find Sidney," the other man stated bluntly striding past him toward the kitchen praying for coffee.

"Oh, is that all?" Luke sagged against the doorjamb. "I thought something was wrong."

"Something is wrong. I can't find Sidney. From what I can figure out you saw her last at that call Smith was having trouble handling. Her car is gone so I wonder if she headed to New York on the spur of the moment…"

"Carl…" The man was pacing like an expectant father.

"I was at the house, Vera and Charlie are no where to be found. Kathleen seemed to think Sid was off running but her room looks too neat…."

"Carl!"

"This is the last thing Kathleen needs." Hands tunneled through his hair in pure agitation. "Hell, what am I saying? This is the last thing Sid needs to deal with."

Luke's eyes narrowed. What the hell was going on? "Carl, we don't have to find Sidney…"

Carl spun around to stare at him like he was deranged. "Shit, Luke. I need to find her like yesterday…"

"Sidney is here. She's been with me."

Carl gaped at him and then shut his mouth to close his eyes, shaking his head slowly as if anguished. "Oh God," he lamented with a groan. He had encouraged this.

The insult stung. "You could sound a little happier. Last night was…"

Carl held up a hand. "Luke, don't…you have no idea…."

"Carl?" Both men jerked around to stare at her pale figure dwarfed in the folds of Luke's burgundy robe. Her hair tumbled in cascades over her shoulders.

Luke moved toward her seeing the distress. Dammit, he had to get rid of Carl so he could finesse this. "Sidney, Sweetheart, I'm sorry we woke you. Carl was just leaving…"

"Get dressed, Sidney," Carl interrupted.

Luke swung around to Carl incensed at his outrageous demand but before he could open his mouth, Sidney began to wail.

"Oh God! No!" She flew to Carl, clutching handfuls of his shirt in a white knuckled grip. "*He's not*! Tell me… he's not!"

Carl firmly planted his hands on her shoulders to gaze into her eyes. "He's alive." She shuddered violently. "Sid, I promise you. I wouldn't lie. Reg was wounded and in surgery but he's expected to live."

Horror owned her body and soul. "The hospital. Which one?"

"St. Mark's."

She was swearing under her breath as she grabbed the phone and punched in numbers she knew by heart. A voice she knew curtly answered the call.

"Tell me he's alive," she asked bluntly.

"Sid! Thank God. Yes. He's still in surgery. Due out any moment."

"How bad?"

The silence was minimal but telling. "He used up another one of those nine lives you badger him about."

"Tell me."

"He took two hits. One was just a flesh wound in the arm."

"The other?"

"A decent hole in his side. He lost a fair amount of blood. The guys are donating right now."

"Any major organs?"

"He lost his spleen and they had to patch up a couple nicks to other abdominal organs. Sid, the surgeon can explain…"

"Any head injury?"

"No, Sid. I'm not bull shitting you…."

Her lip was trembling with the onslaught on her emotion. "Don, promise me."

"I promise, Sidney. I'm giving it to you straight. He was lucky as hell. Just get here."

"In the inside of four hours."

"Safely, Sid, or he'll kill me."

"Think he'll be up to that?"

"Sidney, he'll do one better. He'll be wanting to get busy on that project the two of you are eager to...."

She began to cry softly into the phone for reasons Don knew as well as ones that would shock him.

"Sidney, just come home. We're all waiting for you."

"I'm coming, Don. Tell him for me."

"Safely, Sidney! I won't fix any tickets," Reg's partner warned.

"Got it." She laid down the phone feeling her life sliding away like loose gravel at a cliff. She had felt this way twice before. She groaned inwardly thinking of the old adage about things coming in threes. She glanced up to the rigid countenance of the man she had spent the night with and knew Carl was still in the room. Obviously, they had no secrets. Her behavior last night deserved none. "Can you bring my clothes please?" she asked in a small voice.

He regarded her at length as if trying to determine how best to proceed. Desperation gave way. "Now Luke. I need to leave," she decreed in tortured tones.

"I'll take you," both men told her in unrehearsed unison.

Her expression became shuttered. "I'd appreciate it, Carl."

Luke took one menacing step toward her. "Appreciate it all you like but I'm the one you are going with..."

Her voice hitched on a sob. "It would be simpler..."

Luke's gaze bore relentlessly into hers. *"We're way past simple, Sidney,"* he ground out in barely leashed tones.

Her eyes glistened and she nodded in dismal agreement. "Can we just get dressed and go? I need to stop at Vera's for a second."

"Why don't you call from the car? You must have clothes in New York."

Her expression grew pained as she wrung her hands together. "I need something that is here."

Carl moved forward and took her hands in his as Luke vacated the kitchen. "Sidney, if Don says Reg will be fine, he will be. He wouldn't lie to you." Carl stroked her cheek. "He knows you would shoot him."

She smiled through her turmoil at his obvious attempt at levity. "Thanks for finding me, Carl. You are a good friend. Better than I deserve."

"Sidney..."

She shook her head dismally. "Don't waste your breath, Carl. I know what I've done." *Screwed up one of the sweetest parts of my life. Again.*

"Sidney, just take things one moment at a time. You'll figure it out."

She averted her eyes to the floor. "I hate to ask you to lie for me…"

"Then don't. I know how to be discreet."

She smiled sadly and nodded. "Of course you do. Thanks, Carl."

"I'm sorry Sid. About Reg. About this happening right now…"

"I've had such a pessimistic feeling about this whole cover. I kept telling myself I was oversensitive after last year but…"

"He's alive Sid and waiting for you."

"Right," she agreed softly.

"Your clothes are in the main bathroom down the hall," Luke interrupted and watched her hurry away. "Should I understand half of what I just overheard?"

"Probably not," Carl volunteered. "And you are going to see and hear a few more things that won't make much sense in New York. Luke, a decade is a long time to be apart."

"This isn't impossible," he contended in rigid tones.

"Whatever it is, it won't be easy. Don't underestimate her affection for Reg or you'll be…"

"I am already. Her reaction was leveling," Luke admitted quietly.

Carl gave him a sympathetic look. His guts clenched for all three of them. Reg was one hell of a decent guy. It was clear someone in this scenario was going to end up with a hole through a more vital organ than their spleen.

"Sidney is there anything I can pack for you?" Kathleen was asking.

Sidney stared at her sister numbly. What an about face. Kathleen was so together and she was the head case. She tried to blink her way out of the fog that was stunning her brain. She had to think. Had to hurry. Reg was waiting.

Luke was tapping his foot impatiently, scattering her disturbed thoughts. She glanced from the hall closet she was haphazardly searching through and peered at him irritably. "Could you do that somewhere else?"

He followed her pointed gaze to his shoe and instantly ceased the tapping. "Tell me what you want packed or the afternoon traffic will be building just as we reach the city."

Her mouth worked but nothing intelligible came out of it. Vera had already asked that very same question. Delta was busy packing sandwiches like they were going off on a God damned picnic. Charlie was filling the gas tank and towed Zach along to still his curious questions. Nicole was sweetly off finding her some books to read during the long hours at the hospital. Carlene was loitering on the fringes with wide eyes, stammering about herbal tea. *He* was just standing there. A living reminder of last night that she couldn't shut out. It was even harder given what she was searching for and having precious little luck finding.

"Sidney! Let me help!" Luke yelled.

She whirled to face him as her temper boiled over. "Get out! Just get out and let me...."

"Let you what!" he shouted back as his own frayed nerves exploded.

"Never mind. Never mind! Just go....somewhere... for ten minutes. I'll be ready when you get back," she screamed helplessly.

Luke looked more prepared to throttle her and took a step in her direction. Vera, badly in need of her red rinse, blocked his path. "Lucas, I have a splendid idea. Go pick up the dry cleaning."

Luke stared in the sweetly zany face of a woman he usually found endearing and did a double take. "The dry cleaning?"

Vera's head bobbed. "Yes. Mr. Tanner called about it this morning. It needs picking up *quite* immediately."

He loved Vera but she was nuts. What the hell did they need with dry cleaning when this man Sidney supposedly cared so much for was lying in a hospital hundreds of miles away? Even Sidney's behavior was bizarre. Whenever Kathleen had a crisis, Sidney had always and often recklessly dropped everything to run to her. Now she was rifling through closets!

He threw up his hands. Their logic eluded him. "I'll get the cleaning. Sidney, be ready in five." The screen door banged behind him as she tore up the stairs to her bedroom.

Kathleen stared after her and then over at her aunt, calmly sitting at the breakfast table in the front parlor pouring tea. "Would you like some Kathleen?" she asked quietly. "Carlene made chamomile. Very soothing."

"Maybe we should put some in a jug for Luke to go," Kathleen quipped. "Auntie, do you know what Sid is so frantic about? Why she hasn't left yet..."

"Luke will take care of it," Vera replied with eerie complacency.

"Luke is going to the dry cleaners," Kathleen reminded her in baffled tones knowing that Vera had sent him.

"Exactly," her aunt confirmed while stirring a ladle of honey into her delicate teacup.

Kathleen's forehead creased. And people claimed she was crazy! She shook her head and climbed the stairs to see if her sister was having any more success upstairs than downstairs. Her eyes bugged out at the sight of the attic bedroom. It looked like one of her own better efforts during a manic phase. Drawers were pulled out at odd angles and the rifled contents strewn about, littering the floor and cluttering furniture. Sidney was inside the closet flinging more garments out onto the floor. Suddenly she stilled in the midst

181

of the chaos of her own creation. "Those pants! The navy pair...where the hell are they?!" she cried on the verge of hysteria.

"A pair of pants Sid? That's what this is about?"

"Geez, Kathleen!" she gasped overwrought. Clothes were landing in a growing heap even as she spoke. "Where the hell..."

"Downstairs, Sidney." Two women whirled at the sound of Vera's softly commanding voice.

"What's downstairs, Aunt Vera?" Sidney asked with suffocating panic.

"The dry cleaning. The pants...."

Sidney bolted past her mid-sentence. Puzzled, Kathleen, followed on her heels.

Sidney was heaving for air as she cleared the bottom of the staircase in one bound taking the last three steps in a desperate sprint. The cleaning hung on the hall tree swathed in clear plastic. She recklessly separated the articles tearing at the covering. She gulped realizing the pants were hung upside down. She could barely still her sobs. *Where the hell was it!* She couldn't go to him without it. Bleak hope sprang eternal. Perhaps the cleaners had found it and put it in a little envelope pinned somewhere.....

She crumpled onto the bottom step with the pants clutched to her chest. The torn plastic swirled at her feet. The only thing on the hanger were the pants. Who was she kidding? If a cleaner found some loose change or a button, he might return it. When someone finds a large solitaire diamond...

Two dark shoes appeared in her direct line of vision of the floor. She lifted her ravaged face to his stony one. As she stared pathetically up at him with a tear-streaked face, Luke took her hand and turned it palm upward. He put a small object with sharp edges into it and closed her fingers over top.

"Put it on Sidney and let's getting going," he ground out and spun away toward the door. Zach and Charlie had returned and were watching with morbid interest. Nicole, Carlene and Delta were headed toward them loaded down with things for the trip. Kathleen edged past her sister at the bottom of the stairs to see what was so important to delay her departure. Vera remained knowingly on the stairs.

Tears stood in Sidney's eyes as she woodenly regarded the door, Luke had left like she was something detestable. Knowing it to be true, she slowly opened her hand. Despite everything, she badly needed to see what was there. To remind herself of what it represented. To put it back where it belonged. The brilliant diamond flashed jeeringly as she put it on the third finger of her left hand where Reg had slipped it originally. That moment had been enchanting. This one was guilt ridden. She no longer deserved the honor it represented.

His gaze strayed to the passenger seat for what had to be the millionth time. Her eyes were closed and had been practically since they left Barren's Creek yet Luke doubted she was truly asleep. It was more likely protective camouflage.

"Sidney, we are getting to the point where I am going to need some directions."

Her eyes opened instantly, rapidly scanning her surroundings with palpable alertness. She definitely had not been asleep. She fired off some instructions and closed her eyes once more.

He glanced over at the hand that rested on her leg and his mind wandered to a time when it would have more likely rested on his thigh. He sighed dejectedly. Now the diamond there winked mockingly. Still he felt the urge to reach out....

Her breath caught as his large warm hand covered hers. It felt wonderful but she was wholly undeserving. She turned her agonized face to his and saw his eyes glancing between her and the expressway.

"I'm sorry about..."

"Stop!" he ordered sharply making her jump. "Don't say last night was a mistake! Don't say you are sorry it happened! I am prepared for a lot today Sidney but *not that!*"

She regarded him with sorrowful eyes and felt the pain she had caused. "Then can I ask you to believe something through all of this? What has happened so far and what might..." He waited expectantly. "Luke I care deeply about you and I would never intentionally hurt you."

His hand that covered hers passively curled around her fingers and squeezed. "I know that Sidney. Know this...you need to...I love you...I never stopped. I simply don't know how," he revealed adamantly.

She squeezed her eyes shut in mute misery. He was going to be hurt. This morning was a mere scrape compared to what would follow. "Luke, I think you need to work to on it," she suggested softly.

"Just give me directions, Sidney. The rest will take care of itself. You'll see."

She highly doubted his hypothesis but capitulated nonetheless. There was really nothing else she could do at this given moment. He would see for himself soon enough. Clearly sparing him was no longer an option.

She stepped through the front double doors of the marble foyer of the hospital having left Luke to find parking. He was hardly impressed when she had practically sprang from the car but she had little choice. If there was trouble, she preferred to deal with it solo. Sidney glimpsed the security desk from the corner of her eye and kept walking. She was only steps beyond it when rapid clicking heels descended upon her.

"Ms. Ryan, I must insist..." a raspy voice implored.

She turned crisply to confront a man she once counted as a friend. "Save it. I am not here as an employee. I am here to see a patient as a visitor."

The aging uniformed man frowned deeply truly wishing he could let her by. "Surely you could see this *patient* when they are discharged. I would strongly advise...."

She gritted her teeth and thrust a rigid index finger at his chest. "I would advise you to stay the hell out of my way. My fiancé is lying upstairs with two bullet..."

His face flashed with shock. "Reg? When?"

"Last night. I was out of town."

God, he wanted to give her a hug. She had lent him support whenever he had needed it. It seemed dead wrong not to return the favor. "I'll escort you to ensure you have no further delays."

She took the arm he offered with a weak smile. "Thanks, Bill."

"Sidney, none of this is personal. You do know that."

She gazed up at him with little outward emotion. "I have certainly been assured of that on numerous occasions."

"I need this job, Sidney," the aged security guard divulged, despising himself.

"Now that's a statement I can identify with." She flashed a rueful smile. "Reg is on seventh."

Rapid footsteps pounded behind them. She glanced over her shoulder already knowing it was him. "Luke meet Bill. He is going to walk us up. We're old pals."

Luke nodded and fell into step. This was obviously not the time to exchange pleasantries. As they stood side by side in the elevator, he could sense her growing distress. Her breathing was growing shallow and she shot out of the doors the instant they opened. It was obvious she knew where she was going. Then again, why wouldn't she? This had been her place of employment for years.

The man beside him was regarding him curiously. "You a friend of hers?"

"Something like that," Luke replied noncommittally.

"Damn shame about Reg," the security guard volunteered. "Those two make quite a pair."

Luke did not reply. Truthfully, he didn't have a suitable response. After all, he had never even laid eyes on the man. He saw Sidney walking on ahead, fervently searching each waiting room she came upon. A man's voice suddenly caught her attention. "Sid!"

She whirled at the sound of his voice and took a heaving breath. An incoherent sound came out as she hurled herself into the arms of a short stocky man with shaggy dark hair. He clasped her to him for a long moment without saying anything until she pulled back.

"You weren't hurt, Don?"

"No. Reg was the only officer down," he confided with disgust.

"Because he was in the God damned thick of it," she replied bitterly. "Sidney…"

"I want to see him. *Now!*"

"I just checked. They need a few minutes. The guys are down the hall. Let them have a look at you. Everyone needs a lift."

She gave him a little snort.

"Come on. Everyone knows once you are here, Reg will be fine," he cajoled tugging on her arm leaving her little choice. "Hey look who I found loitering the halls!"

Luke could hear numerous friendly and unmistakably warm greetings and her murmured emotional replies. He suddenly felt like an interloper on a life she had built without him. His eyes caught sight of a smartly dressed woman with flawless ivory skin that he judged to be in her early fifties. She looked preoccupied as she walked but her head snapped up at the sound of a feminine voice in the waiting room. "Sidney?"

Luke watched with stunned fascination as the woman, he had loved for half of his life, sprung from the doorway crying. "Mom!"

"Right here, Honey," the woman answered through her tears opening her arms. Luke stared as Sidney fell into them in a rush. They embraced and Luke could see the older woman was talking soothingly in her ear. The couple of men he could see from the doorway hardly looked surprised by the scene. He felt choked watching them. Sidney had dutifully called his parent, Mother Ryan, at Virginia's insistence and more calculated to make Sidney uncomfortable rather than a sincere gesture of welcome. He could count on two fingers how many times they had touched and those moments never included a quick hug rather than a clutching embrace like this one. Reg's mother obviously cared for Sidney in a way his own mother had failed to. He felt humbled just watching.

Sidney caught her breath and spoke earnestly to the woman before her. "Don says I can't see him …"

The older woman smiled with amusement inflecting clear blue eyes that complimented her pale blond hair. "Honey, Reg is getting washed up for you…"

"What!" she exploded incredulously. "I'm out here and not with him because he is having a God damned bed bath!"

Someone snickered behind her. "Hey Sid, Reg just wants to look his best for you!"

She tossed the man a baneful glare that Luke couldn't completely understand.

Another man chuckled. "It'll take a hell of a lot more than a sponge bath..."

"Enough!" Sidney warned threateningly yet a little wayward smile tugged at her lips. "What room, Don?"

"Sid, just one more minute..."

She stared him down pointedly. "What..."

"749... third door on your right." She was halfway down the hall when he called out. "Take it easy on him. He's a wounded man."

The other men in the room laughed lightly for the first time in hours. "Maybe one of us should go chaperon for poor Reg's protection," one joked.

"And I volunteer you, Hudson," Don retorted.

Reg's mother smiled. She knew her son needed no other protection than the young woman who was coming his way. Just as she went to find a seat to occupy, a large warm hand settled on her shoulder. She didn't even have to turn around to know whose it was. "Sidney's here, Henry."

"I know," a deep baritone voice of a tall powerfully built man murmured. "I caught a glimpse of her sprinting down the hall."

Reg's mother let out a little peel of tinkling laughter. "Obviously you knew better than to interrupt her progress."

"Oh yeah," he rumbled enjoying the grins around the room. "Reg was lucky last night, I hope he is as battle worthy today."

Luke remained anonymous in the hallway. He sensed the security guard watching him curiously and ignored it. He glanced in the waiting room. The woman Luke surmised was Reg's mother stool by a tall very dark skinned man who smiled and draped an arm about her shoulders. His cop's instincts suspected the man might be Reg's superior officer offering moral support.

His feet moved down the hall of their own accord and halted when he saw Sidney standing silently in a doorway a short distance away. From all accounts, she had yet to speak. Tears trickled down her cheek.

"That curtain better open soon if you know what is good for you, Reg Buckman," she warned unsteadily.

The low conversation in the room abruptly ended. Water gently sloshing in a basin reached her ears. "Hey Babe. We'll just be..."

"Get that curtain open," she commanded in a tight voice.

"I didn't break my promise, Babe. I am in one piece."

"That wasn't the promise, you big ox," she complained in a tenuous voice.

"Ooooh flattery…"

"The curtain…" A nurse hurried from the room past Sidney with a secretive little smile.

"Open it yourself, you sweet thing," he told her silkily hoping vainly to lighten the moment.

She folded her lips in a valiant attempt to maintain her composure for another second. Her hand grabbed a fistful of curtain and pulled them open in one forceful swipe. She took in the sight of him expelling a long ragged breath and began crying brokenly.

"Oh Sid…come to me Darlin.…my arms are empty…," he told her, yearning. She rushed forward and his arms wrapped around her shoulders tugging her downward as IV lines tangled about them. His other arm was immobilized in a cloth sling and he swallowed a grunt as her hold tightened around it. He could live with the pain, it was her he couldn't do without, he had decided during the horrendous ambulance ride. From now on, where she went; he went. No matter what. Let someone else save the world. He just wanted her.

Luke could no longer hear their voices only Sidney's muffled crying. He moved a little farther down the hall and glanced into the room. It was time he got a look at his competition. He had already heard more than enough to realize he had some.

It was going to take both hands to close his gaping mouth, Luke figured. He sidestepped the door to sag against the wall. He shouldn't have been so completely thrown but he was. The woman he loved was being cradled by a giant man who dwarfed the hospital bed. His shoulders were massive and from the shape he saw beneath the thin covers, so was the rest of him. He wasn't overweight, merely huge in both frame and build. His hair was just past his shoulders and hung in thousands of thin dread locks with shiny gold beads dangling from each. A large gold hoop pierced one ear. Multiple gaudy rings embellished both hands. He was an awesome sight and his skin was as black as the woman tucked under his meaty arm was white. Luke stumbled backward and wandered down the hall to duck cowardly into a stairwell. He had to get a grip knowing eventually Sidney would remember he was here and come looking.

CHAPTER SIXTEEN

It was no less damaging to his ego that by the time his head felt less dull, his thoughts less fuzzy, she still had not come looking for him. Luke made his way back down the hall toward the room he had seen her last. By the din spilling out into the hall, a party was going on.

"So Sid, how did you get here so fast?" a man was asking.

"You better have driven safely…" another was saying.

"I always drive safely," she retorted feigning insult.

Laughter erupted. "Babe, we've all seen you drive," Reg rumbled sardonically.

She attempted a damning glance but humor lurked beneath when her head suddenly shot up. "Oh hell I forgot." She scanned the room. "Where…"

"Right here," Luke said solemnly from the doorway not quite in the room but not quite out of it either.

Reg, who was cuddling her close, narrowed his eyes at the tall man who stood in the entryway. Sidney gave the man there a small nervous smile. It was all the invitation he required. Luke walked toward the formidable man ensconced in the bed and thrust out his hand. "It's Luke. I drove Sidney. She was too upset to drive," he winked. "I've seen her behind the wheel myself," he added to predicable snickers, one woman's scathing regard and Reg's puzzled regard. "You might know me better as the *door man.*"

Reg studied him carefully as he continued to shake this movie star handsome man's solid grip. Even with his mind fuzzy from painkillers, he sensed he was getting an abridged version. "You don't look any door man I've ever seen. They're typically paunchy old men wearing dorky hats and ridiculous coats chock full of decorative braids."

A couple of the men broke out in deep guffaws. "Reg, you just described most cops in full dress uniform just prior to retirement."

"Actually Luke's a cop as well. Barren Creek's Sheriff," Sidney informed them.

Reg pursed his lips thoughtfully. "A real life Sheriff. I thought you guys were an extinct breed."

"Not in small rural towns. We're alive and well. We get shot a lot less too," Luke observed mildly.

"Sidney, Honey, maybe it is time to take my son home with you," Hilary Buckman sincerely urged.

"Yes, Son. I would like to think of a whole year going by without you getting wounded," Henry readily agreed.

"I didn't say no one ever gets shot in Barren's Creek," Luke felt compelled to add realizing now the man he presumed to be Reg's superior officer was his father.

"So in how many years of policing have you had to draw your gun..." Henry inquired with pointed interest.

"Few enough times that I can recall each one," Luke acknowledged honestly.

"And you have never been injured?" Hilary asked presuming that the answer would help her cause.

"Once."

Sidney's head jerked up off of Reg's chest. "When? No one told me."

Luke remained silent for a moment, privately pleased with her response. "A few years back. You were away at the time. No one wanted to worry you. There were plenty of people fussing over me as it was, Sid." He tipped his head casually. "That's another benefit or perhaps draw back, depending on your outlook, of a small town. Everybody knows your business."

Henry chuckled. He knew that from his own experience growing up. The first time he had returned home with his very white Jewish bride had been a brutal education for them both. "Where did you get hit, Luke?"

Luke's lips curved upward in a rueful smile. "The upper thigh." It was rewarding to glimpse Sidney's concern before she could mask it. The men in the room predictably winced in commiseration.

"Any lasting impairment?" Henry inquired jovially as his wife's elbow met his ribs.

Luke felt himself relaxing in the midst of this lighthearted bantering. "None that I'm willing to discuss in mixed company Sir."

Henry's deep laughter echoed in the room and was joined by his son's. "What's the buzz around town, Sidney? Do the women have any complaints for your Sheriff?" he joked.

Sidney swallowed for reasons unknown to all but one of the people in the room. She quickly checked them and replied to save face. "None that I have heard, Dad, but you are welcome to see for yourself when you come to visit. You would like Luke's father. Charlie's a retired cop too," she divulged.

Reg gawked. "Jesus! This is one fine day! I've been waiting over ten years to get an invite to that berg and my father gets one first."

Sidney laughed and bestowed a sweet smile upon the man at her side. "Your invitation is implied. I plan on taking over for that cute blond who was sponging you off earlier."

"Ooooh, Buckman. We thought you were unlucky last night. We were way off base," Don kidded.

"Sidney, you want Reg to go back home with you?" Hilary asked in thoughtful surprise. "We just took for granted given your sister's circumstances that he would come to stay with us for awhile."

Sidney shook her head firmly. "Not a chance. I'm not letting this man out of my sight. It seems like the only way to keep him in one piece."

Reg threw up the one free hand he had. "Who am I to argue with this tenacious lady of mine? Barren's Creek it is. Come and visit Mom and Dad."

"Yes anytime. I should give you fair warning about my Aunt Vera though." Sidney ran her tongue over her teeth. "I know you've met but when she's at home and she's writing, she's a real... individual."

Luke cracked a grin. "I'm not sure that quite covers it, Sid."

She frowned lightly. "I guess not. She's quite preoccupied most of the time. She writes..."

"For the local paper?" Hilary inquired politely.

Sidney snorted. "Nothing they could print," she declared with amusement and one sidelong glance at Luke told her he concurred.

"Sid's aunt writes romance novels. Steamy ones according to the jacket covers. She's never volunteered to let me read one although lately she has eluded endlessly about the one she is currently working on. I may have to pick it up."

Sidney's eyes narrowed. "Me too. The ongoing saga of Drake and Vanessa."

Luke thrust out a finger in agreement. "That's them. Something about Vanessa's sister being diagnosed with a tragic brain tumor and someone is pregnant I think."

Sidney giggled with fond thoughts of the woman who raised her. "Someone is always dying or procreating in Auntie's books but never fear, there is always a happy ending."

"So true to life," one of the cops mumbled.

Sidney laughed. "Hey, who am I to knock Aunt Vera's novels. They have made her a truck load of money." Several eyebrows were raised at the suggestion. "Have you ever heard of Lara Lovelorn?"

"That's your aunt!" a female voice exclaimed from the doorway.

"Sherry!" Sidney cried coming off the bed to claim a hug from a woman who looked to be about her age. "Luke, this is Don's wife. Don has been Reg's partner for years."

"I gathered that," he said and held out a hand to the attractive brunette standing beside the woman who was still the most beautiful female he had ever laid eyes on.

"You're..." Sherry stammered clearly agog.

Sidney jiggled her brows. "Sorry, my manners stink today. Sherry, this is Luke. We grew up together in Barren's Creek." She felt herself grow slightly warm beneath his intense gaze. They both knew she spoke the truth though she was leaving out some pertinent details.

"Do all the men look like you in Barren's Creek?" Sherry murmured staring.

"I don't know that I have ever thought much about it," Luke confided with amusement. "Sid, do all the men at home look like me?"

Sidney let her gaze slide lazily over him "No. Most of them are better looking," she returned smoothly.

Sherry burst into a fit of giggles. "Sid! You need your glasses changed."

"I don't wear glasses."

"Exactly," the other woman professed.

"Honey, when you are done drooling over Sidney's Sheriff..." Don began to humorously admonish his wife and redirect her attention to Reg, who waited patiently for a greeting.

Sidney remained slightly shell shocked by the depiction of Luke as *her* sheriff. He fit in so well, it was startling. Her worlds, until recently were logically compartmentalized, suddenly seemed to be on a collision course. She fervently hoped disaster wasn't the final destination.

"You're tired, Reg. I should go," Sidney said running a hand lovingly over his hair. Beads softly clinked together. She smiled wryly knowing she wouldn't miss them one bit.

"Is that why you kicked everyone out?" he asked her cheerfully though his side throbbed. "I was hoping you had designs on my body, Babe."

She chuckled at him seeing the pain beneath the grin. "I do but I also know they will keep. In the meantime, rest up."

It was impossible to fool her. She knew when he was exhausted...when he was in pain...she just knew him. God, he loved that, loved her. "I wish you could stay," he rumbled.

"Soon. Tonight you sleep."

"You too. Babe you look exhausted."

Please don't say anything more. I don't want to have to lie. "Reg, I'll be back first thing tomorrow."

"With Luke?"

She blinked suddenly at a total loss, realizing she hadn't thought much past getting here. "I...ahhh...don't know."

"I do. If he can stay for a couple of days, invite him. Better yet, let me.

Call him in."

"Reg…"

"Come on Sid. For me. I don't want you to be alone."

"I'll stay with Don and Sherry," she was quick to suggest.

He automatically frowned. "Not a terrific idea. Brittany is still up a lot at night. Sid you don't need to be around a baby right now."

The stress of this day was getting more difficult to hide. She held up a hand to still his arguments. "Whatever you want, Reg," she conceded.

"Ask Luke to come in."

Luke entered the room and immediately sensed her tension. Reg smoothed her hair. "Sid, can you find out how long before that cute blond plays target practice on my butt again?"

She frowned but left anyway, fairly certain Reg knew precisely when his next shot was coming.

"I don't think my lady likes being asked to go," Reg rumbled admiring her behind as she left.

"Seems like a safe bet," Luke returned admiring those same hips sway out of sight.

Reg's gaze moved to the other man's. The one he couldn't quite get a fix on but judged that he needed to. "I wondered if you would stay with Sid at our place. I'd rather she not be alone right now. She knows how to handle a piece but…"

"Sidney can shoot?"

Reg peered at Luke like he was daft. "Some of her range sessions beat mine." He waggled a finger. "Don't tell her I said so. She just has a lot on her mind right now. This was a lousy week for us before I went and got myself shot…"

"Do you have a spare room?"

"Well, we did." Reg paused as if pained. "We thought we were going to need it for something else but ah…" He shook his head as if to clear it. "Never mind. It isn't important tonight. Sid and I plan on changing that as soon as humanly possible." Reg glanced up and saw the other man observing him curiously. He must sound like a babbling idiot. "We have a great couch, Luke. Ask Sid. I fall asleep there regularly."

"Yeah, he makes a great pillow," Sidney added from the door. "Your shot isn't due for twenty minutes. Can you hang on or should I create a ruckus?"

"God no, Babe." He had seen that too many times. "I'll hang in there. Go home and get some sleep."

She went to the man who laid in the bed and took his heavily bearded face into her hands. Luke could only stare at the contrasts between them. She so pale and petite; him ebony and massive in every respect. The bond between them was so frank and pure that it was grounding to witness. Her words during the drive echoed back. *I care deeply about you... would never intentionally hurt you.* Luke believed her but he was finally starting to realize she may not be able to control that possibility.

Luke counted the locks as she methodically opened them. "Four separate locks, Sid?" he asked relieved he could stay.

"Hey Sheriff, you're not in Kansas anymore. This is the big city."

He not only knew that, but also had worried over it for the most of the last ten years. "How good a part of it are we in?"

She smiled at his lack of knowledge of New York in general. "This is definitely not Manhattan but it isn't Harlem either."

"Is it safe for you to be here alone?" he asked glancing about at the plain hallway that needed paint, better lighting....

"I'm not alone. You're here."

"If I'm not..."

"Reg is..."

"What about when he is undercover, which seems most of the time..."

"*That* is going to change," she said in barely leashed tones that showcased how strained her coping was.

He took it in with a heartbeat, closed a hand over hers. "Inside Sid."

She nodded wearily and pushed open the door. She stepped inside and flipped the light switch. A serene smile came to her lips. This was hers. Her smile thinned somewhat as she realized that most everything was as she had left it. Reg was notoriously messy. Obviously, he had barely been here while she was gone.

Luke glanced around and as interested as he was to see what she called home, he was more interested in her reaction to being here. It was entrancing to see the sense of calm that swept her. She took a deep breath as she walked through the rooms touching something here, turning on the lamps in the living room not meant for a magazine but rather for comfort, checking which plants were dry. Eventually she looked up and noticed him watching her.

"I'm sorry. I wasn't thinking. Make yourself comfortable. We haven't eaten. There won't be much in the frig other than the things Delta packed." She wandered toward the kitchen. "Reg wasn't coming home much. It was too risky to his cover.*" And to our life afterward.*

"We'll order out..."

A knock at the door had Sidney peering through the judas hole. A wide smile graced her face as she threw open the door. "Mrs. Gilpin!"

An elderly woman in oven mitts and a stained apron carried a casserole but Luke was distracted by what was meandering at her feet.

"Sidney, what is *that*?"

"Rauja! You beast! How's my fella!"

"Young man, haven't you ever seen a cat?" Mrs. Gilpin asked incredulous.

"*That* is built more like an ugly dog than any cat!" Luke retorted watching Sidney stroke the huge calico beast.

"Luke Ryan! No one insults Rauja! He was the first present Reg ever gave me," she informed him pertly.

This is how that mountain of a man won her heart? "I guess returning it was out of the question?"

Sidney slid him a glance. "Did Reg mention that Rauja sleeps on the couch?"

Luke groaned dramatically while Sidney flashed an insincere smile rubbing the mangy feline behind his ears. Rauja purred loudly and angled his head strategically.

"I brought you some supper, Sidney. Don called this morning and mentioned that you would be back tonight. How is our fellow?"

Sidney smiled warmly at her long time neighbor. "Cranky but in one big piece, the way I like him. The food smells heavenly and I appreciate you keeping Rauja for us. The poor beast must think we abandoned him."

"Oh poppy cock! Rauja loves anyone who feeds him. Typical male," she commented making Sidney giggle. "Well, Honey, I'm going to go...you get some rest..."

"Wait! Mrs. Gilpin could you ask Terry down the hall to do me a favor?" Sidney asked, rifling through her desk. She withdrew a large thick envelope and fished a scrap of paper out of her purse. "Can you have her send this off first thing in the morning by courier to this address? There is a couple who could use it right away and I can't manage to run out again tonight."

"Certainly, Honey." Mrs. Gilpin threw Luke a glance. "That's our Sidney. Always thinking of others no matter what is happening in her own life."

Luke agreed, privately impressed that she could remember Sandra and Jerry Pensar at all, after the events of the last twenty-four hours. With a quick peck on the cheek, the elderly woman left them alone.

Sidney dished up two plates of tuna casserole and brought them back to the living room. Luke silently accepted one and began eating, noting she did the same.

"You were shocked that Reg is black."

Luke dropped his fork at her stark statement. "Jesus Sid!"

She regarded him calmly. "Well weren't you?"

Luke was thoughtful for a moment. "I was more shocked that he is massive."

Sidney burst out laughing. "Actually that was my initial reaction the first time I saw him too. Built like a Sherman tank."

"I saw Henry first but stupidly thought he was Reg's commanding officer."

She shrugged, kept chewing. "Could easily be true if Henry hadn't retired."

"His parents seem nice. Nice to you."

Sidney saw all of what wasn't said. "They are an incredible couple and have been wonderful to me."

"Did I hear Reg is Jewish?" Luke asked skeptically.

Sidney laughed at Luke's shocked face. "Hilary is Jewish and raised her children as Jews. Henry didn't convert but he doesn't object either. We used to get very strange glances at the Synagogue but it's no big deal now."

"You go to church with him?"

She nodded. "To temple. Yes I do. We plan to be…" Her voice trailed off. She was so tired she hadn't been thinking of what she was saying until the words popped out.

"Married there," he finished with an unwavering stare.

She swallowed and averted her eyes. "I wanted to tell you."

"Getting the ring from Ed Tanner at the cleaners pretty much gave it away."

Tears brimmed in her eyes despite her best efforts to stem them. "Luke…"

He reached for one of her hands. "Sidney maybe we shouldn't have this conversation tonight." He knew there was too much to be said to deal with tonight. "It has been a *long* twenty four hours."

She nodded numbly and removed her hand from his with awkward haste. "I'll get blankets."

Later he lay alone in the dark, stunned that only last night he had her in his bed believing he had gotten his life back. Now he knew better. A muffled noise drew his attention. He made his way down the hallway and stood outside the closed door that he knew was her room. The one she shared with the man he had known about for a decade and hated. The one he had met today and found hard to truly dislike.

He edged open the door. "Sidney…."

She flew to a kneeling position on the bed with admirable agility. "You can't come in here. I have betrayed him in every way that matters. I can't...*won't* do it here," she told him determinedly through tears.

That was lowering. "I would not presume that you would Sidney. I wouldn't either. This is your home with Reg. He asked me to stay with you. I agreed. I wouldn't dishonor that request."

She sniffed pondering. "Is that a cop thing?"

"*That* is just decency. I may have just met Reg but from what I have seen so far, he is a fine man and one you have cared enough about to agree to marry him."

Sidney regarded him thoughtfully in the dark. "When do you need to go back home?"

"When will Reg be able to travel?"

"At least four days and then only with a lot of drugs."

Luke tipped his head slightly. "Then I guess I am going back in about five days."

"Are you..."

"I'm sure. Get some sleep Sid." He left the room knowing there was little else he could do to comfort her. There was precious little he could do to comfort himself. What had seemed so simple last night was fantasy today. He sat down on the couch that a large man regularly fell asleep on with the woman he loved in his arms. It was a morose place to be. Luke sighed and swung his legs up. He was startled, as his feet encountered something heavy and hairy. Two yellow eyes gleamed at him in the darkness easily conveying Rauja was not pleased to share. With one swift movement of his foot, Luke turfed the mammoth cat off his make shift bed. If he could not have the company he desired, he damn well wouldn't settle for that beast taking up half his space. Despite his experience with criminals, unsavory persons in society including his mother, of all things, *this* mangy animal scared him.

Her stomach rumbled as loudly as Charlie when Vera was secluded in her study on a writing jag. However, it wasn't quite enough to make her want to open the ham sandwich she had selected from the vending machine earlier. She knew before sliding in her change that nothing in that machine was fresh but it still beat going to the cafeteria. Far too public for the hospital pariah. She sighed as she watched him sleep, only her love for Reg could bring her back to this building. A place that she had once enjoyed being a functioning part of, but no longer.

A file on her desk from another hospital with the same HMO had changed all of that. She shook her head at the memory. It had seemed so ordinary at the time. A colleague across the borough had wanted a second opinion. There wasn't even a patient name on the file just an insurance code. He had a concern about a mother who regularly showed up in the Emergency room with her infant son.

The inconsistencies had jumped out at her immediately and one phone call concurred that her colleague shared similar concerns for the well being of the child. It was several weeks later the entire matter began to stink after every other professional recanted their opinion and the rotten mess was dumped in her lap.

"Babe, you gonna eat that?"

Sidney glanced up, surprised to find him awake but pleased that he was looking better. Her stomach made a timely grumble. "Do you want it?"

He eyed it skeptically. She was too eager. "Where did you get it?"

"Fifth floor."

Reg grimaced. "Not the machine? The one Kevin used to joke was restocked every leap year!"

She withdrew her hand that held out the sandwich. "I take that as a no."

His gaze turned tender. "I'm sorry you had to come back here for me."

Her lips tugged upward as her hand dropped the sandwich to lay her hand on his thigh, leaning toward him. "I would walk through fire for you, Reg Buckman."

He knew that but didn't mind hearing her say it a bit. "Is anyone giving you a hard time?"

It was imperative not to hesitate. "Of course not."

He held her gaze. "Sidney."

She inhaled deeply before answering. "A few people have gone out of their way to avoid me. Pointedly." She turned away before the shine came to her eyes, which was foolish. Reg knew her well enough to know when she was hurt. "On the other hand, a couple people have done the opposite, which besides being a lousy career move on their part, is very sweet."

It was common decency the way Reg saw it. "I tried to get them to take me to St. Anne's…"

"What?" She popped to her feet like a spring. "You took two bullets and you were negotiating which hospital they took you to!"

She was pacing, hands on her hips. He was making a hash of this rather than improving things. "Come here."

Her teeth gnashed together as she spun to face him. "Dammit Reg! It's one thing to get shot but to be lame brained enough to want to be taken to a hospital fifteen minutes farther…"

"Sidney, come here."

She had stopped and stood with her back to him studying the tiled floor. "The surgeon told me how substantial your blood loss was. How much time did you waste arguing with the ambulance attendants?" She dragged an unsteady hand through her hair. "Jesus! You could have bled to death. Reg, you lug head…"

"Shhh." His arm wrapped around her to ease her back against him.

Sidney started at the feel of his large body behind hers. Her eyes widened as she turned in his arms to see him standing, IV lines pulled taunt. "Reg! What are you doing?! Get back in the God damned bed!"

He was heaving for breath but remained stubbornly put. "Only if you come with me. I won't go alone."

"You will fall down in seconds, Reg, and then what the hell am I going to do. Those gowns aren't flattering at the best of times. Hiked up to your waist letting all of your parts flap in the wind…"

Deep rumbling began in his chest and soon full-fledged chuckling was born shaking him from head to toe, further unbalancing him. Sidney couldn't help herself any longer and a wry smile crept on her face as her hands clutched his ropey upper arms. "Back up Honey. Slowly."

"Coming with me?" he asked in tones rivaling those of a pleading child. The pain was starting to snap at him like a whore who hadn't been paid.

She chuckled in spite of herself. "Do I look like I am coming with you?" She pointedly glanced toward their feet planted together as if engaged in a close dance.

They shuffled backward until his thighs butted up against the bed and he collapsed upon the mattress, pulling her down on top of him. They ended up in an undignified heap on the bed.

"Reg!"

He took a steadying breath. "Don't move Babe!"

Concern poured through her. "Am I hurting you? I must be almost on top of your wound for God's sake!"

His chest rumbled ignoring his throbbing ache. "No Babe. Your skinny bod only covers a fraction of mine. You are on the right half. *Believe me.*"

"Then why can't I move?" she inquired with puzzlement.

His chuckling became full-bodied laughter. "Because in our tumble to the bed, my gown, which was too fucking short to begin with, has ended up around my nipples. If you move, I am going to embarrass myself."

Her laughter tinkled in the small room and one slender hand made a purposeful descent. "Now that you mention it, you do feel wonderfully warm beneath me," she teased.

Reg groaned. "Babe, I am about to look like a randy pup." His huge hand closed over her smaller one in a gentle vise.

Her shriek of laughter echoed in the confines of the room. "Impossible!

You probably didn't look like a pup when you were one."

He grew strangely subdued. "I hate sleeping alone. Even here." He quirked a smile. "Especially here."

Maybe this was the time to say a few things that needed to be said. "Reg, we need to make some decisions about how we are going to live."

"We need to set a wedding date," he claimed resolutely.

Her stare was penetrating. "It's more than that. Smashing a glass won't change what needs to be changed. You need to spend more time around people who are not the scourge of the earth. You need to believe that safe places do exist."

"I do!" he declared nuzzling her neck. "I do when I'm with you."

She was undeterred. "You *need* to come to Barren's Creek. You need to see a place where children play in the streets and their parents' don't worry about drive by shootings. A place where houses have lawns for babies to play on blankets. A place where cops don't get shot every day of the week. Where their wives aren't terrified for them every time they walk out the door."

"Well apparently I am going to Barren's Creek. My sexy nurse lives there right now," he stated glibly hoping humor would diffuse some of the tension.

"Is there anything your sexy nurse can do for you right now?" she cooed.

A sensual smile spread with languid slowness across his dark bearded face revealing rows of white gleaming teeth. "Move."

"Move?" She lifted herself slightly off him, trying to swallow the disappointment.

One big hand clasped her to him and slid suggestively to her buttocks. "Against me."

Her lips curved upward. "What happened to the possibility of you embarrassing yourself?"

"I'll risk it!" Reg confided hoarsely.

She lightly ground her clothed pelvis next to his naked and aroused one. "Does that door lock?"

He chuckled. "Something tells me even if it did, your Sheriff might shoot it open with his six gun thinking the worst."

Sidney paled and fell quiet at the mention of Luke. Other memories came flooding back in a guilty rush. Ones she was determined to banish. It was the only solution that came close to making sense.

Reg's large hand was still smoothing over her hair as she lay half on him, half beside him. Luke entered the room at the low response to his knock on the closed door. His eyes took them in with a heartbeat and he felt an involuntary tightening of his chest. Sidney was nestled by Reg's side, sound asleep with her head resting on his shoulder.

"It's getting late. I thought Sid might want to head to the apartment."

Reg nodded and wondered whether it wasn't time for a second opinion while his lady was safely asleep. "Sidney thinks I need to come to Barren's Creek to see how the other half live."

"Hmmm."

"Guess I'll stick out like a sore thumb in that berg of yours."

Luke's expression remained enigmatic. "You probably won't find too many twins in town."

Reg chuckled abruptly making Sidney stir. Her eyes blinked sleepily. "Hey Babe. Luke is here to take you home."

"Yeah, he's always trying to do that," she murmured and closed her eyes once more.

Reg's gaze flickered from her to the tall lean fiercely handsome man, who filled the doorway. "It seems you have a reputation, Sheriff."

Luke shrugged helplessly and stepped forward to gently nudge her shoulder. "Sid, let me get you home so Reg can get some sleep."

Her head shot up at the sound of his deep voice close to her ear and the heat of another man beneath her. Her eyes were wild and frantic for a second before she thought to carefully bank her reaction. Reg's breath tickled her ear. "Easy Honey. You fell asleep. You're with me at the hospital."

Luke made a motion indicating that he would wait outside the door for her.

She nodded and rose slowly. "I didn't hurt you earlier?"

Reg gave her a secretive smile. "Not a bit. You are better medicine than whatever is in those shots I have been getting."

She smiled back from her perch on the edge of the bed. Her hair was tousled about her shoulders in pretty disarray. "Good thing because starting tomorrow you will only be getting pills for the pain. The shots are done."

He knew the routine. "That must mean they are getting ready to boot my keester out of here soon."

"Soon." She leaned over him and plucked a kiss on his lips. "I'm going to bring you some clothes tomorrow."

"You don't like my gown?"

"It has its uses. Walking to the end of the hall tomorrow isn't one of them." Sidney laughed and ran her hand over the rows of dread locks that adorned his head. She really hoped their days were numbered. "Night, Reg."

"Dream of me, Babe."

She turned back from the door. "I'd rather have the real thing." His delighted laughter followed her down the hall where she found Luke folding one of the many papers he had read through the day. "I just need to use a rest room," she told him motioning down a dimly lit hall.

She swept into the rest room that doubled as a staff locker room and stopped dead when he spoke. "Don't turn around Sidney. Just listen."

Her breath left in a rush. "This isn't a good idea, Kevin. We aren't supposed to talk."

Agitation slid into his tone. "Seeing as I have been hiding in a women's change room for pretty near two hours hoping you would eventually come in, I think I know that."

She held up her hand toward this man who had been her friend, colleague and now someone her lawyer advised her against associating with. "Kevin, it's been a long few days..."

"I'm sorry about Reg. I wanted to tell him." He shrugged sheepishly. "I thought he might deck me if I went in. Even injured I think he could manage it." His hand touched her arm and she bit her lip trying to fight back emotion. "Sidney, it doesn't have to be like this. We can end it without all the lawyers... without the hospital bureaucracy..."

"Kevin..." she began to appeal.

He spun her around to face him and anxiety filled eyes collided with sorrowful ones. "Sidney just make a public statement. Say that you were mistaken. That it was the stress of losing Lily...that it impaired your judgment...."

Something in his face rekindled her determination. "It didn't. Not in this matter at least. I'm sorry Kevin but I can't back down. I can't do that for so many reasons and the biggest one is you and your baby son. You need to..."

"Don't Sidney!" he warned savagely, realizing now that her position was as rigid as it had always been.

"Do you honestly think I want to!? I have no choice. I truly believe that your child is in danger..."

"Funny. The door indicates this is a *Women's* Restroom." Two people whirled to see Luke standing in the doorway. His stance looked casual but Sidney knew better.

Kevin stared at the unknown man; Sidney prayed to disappear. The explanations she would be forced to make now would be humiliating.

"I was just leaving, Luke. Kevin, you should get home to Cynthia and the baby."

"Sidney this isn't done. Not nearly. Consider what I have said. *Consider* your options," Kevin stated meaningfully before turning to leave.

"I don't have any options, Kevin. I never did. There is only the truth."

CHAPTER SEVENTEEN

He didn't take her home and Sidney still wasn't sure what to think about that as she sat across from him in the quiet restaurant. Their dinner had been cordial and Sidney was so famished it made conversation moot. Besides Luke had said nothing about the entire incident with Kevin. He had merely steered her into the car and drove them to the understated elegant dinner spot.

"Did you enjoy the duck?"

She glanced down and smiled. "I almost licked the plate so it won't do to say anything but yes, would it?"

"It's good to see you eat."

For such a simple statement, it seemed loaded with innuendo. "I enjoyed it. Thank you. It was a good idea. Besides the only food back at the apartment are the few things Delta sent."

When the waiter came with the dessert tray, Sidney demurely declined more out of nervousness than anything else. The caramel apple pie made her drool.

Luke's smile gleamed with too many teeth. She wanted to leave so she could get back into that apartment and disappear into a bedroom she knew he wouldn't intrude in. "We'll have two of the apple pie," he continued to order tea as Sidney stiffened. He leaned across the table his eyes peering past every defense she had. "Now Sid. What the hell is going on?"

Her thoughts racing, she opened her mouth.

"Don't bother trying to cover either. You never could lie even badly." She swallowed and stared. "I have sat for four days and watched. You grow tense as we drive to the hospital. More so every day. The first day, you discreetly met with someone upstairs. At first I thought, hey it's work related. Even during a leave of absence, something can come up, right? You haven't gone near the floor social work has its offices on. You eat out of the vending machines rather than go to the cafeteria and you don't ask me to go even when you are so hungry you could fall over. Some of the nurses fawn over you, others watch like you might poison their coffee." He watched her eyes. She couldn't hide the pain. He knew her too well. Luke reached across the table and took her hand. "Is it so hard to talk to me, confide in me?"

Her gaze flickered upward in surprise. "No. That's not it."

"What is it then?"

"It's humiliating." She flipped her hair over a shoulder. "Even while we were apart, I liked to think you might be proud of me." Sidney saw Luke rush to comment and stopped him with a look. "When we were married I was just out of high school. God, I found out about being pregnant on my graduation day. I had no career."

Now he had to comment. "You had the most important job of all. You were raising our child."

Lord, he always knew how to take her heart and turn it over. "When I finished my degree, I think I half pursued my Master's to show you I could."

"I always knew you could do whatever you chose to do. Even when we were married, Vera depended heavily on you to read her first drafts. She still believes the novels you helped create are her best."

He was making it easy for her and she was grateful so she took the chance and blurted it out. "I was fired six months ago. The man you met at the restaurant..."

"Stein."

"Is my lawyer. I'm being sued."

"By the hospital?"

Sidney shook her head. "No but they are named in the suit as my employer and it makes them very nervous. *I* make them nervous."

It was satisfying to see her open up. "What are they afraid of?"

She tilted her head. "Shouldn't you ask what I did?"

"That implies guilt. I may know nothing of the situation but I know *you* didn't do anything wrong."

His belief in her was staggering and she put her curled fist to her mouth. More than right or fair, it suddenly seemed safe to confide in him. "Almost a year ago, I was asked by a long time friend for opinion on a troubling case that kept coming into their Emergency department."

"At St. Mark's?"

She sipped her tea. "No. A hospital not far from ours owned by the same company. It wasn't that unusual for us to share opinions on more difficult cases. I understood as soon as I saw the file. A mother had brought her then eight month old baby boy into Emergency eleven times over a six month period for vague gastrointestinal complaints."

"That's very young. Natalie only went to the doctor for regular check ups. She had never been to Emergency her whole life."

Sidney's eyes shone as she listened to him relate as a father not a cop. "Natalie was very healthy. This child hasn't been. I ran a check to see if this mother and baby had visited any other Emergency wards."

"A check? A computer check?"

"Yes."

"Is that typical for a social worker to do?"

Her laughter brought a sparkle to her eye. "Typical for one who was married to a cop."

And then lived with one, he added sourly.

"I came up with three immediately. At Grace Hospital, the chief complaint was blood in the baby's urine. That resulted in nine visits over six months. At Mercy hospital, gastrointestinal complaints brought them in eleven times over nine months. At another institution, the mother was panic stricken because she believed her son was suffering from apnea spells, which are..."

"Periods when the infant stops breathing for ahhh...half a minute?" Luke filled in.

Sidney gave him an impressed glance. "Yes, at least 20 seconds or greater. How did you know?"

Luke stalled for a moment wondering whether this was the time. "I did some research on SIDS years ago. I needed to understand a little better why we had lost Natalie."

Her eyes bore into his. Did he know something? "You studied crib death?"

"I had to Sidney. After you left, I didn't have my daughter." His gaze hollowed out. "I didn't have my wife. I needed to try and figure out what stole them from me."

Her eyes flitted away. "Did anything you read help?"

He gave a short laugh. "Truthfully no. Natalie doesn't fit the picture of a typical victim of crib death."

"No she doesn't." Still doesn't no matter how many times Sidney went over it and they were countless.

Luke frowned. "Nat didn't have any of the risk factors. For starters, she was older than most babies."

Energy began to sing through her. "Right. Most SIDS victims are under six months! Most occur around or before three months like Sandra and Jerry's baby. What else?"

"She was a healthy birth weight, had no history of any illnesses like breathing problems, she was female, no one smoked in our house or around her. You saw to that." He glanced up proudly. "I'll never forget the night you told Jack to smoke outside or find the door."

"He thought I was pretty demure up until that moment."

"That night you were tough as nails."

Sidney spread her hands. "It worked. He smoked outside away from Natalie."

Luke chuckled. "He did." Then he eyed her as if considering something.

"Another thing, breast feeding is thought to be a preventive factor in SIDS. You were still nursing her at almost a year." He could still remember watching. "And Natalie slept on her back."

Sidney nodded in congruence. "She liked that position best from birth. It used to drive me crazy because at that time, it was recommended for little babies to sleep on their tummies and she wouldn't. I was so desperate to do everything right and according to the book."

Luke laughed out loud. "But Natalie hadn't read the same book. I remember as a newborn, she would scream on her tummy and the minute I flipped her on her back she would calm right down. You were so mad at me I used to think one day you might get my gun."

Sidney flashed him a look of pure innocence. "It's odd. Now it is known that newborns should sleep on their sides or backs to help prevent SIDS so they won't re-breathe their carbon dioxide. Natalie was protecting herself oddly enough in early infancy but ultimately died of crib death anyway," she lamented wearily and a hand reached out to stroke her hair.

It was pleasing that she leaned toward his contact whether she was conscious of it or not. "Nothing really seemed to point in the direction of SIDS in our daughter's case. It was spring when she died not winter, which is more typical," Luke commented.

It was all right to accept his comfort. They were in a public place after all. "Right. The peak month is January." Not the horrible date of March 29th that was etched in their memories.

"And she always kicked off most of her covers except for her blanky and the quilt Vera had given her," Luke recalled fondly. "So she couldn't have been too warm."

Sidney cocked her head as he stirred a memory. One that had recently come to her in a dream. "But she hadn't."

"What?" Luke asked with concern. Her gaze had suddenly become very remote.

"Her quilt was tucked right up to her chin like I had just put her to bed."

That made no sense. She must be mistaken. "Sid, Sweetheart, it was a long time ago...."

Her eyes snapped to his hissing with temper. "You think I've forgotten. Just because we have never talked about those moments don't you dare assume I don't know what I saw." The words were spat from between clenched teeth like sharp nails that neatly pierced his flesh.

He had always avoided asking her about those minutes when she found the baby. After all, it couldn't bring their daughter back and he didn't see the point of her reliving that kind of trauma. "Will you tell me, Sid?"

She pressed fingers to her forehead before drawing them down to rest on her jaw. "I was bounding up the back stairs with the bags of party things you and I had bought after lunch." He blew out a breath. Anything with Winnie the Pooh on it still sliced his heart to ribbons. "Delta said she had checked on Natalie an hour before and she was sleeping peacefully. She was making Carlene tea. Carlene was all in a titter about some errands or something for Vera." Sidney waved that thought away like an annoyance. "Anyway, like all conversations with Carlene, it took all of three minutes. By the time I reached the last landing, you were just pulling out of the drive." That sounded about right. He had spent a few minutes in the parlor comforting Kathleen who was distraught over Nicole's fussiness. He refocused on Sidney to see her smile turn wistful. "I threw open the window to call goodbye."

"I remember." Like it was yesterday. He had had the urge to race up the stairs and convince her to make another child though there was no logic in it.

"Nat and I were rarely apart so even though it had only been a couple of hours I was anxious to see her. If she was still asleep, I planned on waking her up. I thought we'd go for a walk. I half expected her to sit right up at the sound of my voice so I was teasing her." Sidney bit down on her lip until it hurt because it helped the pain she couldn't seem to heal.

"Take your time, Sidney. We don't have to be anywhere. I'm right here, Sweetheart."

She closed her eyes absorbing the comfort of his voice. "The quilt was tucked up to her chin and it had me stopping half way across the room gawking in surprise. It was exactly how I put her to bed two hours before."

That didn't make any sense but his training as an officer stopped him from interrupting.

"I think it was seeing her blanky squashed against the crib rails that started the panic. I raced to the crib then. Stumbled against it and started to cry when she didn't make a sound. She was so still and her color was wrong. Pale, a little mottled and her lips..." Her fingers pressed against her own mouth. "God, Luke, they were blue. I've seen other dead babies since then in my work and I can never stop staring at their little mouths being such an unnatural color."

Her own color was as pale as water. "Maybe this is enough for tonight," he felt compelled to say though as a cop and even more so, a father, he craved the rest.

She shook her head adamantly. "No. I need to finish now. I smelt the dirty diaper then. The scent of urine was strong but the smell of the bowel movement told me everything I didn't want to know. Natalie never pooped during a nap. Not for months." Her forehead furrowed with concentration. "I think I was sobbing by then and awkward. My movements were jerky when I picked her up."

The waiter hovered nearby sensing he was interrupting and Luke motioned him away. She had been dry eyed until now but the tears couldn't be far off. He felt the sting himself. "When you picked her up…"

Her hand cut through the air in self-recrimination. "What a stupid thing to do! As a cop's wife, I should have known…"

He had to speak over her then before things went too far. "Sidney, it wasn't wrong. It wasn't a crime scene."

She looked up and stared without speaking for a full count of five. Anxiety knocked in her chest like it was hollow. In some ways, it had felt that way for the past decade. "I thought I could make her breathe if I picked her up. God, Luke, I think I shook her."

"Of course you did. I would have if I thought it might have helped. Christ, Sidney, don't beat yourself up for anything that day." Their eyes locked.

"I'm sorry for things that happened that day." She didn't have to say more for him to understand and was grateful.

"Sidney, finding Natalie was a shock. It was a horrible day. Pretty near the worst of my life."

She nodded uncertain of whether she could speak. He seemed to sense this and paid the bill.

He hadn't pressed her talk since leaving the restaurant. Indeed, he was still a little bowled over that she had said so much. He had wanted a few straight answers about the strange vibes he was getting at the hospital. Now he had so much more to think about.

Her hand was on the door to her bedroom and he watched her glance over her shoulder to predictably murmur good night.

"Don't go in there Sidney."

The quiet statement left her dumbfounded. She was quite desperate to go in there. It had taken such control to keep herself together this long. She really needed to be alone now. "Luke I'm exhausted."

"You can sleep. Just not yet." Her shoulders instantly squared in protest. "I need you Sidney. And I can't follow you in there. Please just for a moment. Let me hold you. We need to hold each other."

She turned against her better judgment knowing it would be her undoing. His hazel eyes drew her like a magnet calls to metal shards. Like them, she needed him to gather her up and make her whole again.

He felt the resistance as much as her need. His arms wrapped around her and she buried her face in his chest. He bowed his head over her into the silk of her hair. "Yes, Sweetheart. Just let me." He led her to the sofa and bundled her against him. Knowing her ear was over his heart and her arms curled around him, he held her in the dark. A hand to her face confirmed the wetness. There were no sobs just the quiet siege of grief. He closed his eyes on a sigh his hand gliding up and down her back. In some ways this was better than the night she had allowed him her body. Tonight he felt like he snuck back into her heart.

The morning had been awkward. Blinking away the sunlight in the familiarity of her living room and the startling comfort of his embrace. She was grateful to slip from his arms without waking him. Besides, she had somewhere to go and she couldn't take him.

Luke found himself pacing the confines of the apartment she rented with another man. He had a right to be furious didn't he? She left him without a word. Not a God damned word. Only a lousy note, and after cuddling in his arms all night. Well some things don't change. She had left their marriage the same bloody way.

He forced himself to stop, considered ramming a fist through a wall and found himself in front of a closed door. His eyes narrowed. This must be the spare room Reg had referred to that first night. His explanations about it were odd. The agitation festered. Nothing involving Sidney was straightforward. One hand touched the doorknob. It was still there when the apartment door opened abruptly.

Their eyes caught. Hers flew to his hand and panic flashed across her face. She stood frozen in place in the doorway staring at him. Finally, her mind managed to form some intelligible words. "We don't use that room."

His hand fell to his side. "I'm sorry. I was trespassing."

She pursed her lips thoughtfully, recovering. "I guess my absence was getting to you."

Surprise flickered in his eyes. She knew him remarkably well despite the years they had been separated. "I can't say that I appreciated your note. Next time wake me up."

She snorted. "You would never have let me go without a fight."

"I would prefer to think of you accompanied in this city."

She giggled at his comment. "Luke, I have lived here for over a decade. I can handle myself." She patted her purse. "I'm carrying."

He paled. "Where did you go?"

Her expression became shuttered. *To a Jewish cemetery.* "I needed to visit

209

some place I couldn't get to last week. I needed to do it alone."

She knew how to turn a knife. "If Reg were able, would you have taken him?"

Sidney cringed inwardly. Honesty would undoubtedly hurt him. He couldn't begin to make sense of this situation. "I would have taken Reg," she said quietly and watched his gaze become brittle. "You can't understand this Luke and I am not in a place where I can explain it yet." She paused for a brief moment. "It is just too hard."

Luke made his way to the kitchen deciding that distraction was essential to handling this situation. It was difficult to be alone with her and not pull her into his arms despite being furious with her. He had desired her for years in her absence. Since her reappearance into his life weeks ago, it was worse. Honor was the only thing that kept him at bay. She wore another man's ring the way she had once worn his. God only knew what had happened to it. He was afraid to ask.

"Coffee?"

She shook her head. "No thanks. I can't stand it black and there's no cream…"

"There is."

She remained skeptical. "Check it for lumps. Reg hasn't done any shopping for…"

"It's from the cooler Delta packed. She obviously remembers your likes and dislikes."

"It is nice to be remembered," she murmured.

Oh, you're remembered Sweetheart, he groaned to himself. *Your staying power spans a decade.* He fixed her a cup of coffee with a generous splash of cream and handed it to her.

It wasn't to her lips when the phone rang. Sidney sighed and set the mug down. It only took seconds for Luke to know she was talking to Vera. She had wandered to her bedroom. He retrieved the mug and went to take it to her. A quick glance in the room had him changing his mind. She was stretched out on the bed chatting. A bed she shared with someone else. Rationalizing that she couldn't drink the coffee lying down anyway, he shoved the mug onto a nearby shelf and went out on the fire escape to get some air.

Reg squeezed her waist. She had sat beside him while his parents had visited and remained there now but she was definitely distracted. "Babe, tell me about it," he cajoled.

She turned to him blankly. "What?"

"Whatever has you so distant."

She smiled apologetically. "Sorry. I am just preoccupied about a phone call I had earlier from Auntie Vera. She was checking on something for me."

"Whether there are fresh sheets on our bed?" he teased leaning close for a nibble.

She chuckled. "You won't be seeing my room for a bit. It's on the attic floor, three and a half long flights of stairs straight up."

"Oh Sid. Tell me it isn't so," he groaned histrionically.

"Ask Luke," she blurted out and just about swallowed her teeth at the stupidity of her remark.

To her surprise Reg laughed. "Oh yeah…right…the infamous doorman. Something tells me you two can really get into it. He looks like the big brother type."

Sidney gulped. It once seemed that way but they had long since passed that distinction and moved into vastly different territory. Time for a change of topic. "A couple lost their baby the day you were shot. Her funeral is tomorrow morning. I had hoped to be there but you aren't well enough…"

He regarded her with pride inflected in his gaze. "Go ahead without me. Don can drive me up." That was actually preferable in his opinion. He wholly anticipated the drive to be hell and he didn't want her fretting over him. Don, he knew, would handle his cussing without a backward glance.

She frowned. "I won't leave you…"

"I'm asking you to, Babe. That couple will be comforted by your presence like so many couples before them. Don can have me there the following day."

She pursed her lips in contemplation. "You're sure?"

"Absolutely." He drew her close and nuzzled her ear with his beard. "You make me so proud."

"You are remarkably easy to impress."

"Hah!" he snorted humorously. His lips grazed her ear. If she was going to leave later today, he suddenly felt an absurd need to make an impression before she went off into the proverbial sunset with the tall dark and dashing Sheriff. He eased her gently down next to his good side so that her loose hair fanned out beneath her. She enchanted him in every way possible. His mouth covered hers swallowing a sigh he appreciated while lamenting that the door didn't lock. His indelible impression was going to have its limitations.

CHAPTER EIGHTEEN

"Sid! Are you ready? We need to get a move on if we are going to get back for tomorrow." The baby's funeral was early in the morning but he couldn't bring himself to voice it. "From the look of the sky, a storm is coming," Luke called from the apartment door where their bags were stacked.

Sidney glanced around the kitchen quickly and felt a tightness in her chest. Leaving today was far harder than it ought to be though she couldn't really discern why. Some inkling seemed to nag at her that she needed to say some good byes. That she wouldn't be back here in the near future. Which was ridiculous, she chastised herself. Reg would be following on her heels, Kathleen would have her drug holiday and then life would return to normal.

"Sidney!"

"Coming!" she snapped irritably and yanked open the frig. Sidney felt a familiar weight bump against her leg and bent to ruffle the huge cat's fur. "Hey Rauja, here's a treat!" She pulled out the carton of cream and dumped what was left into his bowl. The massive cat purred his pleasure and began to lap up the thick milk. She patted his head one last time and turned to rush out of the small kitchen only to slam into his hard chest with a soft oof.

"Luke! For God's sake!" she stammered blaming her shallow breathing on her shock rather than his nearness. His hands circled her forearms as the warmth of his breath stirred the hair at her forehead. She swallowed hard and licked dry lips. Why the hell wasn't he letting go?

He fought not to imagine that they were somewhere else. At a place and a time where this moment could end differently. So differently in fact that the hot blood rerouting itself to his lap might anticipate some relief. Their unexpected love making the other night had not satiated his appetite. Instead, it had only whet his yearning. Looking and not touching was killing him.

"Tell me we aren't waiting for *him*?" he grumbled with undisguised disgust, watching the cat lapping cream delicately.

Sidney drew herself up regally as if insulted on her pet's behalf. "I won't think of forcing *your* company on Rauja, Luke. Mrs. Gilpin has a key. She'll be by to pick him up."

"Then we can go?" he barked.

"Yes," she snarled back.

"The bags at the front door…"

"There's more in the bedroom."

He turned muttering. "There was a time you knew how to pack light."

213

She gifted him with a placid look. "The other bags are Reg's. I did his packing for him so he and Don can leave straight from the hospital."

"Oh." It was such a wifely gesture that his stomach churned. Luke mechanically went into the room he had not dared enter until now to retrieve the suitcases next to the bed. His jaw clenched seeing the numerous photos of them through the years. He saw the vague images of a huge black man and a petite white woman. He didn't stop to take a closer look, physically couldn't. This room seemed deprived of the oxygen necessary for breathing. He strode straight from the room and out the door. This charming apartment filled with plants, pretty feminine things, detailing the life she had built with another man, was choking the life from him.

Black wasn't her color. Luke had first thought that when they buried their daughter and his opinion hadn't changed. The tailored pinstriped suit emphasized her tiny waist with a short jacket and the fashionably short skirt. Despite his appreciation of her curvy legs, it couldn't alter what the garment was. Funeral attire.

She had pulled her shiny sable hair away from her oval face in a sedate twist making her brown eyes look enormous. Her mouth was set in a grim line as she stared at the small white casket that held another woman's baby. A baby about to be buried. Luke wondered glumly whether she was remembering her own child and a day similar to this, knowing he was.

His eyes lifted to the couple clutching each other for support and he saw himself and Sidney. Luke had to reluctantly admit the similarities ended there. This service was a touching memorial to a little life cruelly lost. The cold ceremony his mother had engineered and bullied Sidney into was nothing like this.

The minister had read a beautiful letter written by Jennifer's parents that they were unable to read themselves but spoke all of the things they wanted said today. Everyone attending received a little pewter angel pin to wear on their collar and a pink sweetheart rose to set on the baby's tiny coffin. Sandra's sister sang a lullaby that she had sung recently at Jennifer's baptism. Her parent's had chosen to bury her in her Christening gown with the stuffed bunny her daddy had given her the day she was born. It was announced during the graveside service that on the baby's birthday in nine months time, a tree planting ceremony would be held.

Sidney stood quietly beside him. Their hands were close but not touching. He wanted to link their fingers but something in her face warned him otherwise.

She leaned toward him and he was slightly shocked she remembered he was still there. "The crowd is beginning to thin. I'm just going to give Sandra a quick hug…"

Luke saw her eyes wander and narrow. He turned to follow her gaze and saw a beige sedan slowly approaching the car-lined section of the cemetery. One hand flew to her mouth but not in time to quiet the gasp that had tears springing to her eyes. The car had barely stopped when the passenger door was flung open.

A long leg in a dark suit was thrust out. A second one joined it and then in a jerky movement that seemed to take a great deal of effort, a large bearded man got to his feet leaning heavily on the open vehicle door.

"That's far enough Reg," she decreed brokenly as she recklessly sprinted toward the car. "You don't have to do any more. This is more than enough." She stopped less than ten feet away just to stare. "Reginald Buckman, you are the most thoughtful human being I know."

He smiled at her tear-streaked face with warm compassionate eyes. "I didn't like to think of you coming here alone."

"Luke's here."

"Without me," he clarified. "I worry about you Babe."

She laughed faintly through her tears. "You are the wounded one."

"My wounds you can see. I worry more about the ones you can't. I worry about you, Sidney. I can't even think straight…"

Her expression grew gravely serious then. "Is that how you were wounded? Were you distracted…"

He sighed ominously. "That Babe is a discussion for another time. Right now I have a problem with my arms."

This was an old line and one she still appreciated. "Oh yeah?"

"They're empty. Fill them, Sidney."

Without another word, she walked into his massive embrace. Luke watched them from a polite distance entranced by what he saw. This man knew her, really knew her. He knew how to reach her, comfort her, and love her….

"Reg, sit back down now before you fall down," she implored from the circle of his arms. He complied without a word and winced as he fell back into the bucket seat like a bolder rocking the car. She glanced worriedly from the giant form to the man, who had remained in the driver's seat. "Don, what on earth are you letting this mule headed man get away with? What time did you leave this morning?"

Don glanced sidelong at the man who had been his partner for years and his friend for longer. "The stubborn son of a…."

"Watch what you call my mother," Reg warned with a hint of humor.

Don gave a derisive snort. "He was banging down my door in the wee hours of the morning demanding a ride *and* that I pay the damned cab fare."

Sidney's mouth fell open. "You left the hospital in a cab, Reg? I can't believe the staff..." She stopped talking abruptly and gave him a scolding look. "You went AWOL from St. Mark's?"

"Sid, I think you can only be AWOL from the army," Reg suggested mildly.

She settled a sullen gaze upon him. "Same general idea, Reg," she giggled spontaneously. "Well at least now we both have reputations there. It was lonely being the only one."

"I'll be company for you Babe as long as you'll have me," he purred.

"And I'll have you tucked into bed in a few minutes," she promised in telling tones.

Reg chuckled deeply and thrust out a thick index finger toward Don. "This is why I made you speed partner. Isn't she worth it?"

Don laughed at the engaging large man that dwarfed him in comparison. "That I never doubted Reg. How do we get this big lug to that bed you are talking about, Sid?"

"You can follow my car."

Three heads turned to where Luke stood unnoticed until now. "Terrific! Sid, go keep the Sheriff company, and we'll see you at Vera's," Reg agreed.

After speaking to Sandra and Jerry, Luke helped her into the car. Sidney had felt her heart fragment in all the same places at the anguished expression on the bereaved parents' faces. She had seen it many times before. It never got easier. Not personally. Not professionally.

She felt his eyes on her several times during the drive. A glance in the rear view mirror confirmed that Don's car followed closely behind them.

"Why did Reg want to you come with me?"

Sidney laughed glad she could. "Oh that. Reg is in a lot of pain now and is likely cursing the air blue. He doesn't like me to hear it. Says it isn't lady like. I used to swear when we first met just to get his goat. It was great form of entertainment."

"And now?"

"I get my thrills other ways," she confided.

That he would rather not think about. "Is everything set at the house?"

"Aunt Vera has the living room ready."

"The living room?"

"Reg shouldn't climb any stairs just yet."

He gave her a studied glance. "You sound like you have been through this before."

She snorted with mild disgust. "Too many times. Things are going to change."

"Are they?"

"Reg and I have a few things to work out but things are definitely going to change. Our lifestyle is no way to raise…" She broke off abruptly as they pulled into the horseshoe driveway. Her door was open even before the car was completely stopped. Vera appeared on the porch within seconds attired as usual in too many frills and liberally applied rouge. Sidney fell into her arms with a glad cry.

"Sidney, it is so good to have you home." Vera craned her head over her niece's shoulder. "Is that our Reginald?"

Sidney looked up as her sister came out onto the porch and caught her eye. "Auntie, can you please just call him Reg?" she pleaded, knowing her request was a fruitless endeavor.

Vera gave her a saucy glance. "Oh poppy cock, Sidney! Men like to be called by their true given names." Her aunt hurried down the steps as Reg's car door was opened by Luke.

The sisters descended the stairs arm in arm. "Funny, she doesn't call Charlie… Charles," Sidney observed wryly.

Kathleen burst into overly loud laughter. "I asked her about that. She said the one time she tried it he went home to his own bed that night. To my knowledge she has never done it since."

"Well unless Reg and Luke want to sleep with Vera, I would say they don't have a hope in hell…"

"Those men definitely have designs on a woman but it's not Vera," her sister observed wryly.

"Kathleen!" Sidney began to admonish when she caught a glimpse of Reg's grimace as Don and Luke assisted him from the car. She rushed forward worriedly. "Straight in the front doors, guys and to the left. The drugs Don? Where…"

"Back seat. Side pocket of the gray bag."

Mere minutes later Sidney held a glass of water to his lips, while he choked down the pills she had popped into his mouth. She eased his head back upon the pillows and lightly caressed his bearded cheek. His eyes closed and he took a huge shuddering breath. Sidney sat perched beside him until she was assured he was asleep. She quietly left the room and headed for the kitchen where Delta was serving Don a heaping plate of food.

"Aunt Sid, are those real dread locks on his head?" Zach asked her excitedly.

"Very real," Sidney admitted ruefully.

"And was that a tattoo on his arm?" he asked in an enthusiastic rush.

"Zachary!" Kathleen lightly reprimanded.

Sidney chuckled and ruffled her nephew's hair. "It's OK, Kat. Lord knows there aren't too many people who look like Reg here in Barren's Creek."

Don laughed before putting another forkful of food in his mouth. "There aren't too many people anywhere Sid that look like that man. Reg is one of a kind."

She shot him a warning glance. "Incidentally, what the hell is he doing in that suit I just wrestled him out of ?"

Don grew serious. "He insisted on it. Said you don't go to a funeral without a suit on. Made me go to your place and get it. You may have had the pleasure of getting him out of it but let me tell you getting him into it was no picnic either."

She could well imagine. "Thanks for putting up with us."

"No problem. You two have kept me amused for the better part of a decade."

She frowned brooding over his comment. "Don, I have known you for *over* ten years."

His shoulders shook. "Yeah but the first few years, you two just scared me. I was sure one of you was going to kill the other when I wasn't available to chaperon."

She broke into full-bodied laughter. "It was entirely possible. We've mellowed."

Don continued to shovel through the heaping portions Delta had served watching this group with a cop's instincts and a friend's concern. Reg, he decided, was going to have an enlightening recuperation. It looked like there were some important discoveries to be made in Barren's Creek. Maybe they would bring some explanations that had eluded Reg for years despite his diligent efforts to unearth them.

Sidney went into the dim living room and smiled hearing Reg's low snore attesting to his comfort. She nearly collided with Charlie in the doorway of the kitchen. Firm hands caught her arms. "Sorry Charlie, I wasn't watching."

The older man snorted like she had bitten him. Sidney frowned as she moved across the kitchen to the refrigerator to find a drink. "What's the matter? You can't stand a week without my muffins?"

"It's more like I can't stand a week where you get amnesia," he told her disgruntled.

She poked her head around the door and stared at him. Her gaze wandered to Vera who shot her a telling glance. She felt a stab of chagrin and went to loop her arms about his neck. "Sorry *Dad*," she whispered into his ear. "It's just while Reg is here. He won't understand."

"Make him understand," Charlie growled back.

"I'll need some time," she replied in an anxious whisper. She noticed that Don's gaze wandering toward their exchange and felt a panicky need to keep his suspicions at bay.

"Your days may be numbered, Sidney," Charlie retorted in a low voice.

She smiled faintly as the phone rang, thrilled for the reprieve it offered. "Mrs. Gilpin! Did I forget…"

Luke lurched around in his chair just in time to see her face fall.

"But he was fine when we left…," she stammered into the phone. "No, of course, I don't think it was anything you did. Nothing like that. I'm just shocked and…" Her voice broke and her mouth worked for a few moments without producing an audible sound. A lone tear trailed down her cheek while others brimmed.

"Sidney, what is it?" Luke asked as he rose to go to her. She turned at the sound of his voice and the blatant pain in her expression instantly disarmed him.

"Mrs. Gilpin, can I call you back. I don't think I can talk right now," she begged brokenly and hung up.

"Sid?"

Sidney tried to swallow a sob with minimal success. "Mrs. Gilpin found Rauja dead on her sofa this morning." Her shoulders shook as Luke pulled her weeping into his arms. Confusion gripped him. That huge beast had seemed well enough yesterday. Well enough to strike fear in him. He hated cats at the best of times and that one gave felines a bad name at a mere glance. His mind reeled back to the last glimpse he had of the grotesque pet. Rauja had been lapping up cream. At least he died after a feast, he thought wryly.

"Sidney? Sidney! Are you crying, Babe? What is it?" Reg called in anxiety riddled tones from the other room.

Sidney disengaged herself from Luke without a backward glance, going into the other room to the man who was calling out. Within seconds, her crying renewed itself, louder and less restrained. Again, Luke felt inadequate next to the mountain-sized man that she relinquished herself to so easily.

Vera breezed into the room and went directly over to Reg to fluff his pillows like she was well used to men occupying beds in her living room. "She's asleep, Reginald."

"You're sure?"

Her smile was patient. "I don't leave until she's asleep. I'm sure."

Reg shook his head in disbelief causing the multitude of fake gold beads attached to his hair to click together. They were so much a part of him now he didn't even notice. "Rauja was the first gift I ever gave Sidney," he said to no one in particular.

Luke couldn't bank his reaction fast enough before Reg caught it and inadvertently laughed.

"He was actually cute as a kitten," Reg revealed with a toothy grin.

Don gave him a pensive scrutiny. "Rauja was the first gift Sidney ever *accepted* from you. You certainly made other memorable attempts."

Reg chuckled and reflexively held his aching side. "Selective memory."

"Sidney returned your presents?" Kathleen asked deliberately.

"Returned is definitely the politest term possible," Don snorted enjoying himself. "It was quite amusing to see your tried and true ploys turned down so resolutely by a beautiful woman. The time she threw your flowers out of her apartment window will always be a favorite of mine. Two dozen long stemmed red roses cascading over the streetwalkers below. It was a shocking sight in that neighborhood."

"Sidney lived near prostitutes?" Luke stammered incredulously.

Don immediately shut up, glancing sidelong at his partner.

"Not for long. I took care of it," Reg revealed in flat tones.

Vera gave him a grateful glance and Luke caught it. She smiled serenely at the burly man as she poured him a drink. Reg eyed it with undisguised appreciation.

"Sidney wouldn't approve of mixing this with my medication," he told Vera with a mischievous edge to his voice.

"Oh poppy cock! Besides she's asleep and that mangy animal was your pet too."

He nodded grimly. "Yeah Rauja and I had an understanding. He agreed to make Sidney smile and I fed him bowls of cream."

Laughter rippled through the room. "From the size of that animal, Sidney's cheek bones must have hurt," Luke jested.

Reg's smile thinned. "Not recently but that's going to change. Sidney thinks coming here is the answer."

Charlie snorted, his eyes bulging. "She does?" Reg nodded gazing off into the night. "Strange. She always led us to believe New York was the answer for her."

Reg shrugged and took a large swallow of the drink Vera had poured, welcoming the warmth that infused his body.

Maybe Sidney was right. Maybe he needed to come to a small town like

Barren's Creek to see how the other half lived. His instincts told him it was not going to be boring.

Luke reread the page of Mayor Pincombe's memorandum for the third time and still couldn't make heads or tails of it. While that wasn't unheard of, deciphering her cumbersome prose for the few directives hidden there, was more tedious today.

It was hard to admit that the man sitting in the open squad room outside Luke's office was distracting. Oh, he wasn't doing anything and that was most curious of all. For the last two hours every time Luke glanced up from his desk he could see through the open slats of his blinds, the man was still sitting there. Patiently. As if he had no other cares in the world.

Luke couldn't put a name to the broad shouldered man. Luke guessed that standing the man would be quite tall and there wasn't an ounce of anything but ropy muscle covering his large frame. The sand colored golf shirt accented with burgundy complimented the navy twill pants giving the stranger an easy sense of style. His hair was so closely cropped Luke wondered whether that was something he could maintain at home. His face was clean-shaven and smooth like he was hoping to impress a date.

The date part seemed off though as Luke watched this large man entertain a whiny child who was accompanying a parent to report details of a car accident. The man distracted the child with such ease and open affection, surely he had a brood of his own and likely a pretty wife to match.

He was interesting to watch, far outweighing the Mayor's cryptic suggestions for surplus budget funds. The man's body language was casual and relaxed, legs crossed at the ankles but his eyes were heedful of any activity occurring and Luke could almost hear the purr of his brain cataloguing everything he observed.

Luke was just considering walking about the squad room to strike up a conversation with this enigmatic man when Jack Walken came strolling in with the monthly stats reports. "Jack, any idea about the man who is waiting just outside my office…."

"He's waiting for you."

"Me? No one told me," he complained irritably. It wasn't his policy to keep anyone waiting for great periods of time.

Jack rolled his shoulders. "He told me and any one else who inquired not to. Said he didn't want to interrupt. He's just interested in a ride home when you're ready to go."

Luke blinked at the inane request. "A ride home?" he repeated lamely.

Jack absently flipped through the report. "Said he has had enough walking for today and this one horse town doesn't seem to have any cabs he can hail."

Luke gave a burst of incredulous laughter as Sidney burst in. "Luke, I can't find Reg. Delta says he left the house hours ago and no one has heard from him since." Her chest was heaving as she spoke on the verge of full-fledged panic. Luke knew he would kill to see that same concern for himself in her lovely brown eyes. Her hands grabbed fists full of his shirtfront. "Luke, I have to find him. That stubborn man…"

Her voice trailed off as she stared over his shoulder gaping. Luke followed her gaze and realized she was goggling at the man, who had also recently caught his attention…the one who resembled a young Sidney Poitier. He seemed to be watching them in return and was now rising out of his chair. An amused smile twitching about his dark lips. Standing up the man was incredibly large…Luke's eyes bulged out of their eye sockets. His shock was full blown when he shifted his gaze back to Sidney. She had moved trance like to the door of his office. The transformation, he witnessed, was leveling.

The hysteria that had gripped her when she had arrived, fell away like it had never existed. Mesmerizing wonder swept her striking features setting them aglow like a gorgeous sunrise. Tenderness filled her warm eyes as they locked on the man who regarded her with a secretive grin.

"It's my man," she breathed in soft lilting tones. "I had almost forgotten how beautiful your face was it has been hidden for so long," she lamented. "I wanna touch."

"Come run your hands over me, Babe," he entreated in husky tones while ogling her playfully.

Sidney glided toward him with sparkling eyes. One hand cupped his bare face as her other slender hand wove through his shortly cropped hair.

One side of his mouth tugged upward in amusement. "You really despised those corn rows of mine but you never once said so."

She averted her eyes guiltily. "I just never said it out loud. They were part of the job, I was just sorry they couldn't be shed at night."

"You're a great cop's wife, Sid," he told her sincerely.

"We're not married," she felt compelled to remind him.

His eyes bore into hers intensely. "That's only a matter of a smashed glass."

She laughed at his cavalier attitude. "I think the Rabbi reads a little more significance into it." Suddenly her head snapped up to stare up at him accusingly. "You *walked* downtown to the barber!"

He casually waved away her concern. "No. I went to the other one that's closer to Vera's."

Deep laughter came from behind them drawing their attention. Several cops stood near Luke, who was watching them closely. Jack spoke through his laughter. "Seeing as Barren's Creek only has one barber, that line won't fly."

"Why on earth would you do that, Reg? I would have gladly driven you!"

Reg grinned unrepentant. He figured his body would pay him back in the morning and that would be plenty. "It would have spoiled my surprise. You deserved the shock of seeing the man you remembered and haven't seen across the pillow for almost two years. This cover has been..."

She sighed with a little nod of agreement. "Yeah, it's been all of that."

He pointed a finger toward her with a devilish glint inflecting his eyes. "Besides I'm in training."

"*What?!* What on earth can that damned commander have in mind now? It's time Mark and I had a long..." she began to rail protectively.

"Babe, my training has nothing to do with work," he interrupted in low sexy tones as her brow furrowed in confusion. "I understand your bed is in the attic. I aim to get to it."

She giggled and shook her head while taking his arm to lead him toward the door. "You are incorrigible, Reg Buckman."

"Only when it comes to you, sweet thing," he promised as he wrapped a long arm around her waist as they strolled out side by side. Reg glanced back at the men who remained watching their departure and waved.

Several cops had the instincts to get back to what they were doing prior to this peculiar interruption. Two men still stood with Luke as he watched Sidney leave the building without a backward glance.

"I didn't want to believe you when you said not to underestimate her feelings for him," Luke said still watching their retreating figures.

Carl turned toward his old friend. "And now..."

"It's hard. I have never seen her with anyone but me," he revealed frankly.

"Luke, Sidney doesn't intentionally go out of her way to hurt you. Her reactions to Reg are just..."

"Unpracticed. Sincere. I know," he admitted grimly. That was precisely what hurt so much.

Jack gave his boss, who often seemed closer to a son, a sympathetic glance. He had been deeply saddened when Luke and Sidney's daughter had died and then sickened when their marriage ended in separation. It was blatantly clear, particularly to him, that Sidney had been insidiously debilitated by Luke's domineering bitch of a mother.

"So what are you going to do about it, Luke?"

Luke turned to the man, who was his father's age but resistant to the concept of retirement. Jack Walden rarely called him by his given name any more, typically addressing him as Sheriff since his promotion. "Is it right to do anything about it? You saw her. She's happy."

"Yes she is," Jack grudgingly conceded. "But once she was *beyond* happy."

Luke sighed tiredly. His skin suddenly felt too tight. "That was a long time ago."

Jack looked him straight in the eye while Carl remained stoically silent. "Sidney has been gone over ten years yet she hasn't married… doesn't have any children…"

"Maybe she doesn't want those things any more," Luke contended stubbornly.

Jack shot him a challenging look. "Luke, Sidney only knows how to give herself completely. Would you agree?" Luke gave a low growl that Jack took as consensus. "Maybe she and Reg have something together but whatever it is isn't enough to make those commitments."

"Jack, you are making a lot of assumptions here. Sidney came home for Kathleen and the kids. When that is sorted out, she will be going back to New York with Reg. At least I now know that he is a decent man who loves her. Maybe I have to be satisfied with that," he ground out and headed for the sanctity of his office.

Jack glanced side long at Carl, who maintained a resolute silence. "Do you think he ought to be satisfied with that?"

"I'm not sure any more. I used to worry about Sidney. When she left years ago, she was a fragile mess. Virginia had been ruthless after Natalie died. For the first couple of years in New York, I was even more worried for her. She was angry and reckless. I thanked God for Reg then. Luke seemed to be coping. He had a different gorgeous woman hanging off his arm every weekend. I was newly married with two tiny kids. Sometimes his carefree lifestyle looked damned appealing until I watched him watch my children and Kathleen's, other people's wives and I knew what he really wanted, and he no longer had. Those early years were just a knee jerk reaction to losing Natalie and then Sidney. When he built that house, I knew without a doubt. And last week when I was searching for Sidney and found her… well you know where I found her." Carl drew a long breath. "I saw something in Luke's face I had almost given up on seeing there again."

Jack nodded knowingly. He knew exactly what Carl was referring to. He had seen what had been missing for over a decade. The love of his life.

CHAPTER NINETEEN

Reg sighed as Delta came barreling through the wide archway leading to his temporary room with Luke and Charlie following dutifully.

"There he is. The foolish man is so stiff from over doing yesterday, he can't hardly move," Delta rebuked freely.

"I just need a slight boost," Reg grumbled giving Delta a savage glance. "This mattress is mighty soft."

"You're soft in the head taking off from the house yesterday frightening Miss Sidney half to death."

"Listen, old woman, I thought you and I came an agreement last time we saw each other about slurs on my character," he challenged.

Luke frowned as he leaned down to get a grip on the heavier man. "I thought this was your first trip to Barren's Creek."

Reg glanced up in surprise. "It is."

"How do you know Delta then?"

Reg pursed his lips thoughtfully. "Delta came and stayed at our place for a bit last year."

"Vacationing in the big city, Delta?" Luke asked though he didn't buy it for a minute.

Sometimes pretending you didn't hear a question made avoiding the answer a whole lot easier. The timely high-pitched shrieking from the kitchen made a fine diversion too. "Must have caught somethin' last night. The alarm just went off," Delta chortled.

"Caught what?" Luke asked still puzzled but now on two fronts.

"A varmint," the old woman cackled through the din of a young woman's screams. "Too bad Miss Sidney isn't back from her run to give us a hand."

"Right! Let's get a move on. Help me into that chair so she won't know how stiff I am this morning. I'll never hear the end of it," Reg muttered.

Delta gave him a wicked glance. "You, I can deal with. I meant that silliness in the kitchen. One little mouse sure can get some females' pantaloons in a knot."

Luke chuckled as he and his father each grabbed one of Reg's brawny arms to hoist him upward. "I seriously doubt anyone in that kitchen is wearing pantaloons, Delta."

"You never know Son. The females in this house are a unique lot," Charlie remarked with a twinkle in his eye. Personally, he liked pantaloons and other assorted female undergarments.

Luke scowled, annoyed that Sidney hadn't wanted company on her run. "Just as well Sidney isn't back yet. She could likely out do that noise." However, he noted, the pitch was escalating.

"You haven't spent much time with Sidney over the past ten years, have you Sheriff?" Reg observed oddly pleased.

The lines bracketing Luke's mouth deepened. "What makes you say that?"

Before he could reply, the screen door sprang open with an endearingly squeaky groan. Sidney came bounding through it and poked her head into the sick room. "Sore eh Reg!" she remarked with a wry chuckle. "That'll teach you about trying to go it alone." Her forehead wrinkled as her gaze involuntarily strayed toward the kitchen. "What are Carlene and Nicole screeching about in there?"

"Something you could give me a hand with, Miss Sidney," Delta replied catching her eye meaningfully.

Sidney burst into ripples of laughter. "Peanut butter and Cherrios tempts them every time." She wrinkled her nose. "I'll go save the women folk."

Luke stared at her back and turned once again to the grinning housekeeper. "Sidney's going to throw the trap away?"

Delta drew back aghast at the very idea. "If she knows what's good for she'll just empty the kill. I might need that trap again." Before her proclamation was out, the din from the other room ended abruptly with a soft thud.

Sidney entered the living room again shaking her head in disgust. "Taken care of Delta but unfortunately Carlene has *swooned*. Vera is fetching the smelling salts. I left the trap under the sink."

"Empty?" Luke sputtered.

Sidney gave him a look like he was deranged. "Of course. It wasn't even a messy kill. I have no idea why Carlene is so squeamish. Gives the rest of us women a lousy reputation."

Reg's chest rumbled in amusement. "Not many women empty traps of rodents half the size of Rauja without batting an eye, Babe."

She fought back the wave of sadness thinking of her beast. "Well that took a little practice."

"There are mice as big as…" Luke began in surprise. One glance told him his father was privately amused by his reaction.

"Not mice, Luke. Rats. New York has a few," Sid informed him.

"A few less once you got on their case, Babe," Reg joked.

"In your apartment?" Luke asked with a gaping jaw.

"Not our present apartment," Sid ruefully revealed.

"I have more discerning taste than that," Reg commented with twinkling eyes from the armchair he was now ensconced in.

"Enough said *Reginald,*" Sidney volleyed back in warning tones.

He raised his bushy brows. "Only Vera gets to call me that."

Sidney smirked. "I know. You have an understanding."

"Yes we do and it is one you would do well to stay out of, Babe," he said meaningfully.

Luke turned to the woman, whom he once married, in growing agitation. "What the hell were you doing living near rats and prostitutes?" he yelled.

The lighthearted atmosphere was effectively broken. "She was broke," Reg stated calmly finding it intriguing that Sidney did not readily volunteer any answers. In fact, she had gone strangely pale.

"Broke! How could you go through a trust fund the size your parents left you..."

"The one she couldn't access until she was twenty one?" a deceptively even male voice filled in.

Luke's eyes widened at that news. She had lied to him. "That was over a year after you left! What the hell did you live on? You sure as hell wouldn't take any of my money!" Sidney stood frozen in front of him. She could feel Reg's penetrating gaze leveled on her as well as Luke's incensed eyes boring into her anxious ones. Things were unraveling quickly. Movement behind them suggested that the contingent from the kitchen were now observing this growing scene. Charlie and Delta stood silent vigil on either side of her.

"Just why the hell would she take *your* money?" Reg asked very calmly. Too calmly for Sidney's liking. A sudden thought dawned. "Sheriff, just what is your name anyway?"

"Luke."

Reg made a derisive snort. "Even in one horse towns, a man must have a last name."

"Ryan. Luke Ryan." the tall scowling man bit out never taking his enraged gaze from her trembling one.

"Sid, tell me this man is your long lost big brother," Reg ground out in low ominous tones.

Sid drew a shuttering breath and her eyes darted around the room appealing for help. "Reg..."

"You didn't tell him we were married?" Luke railed in abject shock.

"Ummm. It didn't seem relevant," she related in a small choked voice.

"That's why you are my Uncle Luke!" Zach enthused from behind them. "Someone at school said you aren't really my uncle. That I was making it up. Wait till I tell him. You and Aunt Sid are married!" His small face scrunched up suddenly perplexed by unanswered questions. "Why don't you live together? Why…" A hand clamped firmly over his mouth. Kathleen stood red faced behind her son.

"You didn't accept any support money because…"

"Because it meant either you would be starving or you would be forced to ask your mother for it. Either alternative was repulsive!" Sidney angrily blurted out suddenly regaining her voice.

"Would it have seemed relevant when we were standing before the Rabbi in the synagogue exchanging vows?" Reg bellowed.

"Yes! I mean no! My marriage to Luke was over. We were only kids when we got married…"

"Speak for yourself, Sid!" Luke yelled.

"How old were you?" Reg asked almost fearing the answer.

"Twenty three," was the deep voiced reply.

Barely leashed violence marred Reg's dark features. "I meant *her!*"

"Eighteen," came the soft reply.

Reg started at that information. "God, that's so young. It's almost like you *had* to get married…"

Sidney's breath left her in a rush and she closed her eyes briefly as if trying to shut out this horrendous scene. She felt an ominous presence before her and slowly opened her eyes to view two men. One tall and lightly tanned regarding her with a mixture of disbelief and compassion. The other man levered himself up from the armchair with an enormous effort. His dark skinned face was carefully shuttered as he peered at her in disbelief.

"You had a baby?" Reg asked softly.

She nodded with glistening eyes.

"Where is this child now?" Reg asked numbly.

"She died of SIDS just before her first birthday," Sidney stammered through little sobs. She watched Luke's expression soften at the mention of Natalie.

· "A daughter," Reg reiterated in awe like tones looking away from her. "Well, this explains… so much, Sidney." His countenance hardened with hurt. "Was your *daughter* not relevant either?"

Sidney's face crumbled as she desperately searched for the words to try and appeal to him. "Of course not! Natalie was…"

"That's a beautiful name," he spoke over her quietly. If memory served him right, he had suggested it for their own child. The pain that splintered through him made his wound seem like a hangnail.

Luke glanced from one of them to the other and shelved his anger. This scene was powerfully charged without it. It was mildly shocking to feel sympathy for both of them.

"Reg, I wanted to tell you about Luke and Natalie. Though at first I simply couldn't. Getting lost in New York was my salvation. It was all I could do to come here for Christmas, Easter and the kids' birthdays. After a while I convinced myself that Luke and Natalie were my past and that you were my present."

Reg was nodding as if willing understanding. "So I guess that brings us to the million dollar question, Babe. Who is your future?"

Sidney gasped in shock and stared at him ass he lowered himself into the armchair, folding his massive arms across his chest. "Reg, how can you say that?"

"Sidney, how can I not? What else don't I know? How many secrets have you kept?" God, he wanted to pace.

Desperate tears trickled down her cheeks as she leaned toward him. "Please Reg…" she begged.

He sighed at her growing distress and took her face gently in his large hands. "Sidney, I need some time to sift through this. I'm going out for a bit." His hands fell away as he tried to shove himself back up from the chair.

Sidney grabbed his freshly shaved face with savage determination. "*No!* You are not going anywhere. You are too weak! You shouldn't have gone out yesterday. The only place you belong is in that bed over there."

"Babe, we need some space."

"I'll go," she stated flatly.

He frowned deeply. "I won't have you leaving your own home."

Sadness invaded her expression. "This isn't my home. It is my aunt's and you are a guest. Promise me you will lay down or at least stay right where you are. I'll go out for a while because we could use some breathing space."

He regarded her indecisively. This was not his preference but she made sense. Truthfully, he wasn't sure he could make it past the door and that would only add to his humiliation. "Sidney, call if you are going to be later than supper and drive *nice*," he warned her meaningfully.

Sidney gave him a weak smile. "Nice. I'll drive nice, Reg," she vowed and without another word turned to go, still wearing the clothes she had worn for her run, with her hair pulled back in a ponytail. She walked past all the still figures that had witnessed their volatile exchange. Kathleen reached out to stroke her hair. Sidney stopped near her and glanced back at Reg beside Luke. Both men silently regarded her progress. "I love you," she said quietly staring into one man's face.

Reg held her gaze steadfast. "Ditto, Babe," he said succinctly. She smiled just a little then and continued on out the front door.

Luke felt his throat tighten as he recalled the number of times he had heard her say that over the phone. He had not understood what it meant then. He knew now.

Carlene leaned over to her employer who stood uncharacteristically silent during the heated exchange. "Vera, I think you just got new material for your book," the young woman whispered eagerly.

Vera did not acknowledge her comment. There was no polite response to that remark. Indeed, it occurred to her that if Carlene weren't so painstakingly efficient, she might just look for another research assistant.

Luke sat at his desk pouring over the stack of reports that piled up routinely at month's end. This month was no different. What was different was that he had absolutely no inclination to read then. They were just words on pages. The object of his attention was out there somewhere despondent and driving of all activities. He could barely stand to think of her behind the wheel at the best of times. Today was definitely not one of those.

Luke caught a small movement out of the corner of his eye and glanced up. Furtively hoping it was her; knowing in all likelihood it wasn't. "Is it important, Carl?"

"Very," he insisted deftly and shut the door at his back. "I'm worried."

Luke sighed tiredly. The last thing he needed was any crisis at the station today. "About?"

"You," Carl said somberly. "Kathleen had coffee with Rebecca this morning. She just called."

"Hmmm."

"That's it?" Carl asked skeptically. "Hmmm?"

Luke threw up his hands in a helpless gesture. "That woman inspires emotions in me I didn't even know I had."

"Like?"

"Compassion for a man, who for all intents and purposes, is my rival."

"Any compassion for Sidney? Kathleen is certainly worried about her."

"Even when I am stark raving mad at her, I have compassion for Sidney. She was shattered today. She didn't mean to hurt him but she did. Enormously. I recognize the signs," Luke acknowledged.

"Sidney has kept some secrets. They were bound to hurt someone eventually."

Luke scrutinized his friend thoughtfully. "Do you know Sidney's secrets?"

He shrugged noncommittally. "It wouldn't matter. If they are Sidney's, they aren't mine to tell."

"Jesus, Carl. You should have been a diplomat not a cop," Luke retorted. Carl chuckled. "I'll keep that option open should my boss ever fire me."

Luke was laughing as a knock sounded on his office door. Calling a response, Jack came striding through the door. "Luke, you should know a neighbor up on the hill just called in a break and enter."

Luke scowled at the mention of the prestigious neighborhood he had been brought up in. It was referred to as the hill because the exclusive homes were built on the bluff that overlooked the rest of Barren's Creek. His mother often told him as a child that they lived up high so they could look down on all of the other town's people who were beneath them anyway.

"Any home in particular?" he asked dutifully.

"Yours."

His expression blackened. "I don't have a house there."

The older officer, who had known Luke all of his life, gave him a challenging look. "You may not acknowledge it but you own that monstrosity that your mother revered."

"Well you're right. I don't acknowledge it. I hate the place. It helped destroy what meant most to me," Luke contended in brittle tones. "Let whoever it is tear the place apart for all I care," he finished bitterly.

One man fell silent. The other man leaned forward as a new thought dawned. "What if it is Sidney?"

Luke shook his head in immediate denial. "She hates that place with almost the same intensity as the mausoleum."

"Exactly," Carl suggested. "And where did you find her a couple weeks ago?"

Luke frowned. It didn't seem logical but he had to begrudgingly admit Sidney likely wasn't rational today. He rose and grabbed his jacket. "I'll check it out on my own. If any further reports come in, contact me and only me. If it is her, I don't want anyone mistaking her for a genuine intruder."

Jack cast him an odd look. "Luke, even if it is Sidney, she *is* a genuine intruder."

Luke shook his head. "No. By rights she owns half that horrid place not that she'd want it."

Jack turned to Carl, who sat resolutely silent in his chair. "Christ, he talks like they're still married."

Carl shrugged. There was little else he could do. This too was not his secret to tell.

Luke surveyed the exterior of the house with a cop's eye and a husband's heart. The dining room window was broken and had been jimmied open with a small tool. Amateur job. The glass was swept to one side but the window was still edged by jagged shards of lethal looking decorative etched glass. He smiled. The intruder had purposely broken one of his mother's beloved custom windowpanes. He entered the same way after removing his jacket and covering the uneven sharp edge but his smile immediately faded. Several drops of fresh blood marred the pristine ivory carpet.

Luke moved stealthily through the foreboding house his mother had treasured above all else including him. He had long ago morosely accepted that Virginia Ryan was only capable of loving things she could own, collect and pay someone else to polish regularly. He covered the entire first floor of the opulent dwelling that still inspired his guts to clench without finding any further sign of her. On silent tread, he climbed the ornate curving staircase that dominated the huge foyer. It was cold and overbearing like his parent had been. Thank God for Charlie, his mind screamed. Only one door was open on the second floor and he smiled wistfully to think that of all places in this tomb, she was in there.

He stood silently in the doorway taking in her still form on the large bed that was still made up as if someone were going to sleep in it this very night. He was considering how to best announce his presence without frightening her, when she spoke.

"Do I have to invite you into your own room?" Sidney asked quietly into the stillness.

"How did you know it was me?" he replied with a flicker of surprise.

"The pattern of your footsteps. I would listen for them lying here in the dark, praying you would somehow come back in the middle of a night shift and make me feel less alone," she revealed sadly.

"You felt very lonely in this house."

She made a small sound. "This house inspires that emotion."

"I'm sorry Sid."

She rolled to her side from her back to look at him where he remained in the doorway. "I know you are. So am I. You can come in you know. I won't bite. Today I don't think I have any teeth," she revealed with maudlin humor.

He glanced around. All of the chairs had either been removed or were covered by dusty sheets to protect them from God knows what. To his surprise, she patted the side of the bed he used to sleep on in invitation.

"You might as well. After all, what else can I possibly screw up. It seems I have managed to mess up everything that ever mattered."

He regarded her with an ache in his chest and stretched out in the space on the bed she had indicated. They lay side by side staring straight up. Close but not touching.

"Sid, I had no idea that Reg didn't know about me and Natalie."

"It isn't your mess, Luke. It's mine. I always knew this could blow up in my face and I let it happen anyway."

"Why didn't you tell him? The two of you seem to communicate well," he asked genuinely puzzled.

Sidney sighed. That was exactly true and further proof of her stupidity. "When I first met Reg I thought he was a pimp."

Luke choked on air. Yet, in his mind he could see the giant man pull it off.

"He was working vice in a skuzzy neighborhood that I could afford so I lived next to him. Of course his real apartment was across town."

"Tell me he didn't try and recruit you."

Sidney laughed but could see from Luke's expression he couldn't see the humor. "No. Reg's girls were vice cops. Someone was murdering young prostitutes and they were working with homicide to catch the killer."

"If you are trying to scare the hell out of me…"

Her hand touched his cheek. "I'm trying to tell the truth. You deserve it as much as Reg. Reg didn't recruit me but he quickly picked out that I was in over my head even though I had a gun."

"A gun?"

"Charlie gave me a gun and some quick lessons when he realized the only way he could bring me back here was cuffed."

"Jesus, Sid."

"Reg pestered me constantly so he could keep an eye on me."

God help him. He was going to have to like this man no matter what he was to Sidney. "When did you find out Reg was a cop?"

Sidney steeled herself for what was surely inevitable. "The night they fingered the perp who was killing the young hookers."

Luke stared at her horrified. "Oh Christ, Sid…"

"Reg got there in time." Annoying tears still welled at the memory. "I was fine." Eventually. "I moved in with Don and Sherry after that and later Reg."

Luke sat up shaking his head barely containing his fury. "None of this would have ever happened if I hadn't allowed us to move in here. Charlie warned me. Vera cried and I mean really cried. Not the way she does over some silly plot line. I heard her in the pool house with my father. She said that we would lose you to Virginia if we moved in here. I believed that somehow I could protect you and that you needed to be away from the room, the place, where our daughter died. And some space from Kathleen who was over constantly with Nicole because she couldn't handle the pressure of a fussy baby and a useless husband who encouraged her to ditch her lithium."

"You didn't really want to live here again?"

He swung around to where she now knelt beside him. "Over Vera's house? Sidney that was my first home other than Dad's fishing cabin. This place..." He drew a long breath. "I may have been brought here from the hospital as a newborn but I was never welcome. The home Vera made for you and Kat was full of love, warmth, laughter and tears. And acceptance. Vera loved Kathleen at her best, her worst, always."

"That's Aunt Vera's way."

His eyes swiveled to hers. "And your way. But never my mother's."

"She tried Luke. In her own way, Virginia tried to reach out to me while you were working such long hours. I wasn't easy to communicate with then. I was young and immature..."

Fury poured through him as his mother's words rang in his head in her voice. "Sidney! Stop it! That isn't the truth! That is my God damned mother talking. She sabotaged you deliberately. In a cold and calculating manner, she destroyed every vestige of self worth you had. And it was such cruel timing. You were devastated after Natalie died. You needed someone loving and supporting you..."

"But you did that..." she staunchly insisted.

He smiled with heartfelt gratitude to hear her express that. "God knows I tried, but I wasn't here enough. Charlie told me what it was like for you."

She shook her head. "That is biased information. Your father and mother despised each other. They fought horribly and I just tried to make peace. Of course Charlie would stick up for me."

He gave her a level look. "My mother told me with glee how she set you up every step of the way."

Her eyes widened in horror. She made a small sound of out right hurt.

"Sidney, you and I were trying to have another child..."

"Yes and she helped me. Virginia took me to a specialist in Ridgetown who dealt with infertility," Sidney persisted.

"And that so called expert put you on birth control pills," he scoffed.

"No! Those pills were to help us conceive. They couldn't have been birth control. They were in a bottle not a pack. I took one everyday. You stop taking birth control pills during the week of your period. I never did. Your mother agreed to keep them in her room so that you won't worry," she protested adamantly.

"Sid, my mother convinced the doctor you were unstable and shouldn't have another child for an indefinite period. The missing week was sugar pills," he informed her feeling responsible for his mother's treachery.

Sidney shook her head in abject disbelief. She bit her lip to stem her

234

roiling emotion as tears clung to her lashes. "So every month when I got my period and cried myself to sleep, Virginia just pretended to comfort me."

He nodded miserably as if guilty by sheer association. "Sidney, I'm so sorry. I wanted us to have another baby too. I knew we couldn't ever replace Natalie but I did believe that a baby might help us heal." Her eyes stared into his and he felt blessed to see tenderness there instead of the hatred many women might have bestowed on him in her place.

"I remember the nights you held me crying in your arms and you tried to be so strong but I felt the tears on your face in the dark. I knew you wanted a child too and that you missed our daughter as desperately as I did," she confessed.

He closed his eyes and reached out to pull her close. As his hands touched her shoulder blades, it occurred to him that he might be breaching her trust. "Sid, I want to hold you. Can I? I won't…"

"Please," she said turning toward him.

She molded against him and the fit was perfect as always. His hand glided over her hair as he rocked her gently the way he once had rocked their daughter.

"I hate this place, Sid," he confided.

She smiled through her tears. "This was the only room in the entire house I liked. The only place I felt safe and loved."

"That's how I feel about Vera's place. I love that attic room. I swear I can still feel Natalie there. Picture you nursing her."

"Can you?" she asked in a bare whisper.

"Yes Sid. People can be lost from someone but no one can take the precious memories." She stared wide-eyed at him clearly unable to speak. "You have memories too. Don't you, Sweetheart?"

Her bottom lip quivered. "Sometimes I dream. It's so real. I had one that night you brought me those remedies for my cramps. It turns out the medicine you bought had a small amount of codeine in it. Codeine does really weird things to my mind."

"I know," he responded evenly.

Confusion claimed her features. "You can't know. I only learned this a few years ago after some dental work."

"That night you thought you were dreaming, I was there. Sweetheart, you were awake."

She gulped and her eyes rivaled saucers. "In my dream, I told you to get into bed…"

"But I rubbed your back instead. Sidney, when did you start sleeping in the nude?" She closed her eyes in embarrassment and her face grew hot. His gentle fingers stroked a reddened cheek. "Sweetheart, you don't have anything to be embarrassed about. I have seen your body many times. It's still lovely."

She carefully averted her eyes. "I think you might have mentioned that once or twice the night Reg was wounded."

"Maybe discussing *that* night is out of the scope of our coping today."

She laughed almost hysterically. "If we work on that premise, it will remain that way indefinitely."

"Maybe that's best Sidney. I asked that night if you were saying good-bye. Maybe you were," he postured.

"That would be simpler."

"Is it what you want?" he asked with deceptive casualness. His entire body tensed as he waited for her answer.

She stared at him for a long spell binding moment. It was as if she were willing time to stand still. "I want to tell you the truth. I am tired of secrets."

His mouth set in a grim line. "What's the truth, Sidney?"

She got up off the bed and moved to stand by the window. "I had another baby last year. Reg and I had a daughter."

Luke gasped as his mind reeled at her stunning revelation. "You had another child?"

"Yes. We called her Lily. She was beautiful," Sidney breathed in wonder like tones.

"Where is she?"

A small whimper escaped her before she spoke and Luke's heart sank as he anticipated her answer. "Where my other child is. Dead. When I was eight months pregnant with Lily, I was at work and received a phone call informing me that an officer was down and they anticipated it was Reg. I was desperate to find out more details. Somehow I believed if I could get to the precinct…" She shook her head in despondency. "I didn't even wait for the elevator, I ran down the stairs and I fell…"

"Oh God, Sid…"

"Down the entire flight. The doctors aren't sure what happened exactly but after the fall, they couldn't get a heartbeat. The ultrasound confirmed that Lily was dead in my womb. When she was born after labor was induced, her cord was wrapped around her neck several times. The medical examiner thought that she likely had the cord around her neck to begin with but my fall tightened it and she strangled."

Her despair was profound and he longed to reach out to her but wasn't certain she would accept his attempts to console her. Her shoulders drooped as she took a shuttering breath and sniffed before she could continue. "Reg

236

didn't even get to see his daughter open her eyes. I remember laying in that bed after I delivered her and thinking at least you and I had that with Natalie. Reg is always marked out because of his size but he was so tender with Lily. He cradled her little body in his large hands and rocked her. I didn't think he would ever let her go. This giant of a man and I watched his heart splinter into a thousand fragments."

Luke frowned. "Wasn't Reg injured?"

Sidney hung her head. "No, it was another cop." Predictable silence ensued. "Her injury wasn't life threatening. She was knifed in an altercation with a prospective John. Reg intervened. The entire incident had nothing to do with the case at all. It was merely a matter of being in the wrong company." She laughed bitterly. "After Lily died, I didn't manage very well."

"Delta stayed with you."

"Yes and Vera."

"She was on an extended book tour last spring…"

Sidney smiled sadly. "There was no tour. Vera was with me. It was a long while before I even felt like getting up in the morning. I actually began making the effort so Reg would worry less about me and be less distracted on the job. Preoccupation in his line of work gets you killed."

"The spare room in your apartment…"

"Lily's nursery. I can't bear to clean it out. I did that once before…" Her voice caught. "Lily was a surprise. I didn't really believe I could get pregnant after… well, I just didn't think it could happen again. I was lackadaisical with protection for only a few weeks when I became ill with what I thought was the flu. When it didn't get better and I began losing weight from persistent vomiting, Reg insisted I go to the doctor for a physical. He bodily took me." She smiled whimsically. "I swear there are still finger nail marks on that examining room ceiling from my reaction after my doctor told me I was pregnant."

"Was Reg happy?"

"I don't think there's a word for what Reg was," she replied as her expression grew dreamy and distant. "He held me so hard our doctor was concerned he might crack my ribs. She was misguided though. Reg knows how to temper his strength. He wouldn't know how to hurt me." She shook her head ruefully. "And how do I show my appreciation, I keep huge secrets. You know I have seen Reg furious, silly, ecstatic, depressed, grieving, outraged… but I have never seen him look like he did today when he learned about our marriage and Natalie. This time the pain in his face was unique because I put it there."

Luke sat on the edge of the bed listening. Sidney hadn't moved an inch.

She was rigidly standing before the window that was covered only by light sheer material. She did not appear to be looking at anything. She stood dejected and alone recalling the painful details of losing her baby.

Luke studied her at length before the pieces clicked into place. She expected him to reject her just like she expected Reg to do the same when she returned home to Vera's. She had come here because in her mind it was where the banished go. He stood up without speaking.

Sidney stood silent before the window. Her sobs were lurking cruelly just below the surface and she wasn't certain how much longer she could contain them. Surely, he would leave soon in disgust and she could give in to the pain. She had been so fortunate in her life to be loved by two remarkable men and had ruined both relationships.

She jumped at his gentle touch on her shoulder and whirled toward him in disbelief. His eyes were tender, nudging her closer to the edge.

His knuckle grazed her cheek lovingly. "Oh Sweetheart. I'm so sorry. I can't imagine losing another baby…"

A strangled sound escaped her as she dissolved into racking sobs and he pulled her against his chest. She clung to him like the only solid thing in her world. A large spot of his shirt became wet with her tears.

"I thought you might leave," she admitted sniffling.

Luke gave her look of measured reproach. "You thought wrong. Sidney that day at the mausoleum, the baby you were talking about was…"

"Lily. That was just after the anniversary of her death. Reg and I met at an inn but he had to leave because of the case."

"And you came back distraught and I acted like an ass…"

"You didn't know…"

"All I knew was that I was incredibly jealous of a man I had never met. A man you were speeding to," Luke admitted in self-reproach.

"I should go. Reg and Auntie Vera will be worried."

He reluctantly nodded his agreement and looped his arm through hers to walk out of the room they had once shared as husband and wife. He stopped her progress at the door. "Sidney the night before you left here, leaving only a note…" He paused and saw her tense. "You made love to me like you knew it was the last time. You knew it was, didn't you?"

"Yes. I believed that you were trapped in your marriage to me. That I was barren and emotionally unstable. I started to think that maybe I was mentally ill like Kathleen and just hadn't been diagnosed yet. I wanted more for you than what I believed I could ever give."

Pain cascaded over him in drenching suffocating waves. "What the hell did you do for money if you couldn't access your trust fund your parents left?

Vera swore she didn't give you money for months hoping you would come back."

Sidney lowered her eyes to the floor. She dreaded answering knowing how deep this poison would seep. "Your mother gave me money to go and sent me more until she was certain I won't come back."

"Was it enough?" Sure that it wasn't. His mother was only generous with herself.

"I made it enough. I made due. I wanted to set you free," she revealed quietly.

He shook his head at the many misconceptions that had riddled their relationship. "I've never been free Sidney. I have always been yours whether you wanted me or not. My heart couldn't accept your choice."

She sighed dejectedly. "Sometimes our hearts don't always get what they want."

He regarded her oddly for a second with narrowed eyes. "You know what I want right now Sid." She froze wholly afraid of his answer. He smiled cagily at her discomfiture. "Sweetheart, I always want *that* but today is not the time." She blinked warily. "Let's go downstairs and break a few things."

"What?!"

His face became illuminated with the possibilities. "How about the damned crystal we had to use every night? Or the stupid china…"

"That Virginia insisted Natalie use at barely ten months and then was angry when the bread and butter plate was chipped," Sidney recalled with blatant disgust.

"That's right. A stupid woman, my mother."

"Luke…" she implored him softly.

He leveled her with a glance. "She was Sid. She surrounded herself with beautiful objects but couldn't see the most exquisite of all… you and our daughter."

Sidney felt herself being drawn in. His words… his gaze… his scent were weaving about her in binding tendrils. She hastily sought to break the spell before it was impenetrable. "I'll race you to the dining room…" she challenged tearing down the hall.

He laughed and ran after her. He marveled that once again her presence had brought some measure of cheerfulness to this torturous place only his mother could think of as home. Luke froze as he stared at her straddling the banister that ran the length of the staircase.

She smiled wickedly. "I always wanted to do this."

He approached her with cautious steps. "Sid, don't. The top of these stairs are more than twenty feet from the foyer."

Sidney scoffed at his concern. "Luke, it's perfectly safe. Come on, follow me down tough cop!" She let out a peel of laughter sliding down the gleaming handrail.

"Sidney!" he cried running forward but too late to stop her descent. She hopped jauntily off at the base of the stairs and held out her hands.

"Piece of cake. Come on Sheriff. A big strapping fellow like you…" Her mouth widened into a beguiling smile as he threw a leg over the banister and slid down after her. She grabbed his narrow hips as he reached the bottom and pulled him to the floor to collapse against him laughing.

Luke smiled down at her. "She needed to see this, to see you, but she just wasn't capable of it. Virginia may have been filthy rich in material things but she didn't have a clue about what was important. You *are* happiness, Sidney Ryan."

"I think that is one of the nicest things anyone has ever said to me, Lucas Ryan. Come on. Let's go break some china. I want the dish Nat broke."

"Can we share it?" he asked with a boyish quality inflecting his tone.

She turned and held out a hand. "Sure, we'll break Nat's chipped plate together."

CHAPTER TWENTY

It was a grounding emotion to enter your childhood home and not be certain of the welcome.

The smells and sounds coming from the kitchen heralded dinner preparations and the kids voices carried from the family room where the TV blared. She cautiously ducked her head into the front parlor to scout out the living room. Tension clawed at her chest to find it empty. Could Don have driven that fast?

"He's out back, Sidney," a gruff male voice spoke from behind.

Sidney turned with a tremulous expression to the man with silver edging the dark hair around his face and hazel eyes that seemed to draw her close. "Thanks, Dad."

"Thought you couldn't call me that," Charlie muttered.

Sidney gave him a guilty glance. "I think my secret's out so it hardly matters now."

Two brisk steps brought him in front of her. "It sure as hell matters to me. Only call me that if you want to."

Her hands rose helplessly. "I didn't mean it like that. Of course I want to. I barely remember my own father. And you have always been wonderful to me."

Guilty eyes fell away from her to study the floor. "No Sidney I haven't. When you and Luke lived on the hill, I should have put a stop to things when I first suspected them. Instead, I waited until I was sure and by then it was too late. Virginia had hurt you too badly for you to want to stay."

Sidney smiled sadly and reached out to touch his hand. "It seems there is plenty of guilt over that to spread around. I am starting to understand Virginia's part in things far more than I did. The responsibility lies with her. Not you or Luke. I don't hold either of you responsible."

He sighed heavily and pulled her toward him for a brusque hug. "I wish I could see it that way Honey."

"Maybe you could ease up a little on Reg, Dad. I would appreciate it."

Charlie drew back defensively. "I am polite."

Sidney gave him a shrewd glance. "And that's all."

"It's all I can manage."

"Manage more," she insisted. "Please."

He groaned dramatically and pulled her close again. "I want you to come home more often."

"I'll work on it. You getting along with Reg would help."

"You better try that yourself. He's sitting on the swing out back." She kissed his cheek and made a beeline for the door.

"She's right, Charlie. Make a sincere effort with Reginald or we won't see her often."

"You talk like she is back in New York already," he muttered disagreeably though he lifted his arm in invitation and Vera slid into it.

"She's not, but Charlie, that is a possibility," Vera felt compelled to remind him.

The face she had loved for most of her life softened and his eyes took on the twinkle that had always had a drastic effect on her senses. "There are other possibilities," he asserted smoothly.

Vera shook her head and smiled at his tenacity. Heaven help Sidney if Luke had learned any of this man's charms while he had been growing up.

She stopped and stared relieved that he had yet to notice her. It was a wonder that she could be this terrified to approach him. The butterflies fluttering in her middle seemed to be playing kick ball with her stomach. She shifted her weight slightly and it was enough to draw his attention.

He glanced around and she froze anticipating the worst. To her tremendous relief, he smiled and extended his hand. With a glad cry, Sidney ran around the garden swing to join him. In her rush, she brushed against something that his uninjured arm deftly lifted off the bench before her bottom landed there.

"Wow Babe, you just about flattened the posies," he told her smoothly.

Sidney gasped at the gorgeous arrangement of pale pink sweetheart roses. She swallowed past the lump in her throat in order to speak. "Reg, you sweet idiot, I am the one who is supposed to apologize."

"You won't get any argument there, Sid. The flowers have nothing to do with our present bone of contention."

"They don't?" she asked with some confusion.

"No. Honey, whatever we need to work out is one matter. The roses are to express how sorry I am that you lost your first baby, your daughter Natalie."

Tears brimmed in her luminous eyes as her lips curved into a sentimental smile. "Oh Reg. I don't deserve you."

"What you don't deserve is to lose two little girls," he corrected. "Vera, Delta and Kathleen told me a few stories about you as a Mommy. You were everything I always imagined you to be," he said tenderly, snagging her arm to pull her close.

"I love you, Reg Buckman."

His dark face brightened with a dazzling smile and show of sparkling teeth. "I'm counting on that, Babe." His arms tightened about her. She felt good there. He had waited all day for this moment. Whatever strife was between them could be resolved as far as he was concerned. Having her at his side was what counted most. It was time to put some strategy in place to keep her there.

That bitch broke the glass. The lovely etched panel, too. She had no respect. She never did. It was one thing to put up with her being in town but to come here to this place was such a violation. One that couldn't be tolerated without retribution.

Heaving with fury, she wiggled in through the small space incensed to see the droplets of blood marring the carpet. Perhaps it was time to get serious and spill some more. First things first, she told herself. She needed to find a dustbin to tidy the intolerable mess when she stopped dead in her tracks. She flew to the fireplace grate onto her hands and knees with a keening cry. Her fingers gingerly picked up one of the larger shards. That beautiful china! Her eyes scanned the huge pile of broken bits with horror.

She scrambled off her knees to the walnut cabinet against the wall. Her eyes were wide with astonishment. The whole set. Moaning she picked up one of the few pieces left and stroked it lovingly. The woman was despicable and had to be dealt with. Virginia Ryan was right all along.

She had known it years ago but this atrocity confirmed it. Natalie was better off not to grow up like her vamp mother. She hadn't committed a sin but a kindness. Virginia had always said so and Mrs. Ryan was a brilliant woman. A misunderstood woman surrounded by people not fit to lick her shoes.

Well Virginia was no longer here to guide her but she felt certain she could make her mentor proud. She would destroy the bitch once and for all and save Virginia's son in the process. She would be a hero then. Luke would see. They could live here as they were always meant to. On the hill among the more refined citizens. She would give him what he needed in a wife. Everything he had never gotten from her.

Clear now in her purpose, she found a broom and dustbin and set to work.

It gave Sidney a shiver but she knew it was the right thing to do. She slipped to the back door and quickly picked the lock. She could have easily done this yesterday but it was so much more satisfying to bust Virginia's gilded window.

A shudder rippled through her as she stood in the utilitarian kitchen. It was equipped with state of the art appliances, dominated by sleek stainless steel surfaces and shiny black and white tiles. No decor had been wasted on this room. After all Virginia only permitted the help in here. Sidney quickly found a broom and dustbin and strode purposefully toward the dining room. She didn't want to waste a second in this place but still it felt wrong to leave the mess.

She stopped in her tracks, baffled. The fireplace was immaculate. There was not a sliver of china anywhere and God knows the place had been covered. Sidney cracked a smile remembering. She had only thought they would smash a dish or two but hurling that china was such a release. She would have kept going and finished off the set if she hadn't started to feel such electricity sparking between her and Luke. It was undoubtedly just a carry over of the delightful purging. Money had never been so well disposed of.

Her lips curved with affection, Luke had obviously come back and tidied up. She did a double take and blinked at the china cabinet. Another set of fine china, equally ostentatious as the last, had been put on display and quite artfully. That was odd. She shrugged it off, concluding that Luke wanted to avoid any questions from Charlie about where the dishes had gone. Lord knew that man wouldn't recognize one set from another. Relieved that the chore had been so easily dispensed of, Sidney slipped back out the same way she had come.

Sidney rolled over and punched her pillow for the umpteenth time. Nothing seemed to help. She was wide-awake and restless when she first heard it.

Her brows drew together as she listened intently in the darkness. The entire household was in bed so she hastened down the stairs belting her robe as she went. The low sound reached her ears again and Sidney smiled girlishly. Her feet couldn't move fast enough. His tone was more insistent the next time he called and she began to giggle. Suddenly she skidded to a halt halfway down the last set of steps. An enormous shadow blocked her path.

"Reg! What on earth are you doing?" she asked swallowing a laugh.

A slur came out of the darkness. "Calling my lady love."

"Is she a moose?"

"I've never thought of you as a moose," he replied inanely.

"Good thing," Sidney chortled, impishly skipping down the last of the steps. She looped her arm through his and almost lost her balance when he leaned so heavily upon her. "Just what have you been drinking anyway?"

"Whatever used to be in that crystal decanter in my bedroom."

Her mouth fell open. "You drank Vera's entire decanter of sherry? Whatever will she do at noon on Saturday?" Sidney teased. "Come on, Reg, I'll get you back to bed."

He grunted before he grudgingly began to move. "I don't like it there."

"Where? Your *bedroom*?"

"Yeah," he pouted.

"What's wrong with it, Honey?" she asked tenderly. It was unusual for him to drink more than a few, let alone so indiscriminately. His tastes would not typically run to sherry of any variety.

"You're not in it," he said flatly as she eased him onto the bed.

Sidney smiled and laid a small hand on his cheek. "I think I could probably remedy that." She pulled the blankets up over him and lifted them to slip inside.

He groaned and pulled her against his massive chest. "You are the best medicine I could hope for," Reg said running his hands over the folds of her robe. He slid a hand inside her lapel and fondled her breast. "But you're overdressed, Babe."

Her light laughter tinkled in the night. "Your bedroom is the living room, Reg."

He grumbled something under his breath. "I gotta talk to Vera about reassigning my room."

"Vera has little to do with it. Letting that side of yours heal is more the point. Hold me close and go to sleep."

He readily wrapped a brawny arm about her. She relished the security of his bear like embrace and felt the restlessness she had battled upstairs melt away. Within seconds, his breathing became the rasping snores she was well used to. She smiled serenely, snuggled closer to his furred chest and drifted off to sleep.

Sidney blinked, trying to shut out the blinding light. She covered her eyes with one hand and felt the covers slide off her shoulder. As she squinted at the sun streaming into the living room, she belatedly recalled crawling into bed with Reg during the night.

His sturdy form was a firm presence at her back and his rasping snore assured her he was still asleep. One glance at her bare shoulder suggested that she was naked beneath the covers. She spied her robe lying a few feet away.

Sidney chuckled to herself as vague recollections of Reg peeling it off her during the wee hours of the morning flooded back. A wandering hand assured her that he at least still wore boxer shorts. One of them was decent.

Her ears slowly became attuned to the low murmur of voices in the kitchen. Obviously, Delta was preparing breakfast while Charlie enjoyed his first coffee of the day. The screen door squeaked opened and banged shut as another voice joined the dialogue in the kitchen.

Sidney shuddered suddenly feeling ridiculously exposed. It was an unsettling thing to be ensconced naked in a bed in the living room knowing the only other man she had ever been intimate with was only a room away.

She gasped as she realized that was no longer the case. Luke strode in with a steaming mug in his hand. "Reg, I thought you might…" The words died on his lips as he froze in his tracks and stared at the sight of her cradled in the other man's arms. His eyes were locked on creamy shoulders peeking above the covers as he stumbled over her robe.

"He's still asleep," she whispered feeling the flush climb into her cheeks.

"I see that," Luke stated evenly. "Would you like the coffee instead?" he offered holding the cup out to her.

She averted her eyes nervously to the floor. "I would rather have my robe."

"Uh huh."

"You're standing on it."

He stooped to scoop it up and handed it over like it was a cloth of nettles. Pivoting on his heels, Luke headed for the kitchen again like the hounds of hell were chasing him. Just as his escape was almost complete, a low rumbling voice reached his ears.

"Hey Babe, what is that robe doing back here? I thought I settled that issue last night."

Sidney's soft voice sounded like a shout in his ear. "You can't settle everything in the night, Reg."

"I can try," the man claimed smugly. "And have a hell of a lot of fun at it."

She leaned closer to murmur something Luke was certain he didn't want to hear. Suddenly Delta's mouth-watering waffles lost their appeal. He wrote a hasty note to Kathleen and headed to his office.

Luke saw him from his office window and could only wonder what had taken him so long. Truly, he had expected the man to make an appearance all day.

He marveled at the transformation in body language from the last time Reg arrived unannounced. One could easily see how he might intimidate a perpetrator with a mere glance.

Reg was taking long purposeful strides toward where he stood, bearing down on him like a freight train and Luke was certain the buzzing of his intercom was Constable Dennison terrified at the front desk. One would think that such a pace might tug at the wound that was still healing on his left side but if that was the case, Reg didn't let it show. His expression was tense and unsmiling as the formidable man came to a crisp halt.

"We need a moment, Sheriff."

"Seems like," Luke agreed tersely.

Reg lowered himself into one of the chairs near Luke's desk crossing mammoth arms over each other. In one hand dangled a ring with a lone key on it, that Luke knew with a certainty fit Vera McCorkidale's Victorian home, because he had one too from years gone by. One he was never asked to return. Dark fingers fiddled with it in a clear gesture of possession prompting Luke to lean in an outward casual stance against his desk rather than sit behind it. And waited.

Their eyes met and held. "When we met, I was clearly on too many drugs. I mistakenly thought you were like a big brother to Sidney."

Luke maintained his a level gaze. "Actually for years, I was exactly that to Sid. I even dated Kathleen for almost a year."

Reg took that in and burned. "Get tired of one sister and decide to move on?"

Luke envisioned his balled fist connecting with that thick jaw. "Kathleen was starting to experience more obvious symptoms of bipolar disorder and quite frankly didn't see herself as a one woman man. Sidney was extremely protective of her and spent a lot of time keeping her sister out of trouble. Somehow I ended up trying to keep Sid out of trouble."

Reg's eyes narrowed. "The way I understand it, you got Sidney in trouble in the oldest way possible."

Luke remained calmly aloof although somewhere deep the insinuation stung. "A lot happened before that happened."

"Well as far as I'm concerned, it is all water under the bridge. It must be because Sidney has never spoken of you or alluded to your relationship in over ten long years," Reg stated caustically.

"Things were a real mess by the time she left," Luke acknowledged grudgingly.

"The loss of a child that was the reason for being married too young..."

"It was far more complicated than that," Luke bit out stringently.

Reg peered steadily in his direction. "Consider it simplified. Sidney and I are engaged to be married. We are trying to have another baby. I intend on staying here with her until Kathleen's drug holiday is over..."

"What about work..."

"I will take a leave of absence. Sid and I could use some uncomplicated time together away from New York."

Luke blew out a breath. "Are you telling me to stay away?"

"Absolutely not. You are clearly part of the family and your presence will not affect Sidney and I. Perhaps she even needs to resolve some of the things she has bottled up all these years. Regardless she and I *will* return to the city. We *will* get married as planned and as soon as humanly possible, I will put a baby in her arms," Reg informed Luke in resolute tones.

The two men regarded one another for a long space that was highly charged and completely silent. A knock on the office door didn't budge either of them an inch. Carl framed the doorway a few seconds later at Luke's bidding to enter.

"Luke, the DA…" Carl stopped speaking abruptly as he registered Reg's presence. As he did, Reg rose out of his chair and gave his first cordial smile to Carl, visibly willing himself to relax.

"I was just going on my way, Carl. You and the Sheriff obviously have important business to conduct," he stated smoothly and left without further comment.

Carl watched him go and turned back to Luke, who remained leaning on his desk maintaining his stoic silence. "It looks like the important business was conducted before I arrived."

Luke readjusted his gaze to meet his friend's. "Reg felt compelled to remind me that Sidney is his woman."

Carl regarded the tall fierce looking man who emanated barely leashed violence that hardly befitted his title. "And…"

"And I knew that of course. What he doesn't know is that *his* woman is *my* wife."

CHAPTER TWENTY-ONE

"Jack, I just need a few more seconds…"

"Gee, I had better change my perfume if I am starting to be confused with a crusty old cop like Jack," Sidney joked shakily hoping to hang onto the last shreds of her bravado until the door was shut.

Luke's hand stilled completely at the melodic sound of her voice and a sensual smile curved his lips upward before he lifted his gaze to hers. She was similar to the figment his imagination had put in that very place a thousand times before. She wore a simple calico sundress that clung to all the right places and her loose hair flowed in waves around her shoulders. Large chocolate eyes shone behind long thick lashes as she regarded him steadfastly.

"I could never confuse you with Jack," Luke told her firmly as he rose to greet her. His lips quirked into a sexy grin. "His beard is far coarser than yours."

Her smile was sorely in danger of flip-flopping and for the first time he saw that she was trembling. He was upon her in a minute nearly toppling over his chair in the process. "Sidney? What is it?"

She stared up at him unaware how her chest was heaving and the view her dipping neckline afforded him. "Sorry. It's nothing really. I just figured out where I got my driving skills."

She had driving skills? Luke's mouth hung open as his eyes strayed to the valley of her breasts. "Where?"

"I inherited them from Kathleen."

His laughter bounced off the acoustic tiles. "Is that what's wrong?"

Sidney shoved him away. "It's plenty! And you won't find it so funny when you see what's left of your bike rack!"

"Oh Jesus!"

"And Hallelujah!" Sidney quipped unable to hold back her laughter though she still shook. "At least Mrs. Carmicheal and her poodle Precious were spared."

"Kat almost took out Mrs. Carmicheal?"

Sidney nodded. "And the dog. It's OK. I smoothed it over. I'm compensating her trauma with a cranberry banana loaf for her bridge game next week."

Luke smiled as he ran hands up and down her arms. "You're shaking."

"It unhinges me to see her like this again. It's been a long time." Sidney sank into a chair. "She was coming on to the meter reader yesterday." And Reg but she wisely left that out knowing Luke would only applaud.

Luke poured her some water from the cooler. "The kids seem fine. I had them over last night."

"They had a good time. Said your pool is warmer than ours but I think it's your company they love most."

"It's mutual."

She could see that. "You are good for them."

"Zach has a lot to say about Reg."

"Which should make up for what Nicole says. I hope."

"I could talk to her."

Sidney smiled appreciatively. "No. She feels disloyal to you if she cares for Reg. He understands."

"You don't."

She held up a hand. "I do. It's just hard. Charlie doesn't care for Reg. Nicole is snotty to him. And if Carlene swoons one more time with that moony eyed vacant look, I'm going to put smelling salts in her tea like sugar."

Luke turned away, his shoulders shaking.

"Luke Ryan."

"I'm not laughing. Really Sid." He turned sobering and then lost the battle. "All right I am laughing but frankly I think Reg can take it."

She gifted him with an irritated glance. "I'm leaving. This is getting us…"

"To where we belong," his deep suddenly solemn voice said from behind. She stopped in her tracks but didn't turn around. "Sidney, I have watched and not touched for weeks now. Reg is as subtle as a sledgehammer. For years, I was desperate to hear anything about you. I had too much pride to ask so I waited for any little comment no matter how inconsequential that Kathleen, Vera or even Charlie would let slip. But after a couple of weeks of Reg's company, I have heard more about your life in New York than I swear I ever wanted to know."

Sidney sputtered her water. "I'm sorry. You aren't seeing Reg at his best. He's not typically possessive. I don't know what's gotten into him…"

Luke shot her an incredulous glance. "Maybe it's finding out that another man he knew nothing about is in love with you."

Sidney opened her mouth and closed it again.

Luke edged closer. "You're shocked. How can you be? Sidney you were in my…"

"Don't! Just don't," she implored with pleading eyes. "You and I have been apart for years."

He caught her chin with two long fingers. "We were very together about two months ago."

Sidney closed her eyes as anxiety claimed her in a rush. "Please...that was..."

Two strong arms gripped her arms. "Not a mistake Sid. Something that beautiful couldn't have been wrong."

Sidney averting her glistening eyes from his penetrating gaze. "It wasn't honorable," she insisted hating how her voice trembled.

"It was inevitable."

She stood up stricken. "I have to go."

"To get in a car with Kathleen. Nice to know which way you gamble." Knowing his temper was a hair trigger, he caught himself. "Sidney, if love survives a decade apart isn't it worth exploring? Let me compete. Let me touch you that way he does..."

She hit her fist against the door making his head snap up. "Dammit Luke I didn't come here for this. I wear his ring. I am going to be his wife."

His hands bit into flesh to lift her up to his snarling face. "What about being my wife?"

"I am no one's wife now," she reminded him thinking he needed to hear it.

His features hardened into a stony mask. It took every ounce of his formidable control not to reply. They stood nose to nose for several long moments staring into the depths of each other's eyes.

The door swung open behind them without warning and they spun apart. Jack framed the doorway holding a brownie on a napkin. "I brought you a brownie Sheriff so you wouldn't miss out. The pan you brought is pretty much licked clean Honey."

Sidney smiled thinly trying to gather her wits before having to walk through the squad room.

"Thanks Jack but Sidney brought my sweets personally."

Jack knew that. He had seen her go in. He also knew by Luke's tone and Sidney's pallor barging in was the right move though by the glint in the younger man's eye he might be retired without a party for it later.

"I have to get going. I left Kathleen alone with Dennison." She lifted her eyes upward as if praying. "It probably wasn't wise but..."

Jack eased out of the office thinking he could now. "I'll go check on Kathleen while you two finish up."

Luke eyed the solitary brownie pondering. "You didn't come to bring me baked goods..."

"I just felt I needed to come."

"I'd be interested why you did. I think this is the first time we have been alone in what…a month, six weeks?"

"I came to bring you these and let you off the hook." She tossed something in foil that he caught against his chest.

"A bribe and a fishing analogy?" Luke unwrinkled the foil to uncover more fudge brownies. "These are squashed. You lose marks on presentation."

"I had to grip something with Kathleen driving."

The look in her eye told him she wouldn't mind if he volunteered his neck. He licked his lips and dipped his finger into the chocolate goo. "God these are wonderful even if they look like mud pie."

She was mentally mashing them into his smirking face.

"What hook, Sweetheart?"

"I'm not you're Sweetheart." She batted his chest. "Stop grinning like an idiot."

The confusion brewing in her expression dampened his fun. "Seriously Sid."

"It would be simpler if we celebrated the Fourth of July separately."

She knew how to pack a punch and changed his plans considerably. "Well I guess I have had Kat and the kids and Vera and Charlie with me for the past…"

Sidney huffed out an agitated breath. "What are you talking about? This has nothing to do with the family." She knew where their preferences lay. "I just meant Reg and I. We can spend the day alone. We don't belong…" She was already edging toward the door.

His hands snaked out to catch her arms. It felt so good to touch even if she did stiffen. "Hold on. Just hold on. You belong…"

"I'm with Reg. Your men know we were married."

"My men are not interested in my private life."

She laughed. "Do you know how many conversations cease when I walk through that squad room?"

His mouth was open to deny it and realized it was pointless. To some extent, he experienced something similar. "They are curious." Something else occurred though. "They are respectful? They don't say anything…"

"No Luke and that isn't the point. The point is…"

"The point is I want you at the pig roast. I want to watch the fire works for the first time in ten years and see you across the lawn."

"It won't be the same."

It couldn't possibly be the same. They had a child between them before. "I accept that. Just like I accept Reg coming."

"Luke…" She was shaking her head but her eyes were indecisive.

"Come to my party. Vera and Charlie won't enjoy themselves if you aren't there." That was a huge chink in her armor and he wasn't above exploiting it any longer.

She sighed. "I would feel better being there with Kathleen. That's a lot of people…"

His fingers linked with hers. "We'll both be there."

"We'll both be there," she agreed wondering whether her sister's psychiatrist gave two for one specials.

Luke smiled like a Cheshire cat as he watched her vacate the building like there was a bomb scare. He felt Jack's gaze upon him and turned toward the older man, who he admired in ways he confided to no one. "So Jack how am I doing?"

"I'm trying to decide if you know what you're doing," the older man stated dubiously, dragging a hand through salt and pepper waves of hair.

"I know."

"You're turning her inside out," Jack clarified.

"Then it's working," Luke replied smugly with burgeoning hope.

Luke broke his stride and stopped running altogether to do a double take. It was unusual to see Charlie out running since his retirement from the force but his companions were an even greater shock. He was under the impression Charlie could barely tolerate Reg and Zachary's wiry frame seemed absurdly dwarfed between the two men as he valiantly struggled to keep up.

"Hey Dad…Reg…Zach! The crossword not part of the paper anymore Dad?" he asked, ruffling the youngster's blond mop of hair.

"It's the first day of summer vacation for the kids," Charlie stated bluntly as if that should clarify things and ran ahead with Zach eagerly on his heels.

Reg shrugged his wide shoulders. "I was perfectly content to wait for the batch of biscuits Delta had in the oven when Charlie pretty much dragged me out of the kitchen," he puffed.

Luke took in the other man's endurance at a glance. "How's your side holding up?"

Reg snorted. "Felt fine at the kitchen table."

Charlie frowned over his shoulder, at their on-going conversation. "Are you two going to chit chat or run because if we don't get a move on, we're going to miss them."

"Yeah!" Zach agreed enthusiastically.

Reg and Luke exchanged a questioning glance. "Miss who?" they asked together.

Charlie's grin was wide and toothy. "You'll see," he promised and took off with Zachary bobbing by his side like an eager pup. They entered the conservation area when Charlie left the main path.

"Dad, you don't want to go that way. It's all marsh land down there at that end of the pond," Luke warned.

"Exactly. That's where they'll be," he claimed gleefully with Zach nodding in agreement.

Reg and Luke stared after the two of them and then followed in hot pursuit. When they came upon the oldest and youngest of their strange running contingent seconds later, the only saw their hind ends. Zachary and Charlie had their heads stuck in some brush by the edge of the pond. When a feminine peel of laughter rang in the air, Luke and Reg shared a communicative look. They both knew that voice by heart. Their pace quickened.

Reg thrust his head through the shrubbery ignoring the scratches incurred and stared agog at the sight below. Sidney was wading at the edge of the pond intently studying the rushes nearby. She wore a white shirt knotted at the waist above her cut offs. Her hair was gathered into a long ponytail. "God, Sidney looks so young!" Reg marveled to no one in particular.

"Shhh! They'll hear you!" Charlie admonished sternly.

"Yeah, they'll hear you!" Zach echoed in camaraderie.

"What are they doing?" Reg asked in a rough whisper genuinely at a loss.

Luke chuckled as he gazed at the figure of a woman, he didn't know how to forget, looking so much like the young girl he had fallen hopelessly in love with. "Sid's catching…" Reg frowned as Luke's voice was drowned out by loud ripples of laughter and Nicole's excited squeal.

Sidney turned with her arms akimbo and a disapproving expression gracing her pretty features. "If you two can't keep quiet, I am going to banish you to the bank," she scolded mother and daughter, who were wading just behind her and tittering with giggles. "Shhh. I think I have figured out where he's hiding. I won't have a chance of catching him with you two laughing hyenas backing me up."

"Hey Nic. Sid thinks we're her back up…like cops assisting their chief," her sister laughingly told her daughter, nudging her with an elbow.

"Aunt Sid, you hang around too many cops," her niece suggested somberly.

Sidney made a little scoffing sound. "There have been a few moments lately when I would agree with that, Nicole." Two men frowned reflexively.

"Well you better find a different breed of men to sleep with then, Sid," her older sister stated boldly.

Sidney gasped and whirled to face her sibling. "Kat!" She jerked her head toward Nicole and narrowed her eyes.

"My daughter knows about sex, little sister, and that you have had it before. Hell, I had it twice before I decided I didn't like it," she remarked blandly.

Sidney put a hand to cover her gaping mouth but was unable to contain her mirth.

"Mom, is twice really enough to decide whether you like it or not? You always make me and Zach try new foods at least ten times before we can say we don't like it. Shouldn't sex be the same?" Nicole asked with grave seriousness.

"Sex should be what it is," a melodic voice entered the fray as Vera came wading in from the far bank of the pond. Her frilly skirt was gathered from behind and pulled forward between her legs to tuck into her waistband in the front. Her filmy blouse was delicate looking and too low cut to be worn this early in the morning by most women. Red curls gleamed in the bright sun. "Sex, my Dear Nicole, is….."

"Miraculous with the right person," three women suddenly chorused in a singsong manner. Two wore huge grins; their elder rose her penciled eyebrows in feigned reproach.

Nicole eyed them all skeptically but enthralled just the same. "A miracle like as in God?"

Sidney's smile turned warm. "Making love with a man who loves you in return Honey is as close to heaven as you can get while you are still alive."

"Was it like that with Uncle Luke?" the young girl asked starkly.

Sidney made a little choking noise. "Ahhh…"

"That would be telling tales out of school, Dear," Vera interjected smoothly.

Nicole frowned deeply in her disappointment. "Isn't that why we are here? The ritual of welcoming summer on the first day of school holidays? Isn't that why Aunt Sidney baked cream scones at six o'clock in the morning for us to eat for breakfast?"

"With chocolate butter," her mother piped in like it was of dire consequence.

"Uh huh," Sidney agreed.

Nicole gave her a challenging look and made a little splash in her aunt's direction. "Then we are out of school and I want to hear the tale!"

"Well Nic, I'm here to catch that granddaddy bullfrog that I haven't managed to snare after years of trying. Cut the chit chat or hit the bank over there," her aunt decreed firmly.

The eleven year old made a derogatory noise that made Sidney glance over her shoulder in time to catch the splash full in the face. She sputtered through the water just as an enormous warty frog leapt in front of her. Sidney hit the water face first with both hands outstretched expectantly. She surged back out of the pond spewing water and triumphantly clutching a huge amphibian in her hands. She turned toward the three generations of gaping women with a spectacular smile. "I got him! Look!" she cried at the top of her lungs. Just then, the large frog wriggled from her grasp and leapt toward the three females directly in his path. High pitched squealing rent the air as the panicked females sought their escape tangling with each other as Sidney laughed at them. Heads bumped and bodies collided until they collapsed in a jumble of limbs and floral frills that were never meant for any pond before sinking into the shallow muddy waters.

Sidney slapped her thighs in gut wrenching gales of hilarity at the sight of her niece, sister and aunt rising out of the ripples they had created. The three women glanced at one another's sodden condition and then at Sidney whose own hair was plastered to her head.

"Let's get her!" Kathleen exclaimed and Sidney's mouth formed a silent 'O' at the sight of her family charging forward with outstretched arms. She squealed and turned in the opposite direction, purposelessly leading them toward the deeper part of the pond often used as a swimming hole.

"It's getting deep Mom!" Nicole complained.

"Chickens!" Sidney yelled at the three whose pursuit was slowing and began to make clucking sounds while flapping folded arms, hands tucked under her armpits. Vera disappeared from sight as she plunged under the water.

"Auntie!" Nicole cried, her eyes glued to the spot where her elder had disappeared. Vera suddenly surged upward with a show of white shoulders.

"Auntie! Where's your blouse?" Nicole cried mystified.

Sidney and Kathleen burst into fits of giggles as Vera flung the wet mass of frills toward the far bank where it landed on the muddy edge. Seconds later her skirt followed. "Sometimes clothes are too restrictive," she declared adamantly.

Two sisters, flushed with amusement, shared a knowing look. Sidney dove under the water and when she resurfaced her shorts were in her hand. They joined her aunt's garments in short order followed by her white shirt. Nicole stared wide-eyed as her mother followed suit.

Sidney gave her stunned niece an understanding glance. "You don't have to join us if you don't want to, Nic. It took me a couple years before I dared when we came to live with Auntie Vera."

"You were so proud of yourself the first time you skinny dipped, Sid,"

Kathleen recalled fondly.

"I couldn't believe how free it felt once I got over the embarrassment," she admitted.

"You certainly weren't mortified as a young married woman in our backyard pool late at night, Sidney Ryan," Vera acknowledged silkily.

Sidney gasped. "You knew Luke and I..."

"Snuck out around midnight to skinny dip whenever the opportunity presented itself. Of course I did, Dear. It was sweet to see you so happy."

Sidney smiled self-consciously and averted her dreamy gaze.

"Do you think Uncle Luke ever skinny dips in his pool?" Nicole asked innocently.

Kathleen rolled her eyes dramatically. "Maybe with Jack and Carl after poker but to my knowledge no woman other than us family has ever been invited to that house."

Sidney swallowed. "I'm sure Luke is just discreet. He is the Sheriff after all. He has a reputation to worry about."

"I remember when he didn't care about his reputation...."

Sidney moved toward her sister with a menacing expression. "Don't finish that Kat..."

"Stop calling me that then..."

"Kat suits you. Dad used to call you that. I like it," Sidney stubbornly insisted.

"Why didn't Uncle Luke care about his reputation Mom?" Nicole asked predictably.

Kathleen batted her eyes at her sister. "Because all he cared about...."

"Kat..." Sidney growled low, tackling and dragging Kathleen under the water before she could finish.

Nicole watched her mother and aunt cavort like schoolgirls and glanced over at her great aunt. "What was all that Uncle Luke cared about Auntie? Mom didn't say. Aunt Sid didn't let her. Doesn't she want to know..."

Vera smiled at the perplexed young girl by her side and put a ghostly white arm around her shoulders. "Your Aunt Sidney does know. Better than anyone. Your Uncle Luke didn't care about his reputation years ago because all he cared about was your Aunt Sidney."

Awe swept the young girl's visage. "That's so romantic!" she breathed wide-eyed.

Vera smiled gloriously. "Yes Dear. It was more romantic than even Lara Lovelorn could write."

The two sisters stopped for a second to glance upward at the bank where a movement caught their eye. "Hey Carlene! Come on in! The water's fine!

But you have to ditch that fancy running outfit!" Kathleen yelled to the startled figure that gawked at them from a safe distance. She hesitantly returned the wave she received from her employer. Carlene was visibly shaken as she took in the tops of Vera's shoulders peeking above the water. Her mouth opened and her eyes rivaled saucers as the realization struck her that Vera was naked. "Why you're...you're...."

Kathleen and Sidney snickered at her reaction.

"Come on, Carlene! We'll give you a hand!" They teased relentlessly and rushed toward the bank until the only part of their bodies still covered by water were their shins. Carlene went whey faced like she was on the verge of a coronary.

"I...I ...gotta get to the library," she stammered and ran in the other direction. "My books are overdue."

"I said to cover his eyes!" Luke whispered urgently from his position in the brush. "Have you got him?!"

"I do! I've got him!" Reg retorted with undisguised annoyance. This entire scenario was agitating. Hearing intimate details of Sidney's marriage was arousing rampant waves of jealousy he didn't know what to do with.

"If you have Zach's eyes covered, why is he standing over there gaping at his mother and Sidney!" Luke cried.

"Because the big lug has a hold of me!" Charlie snorted finally breaking free of Reg's slackening grip.

The three men turned together to grab the young boy, who stood riveted to the giggling scenario playing out near them and almost flattened a stupefied Carlene, who was blindly fleeing the area.

"Oh! Oh! I... didn't see... why you... you're... *you're watching!*" she stammered with unbridled horror.

"Ah no, we're not, Carlene," Charlie told her smoothly. "We're just looking for little Zachary. He wandered off the path. Ahhh... there he is, fellows. We'll just go collect him and be on our way."

The three walked nonchalantly to where Zach stood mesmerized and yanked him back toward the running path. Carlene watched them leave and felt a heaviness in her chest as she witnessed Luke take one last parting glance toward the pond. She followed his gaze and knew the only one he could see from his vantage point was her. Her long hair was soaking wet and matted to her skull. She was absolutely devoid of any make up or clothing yet he stared at her hungrily with longing teeming in his gaze.

Carlene knew then that despite her designer outfit, perfect coiffure and skillfully applied make up that she couldn't compete with this woman. More drastic measures would have to be taken.

CHAPTER TWENTY-TWO

It was a picnic for chrissake not a funeral.

Somehow, the two occasions had blurred in distinction as Sidney fussed over the contents of her bag for the millionth time. Her stalling was reaching its limits though. The house was empty now except for her and Reg, who from the sound of his footsteps, was pacing in the hallway below.

It was time she decided, flinging her bag over her shoulder, when the soft purring of the phone interrupted like a death knell.

"Sidney..." his voice responded to her lackluster greeting and she was instantly annoyed that her pulse quickened at mere sound of him coming across the line.

"Yes."

"Sweetheart, the celebration can't really begin, at least not for me, until you arrive. Are you coming soon?"

"Ummm..."

"Sidney, there's nothing to be nervous about," Luke calmly reassured her. It was a relief that there was no one to witness her stunned reaction to his astute perception behind her procrastination. "There's no one here but friends. I promise."

"Luke, you can't make a promise like that. Given who you are in this town, practically anyone could show up and it would be difficult in your political position to turf them out."

A little scoffing sound blew into her ear. "Try me," he told her silkily.

"It's more than that..."

"Sidney, my staff are well aware of our history and that you are coming with Reg..."

"I don't want anyone to think I'm flaunting Reg in front of you," she admitted candidly.

He smiled reflexively and wished she could see it. "I know you're not and the people who are important know the same thing. Please just come. Jerry and Sandra Pensar have just arrived and they are putting on a brave front but I know Sandra is desperate to see you."

A brief silence prevailed. "Tell her and Aunt Vera, Reg and I are on our way."

"How did you know Vera was concerned?" he asked with sincere interest.

Sidney laughed for the first time in their conversation. "Vera is typically far more concerned than she ever lets on. In fact, lately, she has been leaving me chapters of her newest book in the most peculiar places. I believe she thinks they might be therapeutic."

"Maybe you should indulge her and pick it up. You used to be one of her best editors."

"Hmmm. I had almost forgotten."

"She still maintains that your suggestions to her story lines and characterizations resulted in some of her best work," he reminded her.

"That was a long time ago," she stated with a tinge of sadness.

"Babe...If you still want to go, we had better get a move on or we're going to look rude," Reg hollered up the stairwell.

"You don't want to look rude, Sweetheart. What will your host think!" A deep voice ribbed her over the line.

She made a disgruntled noise into the phone making Luke laugh. "We'll be there in a few minutes."

"I'll be looking for you," he said with a pleased smile and clicked off the phone.

Reg deliberately squeezed her smaller hand in his as they walked around the side stone pathway of Luke's house toward the din coming from the backyard. The party was obviously well underway.

"They're here!" Zach yelled excitedly as he rounded the house at top speed skidding to a halt near them. "I knew I heard your car. You squealed your tires coming around the curve."

"Zach! I did..." She frowned as she caught the challenging look Reg leveled at her. "All right, they made a little noise. My car needs a brake job."

"Now why would that be, Sid?" a familiar voice joked and they both spun toward the sound.

"Don!" Sidney cried and moved forward to collect a hug. "We didn't expect to see you!"

Don snorted. "I hope not because otherwise the bunch of us might take it personally that the two of you have taken your sweet time arriving," he admonished them with humor-laden tones as they were bombarded by numerous raucous greetings.

"Your mother was getting antsy," Henry's baritone voice rumbled as he clamped a hand on his son's shoulder. "It isn't like the two of you to be so late for a party."

"Dad!" Reg exclaimed with open amazement that grew as he quickly scanned the crowd. Not only were his parents there, so were a number of cops from his precinct interestingly mixed with men from Luke's force. He glanced over at Sidney and saw a similar stunned reaction on her face, by the combination of guests they saw before them. His dark brown eyes flickered over to where Luke stood with Kathleen and when their eyes met, Luke's smile quirked upward ever so slightly.

"Sheriff, does your office have some connections to my personal phone book?" Reg queried sardonically.

"Didn't need it," Luke returned smoothly. The few strategic calls weren't tough to place, Reg, he had found, was well liked. His gaze wandered to the beautiful woman, who remained by the large black man's side. Their eyes caught and he was privately pleased by the heartfelt gratitude in her eyes.

A little while later when Reg was satisfied that Sidney was duly occupied talking to Sandra in the pretty gazebo down the yard, he wove through the crowd calling out friendly greetings to people he hadn't seen for weeks, until he located the officer he wanted most to address. Luke glanced up at his approach and made excuses to disengage himself from his present company.

The two men stood just off to the side, where the woman of their mutual affections was still within sight. "It was a very thoughtful gesture to ask my family and friends to your pig roast today, Sheriff," Reg rumbled cordially, one hand thrust in his pocket, the other holding a beer.

Luke nodded a casual acknowledgment. He didn't want or expect thanks.

"I think it made Sidney more comfortable. I wasn't certain I was going to get her out of the house. The idea of coming seemed to make her strangely nervous," Reg told him.

"Sidney hasn't seen many of these folks since she left home." *Left me.*

"Just coming for holidays doesn't leave a lot of time for socializing," Reg commented.

"She spent most of that time with just the family and Carl and Becca."

Reg studied him now with a frown. "Where were you, Sheriff?"

Luke gave him an expressionless sidelong glance. "Anywhere else. At first, seeing her was pretty much an obsession but it was made crystal clear she wouldn't be in the same room with me. I saw how much Vera, Kathleen and my Dad missed her. When her visits became more sporadic, I decided to stay away completely to ensure she would show up even occasionally."

Reg regarded the lean man beside him keenly. "So when she came home a couple months ago…"

"I hadn't laid eyes on her except in pictures for pretty much ten years," he admitted though it cost his pride.

"What about court appearances for your divorce?"

Luke shifted his gaze purposefully. "There weren't any. It was all handled through correspondence."

"Christ!" Reg expounded. "She shut you out completely. I can't imagine…"

Luke flipped the tab off his beer can. "Believe me neither could I." Time to change the topic for a number of reasons. "But just to set the record straight, I didn't invite your friends and family to make Sidney comfortable. I was relatively certain that within a few moments after arriving, she would be fine. Many of my guests were eager to think they would get to see her again."

Reg turned to him bemused. "Then why bother to invite my folks and friends?"

Luke met and held his gaze. "To express my gratitude that you have kept her safe all these years and taught her to defend herself. I will always hate that she left the way she did, when she did and that my *mother* helped and encouraged her to do it." He blew out a breath. "But I'm damn glad she found you."

Reg stared at him too stunned to respond. After a long moment, he thrust out a large dark skinned hand. Luke gripped it without hesitation. "Your thanks are appreciated, Luke, but not necessary. I was compelled to help Sidney when I met her. She is the most intriguing woman I have ever known."

"You won't get any argument there," Luke agreed. His eyes narrowed suddenly. "Did you just call me by name?"

"I did," Reg replied succinctly.

"You never do that."

"I know," Reg agreed flatly.

"Why exactly?" Luke asked, genuinely interested in the answer.

"Because I might just learn to like you," Reg remarked dryly, smiling as he became aware of Sidney's imminent approach. "Hey Babe. How are Sandra and Jerry managing?"

Sidney slipped into the arm that Reg held up for her and cuddled next to his side to glance between them warily. It had been unnerving enough seeing them shoulder-to-shoulder from the other end of the yard to excuse herself from a gripping conversation with Sandra. "They are holding up fairly well considering there are some babies present." Sidney knew from brutal experience that when you lost your child the world suddenly seemed too full of other people's children. "They have some plans to travel next month which will be a good distraction. I'm glad they came. It's good for them to be among people."

"Are you glad you came?" Luke asked bluntly.

She glanced up with a smile. "Yes as a matter of fact. I am enjoying seeing some people I haven't seen in ages."

"Not as scary as you first thought, Babe?"

She shifted her eyes from one man to the other cautiously. "What have the two of you been talking about over here all alone?"

Reg chuckled and Luke soon joined him, sending her stomach diving. "Worried Sweetheart?"

Unsure of what she felt, Sidney quickly rallied. "What on earth would I have to be concerned about? It is a beautiful summer's day, a pig is roasting on that spit over there, being argued over by Jack and Charlie, I'm surrounded by family and friends..."

"How about us, Babe?" Reg asked jerking a thumb at himself and Luke.

"You two are easy enough on the eyes. You can stay," she added flippantly as she shrugged out of Reg's embrace. "I need to go find Kathleen and make sure she stays out of trouble."

Luke smiled knowingly. "Old habits die hard, eh Sid?"

Her mouth widened into an easy smile. "Something like that."

Reg suddenly felt tension rifle through him at her off the cuff remark. He was becoming increasingly concerned that Kathleen wasn't the only hard habit she didn't know how to break.

Of all places, Kat had to be here, Sidney lamented ruefully. It seemed ironic that the delicate rosebud walls displaying such beautiful family scenes inspired such an onslaught of anxiety. Being here once before had led her to a momentous decision, the consequences of which, she still had yet to face.

Despite the guilt it inspired, Sidney would have rather found Kathleen flirting with Father Pat, the local parish priest, in earshot of school board officials than find her here alone quietly studying portraits.

"Natalie was a gorgeous child, Sidney," Kathleen commented nostalgically into the stillness.

Shaken both by the sentiment and the fact that her sister had noticed her at all, Sidney needed a minute before she could speak. She moved, as if drawn by the sheer magnetism of the pictures, to stand beside Kathleen. Her sister was gazing intently at the family shot of the three of them that she had masterminded. It was eerie that the frenzy of that moment could still be summoned up so easily.

"Sometimes I watch Nicole and feel incredibly sad that she and Natalie don't have each other the way you and I do," Kathleen expressed wistfully.

Sidney laid an arm about her sister's shoulder. "It would have been a little different for them being cousins instead of sisters."

Kathleen leaned her head toward the petite brunette by her side. "I don't know I couldn't feel differently about you if you were merely the girl next door. And for the last decade you sure haven't been easy to entice home."

She felt Sidney stiffen beside her and felt a mild stab of regret at her comment. But not enough to stop.

"I tried, Kat. This was very hard to face," Sidney whispered as she continued to gaze straight ahead at the picture of the two people, who were once her life.

Kathleen ran her free hand over the length of her sister's tumbling hair. "But Sid you never did face it, Honey. You just left it. Left Luke. He has needed you..."

Sidney broke free of her sister's light hold, raising a hand in warning. "Kat...don't! Please. I know I didn't handle the end of my marriage well but I was so broken then. After we lost Natalie..."

Rather than softening, Kathleen dug in like carving a trench needed for war. "And you went to live in that bitch's house away from us. We couldn't even visit you there. It was abundantly clear the sentiments on Virginia Ryan's welcome mat didn't extend to us."

"We came for dinner..." Sidney interjected weakly.

"Barely once a week and then even less thanks to Virginia's manipulation."

Sidney grappled to explain what couldn't be easily rationalized now. Somehow, it had made so much more sense years ago. "Occasions came up that required our presence..."

Kathleen's face contorted with rage. "Virginia strategically kept you from us so that she could crush you."

Sidney felt tears smart behind her eyes and lowered her crumbling gaze to the floor. "And she did. I wasn't strong enough. Luke deserved better. I left so he would be free to find it. To find you if that's..."

Kathleen spun her around and Sidney's eyes jerked up to hers in shock. "Luke doesn't love me as anything but his sister. He never has."

Sidney's eyes grew hard in an instant. "That hasn't always been true, Kat. Years ago..."

"I have never slept with your husband, little sister!" Kat expounded vehemently. as her blue eyes bore into Sidney's. Incensed she had to explain what seemed so obvious though her sister couldn't see it.

"Of course not... not when we were married..."

"Not ever, Sidney! Not while we dated and not since," Kathleen ground out emphatically. She had always known which sister that man had wanted.

Sidney gaped at her and then swallowed hard. "Kat, while you dated Luke you must have..." she began hesitantly.

"Come on to him like I came on to so many guys during that time before I was diagnosed and without lithium. Yeah, I did, Sid. I have eyes. Luke is gorgeous, sexy and an incredible human being to boot. The human being part is what prevented us from having sex. Luke knew something wasn't right. He spurned every attempt I made, until I saw he wasn't really looking at me anymore. Oh, he continued to try and keep me out of trouble but his eyes were on you." Kathleen paused, found herself staring at the small oval of Virginia Ryan. "For a brief time, I was horribly jealous of you. I still believe that is part of what was behind that horrible incident up on the bridge."

Sidney stared both mesmerized and astounded at the turn of this conversation. "Why are we talking about this, Kat? It all happened so long ago."

"Because it still isn't finished. You look like you have moved on. You wear Reg's ring on your finger but what does it really mean? You haven't married him..."

"I explained that. He asked me right before we realized I was pregnant with Lily. I couldn't marry another man under those same circumstances."

"Right. So you were going to do it immediately after her birth..."

Hurt teemed in her eyes at her sister's callous insinuation. "Kathleen, Lily died. It hardly felt appropriate to run out and have a big wedding."

"It didn't have to be big. Reg would have settled for a dozen people in the synagogue. Hell, he would have settled for just you, the Rabbi and a witness to make it God damn legal," Kathleen contended adamantly.

Sidney expelled a staccato breath. "And we're going to do that..."

"*When?* And if you do, what about Luke?"

Sidney gave her head a little shake as if to clear it. "*What about him*?!"

"How fair is it to marry one man when you love another?" Kathleen accused bluntly.

"Kat! For chrissake! Shut up!" she yelled in low frantic conspiratorial tones, grabbing her sister by the shoulders.

Kathleen gave a little hysterical laugh and shook her head at her younger sibling in disgust. "If I do will that make it go away? Hey Sid?" she taunted. "Because I doubt it very much. After all hiding in New York *didn't!* Pretending Luke didn't exist when you graced us with your rare presence here, *didn't!* Figure it out, Sidney. For yourself, for Luke and for Reg." Sidney's eyes narrowed dangerously at the inclusion of Reg. Kathleen saw it for what it was and scoffed. "Yeah, Sidney, for Reg, too. He deserves better than leftovers. Any idiot can see what he feels for you..."

"Yes, and I feel the same way," she ground out between clenched teeth.

Kathleen shook her head with a brittle gaze leveled on her as she moved to leave the room, carefully spacing her final words. "Yes you do. It just happens to be for another man."

Sidney closed her eyes in roiling exasperation as she listened to her sister's footsteps move down the hallway. Her entire body was rigid with indignation as she sank onto the love seat that was one of the few pieces of furniture in this small room filled with haunting visions of her past. Her lower lip quaked and she dissolved into racking sobs. Panic assailed her that she might be heard and rose quickly seeking escape. Sidney stood in wide-eyed alarm trying to think of a place she could go to pull herself together. There was one room that was unlikely to have any intruders. She impulsively slipped inside and closed the door.

Sidney was barely inside before one sweeping glance of the master bedroom renewed her distress to greater proportions. Her weeping became mindless and she sank to the floor near the bed, burying her face in the edge of the bed linens.

Two solid muscular arms closed around her and she shuttered while struggling to break away. "Shhh, Sweetheart. No one knows you are here. Reg is talking with his parents and his lieutenant. Relax. Let me hold you."

Sidney stared up at him with tortured eyes, which she finally squeezed shut and clung to him. "God damned drug holiday," he heard her mutter brokenly into his chest.

"What about it, Sidney?"

"Kat says things. Stupid… utterly stupid things," she mumbled tearfully.

"Want to talk about them?"

She gave him a choked edgy laugh. "Don't think so!" Trying to rise. "I should get back outside before…"

"He's occupied," Luke reiterated firmly, planting his palms on her shoulders.

The resolute tones of his words made Sidney regard him intently for a minute. "Because Kathleen is with him! *She* sent you in here!"

Luke studied her cautiously. "Kathleen told me you were upset and needed me…"

· "I'm going to kill her!" she spewed venomously but his hands held firm despite the furious gaze she pinned him with.

"Why Sidney? From what I have seen in the past few minutes, Kat's right on the money. Besides if you leave *this* room as distraught as you are right now I can guarantee there will be an ungodly up roar."

Sidney rubbed her red swollen eyes with frustration and broke away to flop into an armchair. She instantly realized her mistake. The chair faced the spectacular bed with its massive columns and coupled with Luke's charismatic presence, sensual memories assaulted her savagely.

He followed her tremulous gaze well understanding her discomfiture.

"Try laying in it night after night wondering whether it was all just a glorious dream or not."

She covered her face with her hands in despair. "My life is so messed up. I should have never come back here."

He closed the space between them with stunning speed and framed her face roughly with his hands. "Or maybe you should have never left. Have you ever considered that, Sidney?!"

Confusion claimed her in a sweeping instant. "I love Reg," she murmured with glistening eyes.

"Do you?" Luke asked so softly she had to strain to hear him.

"Yes," Sidney reaffirmed breathlessly.

When his lips plummeted on hers, they were bruising, impatient, teetering on punishing. Slanting and shifting across hers relentlessly until there was no more breath and then no more fight. Only abandon, and a desperate need that was curling out in vicious licks, delivering a swift punch of lust to his groin as her tongue darted into his mouth and slender arms locked about his neck. "Say it, Sidney," he spoke hoarsely into her mouth.

"No," she moaned softly.

"Yes," he demanded savagely and assaulted her senses again with another shattering kiss leaving her limp, pliant. "Admit it," he ground out huskily as her chest heaved.

"I can't," she whispered desolately.

"You can." His hands were in her hair holding her in place. "You do without saying the words," he declared with his lips only a fraction of an inch from hers. Their breath mingled as he spoke.

"Then let that be enough," she pleaded with woeful eyes.

"Until you are mine alone, it will never be enough," he vowed with a tenacity that sent quelling emotions breaking over her as he abruptly broke his hold on her.

"I love Reg," she stubbornly asserted in a raw voice as she fell back into the deep chair.

"That's the crux of the problem, Sweetheart. You can only have one of us."

Defiance surged through her despondency and she sat up in rigidly. "The choice is made. I wear his ring," she spat angrily thrusting her left hand into his face.

Fingers made a skirting pass across her breasts to catch something in his hand tugging her neck. She gulped knowing the diamond pendant she wore on a long chain and rarely if ever took off, was clenched in his fist. "What's this I would like to know?! It looks a hell of a lot like the solitaire that I put on your finger." The realization had clicked for him a couple of days ago after Kathleen made a careless comment. The setting was different and it was around her neck rather than on her finger, where it belonged, but the stone he finally recognized. "The same one I worked two solid months of overtime for."

Her eyes darted guiltily away. She remembered that and loved him for it.

"So you wear mine as well. I remember it brushing against my chest while we made love weeks ago." In an instant, his hand opened, he stood up and swift steps were propelling him to the door. It was either go or throttle her. Just before leaving, Luke spun around and skewered her with blazing hazel eyes. *"And as I recall, the night you laid in my arms in that bed, you weren't wearing his ring! Only mine."*

The door shut with obvious restraint behind him yet the echo of the quiet click reverberated in her mind as she sat stunned and defeated in his room. Woodenly she made her way to the bathroom to splash water on her face. Cold water dripping from her face, she caught sight of the luxurious sunken tub reflected in the mirror. Memories made there riddled her mind despite dire attempts to shut them out. She grabbed at the hand towel near her side, desperate now to compose herself and get out of this torture chamber before she was crazier than her sister.

Kathleen's unsmiling face in the mirror made her jerk knocking a glass from the vanity. Her sister calmly picked it up, unbroken and returned it to the marble counter. "Sidney, I brought your bathing suit. You probably want to change and jump right in the pool. If you are all wet, people will be less likely to notice that you've been crying."

Sidney accepted the bag with outward passivity; grateful yet unwilling to admit to it. "This isn't my suit," she ground out irritably less than a full second later, holding a garment at arm's length as if it was offensive.

"Sure it is. It's the one we bought last week with Auntie," Kathleen replied mildly.

"Kathleen, you dragged us into a place called the Tender Trap. This suit is barely more than a few strings. All it needs is a few tassels and I could gain a whole new profession," she spewed angrily.

"Consider the switch a favor, Sid. Vivian Filmont arrived a while ago and she's wearing an exact copy of your other suit. I hardly think you want to caught in something she is parading around in. She had some enhancement done, you know," Kathleen divulged with a wicked glint.

Sidney's eyes were wild and incredulous. "Kat, at least *I* won't be noticed! All eyes would be on vampy Vivian."

Kathleen smiled as she heard her sister recall the nickname they had given the other woman years ago when they were all teenagers. She put her finger to her tongue and licked it dramatically, stroking the air in a deliberate action. "Precisely." Kathleen turned to go and then seemed to reconsider it. She glanced over her shoulder as she spoke. "You never know a quick swim might help hide some of the whisker burn too," she added smoothly and before Sidney could recover, the bedroom door closed behind her.

Sidney stepped through the French doors that opened onto the flagstone patio, eyeing the diving board like a plank off a doomed ship. In the process, alert eyes caught sight of Vivian's voluptuous figure predictably surrounded by a number of male admirers. The other woman turned as the men who had been fawning over her realigned their gaze. Vivian's glance was murderous as she took in Sidney's entrance.

Sidney squared her shoulders, thrust out her chest and stalked through the thong of people, who seemed to naturally part to let her by. If she was aware of any of the shocked expressions, she didn't let on. Her movements bespoke of the singular purpose of reaching the far end of the pool. She nimbly climbed onto the diving board and sprang forward into a clean arcing dive that ended as her body cleaved through the water causing barely a ripple.

"Was that *our* Sidney?" Hilary Buckman queried with uncertainty.

"Appeared to be. Nothing like the Speedo she wears at the cottage," Henry replied while casting a furtive glance at his son. By the shell-shocked expression on Reg's face, he seemed to agree. A glance in the direction of Sidney's former husband gave Henry to believe the Sheriff had never seen her sporting such skimpy attire either.

As Sidney cut through the water the entire length of the pool in strong clean strokes, Charlie stalked toward the shallow end. "Where in God's name, did you get that suit!?" he thundered as she stood up in the chest high water.

Sidney sputtered slightly, noting his barely leashed fury. Annoyingly, her sister began laughing conspicuously from the other side of the pool. Sidney shot her a quelling glance that she rapidly noted had little to no effect. She privately fantasized about putting lithium salts in her sister's beverage.

"I'm waiting," Charlie yelled.

"Charlie... Dad... I'm thirty one years old!" she hissed softly hoping to avoid a scene though heads were already turning.

Kathleen was doubled over by the side of the pool and Sidney drenched her with one vicious swipe of her arm. Sidney sighed when her sister guffawed swiping a hand over her dripping face, undeterred and unrepentant.

"I don't care how old you are..." Luke's father persisted loudly.

"I bought her the suit, Charlie. Isn't it darling?" Vera purred in melodic tones as she looped her arm through his to draw him away. Charlie growled and cursed beneath his breath. He caught his son's carefully blank expression and narrowed his eyes.

"What do *you* think of her wearing *that*?" he asked bluntly in a loud voice that made Sidney feel like a chastised teenager.

Luke glanced over at the slick wet figure, who was watching him with avid interest. He deftly grabbed a small bottle from a nearby table, smugly noting the blush that was creeping up her neck. "I think some sun screen would be wise. Come on out, Sid and I'll...."

A number of out-of-towners tensed as the formidable figure of a man, they knew well, stood up and with several long strides was at the pool's edge. Reg grabbed the oversized towel that Charlie was clutching and swiped the bottle of sunscreen from Luke only a few feet away. "Thanks Charlie, *Sheriff*. I'll handle it from here. Hey Babe, come on out. You look like you could use a drink along with the lotion."

He wrapped the thick towel about her body before she even cleared the water completely with a cagey smile. His low voice rumbled into her ear alone. "I love that bit of thread you are wearing but in the future, Babe, I wish you would wear it for my eyes alone. My cock is so hard I could drill holes with it."

Sidney's eyes widened and tired to squelch the laughter that gripped her as a deep flush crept into her cheeks. She abruptly choked as her gaze flitted to Luke's stony expression. His eyes were glittering dangerously. Carl suddenly materialized at his side distracting him with something he said. She watched as Luke muttered an answer and then disappeared into the house.

CHAPTER TWENTY-THREE

The pig was roasted a crispy brown and the aroma of it being carved wafted through the line up at the buffet table. Sidney's nostrils flared and her stomach did a little flip-flop that made her want to bare her teeth. A proverbial feast was laid out and she had so many nerves vibrating she couldn't appreciate it.

Her hand snagged Reg's arm. "Reg, your mother doesn't eat pork!" Sidney whispered panicky.

Reg tipped his head. "That's why she's over with the Sheriff."

Her heart sank for Luke. Of course he won't have thought of this. It was the kind of glitch wives took care of. Her eyes widened to see Hilary chatting amicably while Luke took something off the barbecue spit. Her mouth watered as she saw a row of Cornish hens. "Reg, I'll meet you at the table."

She made a beeline for the poultry barely able to maintain civility trying to dodge the people milling about with plates of food.

"Perfect! I've caught you before you ate."

Sidney's lip lifted in an automatic snarl. "Stein, I don't know how you found me but this is a private party."

The sleazy lawyer gave her a haughty smile. "We just need a few moments. Who knows, you may enjoy the festivities more after we've met."

"Doubt it." She stretched out an arm to clear her way.

"Mr. Stein. When I think of someone crashing a party you didn't spring to mind." Luke smiled, protectively flanking Sidney.

"It's a holiday Stein. Go get yourself a room. We can talk tomorrow," Sidney claimed snidely.

Air strangled in his throat. "Does this berg have a five star hotel?"

Sidney's eyes roved mischievously to Luke's. "Would the Rest Easy qualify?"

Luke shrugged. "John's seem to like it."

Stein shifted his briefcase. "We can deal with this expediently."

"Stein it's a national holiday," Sidney ground out. Her gaze strayed to where all but one of the Cornish hens had been snapped up.

The lawyer gave her a placid smile. "Yes and I'm afraid the holiday rate is in effect."

Sidney narrowed her eyes as if sighting a target. "Of course. Well what are trust funds for. I am going to eat first. After seeing you Stein, I never have an appetite."

She was a most tiresome female. Beautiful though. Too bad there wasn't some way to shut her up while a man enjoyed the view. He whiffed the air delicately. "Perhaps some refreshment is called for."

Known to be a consummate host, Luke suddenly felt boorish. "Help yourself to the buffet line, Mr. Stein."

The man angled his head wrinkling his nose at the idea of the lengthy line where he likely would be forced to converse with simple folk. His eyes shifted toward the house and an idea struck. "It's pork. I'm Jewish." He turned his head innocently as if for the first time. "Is that fowl on the spit?"

"What it is, Stein, is my hen."

"Ms. Ryan, I can eat poultry. You can eat anything." His fingers snatched up a plate and sidled toward the barbecue.

Tell her cranky stomach that. "Stein you are becoming foul and I'm not opposed to putting you on a spit."

"Yeah, Sid will do anything once. Ask her about Virginia Ryan's lawn art."

Sidney's mouth opened as her eyes darted to her sister. "Kat, Mr. Stein is a very important attorney. He has no interest in lawn ornaments of questionable taste."

"Ohhh, that is refined, Sid. The night we hauled that ugly bit of junk away you called it far more colorful names."

"Kathleen, go find something to eat," Sidney ground out.

Charlie patted her shoulder in approval. "You were behind swiping that butt ugly statue years ago."

Her gaze wandered to Luke's and was relieved he seemed amused. "I didn't do it while we were married."

Luke snorted barely resisting the urge to scoop her up. "Of course not, Sid. You were a model law abiding citizen."

Her smile grew strained as her tummy rumbled. She really wanted that hen.

· "Ginny Ryan had me all over the county looking for that silly thing that looked like Aunt Jemima. It was heavy as hell, left some deep grooves in the grass," Jack Walden hedged. "Who helped you two girls?"

Sidney wiggled through the crowd to Kathleen's side. "No one." Elbowing her sister. "Right, Kat, *no one.*"

Charlie considered Luke. "Were you in on that?"

"No." He was feeling miffed about it.

Green eyes sparkled as Becca's lips twitched.

Vera gave her neighbor, who had grown up along side her girls, a cagey smile. "How delightful? You did it together!" She frowned suddenly. "Where was I that evening?"

"Auntie!" Sidney cried dismayed. She remembered only too well, where her aunt was and it wasn't for public consumption.

Kathleen felt no such restraint. "Occupied in the pool house Auntie. Besides we had some muscle, it was no big deal."

Sidney kicked her sister's shin. "Leave him out of it. It was my idea..." Her eyes flitted about sheepishly. "Well the stupid thing was commissioned. Virginia had it made to look like Delta on purpose."

"It was you!" Charlie turned on his son.

"No it wasn't," Luke grunted. "I was left out."

"It was me," Carl admitted figuring it couldn't be held against him all these years later. "Rebecca kissed me into it."

Kathleen thrust a fuchsia fingernail toward Luke. "You left yourself out by taking Gloria Bondy to the drive-in to examine her tonsils. You made Sid sad."

Brows lifted. "You cared if I..." How did someone phrase this in public? "Played tonsil hockey, Uncle Luke?" Nicole supplied.

Luke blinked. "Ahhh..."

"Can I eat now?" Stein asked piously.

"Stick a fork in that bird, Stein and..." Sidney broke off aware there were too many lawmen there to issue any kind of a decent threat.

Deep rumbling came from behind her. "Sidney, you promised Judge Claymor you would stop uttering threats." She rolled her eyes and sighed. The hen was as good as gone. "I however made no such promise. Babe, grab your pigeon."

Stein met Reg's toothy grin with beady eyes that fairly glinted violence and he moved off toward the other line. Sidney glanced over to see Carlene helping him find a plate and beverage. "Guess who is kissing ass?"

"Is Stein a free agent?"

"Oh please, Kat," Sidney complained as the thought of anyone coupling with Stein gave her nausea. "I am finally going to get to eat."

"It's almost dusk, Stein. Get on with it," Sidney snarled. She had missed enough Fourth of July fireworks for good reasons. This man wasn't one of them.

"You have to agree to the deal now."

"Why? It is the same deal I turned down last time." Sidney rose shuddering out an exasperated breath. "Stein, I'm well aware that you want this settled so you are well rid of Reg. I don't know exactly what he has on you, only that there is something. Get this. I don't like you." She smiled insincerely. "Hell, you don't like me. However, I've seen you in the courtroom and I recognize your skill there. So, we put up with each other. I won't recant my opinion. Kevin Salenger's son is in danger."

"Stop right there."

She ignored him out of well-formed habit. "It may be rare but Kevin's wife is a text book case of Muchausen Syndrome by Proxy. I don't give one iota how much Cynthia's blue-blooded family is worth. She is going to harm that child and I won't be party to it."

"They raised the figure of the suit."

That tightened her chest but she didn't let it show. "It's only money, Stein. I have spent very little of the trust fund my parents left me when they died."

"If you fight this and lose, you'll never work again in a profession you have excelled at until this situation."

She narrowed her eyes. "Listen you weasel. I made my opinions without knowing who the parties involved were. It was unbiased and accurate."

"And for one child, even if he is in danger, you are willing to throw every penny you have away as well as your career."

Sidney drew a shaky breath. She was willing though she wasn't happy about it. "If that's what it comes to."

Stein tipped his head with a sly smile. The woman should have let him have the Cornish hen. He would have proceeded regardless but he might have finessed the telling. "Do you think your husband will agree? After all his assets could be called into question as well."

Sidney turned from the bookshelf in Luke's study where she had been studying pictures of him with the kids taken through the years. "Stein, Reg and I aren't married yet." Maybe this man hadn't really earned the diplomas on his office walls.

Stein's thin lips curved into a cold toothless grin. "Of course you haven't. Which is a very good thing or we would have another legal dilemma on our hands."

Cold dread was squeezing Sidney's heart. Stein was entirely too pleased with himself. "What are you talking about?"

"Bigamy." Stein extracted some documents from an envelope immensely satisfied with her pallor. "Perhaps you should peruse these."

Luke tapped a foot impatiently. It was close to dusk and he wished Sidney would come back out of the house. He hated the fact that Stein had insisted they meet alone to begin with but he took some solace that Reg had been left out as well. A glance in that man's direction drew his immediate attention.

Reg's head snapped toward the patio doors with instant alarm.

"Babe, what the hell is…"

Sidney slapped him back. She had only one man in her sights now. "Luke Ryan!"

Luke pivoted gaping. He wasn't sure he had ever heard her that incensed and never at him. "Sweetheart…"

The endearment was barely uttered before her small fist solidly connected with his abdomen. "Christ Sid!" he grunted out doubled over, shocked at the strength behind her wallop. Luke had barely straightened when she launched herself upon him with an animalistic growl. It was humbling that for such a difference in their body sizes she knew how to use hers to its best advantage. He staggered backward with a wild armful of enraged woman mindful that the pool was nearby. "Jesus, Sid…" he panted out as the crowd drew back to give them room but close enough for a good eyeful.

"You son of a bitch!" she snarled. It was one endearment that truly seemed apt. "How could you?!" Tousled hair obscured her face but her contempt was visible enough.

"Charlie!" Vera tugged at his sleeve. "We should do something."

"Stay behind me," Charlie ordered his eyes narrowing on the smug expression of the slimy lawyer observing the tense scene from a cautious distance. One glance was a decent gauge as to what had set these early fireworks off.

"We can't just standby and…"

Charlie gave her a meaningful sidelong glance. "Darlin' you did that part already and if my guess is accurate, this is what has come of it."

Vera cringed as Sidney's fist connected with Luke's jaw in a brilliant crack.

"Christ!" Charlie goggled and skewered Reg with an admiring look. "Did you teach her to fight like that?"

"So what if I did?" Reg tossed back, feeling surly knowing he would have to step in soon.

Charlie gave him a brisk nod. "Well my son may not appreciate it at the moment but I'll thank you for both of us. She's no push over."

The crowd gasped as the scuffle neared the buffet table. Reg shook his head as he made his way closer with heavy tread.

Luke stumbled forward blindly intent on getting a hold on her before she could do more physical damage. His reputation was already in tatters from the tittering of the crowd. What really mattered was getting the little hellcat somewhere private to find out what had set her off. His hands locked on her upper arms and he was giving himself a mental pat on the back for subduing her when her knee came up sending him crumpling to his with a groan.

"Let go, Reg," Sidney shouted, squirming wildly, as brawny arms lifted clear her off of the patio. The damned man was on his knees now just where she wanted him. This was no time to get detained. "Put me down God dammit," she spat as her mouth opened intent on biting his meaty forearm.

"Try it, Babe, and so help me you'll be over my knee," Reg warned her fatefully.

Her mouth closed with a click of teeth knowing the man was as good as his word. Her red haze of temper almost had her forgetting his recent injury. Reminding herself grimly that this was not his battle, she ordered herself to capitulate. "Let me go."

"Not until you cool off," he growled into her ear aware that some of mad seemed to be waning. Lord, it was a grounding to see that she had this much emotion for the Sheriff even if it was hazardous to his health.

She stilled in his hold knowing only too well struggling was pointless. "I'm cool, Reg. Let go."

He grabbed her chin to pin down her gaze and stare meaningfully into it. "Pull another punch and we're gone," Reg pledged thinking otherwise she would likely end up in a cell. He released her and watched with interest as she shook him off, straightened up and raised her chin with dignity though her body still vibrated with potent fury.

"Sidney," Luke said in the same controlled tone he would use as a hostage negotiator despite the pain in his groin that would make his eyes cross if he gave in. "Obviously we need to talk." She eyed him with hostile insolence not caring an avid crowd of more than a hundred looked on as he struggled to his feet with Carl's help.

She brushed off the grass that was on her light linen slacks like she was alighting from a picnic blanket. "A lovely gathering, Luke."

His throbbing head shot up at her stiffly polite remark. With aplomb, he decided to match it. "It was wonderful of you to come." He swiped at the blood trickling from his lip.

She nodded curtly, brushing tangled hair away from her face. "I apologize for not pulling my weight."

He squinted his good eye, the one she hadn't poked with a well-aimed elbow. "I felt your weight, Sweetheart. Every ounce." The crowd, who had watched their brawl with keen interest, began to snicker at this bizarre twist.

Sidney drew a big breath and looked him straight in the eye. "Well in all fairness the party planning should have been more evenly shared."

Some glimmer of where she was headed started to tweak Luke's befuddled brain but her step forward kept him busy cautiously retreating.

"Don't worry about the preparations. I hire out."

Her smile was coy and hackles rose on his neck. What could be more dangerous than an agreeable woman who had just pummeled you into the dirt? "Oh but I do worry," she told him silkily.

He drew back vigilantly as she began to flutter her lashes. One delicate hand, that he now knew could effectively snap his head back, reached toward him. He couldn't decide if he felt more foolish that she had given him a decent tussle on the ground or that now a mere sweet glance had him wanting to cringe. He forced himself to remain outwardly docile but his eyes were heedful of her hand as it smoothed the torn pocket on his shirt.

"There are certain things that a man should be able to expect."

"Oh?" To be beaten up after a fine supper, he wondered, in front of spectators.

"Yes," she fairly purred. "And had I known I would have never shirked my duties but you see I had no idea."

"No idea?" he echoed astute enough to realize that invisible jaws of a trap were snapping around some vital part of him. Just what remained to be seen.

She raised up on her toes like she might press a kiss to his lips. "None whatsoever."

This method, he hastily concluded, was more lethal then violence. She was planning to arouse him publicly. Her fingertips were gliding up and down his chest as she lowered her lashes at him. "Sidney."

Her hand threaded through his hair. "In order to do what's expected of her, a woman really needs to know when...."

"When..." She was drawing him mindlessly in to what all logic told him was a very sticky web.

The hand in his hair fisted around a generous clump of hair to pull while the other one shoved hard against the chest. "When their fucking divorce hasn't gone through!"

She whirled to stomp through the crowd that was reeling with shock but he was on her like fly paper. His own temper hazing his vision, blocking out the occasion, his guests, until there was only her and this time he had no intention of letting her get away.

A steely hand clamped down on his shoulder. "Let her go, Luke."

His lip lifted in a savage baring of teeth. "Not this time." Though the fact Reg had called him by name stole some of the edge of his animosity.

"I've spent years butting heads with her..."

"I don't want to hear about your years as her lover for chrissake."

Reg tilted his head. "I won't tell you then though it would be only about three."

"Three what?"

"Years. We were just roommates before that."

Luke could only stare. "Roommates? As in dating other people?"

"Well I dated plenty. Sidney just went to school and worked hard."

Why was he just hearing this now and from this man of all people?

Reg could see the shock and still wasn't entirely sure why he had volunteered that. Probably because the man had just had his personal business brutally displayed. "Let me talk to her. The two of you can finish this another time when she is less likely to draw a weapon."

Luke lifted a hand in defeat. What other choice did he reasonably have with a house full of guests? He turned around and faced the crowd. "I guess it's time for the fireworks."

Charlie walked toward his son and although he wasn't a man prone to displays of affection, put an arm around his shoulders. "I think you covered those, Son, but we could grab a stiff drink and watch some pretty colors in the sky."

Luke chuckled, grimacing as pain sang up his jaw to pound in his head and gratefully accepted the liberally poured glass Carl pressed into his hand.

"Refills are on the house," Carl told him and jerked his head toward Stein. "But drink slow. I need a few moments to put out the trash."

Reg saw her sitting on the curb and his heart softened. She looked miserable staring upward as brilliant colors burst against the night sky, and terribly alone.

He lowered himself to the spot beside her, praying he would be able to get back up when the time came. They sat for a long moment both watching the fireworks display saying nothing.

"Well that was mature of me," she finally said.

He couldn't have suppressed the gales of laughter if he tried. "Did you shoot out his tires before you left?"

She smiled. "No. I need to save a little something for tomorrow."

Their heads tipped toward one another and hers found his shoulder. "Will that be before or after you eat crow?"

Her head jerked up. "What?"

"Babe, did you ever meet the man in court?"

Her eyes lowered to the ground she couldn't see in the dark.

"Did you ever sit with him to discuss the end of your marriage?"

She sighed grumpily. "I asked Vera to help with the paper work."

"Sounds fair." The economical reply was liberally infused with sarcasm.

"Reg..."

He levered himself up with an effort. It had been a long day and it was disturbing that he could more easily feel for her husband's side than hers. "Fix it,Sidney."

CHAPTER TWENTY-FOUR

Waiting was never easy especially when it involved humbling yourself, but she did it just the same. Timing was everything today. When she entered the police station, the squad room was buzzing. One sight of her standing in the doorway brought a hush worthy of a funeral. She had been prepared to walk through it but when he strolled out of his office with several files in his hand, another idea struck.

Luke halted abruptly at the sight of a woman he hadn't dreamed would seek him out. He had already decided to stop at Vera's after work and do what had to be done. He wasn't particularly looking forward to it but he was resigned. Seeing her there, looking so delicate dressed in a butter yellow summer blouse and navy slacks with sandals, stopped him cold. Surely, this couldn't be the same woman who had wrestled him to the ground yesterday?

He was just standing there. Staring and for all her professional skills at gauging people's reactions, she didn't have a clue. Not that it truly mattered, Sidney told herself sternly, she knew what had to be done.

"A lot of things about a person change over ten years," she began softly not quite prepared yet to meet his eyes so she gazed at his chest instead. "I have developed a rather nasty temper." Drawing in an unsteady breath, she raised her chin so their eyes met. He deserved that. "I shouldn't have used it on you. And I shouldn't have done it at your home."

Luke knew he needed to say something, but for a long moment, he could only continue to stare. He knew what time it was and that she did as well. She had purposely come to this very public place during shift change when the greatest number of his staff would be in and rather than seeking the privacy of his office, she was apologizing to the room at large. Digesting all of that, the words came easy then. "Technically, my home is your home."

She nodded as either worry or regret seemed to flicker in her eyes. "We have some things to work out."

"What's in the bag?" he asked quietly.

She blinked blankly at him having forgotten about the little paper bag though her fingers were blanched as they curled around it. "Oh. Muffins."

"What kind?"

"Carrot."

His mouth quirked to one side. His favorite and a variety she hadn't made since coming home. "Are they for anyone in particular?" His gaze swept the room beginning to warm to this conversation. "Dennison?"

Her lips twitched. "They are meant for you but you may want Dennison to try one first."

Dennison sat at his desk rigid and growing increasingly uncomfortable, his eyes darting about the room. He may have fantasized about the petite beauty before but after yesterday he decided that she was more than he dare take on. Jack smacked him companionably between the shoulder blades.

"Yeah Dennison. That would be a good job for you. Checking the Sheriff's food before he eats it."

"Why? Her brownies were good enough. Those are likely edible," he stammered wishing the attention in the room elsewhere.

Sidney's lips curved with chagrin. The naïve rookie was out of the loop. "For poison Dennison."

The young cop wheezed in a breath.

Luke smiled at her outward composure. She was swallowing her pride like a pro. He walked toward her noting now that her posture was stiff. Her tension fairly vibrated. He took her free hand in his and felt his ego expand feeling the dampness there. He lifted her hand up to shoulder level and studied it at length, turning it over in his. "Amazing."

Mortified that he might notice the tremble, she ordered herself to relax. "What?"

"That these small elegant hands can pack such a wallop."

She put her tongue to her cheek. "It helped that you didn't fight back."

He fought back more than he cared to admit. "Reg teach you those moves?"

She nodded. "He's the original drill sergeant."

"You must have been an enthusiastic pupil."

She rolled her shoulders relieved that quiet conversations were renewing themselves in the room. "We should probably have a conversation soon and see if we can't tidy up our loose ends," Sidney proposed demurely.

"I'm free now." He saw the panic and heard the soft whirl of her thoughts so he tucked her hand in his arm decisively and steered them toward his office. "Julie hold my calls until my wife and I are through please."

Jack and Carl shared a communicative glance as the door closed behind them. "That took guts."

Carl nodded in agreement though he wasn't sure if Jack referred to Sidney coming to the lion's den or Luke referring to her publicly as his wife.

"You didn't have to do that."

They stood three feet apart baffled by the statement they had spoken in unison.

A slow grin spread across Luke's face steeped with enough satisfaction he could overlook the discomfort of his jaw. He leaned back against his desk stretching his legs in a lazy stance and enjoyed the view. "Your coming here meant something Sidney."

She wasn't sure what to do with herself in the small space, so she moved to stare out the window. "It was the least I could do. You are a public figure and I made a spectacle last night," she glanced over her shoulder. "You didn't have to ask me in here. I'm sure you have things to do…"

"Yes I do," he spoke over her. "I need to talk to my wife."

Sidney shuddered out a breath. "I think we need to make an appointment with a lawyer, maybe two, and sit down and figure out what needs to be done. I have Stein though I would rather not use him." The man found far too much glee in ending something that had been precious to her.

"Then don't."

His tone had her turning around. "Do you have someone in mind?"

It was hard not to rush his fences when it had taken so long just to get to the damned gate. "I have something in mind," he corrected and her apprehension fairly hummed. "Sidney, why were you so angry last night?"

She blinked at him, opening her mouth to speak though the words won't come for a minute. "I was shocked. I assumed that our divorce was final, the final decree had been granted."

"But you never asked for it. You didn't attend one divorce proceeding, not one meeting between our lawyers about property…"

"We had so little then. There was not much to…."

It was hard not to take her words personally. As far as he was concerned they had more in those days of being a broke young couple, then he had since inheriting his mother's large estate. "Do you know I changed my tie four times before one of the meetings with the lawyers just hoping you might show?"

She bit the inside of her cheek. The man knew how to aim a slingshot directly at her heart.

"But like all the others you didn't show. So, I stopped the proceedings thinking you would restart them and agree to come to the table. Sidney I needed you to come to sit in the same room so I could at least understand why the best part of my life was sliding away like an avalanche."

Fix this. Fix this. Fix this. Reg's economic advice was a chant in her head but the problem was so huge. She couldn't fix it years ago and it wasn't any easier now. "So when I didn't restart things…"

"I waited. And I'm still waiting." He moved closer, now more confident that he could, but after last night, he wasn't fool enough to touch. "Sidney, look at this from my perspective just once. One night you were in our bed. Loving me with your hands, your body, your *mouth*...." He paused pleased to see her eyes glaze over knowing that she was recalling the event with the same clarity. "I went off to work the next morning, exhausted but more hopeful than I had been in months that we could heal the pain of losing our baby." He did touch then just with two fingers to tip her chin up so their eyes met. "That we could start again...but I came home to find a pathetically simple note where you should have been. My mother was in her glory. I thought after all the years of animosity between them, Charlie might actually hurt her and ruin his life and career over it."

Sidney closed her eyes. The repercussions of her actions were more widespread than she had ever wanted to fully admit.

"I left them in Jack's hands to referee and ran to Vera's. I didn't trust myself to drive. I told myself a brisk walk would help me clear my head but before I knew it, I was running. Somehow, it seemed that if I went fast enough I might be able to catch up with you...go with you. Because Sidney if all you needed was to leave town and start over, I could have done that. I would have done that. I don't particularly like big cities but if it was what you needed...."

"Please stop."

"I can't. I have saved this up."

Yes, he had. She could see that now and it could no longer be explained away.

"I found Vera in the pool house. She was waiting for my father. I know you have never understood what is between them. That it never seemed right to you but there is love there. Strong and enduring. Perhaps not sanctioned by any church or court but it is there just the same. I could tell by the little table set for dinner that they were celebrating. My optimism during the day had obviously rubbed off on my Dad."

She could envision it all too clearly. Vera standing by the china service in a frilly blouse and a sentimental smile waiting for a man she couldn't be seen with in public.

"She knew immediately when I burst in that something was wrong and Sidney when she read your note, she cried. Not the way Vera cries over a silly plot line. I heard her heart break and with it mine." He shuddered as the memory swam back as clear as yesterday. Vera sobbing in his arms babbling about Virginia finally taking what mattered.

His hand moved to cup her cheek stealing what was left of her breath. "And it never got better because you wouldn't see me or talk to me in any meaningful way. My mother stipulated that when she helped you leave, didn't she?"

Sidney hesitated to answer. It seemed wrong even now to incriminate the dead.

"Didn't she?!"

The sudden furious rise in his voice coupled by his hands digging into her shoulders made her jolt. "Yes. Virginia wrote the note, I only copied it. She said more didn't need to be said to make a clean break. I agreed because I wanted what I believed was best for you."

"You are what's best for me. We don't need to make any appointments with lawyers to tell us what needs to happen next. We know." Luke saw the confusion swirling in her eyes. "We admit that we made a mistake...."

"You're right. We can be mature and civilized about this entire situation. Cooperate with the attorneys..."

Luke shook his head at her misconception of his intentions. "We can admit we love each other...that we never stopped and remained what we are...married."

For one bright sparkling moment, it seemed that she could reach out and grab what he offered. Reality butted in ruthlessly. "Luke, it is time for me to grow up and honor the commitments I have made. I made a pledge to Reg..."

His voice was raw and rough. "You made vows with me. *First.*"

"Don't you see, Luke? Don't you know through all of this what I have become?"

He blinked at her blankly, his lips slightly parted.

"I bore another man's child while I was married to you! I sat down with our Rabbi and professed my love and life to a man, who has repeatedly saved me....cherished me!" Silent tears traced down cheeks that seemed as fragile as fine porcelain. "I love Reg."

"He took my place," Luke ground out vaguely aware that his fingers were digging into her arms.

"He made his own place." The words were harder, even harder than she might have expected, to say.

Luke averted his eyes and nodded his understanding but thought it was high time she faced reality. "Loving your best friend is not necessarily being in love... it doesn't necessarily make your best friend marriage material..."

"You're wrong," she said tightly, reverently wishing her own words didn't sound so forced.

"You love me, Sidney. *I feel it,*" Luke decreed like he was reciting a sacred vow. "And what's more, maybe we need to put a few things out on the table about that man you live with."

Sidney went board stiff. She had still held out some futile hope that Reg could remain out of this mess.

"Has it ever occurred to you that despite our obvious physical differences, Reg and I share a number of similar characteristics?"

She studied the pattern of the floor tiles.

"We're both cops."

"Coincidental."

"We're both devoted to you and want children with you."

"So do most men." Annoyed at his over generalization, she inadvertently tossed out one of her own and was startled by his shout of laughter.

"Well, Sweetheart, your ego has finally blossomed. And you are right, any man would have to be an idiot not to want what you could offer..."

Her teeth clicked together. "That's not what I meant!"

He waved away her indignant response. "Have you ever noticed that Reg and I just about echo each other sometimes?"

She had noticed that disconcerting fact during Reg's first phone call the night she arrived in town. "I often thought the two of you would make good friends," she said very quietly.

"Yeah, if we didn't kill one another over you first!" Luke retorted cynically.

"I'm going to marry him," she told him, forcing herself to look him straight in the eye.

"You are married to *me*!" Luke declared pointedly.

"Stein may be working that out even as we speak," she said though she didn't really have a clue.

"Don't think so," he said with confidence remembering the few parting words of advice he had given the slim ball last night.

She gifted him with a grounding glance. "While you may be the head honcho in Barren's Creek, Stein still answers to Reg."

"We'll see," Luke returned mildly. "Irreconcilable differences is no longer grounds in this state."

"Adultery is."

"Charming, Sweetheart!" he clipped caustically.

"Merely the truth."

He pinned her down with hooded eyes. "Whose will you use? Mine or yours?"

"Take your pick. It hardly matters now although it bears stating that at least when I was committing adultery I didn't know it!" she replied defensively feeling spent in every sense of the word. The hurt she felt knowing he had been with other women was irrational perhaps but also very deep.

This was getting them nowhere so she made the unilateral decision to head for the door. Her hand on the knob, she paused and turned to see his eyes trained on her. "Our marriage up until we lost Natalie made me beyond happy but it is ludicrous to think that after all this time we can recreate that. Maybe Nat was largely responsible and God knows we can't ever change what happened to her. What exists between us right now, Luke, is wrong." She paused to lick her lips but his eyes never left hers. "I have become a woman without honor. You seek me out at every turn. You kiss me with no regard for my commitments to another man until I can't think straight to protest. I need to set things right in my life. The sooner the better for all of us." Without another word, she quietly left the room.

Her eyes self-consciously flitted around the squad room. The few cops that were still present hastily busied themselves and averted their gazes. She was half way across the room when his low solemn voice startled her to a dead stop.

"You have more honor than any woman I have ever known," Luke declared meaningfully from his rigid stance in the doorway.

Sadness rippled through her before she carefully masked it. She turned back to face him, vividly aware that while the men in the room may not be looking directly at them, they were undoubtedly listening. Intently.

"Then Luke, I feel obliged to tell you that you need to get out more." She paused briefly to lower her eyes as his expression turned cold. "For the sake of your reputation though, wait until we work out the paper trail."

Luke maintained his silent vigil in the doorframe until she was out of sight. Mindful of the concerned gazes, he felt obliged to make some kind of statement. "I apologize for the disruption. My wife and I have a few *wrinkles* to work out."

Sidney fumbled with her keys through the blur of tears. In her distress, they slipped out of her hand to fall on the pavement. She choked back a sob and crouched to retrieve them only to jump backward with a hand to her chest when Carl suddenly appeared in her field of vision.

"Shit, Carl! Can't you cops learn how to make some fucking noise when you approach someone you aren't trying to lock up!"

He smiled warmly and laid what he hoped was a comforting hand on her shoulder. "You did good in there, Sidney. Coming in can't have been easy."

"Nothing seems to be easy these days."

He squeezed her shoulder. "You will work things out."

She rose to gaze intently into his concerned face as he dropped the keys into her palm. "Tell me you didn't know."

"Sidney…"

She pulled her composure together with an effort. "Would you have said anything before I married Reg? Or would you have just sat in the synagogue and let it happen?"

He wished he had an answer to give her. "Sidney, I…."

She heard enough to knock him aside with one hand so she could stick her key into the lock. Before getting in, she looked him straight in the eye one last time. "Tell Becca to come see me some time at Vera's."

Carl sighed knowing that inferred she would no longer be frequenting their home. "Sid…" He almost gave into a reckless attempt to repair damage that wasn't truly his.

"Save it, Carl," she told him feeling incredibly used up and sped away squealing her tires.

The grilled steak, corn on the cob and salad should have been more appealing given that she had barely eaten all day. Instead, the aroma of the meat was inspiring her stomach to do interesting little dives and rolls. It took every ounce of willpower not to push the plate away except that she needed it as camouflage. Toying with her food gave her something to do and given the glower Charlie had settled upon from the instant the meal began, it was necessary.

"Aunt Sid? Aunt Sid?" Zachary frowned eyeing the corn on her plate slathered with butter and without a nibble in it. "Aunt Sid!"

She swung her head toward her nephew. "Zachary! Whatever it is, you don't have to shout!"

Kathleen wrinkled up her face. "Maybe he does, little sister. That's the third time he's tried to get your attention." She smiled at her son, knowingly. "Go ahead, Zach. Sid isn't going to eat it."

Sidney watched a little indignantly as the cob of corn slid from her plate straight to her nephew's nimble teeth. "Well, I might have gotten to it." Zach stopped nibbling mid row. "No, it's fine, Zach. Go ahead."

"Maybe if you had less guilt weighing down your conscience you might feel like eating some food rather than just playing with it," Charlie contended accusingly.

Sidney lowered her gaze once more wishing she had made it back to the house in time to catch Reg before he went out *exploring* according to Delta. Sounded more to Sidney that the man just had the good sense to know when to vacate a building before an imminent explosion. If Charlie was aware of her trip to the police station, he sure wasn't letting on or judged it too little, too late.

"She hasn't eaten all day either," Charlie muttered meaningfully.

Sidney sighed wearily. Fatigue seemed to have sprouted hands and planted them firmly on her shoulders weighing her down. "I'm sure Delta could make up a tray..."

"That isn't Delta's place!" he roared slamming a fist onto the table making the place settings jump.

Sidney shook her head in roiling frustration. "So whose bloody place is it? I seem to need a score card in this damned house."

"Don't you start cursing at this dinner table, gal."

"Why? You do!" Sidney shouted back. The anger that had dulled down to a simmer after last night was rapidly recouping to a rolling boil.

"I live here. You are a guest," Charlie yelled wishing the ugly words back when her face fell.

The direct hit was so well aimed, Kathleen saw and felt guilty over it. "Charlie... that's not fair."

He leapt to his feet now shoving back his chair, ignoring that it toppled backward causing the kids mouths to fall open at the level of his fury. Charlie was often blustery but tonight he was furious. "She took you into her home. She took you into her heart when your folks died in that car crash. I remember how little you were, gal. Little and shy. Vera let you sleep in her bed most nights for a whole year rather than alone in that pretty room she made up for you. You wiggled into her heart and sank in your teeth. Well that was just fine. It was even fine when on your high school graduation we find out you are expecting. Did your Auntie rant and rave at you? No! She held you while you threw up in the mornings, took you to buy pretty maternity clothes out of town where you wouldn't hear gossip."

"Charlie please...."

"I'm not done!" he yelled with blazing eyes that had her weakly sinking back into her seat. "And on that horrible day when you found little Natalie, whose arms did you cry in?"

Her mouth worked as hot tears sparkled in her eyes. "Charlie, I haven't done anything. I didn't yell at her even though it obvious Auntie knew Luke and I were still married."

"No you haven't. Well maybe you should."

She threw up her hands unable to see his point or even if there was one. "Maybe I should what? Scream at her?"

"If that's what you need to do. Yes."

She gaped at him for a moment utterly lost. "What would be the point?"

His fingers uncurled from where they had clenched the edge of the table as he sat down on the chair he righted with a thud. "At least then it would give her something to work with. Right now she's sick with worry that you'll say nothing, pack your things and go." He watched her frown and leveled her with a look. "You have been known to do it before."

She rose from the table as the exhaustion tightened its grip, leaving the room with a heavy sigh to head up the stairs.

"You could have taken it a little easier on her Charlie," Kathleen complained. "She had a shock yesterday."

"Well that's the whole point." Charlie saw her arched brows. "Sidney isn't known to cope well with shock. I think a firm hand is called for."

Her heart loosened at the cantankerous man her aunt loved beyond what made sense and smiled sadly as he stomped out. She turned to see Zachary putting the half eaten cob back on his aunt's plate.

"She might get hungry later." He wrinkled his nose. "I don't like when Charlie acts mean to her."

Kathleen smiled and angled her head to see that her daughter was deep in thought. "What do you think Nicole?"

"I think Charlie's scared," she said.

Kathleen reached out to run a hand over her daughter's shining hair. "I think you are very smart."

"Aunt Sid won't really go. Not yet. Will she?" Zach asked rapidly with wide eyes.

His mother shook her head. "No Zach. Aunt Sid has a few things to work out but I don't think she'll leave." *I'll stop her first.*

Leaving was looking good as Sidney peeked through the crack of her Aunt's bedroom. There was a book in her lap but Vera's gaze was too remote to be reading it. A tray of supper sat on the table beside her and it was as untouched as her own downstairs.

Before she could knock, Vera mysteriously turned toward the door. "Sidney?"

Caught, she pushed the door open. "You haven't eaten your supper."

Vera shrugged fending off the disappointment. Delta had sent her up for the tray. "I was too caught up in my reading I'm afraid."

Sidney sat on the edge of the bed where she could face the wing back chair Vera occupied a few feet away. "What's happening in the book?"

Vera opened her mouth and let her imaginative mind churn. Surely, she could come up with something to say. It need not be accurate.

Sidney reached across and took the novel out of her loose hold. "Decent author," she said turning the book over in her hands. "Not as good as you of course Auntie. Is she a friend?"

"Well yes. We speak occasionally on the phone and if I can ever convince Charlie that puzzles pack, well we might go for a visit. She lives in San Francisco."

"And she counts on your opinion?"

Shadows crossed Vera's eyes. "I suppose."

"The way you used to count on mine."

Vera smiled then remembering. "Perhaps not that heavily."

"I counted on you heavily. Didn't I? Too heavily." Sidney set the book aside and took one of her aunt's soft hands in both of hers. "I had no right to ask you to be responsible for my divorce. If I wanted one, I should have shown up and been present at the proceedings myself."

"I wouldn't have let you and Reg get married, Sidney. I would have stepped in first and explained but you didn't have a date and up until this trip, I knew nothing of a ring," Vera needed to say and felt better for it.

Sidney sighed and pursed her lips in thoughtful silence. Nothing was ever rushed in this room. "I made a mess out of things."

Vera joined her on the bed and drew her close. "Honey, sometimes things have to get messy before you can clean them up."

Sidney laughed. "That sounds like something you might get out of a fortune cookie."

Vera giggled. "Close. Charlie says it."

Sidney jiggled her brows. "Charlie says a lot of things."

Vera tipped her pretty face so she could get a good look. "Charlie's scared you are going to leave."

Sidney was already shaking her head. "Not this time. I have to stay and see this through for all of us."

Vera relaxed beside her. A great deal of the heady anxiety that had made her chest feel tight through the day was loosening now. "I think that sounds like Reginald downstairs." She cocked her head and fought back amusement. "And Luke."

"Together?" Sidney sputtered leaping from the bed to scramble toward the door.

"Sidney Ryan!"

For one frantic second, she turned back.

"You play nice with those boys and keep your hands in your pockets."

Sidney giggled and dutifully made a show of putting her hands deep into trouser pockets.

CHAPTER TWENTY-FIVE

She stopped halfway down the last flight of stairs. Reg and Luke sat at the long kitchen table with stacks of books in several piles between them. Delta placed a platter of sandwiches on top of one pile and turned back to the kitchen island to pour iced tea.

"What are you two doing?"

Two heads looked up with casual smiles. "I went to the library to do some more research on Munchausen By Proxy and I ran into your husband doing the very same thing. So I suggested…"

Sidney blinked open mouthed. "What did you call him?" God she felt lightheaded.

Her hearing was acute as usual, Reg noted. He stood up to meet her at the base of the stairs. "I called the Sheriff exactly who he is for the time being, your husband." Reg angled his head. "It is time we started looking at things just the way they are and dealing with them."

"We thought it might be good to start with the case against you," Luke said evenly taking a bite out of a sandwich, wincing when his jaw complained.

Sidney sighed disgustedly. She wandered over to the refrigerator and Reg took it as a sign to sit back down. Minutes later as she neared the table, Reg pulled the chair beside him out for her. His eyes shifted to see her sit next to the man she had married years before and press something against his face.

"Hell Sid. That's cold."

She held the ice to his jaw just the same with a sweet smile. "Oh, don't be such a baby. This will make it feel better."

"Doubt it," he grumbled. It didn't really hurt there despite the swelling and redness. He had *referral pain*. The kind she clearly wasn't going to do anything about.

"Anything else that needs attention, Sheriff? Sidney only has two hands but I bet Carlene would be more than…"

Luke slanted the larger man with a look. "I thought we had an agreement."

Sidney shuddered beside him. "What agreement?"

Reg laughed at her dismay. "To act civilized and incidentally that includes you." His index finger stabbed the air in a parental gesture. "Hands off."

She drew her hand away that held the ice to Luke's face. He pulled it back. "Only the ones balled into hard little fists, Sweetheart."

She fluttered her lashes coquettishly. "Auntie already told me to play nice."

Reg grinned rolling his eyes devilishly. "That could imply a lot. I picked up Vera's new novel last night." He shrugged. "Couldn't sleep." Really couldn't sleep after knocking back a few chapters. The pages fairly steamed. What he couldn't figure this morning was why Charlie seemed so crotchety when he cozied up to that woman at night.

"Tell me about it later will you so I can say something about it to…" She swallowed as Reg pinned her with a look.

"Read it yourself Babe. Consider it part of cleaning house," Reg decreed in steely tones.

Luke flipped through a book in front of him as he circumspectly listened to their banter. He frowned down at the material at hand. Mothers intentionally harming their own children for attention. Sidney would have died for Natalie. It was brutally unfair.

Sidney offered Luke a sandwich but he waved it away. "Does your face hurt that much…"

Luke looked up to see both of them watching him. "No. This material ruins my appetite."

Sidney nodded with a sad smile. "Me too. Even though it isn't the same thing, it reminds me of Natalie."

Reg watched as hands linked on the table. It was such a spontaneous movement he wondered whether they were even conscious of it. "Kathleen told me you found her, Sidney."

Sidney nodded grimly as she stared at her hand in Luke's and tugged it away guiltily.

Reg made a noise low in his throat. "It's an awful sight."

They both turned to look at him. "What do you know about it?"

"Been first on the scene a couple of times. Poor babies look like they have been at war in their own beds. Huddled and tangled in their blankets. One sad little thing I found was clutching his blankets so tight like he had been having a nightmare. The first time I saw a case with all the bloody fluid in the mouth and nose, I thought the baby had bled to death."

"Natalie didn't look like that."

Reg's head snapped to Sidney's. She was quaking with fright like a small child. "Babe, you need to drink something. You are as white as a sheet."

Desolate brown eyes lifted to Luke. "I told you she looked like I had just put her down. It's so wrong. None of it fits." She shoved at a stack of the big books in exasperation sending them tumbling to the floor. "Nothing in these damned books explains why we don't have our daughter!"

"Maybe it doesn't fit because it hurts too much for it to fit," Luke suggested though he was hard pressed to believe that himself. He pushed out his chair and lifted her into his lap. He expected resistance but instead she burrowed against the same chest she had pummeled only the night before.

It was comfort, Reg told himself and with an effort sat still. "What did the autopsy show?"

Sidney lifted her eyes to Luke. She had never heard the results. At the time she had been too naïve to ask.

"There wasn't one."

"Excuse me," Reg gawked. "Are there different rules in backwoods towns?"

Luke's mouth flattened as he felt tension stiffen the woman in his lap. "Rules are bent occasionally. Natalie was the granddaughter of the longtime Sheriff and I was a cop as well. Everyone knew Sidney was a loving doting mother. It seemed like a further cruelty. The coroner agreed to the gesture."

"Who suggested it?"

"My father."

Sidney scrambled to her feet. "Charlie? Charlie did that? Why? We had nothing to hide."

Luke took both her hands. "Sidney, he was worried for you." Her eyes narrowed intently. "You frightened him that day."

She released an anguished sound and turned away.

"Frightened Charlie? The man who spits tacks at the breakfast table?" Reg spewed incredulously.

"Reg." Her tone had him giving notice. He knew it and never liked what came after it. "I was very upset when I found Natalie." She put her tongue to her lips for a second. "I was even more upset when I realized they were going to take her from me. I crushed her against me and threatened to jump out of the attic window."

Reg dragged a hand over his face and Luke could have sworn the man paled. He gathered her close in those massive arms and rocked. "Sidney....Oh God..."

She tipped her face up toward him. "I'm sorry. I'm so sorry this brings it all back."

He released her, nodding bleakly and looked around. "Does Vera keep anything in the house stronger than sherry?"

Luke rose and retrieved some Jack Daniels to pour it into a tumbler. He grabbed a second glass, judging he would need it as he watched the massive man take big swallows of the potent liquor. "Sidney, why do I think I'm going to want this?"

She glanced between the two men. Luke watched as something meaningful passed between his wife and the large man before she turned to him decisively. "I tried to hurt myself after we lost Lily last year."

His jaw, he discovered, hurt like a bitch when it fell open. "What?"

"I was in a very bad way. I went back to work quickly and all of this happened with the Salenger baby. Reg had taken time off but in order to not blow his cover he really needed to spent a lot of time away from home." Seeing his guilt, she sent him a tender smile. "Reg, I am responsible for what I did."

He held up two large hands. "We've been over this, Babe. You can't absolve me of my guilt."

She agreed. "No. Only you can and you should. After all I wouldn't be here if you hadn't followed your instincts and come home."

"You found her."

Reg nodded as he shuddered. The moment, the horror of it, would be with him forever. "I was barely three hours into my shift and something just wasn't right. I left without even telling anyone."

Black rage settled over Luke's features. "Who knew about this?" When Sidney shrunk away, he had his answer. "My Dad? Kathleen? Carl?" He was pacing the length of the kitchen in fury. "*Carl knew!*"

"Everyone knew," Reg said quietly. "I needed everyone to make sure it wouldn't... couldn't happen again."

Luke marched forward to where the man stood separating him from Sidney and rapped him hard on the chest. "Well, not everyone knew. I sure as hell didn't know!"

Reg buried any urge he had to fight back, surprised it was not as difficult as it might have been weeks before. This man was incensed because he cared. It was a hard thing, Reg discovered, to hold against him. He searched for something to say and was mildly surprised to see the other man slam out of the kitchen.

Reg turned around to see Sidney, pale and drawn, staring after him. "You don't think he'll get in a car like that."

Sidney shook her head. "That isn't where he's going."

Luke didn't see red when he stormed into the kitchen where Carl was watching his wife make lunches for the next day. He saw pure black.

"Jesus, Luke!" Carl cried springing to his feet. "What the hell..."

Rebecca's eyes bulged as her husband was lifted off his feet by his shirtfront. "Luke! What are you..." Her head flew around as the door banged for the second time in hardly a minute, Sidney and Reg stood stacked in the doorway.

Rebecca ran frantically to Reg. "Stop him before he hurts Carl!" she appealed through terrified sobs as Luke intermittently swore and threw punches.

"You bastard! You were supposed to be my best friend! *Mine!*"

Carl lay sprawled on the floor trying to curb the steady stream of blood from his nose. From where he was sitting, this friendship was something he might have to reconsider in the future.

"Get up!" Luke shouted.

"I'm trying to make sure I can, you son of a bitch!" Carl yelled back. "Just what the hell are we fighting about?!"

Teeth tightly clenched as he heaved for breath, Luke loomed over him. "My wife needed me last year..."

That softened his heart though it did not stem the blood pouring out of his nose. "Oh Christ! Luke, you were away. I had no idea what to do..."

"Interrupt the fucking conference!" Luke shouted trembling with rage.

Carl was shaking his head. How the hell did he get into or out of this mess? He had been in it for years and could never find his way clear of it. "You weren't at a work function. It was personal time." He saw something flicker across Luke's steely expression and knew he was catching on. "Think about it, Luke. You were on your first vacation in years. I wanted to find out more about Sidney's condition before interrupting that. You didn't even know about Lily..."

"You think any of that would have mattered? For chrissake, she's my wife. She's always been my wife. I could have helped. Maybe it was the one time she would have let me." He was gripping Carl by the lapels of his shirt yelling into his bleeding and battered face when a slender arm wrapped around his chest, dragging him back with shocking strength.

"Shhhhh." A hand feathered through his hair and his eyes fluttered closed with the recognition. "It's OK, Luke. I'm OK," Sidney spoke softly, relieved that although he was board stiff he didn't try and shake her off.

Her hand reached up to stroke near his temple as she molded herself against his back. "This isn't Carl's fight. None of it. You and I have put him in a lousy position for years." He was relaxing enough that she could ease him into a rocking motion. "Carl loves us both and for that we should only question his taste."

One guttural noise escaped his throat as his eyes became hooded. He let himself get lost with her. Sink into her. Her voice in his ear. Soothing. Gentle hands gliding over him until the need to fight was over powered by the need for her. He turned in her hold mindful that she didn't get away.

Luke buried his face in her hair remembering the scent that had haunted his nights for years. "Nothing can happen to you. Nothing ever. I can bear anything but that," he decreed fiercely into her neck.

"Nothing will happen to me. I promise."

His hands caught her face roughly. "You promised to stay with me forever. You didn't do that."

Guilty tears slipped off her lashes onto his hand. "I'm sorry. I made a mistake. I made a mistake," she cried incoherently into his chest. Arms wrapped around each other, they clung and rocked.

Books! Books and books and books!

If she didn't believe so strongly in the power of literature, she'd burn them.

The little bitch was getting too close. They were all getting too close. It was time to pull out some stops. This trollop could only be tolerated for so long. She was destroying a good man's reputation! *Her* man's reputation. It was one thing on the Fourth of July. She only looked the fool then but now he had struck his best friend and broke his nose.

She had to be stopped and made to suffer. Oh, it was true she thought that had been accomplished years before but now it was worse. Her mentor would agree. She wouldn't want Luke's reputation to be sullied. Besides, it was safe, wasn't it? No one had ever thought twice the last time drastic measures had been required.

Tragedies were a part of life after all and who better to stage one. Her years of experience would come in handy now. She smiled dementedly leafing through the books enjoying the autopsy photos. Yes, this would have to be taken care of soon or there would be one more to dispose of.

Sidney opened her bedroom door wondering how much longer her rubbery legs would hold up. Her face relaxed into a bright smile when she saw him in the doorway. Her fingers curled around his arm to drag him in. If ever she needed him, it was tonight.

"I knew you would finally make your way up here."

Reg walked past her cheery reception to take in the room that he had only been able to imagine up until now while sleeping in his own lonely bed. The subdued sage striped walls and unique antique pieces suited her though somehow he had envisioned flowers on the walls. The dormer windows were plentiful and homey but it gave him a shiver to think that it was from one of these she had threatened to jump.

She looped her arm through his mildly disturbed by his lack of conversation. It was time to drag him to the bed and do what came natural. "Where did Natalie sleep?"

She lifted her stunned face to his. "Over there in the corner out of the drafts," she replied numbly. "Are you asking as a cop or my fiancé?"

Reg took the coward's way out. "Merely curious."

"Oh." That took the wind out of her sails. "Come to bed, Reg."

He could do that. For a moment anyway. Couldn't he? Lying on his back with her curling warm and inviting to his good side, he was reconsidering his will power. He began to doubt his sanity when her nails lightly raked his chest making his large frame quiver. It had been a long time.

Her lips were doing delicious things to his ear. "Reg, I've missed you." Her mouth curved. "I've even had some fantasies about you in that damned hospital gown."

He growled low as one hand stroked his thigh while she bent over his shirt spreading it open. Her mouth found his nipple and suckled until the animal in him could no longer be strapped down. His hands settled her on top of his body that was hungry to remember. He wanted to savor her softness and blanket himself in it. He needed the kind of comfort she could offer....

"Reg, why are you getting up?"

He sat on the side of the bed knowing she was crouching behind him. Her hands were about to wrap...he had to brush them away or go insane.

She goggled at him when he rose and stood a few feet from the bed. "Reg! What is it?"

"I think we need to talk about..."

Sidney waited but he seemed reluctant to finish. "About?" she prodded.

"About your husband."

She licked her lips. "That's a technicality..."

His eyes narrowed and locked to hers. "What I watched tonight in the Swanson's kitchen was no technicality."

"Reg, he needed me. I know Luke very well. I knew I could reach him and make him understand."

She had. He had watched as his heart broke open and poured blood no one could see. "After ten years apart that is rather extraordinary."

"We had a close..." She hesitated.

"Say it Sidney. We need to talk straight."

Maybe they did. "Marriage. Luke and I had a good marriage."

Why didn't the past tense sound like the past? "He loves you. I see it."

"I didn't give him a chance to say goodbye..."

"Dammit Babe. That man is not saying goodbye. He's..."

"This hasn't been fair for you. To bring you here wounded into the middle of things I left dangling. We can go back to New York. Kat is coping..."

That snapped his temper like a twig. "Go back and what!? Forget all of this. Leave it undone until the next time. Babe I don't want to be married like this."

Sidney couldn't say whether it was her heart that thudded to her knees, or her stomach. From where she knelt on the bed, nothing felt solid any longer. "Reg what are you saying? It's just been a long day! We're both tired. Come to bed and let me hold you."

His eyes swept the bed, took in its comfort and its lure. "Did you share this bed with him?"

Her lashes lowered. "That was years ago."

Somehow given the last twenty-four hours, that distinction was no longer a comfort. "I have to go back downstairs." *While I still can.*

"No! Reg!" she wailed softly, kneeling on the quilt with outstretched arms. "Don't go! It's been so long. We need each other."

He could only argue half that statement and it was what kept him retreating.

"Please..." She had never begged him before but she was willing.

He hated the tears streaming down her cheeks, knowing he had put them there, knowing too that he could chase them away. At least for the night. He wanted more than now. He wanted the long haul and chanted it like a mantra until he was safely in the hall.

Sidney's feet flew down the darkened hallway barreling toward a place where she could find peace. She needed it so badly. She stumbled backward when she saw the figure in her path.

"I didn't mean to scare you, Sidney." A hand reached toward as if to draw her close.

"Oh you didn't," she lied forcing a smile, taking a safe step back.

"I'm used to the dark. Would a light help?"

"No. I'm fine." She frowned grappling for an explanation. "I was just hungry..." She pointed feebly toward the stairs.

The front stairs. Odd when she had started down the backstairs that went directly to the kitchen. "Oh. Do you want company?"

"Company? No. I was just going to grab something and take it back up anyway."

"Sid?" Experimentally she reached out to stroke her hair and felt the quaking. She sensed it took considerable effort for her to hold still rather than bolt. "Why don't you get your food and go back to bed? You look tired."

"I am."

In a maternal gesture, she pressed a kiss to her forehead and went back into her room. Bare feet were flying in the opposite direction. Was she afraid or angry? Did she know something? Kathleen leaned against the inside of her door and heard quiet footsteps return.

She had predictably lied. Sidney wasn't hungry, at least not for food.

"Don't move!" he barked out in a low hiss and reached over with his free hand to click on the lamp.

"Sidney!" A high-pitched feminine voice exclaimed.

She stood small and fearful staring down the barrel of Charlie's gun, who swore viciously as he put on the safety and set it aside. Vera was scrambling toward her but Charlie had the advantage of the closer side of the bed. His arms wrapped around her and pulled her toward the bed as he muttered apologies.

Rough hands smoothed back her hair as he framed her face. "Sidney, you need to knock."

Finally finding her voice, it squeaked pitifully. "I shouldn't have come."

"Bullshit. Say that again and I won't let you go till morning."

That made her crack a smile. "I didn't stop to think." *I didn't want to make any noise.*

"You look upset," Vera ventured softly reaching out to caress her cheek. "Were you dreaming?"

Sidney kept a pained silence wondering what to say. She had a dream all right and then an encounter that was as frightening though nothing menacing happened. "I dreamt about the time on the bridge."

"Oh Christ and I draw a gun!" Charlie shook his head in self-reproach.

Sidney laughed nervously. "It woke me up!"

"Oh gal. No one is ever going to pull a gun on you again. That only happened the once before we knew what we were dealing with."

"Kathleen won't have really done it. Even without drugs to stabilize her," Sidney felt obligated to both say and believe.

Vera nodded because she desperately needed to believe. "It was a horrible time. I'm sorry you still dream of it."

Sidney sighed. That wasn't the half of it. Then she had dreamt the fallout of that day. A stolen night in Charlie's fishing cabin when Luke had taught her about intimacy and she had taught him about love. The night they had made their daughter.

"Sidney?"

"What?" Vera was looking at her oddly.

"Are you all right?"

"Yes." She lifted her eyes to both of them sheepishly. "No. It's been a long night. Dad, is Luke…"

"I talked him into staying in the pool house for the night. The place is comfortable." A smile ghosted around his mouth remembering how comfortable. "And I convinced him we would feel better if he was close."

"I hurt him again."

Charlie stared at her. Saying things was never his strong suit. He did better figuring out puzzles. That's why police work always suited him. "You help him too. He doesn't let go with many people, Sidney. Because of Virginia. She was a cold mother. You reach him."

"It'll hurt him when I go."

Don't go, he ached to say. *Stay married. Make me a grandpa again.* "Let's work on tomorrow, tomorrow and deal with today, today."

Sidney giggled. "Dad that's funny."

He frowned insulted. "I thought it was good advice."

Sidney tipped her head. "It is. I say it often to patients."

He grinned proudly at Vera. "Look at that Vera. I missed my calling. I should have been in social work."

"Yes Charlie and I should write the phone book for a living."

He spread his hands. "Might spice up the copy."

"Might? Dad! No one under eighteen would be allowed to pick it up," Sidney teased as she rose. "Thanks, I feel better." She moved toward the door but turned about uncertainly. "Dad, Luke said tonight an autopsy was never performed on Natalie."

Vera was grateful for the foundation she had left on as the blood drained from her face. Her hand squeezed Charlie's under the sheet.

"No Sidney. Frank Barrett didn't think one was called for," Charlie told her calmly. He may be off the clock but he still remembered the skills that kept him a cop for thirty years.

"But it's routine when someone dies at home to determine exact cause of death."

Charlie held her steadfast gaze knowing it was necessary. "Crib death was determined from the scene. We knew the cause of death and it wouldn't bring your baby back."

"No of course it wouldn't. I'm sorry for frightening you. Earlier."

"Sidney."

"Yes Dad."

"Don't stay away. Just knock first. I'm not that retired."

She was giggling when she left the room but the merriment left with her.

Vera turned to Charlie, her eyes teeming with panic. "Oh Charlie! Do you think she knows anything?"

"You mean more than we know?" He spread his hands wishing he could wipe the distress away. "Darlin' we can't change the past. What's done is done."

"Charlie, she'll hate me. I couldn't stand it if she hated me."

He had tenderness for her and she was the one woman he could always express it to. "Darlin no one could hate you."

Tears sparkled. "Your wife did."

"No one *human* could hate you, Darlin'."

"Charlie, many people are important to me. Kathleen, Luke, the children but Sidney..." She began to cry.

He nodded his eyes lit with pride. "I know, Darlin'. She was so young when she came to you. Five years littler than Kathleen. She barely remembers her parents so she wiggled in that much closer to you."

He didn't know the half of it and might detest her for it. So, she stayed mute and absorbed his love.

"I only have a few huge regrets Vera. Well Virginia, of course heads the list and takes up several spots but the only other big one is that we never shared a child. It's been a pleasure to see you with your girls. I just wish I could say they were mine."

For a woman skilled with words for all occasions, this time there weren't any to be uttered. Instead, she took the time-honored method known to hush any man. She slipped a hand under the covers and sidled closer to brush her lips over his, once and twice to tease and then purposefully, skillfully, deepened it until she knew his mind was wiped clean.

CHAPTER TWENTY-SIX

Sidney closed her eyes relishing the quiet and the sun. It had been a long day but satisfying too. Her mind was churning with pieces of a puzzle that begged to be put together. As difficult as it was after too many years, she was determined to do it. She just had to find away to finesse her *husband*.

That was what was behind the dinner plans she had concocted. She shaded her eyes to the welcoming glass patio table where three places were set. It was odd how right it felt being here, cooking in someone else's home. Glancing at her watch she gauged they ought to be along soon. Other than the chicken that was marinating, dinner and dessert were inside ready and waiting. Her eyes sagged heavily. The past night had been anything but restful. She yawned and let her mind drift.

Lips pressed against hers light as thistledown drawing her out of sleep. His scent brought her comfort and set off a chain reaction of tingling nerves as he changed the rhythm of the kiss. The slant of his mouth shifted. Gentle teeth nipped her lower lip begging for a response to be matched. Her arms lifted to curl around his corded muscular neck to drag him down.

"Let me take you inside. I want to do this properly," he pleaded hoarsely.

Hers eyes flew open at the sound of his voice struggling to remember where she was. If this were real. His hand brushing against her nipple settled part of the confusion. "Luke."

Strong arms were already lifting her off the chaise as she stared into the heat of his gaze.

She slapped a hand on his chest. "We can't do this here."

His eyes moved back and forth as one side of his mouth, that only just left hers, tugged upward. "Sweetheart I own the place. I think we can."

"Reg is coming."

Disappointment couldn't have been more acute. After the day he had put in, miserably trying to make things right with Carl, he had gotten through by thinking of tonight and her. He could not have been more pleased or startled when she asked to make dinner in the home he considered hers as much as his own.

"Reg?" he bit out setting her down but determined not to let her loose.

"We were going to work more on my defense." She averted her eyes uncomfortably and very aware that tanned sinewy arms rested on either side of the lounge chair caging her in. "Stein contends that if the Salengers become aware of our marriage, they could have a lien on your assets too."

305

"I contacted my own lawyer today. He felt given the unique history of our marriage and the fact that it can be documented we had no contact with one another for years and...." He hesitated not wanting to put a pall on the evening.

"And..." This sounded like it pertained to Reg.

"And that you have been living with another man," Luke finished on a sigh.

"I'm sorry. That couldn't have been a pleasant phone call." Tears smarted and she felt powerless to stem them in her embarrassment. She rarely cried in New York. Oh, she got mad regularly and hit the gym but she didn't do a lot of leaking. Now it seemed to be an everyday occurrence.

His eyes squinted as he cupped her cheek. "What's this?"

She smacked her lips buying time. "I'm still a source of embarrassment to you."

His shoulders shook as his grin spread revealing rows of gleaming white teeth. He was suddenly the wolf she would not mind seeing made into a throw rug.

She gave his quaking chest a shove. "Just what the hell is so funny?"

Luke leaned closer to show her he was getting a handle on her variety of intimidation. "You are gorgeous and incredibly sweet." It seemed appropriate and wonderfully playful to accentuate his points with little kisses so he indulged. By the look in her eye, the next time he got close she might bite. "I know an embarrassment, Sweetheart. Look the word up in the dictionary and my mother's picture will be glaring at you."

Sidney felt a prickle rush down her spine as she could envision that image all too clearly.

"Sid!" His eyes widened with concern. She was as clear and as cool as ice. "Sweetheart, I'm sorry to have brought my mother up."

She tried to smile but the result was only marginal. "No. Really I'm fine."

His voice lowered a husky octave. "Sidney you turn my even temper into anyone's guess. You have tried to poke my eye out with a lobster claw, wrestling on the lawn in front of invited guests and once I believe while we fell into a tub naked together. I bought a most unusual garden shed that I just learned today will cost me more to transport here then it did to purchase." Her lips were twitching and though he wanted to taste he ordered himself to finish first. "I hear our names whispered behind hands in most public places though usually with a wink and a smile. You turn my life upside down and me inside out." Her brows rose dubiously. "You make smashing fine china arousing. You are my happiness Sidney Ryan. Stay here and be my wife."

His lips were moving over hers but rather than partake in the kiss all she could manage was to hold back her sobs. "Luke…."

"Hey Luke! I hope you don't mind but I figured by dessert we could use some more company." Reg's face hardened, taking in the scene as he rounded the path that curved around the house. Sidney flustered and moony eyed; the Sheriff oozing testosterone. His eyes shifted to the table. It was still set for three but somehow welcome wasn't in the air.

It was the first time Reg could recall disliking pie but by the time it was served with tea, he despised it, or at least he despised eating it at the Sheriff's home. In fact, the entire house was beginning to grate on him. Sure, it was a pleasure to look at but that was much of the problem. He could see some things too clearly for comfort. Sidney dusting the mantel clock on a lazy Saturday morning with the sun streaming in; her and the Sheriff sharing a glass of wine over an intimate dinner; her curled cozily in an armchair with a baby at her breast….

Her laugh distracted him as she set down a slice of pecan pie slathered with a generous dollop of whipped cream in front of him. His mouth should have watered but instead his stomach churned.

Sidney put her hand on Reg's arm after setting down his pie. He was brooding over something but before she could ask the phone distracted her.

The living room was full of friends and family enjoying dessert. Major moral support Sidney considered as she prepared to jump into her agenda as soon as Luke finished on the phone. It changed all of her carefully laid plans. The brief call Luke took in the kitchen proved his earlier point with clarity. She did turn him inside out.

Luke glowered at Sidney as a muscle began to flex in his lean angular face. He rapidly closed the distance between them until they were barely a foot apart, looming over her as he stared stonily into her puzzled face. "Did you speak to Frank Barrett today?"

"Ahhh…"

He leaned in close. "He seems to be under some preposterous impression that we are considering exhuming our daughter's body!"

Perhaps it was the contempt in his tone or the fact that his words were fairly shouted into her face. Regardless, Sidney went whey faced and clutched a nearby sofa for support as her knees turned to jelly. "I…"

"Yes," Luke ground out through clenched teeth and took another menacing step forward until their breath mingled.

"I realized over the past weeks, over the years really…" she faltered unnerved by the fury he was barely strapping down.

"Go on," he growled impatiently.

"I realized that I don't understand why we lost Natalie."

"I will buy you a book on SIDS," he told her coldly. "Natalie stays were she is."

She was shocked and stung by his rigid stand. Tears fell now making silent streaks down her strained face but her temper flared. He wasn't the only one whose moods were unpredictable. "Of course Luke. That crypt is such a lovely place to be. Heaven forbid we disturb her. Maybe she's even having a tea party with your God damned mother!" she shouted sarcastically ending on a choked sob.

"That's what this is really about! My mother," he accused her icily.

Sidney made a scoffing sound. "No."

"Yes."

"No!" she emoted in a raw voice.

Her husband was clearly unconvinced as he began pacing the length of the living room between the sofa and the hearth. "I don't want our baby to undergo an autopsy. It's unwarranted and..." His voice trailed off unable to finish.

Sidney sighed heavily as she glanced around at their aghast guests. "It could answer a number of questions..."

"Honey, after all this time..." Charlie paused uneasy at how to proceed. How does one delicately talk to a mother about the decomposition of her lost child?

Sidney adeptly read his thoughts. "Actually as much as I hate that stupid crypt Virginia insisted upon, it is an advantage now. According to Frank Barrett, bodies decompose much slower...they are almost mummified..."

Two rough hands gripped her slender shoulders and the snarling face of her husband leaned down to hers. "Don't talk about Natalie that way!" he yelled shaking until her teeth rattled.

In a heartbeat, his presence was magically lifted from hers. Sidney blinked through the blur of her tears to see Reg holding Luke in an unrelenting hold. Compassion resounded in his dark beautifully chiseled features. "Cool down Luke. It's understandable that you are very angry but Sidney is no match for you. You weren't trying the other night."

An arm pulled her back against a solid frame not unlike that of her husband's. She glanced back anxiously before realizing Charlie was merely offering support. "Relax Honey. Take a deep breath. You are very pale." Vera was pressing a glass of cold water into her trembling hand.

Sidney accepted it with a grateful smile. She wrapped her hands around the glass until they were white-knuckled as Luke and Reg took seats beside one another to face her.

"I'm sorry, Luke. I have handled this very badly. You must think that I was going behind your back looking up old records and talking to the coroner. I wasn't really. I have never seen any of those documents and I have realized over the last few months more and more that I needed to. The more I questioned things, the fewer answers that seemed to make sense. I merely ended up with more questions. Initially my inquiry about exhuming Natalie was impulsive and just speculative."

"Keep it that way. I hate it," he snarled.

She bit her lower lip to keep from crying. "I need to know what killed our child."

"Crib death."

She leaned forward as if that could help her reach him. "Without an autopsy, we don't really know that."

"I know that. Natalie was asleep in our bedroom. No one in that house would have hurt her," he stated with an almost eerie sense of calm.

"Luke, I am not inferring that someone deliberately…" She was vividly aware of the many silent observers in the room and it no longer seemed prudent to continue. "Natalie could have died from an aneurysm for all we know. Luke, I need to know."

"Not this way."

She drew a tedious desperate breath. He was immovable. "I won't pursue the divorce if you agree." The words were out of her mouth before she registered either their origin or gravity.

Two startled men gaped at her and it was all she could do not to bolt from the room but the impulsive words were already spoken. Nothing could take them back.

His voice was strangely even and bore no hint of his earlier tender appeal. "Will you live here as my wife with all that that entails?"

Sidney thought her heart had stopped as she heard both the words he said and those implied. *Sharing my bed.* The silence stretched and lingered uncomfortably.

"If I do, will you agree to the autopsy?"

"Yes," was his clipped response.

Sidney studied the oak floor in bewilderment. "All right," she finally said in a bare whisper.

Reg closed his eyes and exhaled in untold anguish.

"Frank said he gave you documents. Do you have them?" Luke asked in deadened tones.

"In my purse," she numbly retrieved the thick rolled consents. He took them from her grasp in one savage swipe. He scrawled his signature across the bottom and flung them back at her roughly.

"Now get out," he said so softly as she stared up at him thinking she must not have heard him correctly.

She peered up at him with large desolate eyes.

"You heard me correctly. I want you out of my house. We can communicate through our attorneys and settle our legal difficulties...."

"Lucas..." Vera's voice softly interrupted and he ceased speaking abruptly.

Sidney stood up, unsteady and feeling utterly foolish. Her eyes were downcast, unable to meet anyone's gaze in her roiling humiliation. His cutting voice stilled her movements.

"Since you have been back, you have repeatedly told me things are different... that you have changed... that you weren't the wife I remembered." She glanced up when he paused and was instantly disarmed by the contempt she saw in his eyes. "Well, I finally agree with you. The woman, who just bargained herself away in order to get what she wanted, is not *my* wife. My lawyer will contact Stein first thing in the morning. We should be able to reach a settlement within 10 days."

Sidney's breath left her deflated and defeated. She turned slowly away and without another word left the house. Kathleen and Rebecca hurried out behind her but came back in within mere moments. Rebecca looked up at her husband. "Sidney says she wants to walk. Alone."

"She insists, Auntie," Kathleen verified worrying over Vera's distress.

Reg stood up decisively and spoke quietly to Vera. He walked out the door without a backward glance.

"You think he is the better man," Luke said in a low voice staring directly at Vera.

She turned very slowly to look into his eyes. Her eyes were riveted and alert. There wasn't a trace of the flighty romance novelist tonight in her gravely serious face. "Lucas, you and I will discuss this at another time."

"Now."

She gave him a cool scrutiny. "Well, Lucas, if you insist. Tonight is truly the first time I saw any evidence that you had actually *been at your mother's knee*." Their eyes held for a long moment before Vera turned and left through the front door. Charlie frowned and followed her.

After Vera's departure, the others left in short order with hardly a word. Luke presumed he was quite alone standing before the empty hearth when a deep voice spoke.

"Just what exactly were you hoping for?"

Luke turned and saw Jack regarding him silently.

Jack shook his head at Luke's lack of response. "Did it ever occur to you that maybe, just maybe, Sidney might have said yes because she wanted to live here as your wife?"

"I don't want her that way," Luke said starkly.

"Well, you pretty much fixed it tonight so no one will want her." Jack stated pointedly. "Reg has some pride too. His reaction was certainly not lost on Sidney. You didn't see his devastation because you were standing beside him when Sidney agreed to live here as your wife. That was your ultimatum, wasn't it? Although certainly there were other duties implied," he remarked in a disapproving tone.

Luke frowned disgruntled. "It wasn't an ultimatum. I wanted her to make a choice."

Jack snorted. "Some choice. To find out at long last something definitive about her daughter's death as well as the opportunity to explore what has become of her marriage or go with the status quo of not knowing where the hell she stands with anyone. She goes for it…" Luke made obvious motions to interrupt and Jack narrowed his eyes and stuck out an accusatory finger cutting his attempt off at the knees. "She goes for it and you reject her. Completely. At this very moment, Reg is likely doing the same. Bravo, Luke. Tonight will definitely not enhance your life, son," he finished tightly.

Luke's head snapped up suddenly thinking perhaps he hadn't heard him correctly. Surely what he said was a slip of the tongue but Jack was already disappearing out the door and Luke hung his head dejectedly. He sat alone in the incredible house, he had built from all the dreams he and Sidney had once shared and thought of his mother.

CHAPTER TWENTY-SEVEN

"She looks awful and it's your fault."

Luke's head snapped to see Nicole and Zachary hip to hip in the doorway of his office. Julie had apparently let them by. Hardly surprising. His young impressionable secretary didn't think much of him at the moment.

"How awful?" Luke asked opening his desk drawer and pulling out a couple of Hershey bars.

Zach ripped the wrapper from one. "Her eyes are all red."

"She hardly eats." Nicole slid the candy bar back toward her uncle in an eloquent gesture.

Trying to remain neutral though her rebuff struck a chord, Luke spoke evenly. "Nicole, not eating isn't unusual for your aunt."

"She got dizzy the other day on the stairs but Reg caught her before she fell," Zach told him from a mouth stuffed full of candy.

"It's been very warm out, Zach. Heat can make anyone feel faint," Luke explained hoping to convince himself.

"Charlie's so worried he's nice to her all the time."

Luke glanced up sharply. That was significant.

"Mom explained to us about your baby. We're sorry," Nicole told him with grave seriousness that had him glimpsing the young adult she was growing to be while Zach nodded wide-eyed.

Luke looked up at the two children he had helped raise and missed his own. "I could use a hug."

They surged into his arms and loosened the tight chain around his heart.

"Aunt Sidney could use one of these too," Nicole told him defiantly.

"Well remember that when you get home..." Luke began to say.

"From you," Nicole corrected.

Zach gave him an eager smile. "A Hershey bar might help too."

What was a man supposed to feel as he watched another man labor to open up the cold marble wall that had sealed his child in a tomb for the past decade. Luke stood oppressively silent and only concluded that whatever it was, it wasn't comfortable. He was learning to accept it.

Lately he was accepting a lot, he considered morosely. It almost seemed fitting to have Reg there, standing equally reticent behind him. It was just as fitting that Sidney wasn't.

Whatever acrimony existed between them, Luke didn't wish this moment on her. It was still far too easy to summon up the horrible instant when their baby had been pushed into this frigid wall and sealed behind it. Her tear streaked face burrowed into his shirt sobbing like she might never stop, fingers digging into his ribs even through his suit jacket. The helplessness of that moment, Luke knew, would never really be banished from his memory.

The little gasp flung him headlong back into the present. He whirled knowing the tiny sound so steeped in grief could only be hers. Invisible talons sunk into his chest as it registered the kids were absolutely right. She did look awful. Small, fragile like thin crystal that could shatter with the faintest effort. He had heard quite definitely from Charlie that the divorce papers had been delivered two days ago. Had they done this to her? Kathleen stood directly behind her, car keys clutched in her hand, looking guilt stricken that they were there at all.

Sidney's wide reddened eyes were staring past him where the man from the coroner's office was lifting their daughter's small, too terribly small, coffin out.

Reg sighed at the sight of her, automatically moving forward. "Ahh, Babe, we agreed you would stay…"

She didn't meet his eyes. Couldn't. They were riveted to the glossy box that held her child who by rights should no longer fit in such a small space. "I tried to stay away. Couldn't. I just want to touch. For just a moment." Her eyes lifted to Frank Barrett's. "Please. I know it must seem stupid. But it's as close as I can get to her."

Considering he had been in this business damned near forty years, her plea shouldn't have touched him but it did. This case had always done that. It triggered every emotion including those he steadfastly strapped down. He had smoothed the way for this exhumation, half out of longtime friendship to Luke and half for himself, he had dismally admitted last night over several glasses of Jameison's. Something had never rang true about this sad event and needed to be settled. Studying her now, Frank glimpsed the same savage grief that he had never quite been able to shove from his mind even after over a decade.

Frank gestured to his men to move away for a moment and nodded to Sidney. "It isn't stupid Mrs. Ryan. I only wish I had understood that better when this tragedy occurred years ago."

A grateful tenuous smile ghosted about her lips as she took steps toward the little white coffin. She vaguely sensed eyes upon her but was rapidly so overwhelmed none of it mattered. Her fingertips strained toward the surface lightly touching before she flattened her palm. Her chin quivered as tears sparkled and began to flow.

Sidney angled her head to look at him. It was hard. The connection and the surge of pain that it prompted were vicious but it had to be done. He had predictably been watching her and their eyes met recognizing one another's sorrow.

Though she looked at him, she spoke to another man. "Dr. Barrett, the town sheriff is known to have free access to your facilities, isn't he?"

Frank Barrett's pale blue eyes flitted between this troubled couple. "It is a courtesy."

"Withdraw it in this case," she stated flatly.

Frank's head whipped to Luke. He had never considered this man would attempt to come into his facilities during this particular case but something he saw in the other man's face told him he should have.

"Sidney..."

"You have thought about it," she insisted quietly and calling upon her courage reached out her free hand. It was a relief that he took it rather than publicly rejecting her. For a brief moment, they were strangely connected again with their daughter. "Don't do it. You won't get close to her that way. Remember our laughing beautiful girl Luke, not what the cruelties of time do to a little lifeless body."

"I..." Lying into those eyes was never a possibility so he broke off his reply.

"Promise me. You need never give me another kind gesture..."

That remark was better aimed than her knee had been weeks ago on the fourth of July and that had brought him to his knees. "I promise." He paused. "On the condition you see a doctor. You don't look..." Good seemed too harsh. "Well, Sidney. The family is worried. The kids..." *Me.*

She nodded letting her hand slip away. "All right." Her eyes flitted about nervously and as always found solace with Reg. "Will you take me home? Kathleen is going to stay for a bit."

The need to protect was as strong as the day he had met her. "Sure, Babe. Let's go and we'll make that appointment." Then he planned on tucking her into bed if it meant holding her there.

Luke watched the man, who dwarfed her today more than ever, wrap a brawny arm about her shoulders and her head tilted to naturally rest there. For such an odd pairing, there was no denying their bond.

Luke turned when a gentle hand touched his arm. "I'm sorry, Luke. I tried to keep Sid at home but she was determined to come and was prepared to drive..."

His breath shuddered out in a rush. It was a toss up who should be behind the wheel, with Sidney distraught and Kathleen off her meds, but as he gazed into her eyes, she seemed remarkably steady. "Thanks for bringing her."

"She came for more than Natalie you know. She was beside herself thinking you might try and see Nat."

He lowered his eyes staggered how well his wife knew him beyond anyone else when something was pressed into his palm.

"Sidney said she promised to get these to you sometime. Today seemed to be the day."

Luke stared at the little while envelopes neatly bundled and tied with a pink ribbon. "These are the letters she wrote to Natalie over the years."

"Apparently. I didn't know anything about them," Kathleen confessed not quite able to suppress the twinge of resentment.

"She told me the night Sandra and Jerry's daughter died."

"The night she didn't come home," Kathleen added meaningfully peering into his face.

Hazel eyes held clear blue ones knowing what was implied. "Kat, I don't want talk about that night."

She gave him a conciliatory nod. "Have you and Sidney talked about that night?"

Considering the floor beneath him was granite, it was shifting like sand. "I'm not sure it would matter one way or another. It may have only been a few months ago but it seems like an eternity. So much has happened in the meantime." He rolled his shoulders feeling more than the usual weight there. "What could it possibly mean now?"

Kathleen saw him take a step toward the door and fell in step, threading her fingers in his and squeezing. Words weren't the best tact now. There was far too much to give away.

His desk blotter was buried beneath things requiring both his attention and likely his signature. He cared about neither. His in-box was jammed with the overflow scattered on the floor. If the intercom buzzed one more time, Luke was reasonably certain he would shoot the damn thing. Work was piling up everywhere and for the first time since taking the position of Sheriff, he couldn't give a damn.

Luke was staring morosely out of the window when Carl found him. A sweeping glance of his office was telling. "Frank Barrett mentioned that the autopsy will only take a couple days at most."

"Hmmm," Luke murmured.

"Then what?"

Luke swung around puzzled and sighed. By then, he would likely need a forklift to get to the door.

316

Carl gazed at him compassionately. "Have you considered giving your daughter the memorial you wished she had years ago?"

Luke considered that without comment.

"You could buy a burial plot..."

"Instead of the crypt that Sidney hates..."

"And you hate, too," Carl challenged gently. "Think,Luke. There can be several positives of all this. You can put your daughter to rest the way you have often regretted didn't happen years ago. Maybe that will help both of you heal as much as finally hearing the cause of death substantiated."

Luke stoically regarded something far off.

Carl gave him a sympathetic look. This entire situation was beyond trying. "Luke, is there something...."

Luke turned to skewer his friend's eyes but said nothing.

Carl's eyes flew wide. "Christ! You are afraid that Natalie didn't die of SIDS! You are afraid that..."

With stunning speed, Luke was looming over the other man. "Some things shouldn't be said out loud."

"Are you ready Honey?" Vera touched Sidney's arm.

Sidney turned toward her Aunt's voice and away from the tree lined roadway of the cemetery. She wasn't ready when she and Luke had to do this the first time. Twelve years later, she didn't feel any more ready to commit her little daughter's body to rest but at least this time the sun was shining brightly and the sound of birds in the trees could be heard. Natalie was finally going to be buried in the ground instead of shoved into a drawer in the wall and sealed shut behind a cold glistening sheet of marble.

She sighed as anxiety congealed in her chest. Where on earth was he? Reg was nowhere to be found this morning or even now that it was mid afternoon. The intimacy between them was fading. She could feel it a little more everyday. They were becoming what they had started out as. Friends.

Her eyes shifted to where Hilary and Henry stood solemnly off to one side speaking quietly to Don and Sherry. Her heart swelled thinking of them being here at all. She had certainly not expected it. This memorial was intended to be small and private. After all, it was under the most unusual of circumstances. She and her husband stood politely side-by-side but certainly not clinging to one another as they had at Natalie's funeral.

"Sidney, we really need to get started," Luke told her reluctantly. "Do you have any idea where Reg might be?"

She summoned all her courage to turn to him. "Reg was gone when I woke up. He did feel strongly that you and I needed to do this together as

Natalie's parents but to not attend…"

"He'll be here, Sidney," Henry Buckman's baritone voice assured her.

Hope flooded her features. "Do you know where he was going?"

"No, but my son would not leave you at a time like this."

She lowered her eyes. "Maybe Reg hasn't confided to you that things between us are somewhat…"

"Sidney, our son loves you. Whatever the two of you are dealing with at the present time, it would not affect his being here today," Hilary decreed as she came to stand beside her husband. -

Sidney gazed at them, desperately wanting to believe. "I have no right to expect Reg to be here today. I thank the two of you from the bottom of my heart for coming. I certainly never expected…"

Henry looked insulted. "Well damn it, you should have. Our affection for you is not dependent on what becomes of your relationship with our son."

Tears sprang to her eyes when simultaneously the sound of a car could be heard in the quiet cemetery. Her head whipped around and a relieved cry broke from her lips. The car was barely stopped before the door was thrown open. His eyes found hers and held for a communicative second that transcended speech.

Reg grinned gauging she needed him to and held up a solitary finger that signaled he needed a moment. Sidney watched intently as he stooped to retrieve something from the back seat. A hand flew to her lips as the pieces fell together.

Luke watched the amazing transformation overtaking the mother of his child and the massive man who was causing it. Reg was cradling a box with the utmost care.

Reg's eyes never left hers as he approached them. "I'm sorry Babe…"

"I love you," she breathed through her teeming emotion.

His grin spread. "Ditto, Babe. I know I wasn't very clear in my note…"

"A note?"

He frowned sharply. "Hell yes. Babe, you didn't think I had just…"

"I didn't see any note. Truthfully, I was worried. I knew you wouldn't not be here…"

His volume and pitch were escalating. "Of course I wouldn't! These beauties were a little tough to track down. It ended up to be quite a drive."

Her eyes fell to his light but precious burden. "Natalie loved…" Her voice cracked and broke off as Don gently eased the box from his friend's arms so Reg could step forward and fold her in his embrace.

Luke watched in silent awe as this man was able to do so effortlessly, what he seemed unable to accomplish. Sidney was coolly polite in his presence but she absorbed this man's comfort.

Luke was stunned when he saw Reg gently disengage himself from her to stand just behind them as the service began. He did not attempt to take a place on her other side. Vera came to stand there instead.

The minister offered several prayers that Sidney had chosen and Nicole read a short poem. Luke glanced between the little white coffin that held the small body of the child they missed everyday and Sidney's hand that hung listlessly by her side. Her other hand was clasped in her aunt's grasp. His hand itched to close over hers but he was mindful of the distance between them. Surely, she didn't want his touch.

After the prayers, Luke moved to where the minister stood. He felt his wife's inquiring gaze as he withdrew a small envelop from his suit jacket.

"Recently I had the privilege of reading some beautiful letters written to my daughter by her mother. I would like to read one of those now. Natalie's short life was extraordinarily happy because the most incredible woman gave birth to her. Here's proof.

My Dearest Natalie,

Today would have been your fifth birthday pumpkin. In my mind, I have baked you a castle cake that would befit my little princess. Upturned ice cream cones are the corner turrets. Daddy has cut out little flags and attached them with toothpicks. The frosting is sunny yellow that I know you will stick your finger in with a beaming smile. The castle walls are decorated with candies of every color. And I will pretend not to notice when you sneak one. The drawbridge is chocolate ladyfinger cookies that Grandpa will grumble ought to be on his plate but I know he will gladly share with you.

There are streamers and balloons everywhere and Daddy is still busy putting your birthday present together in the garage. It is a pink two-wheeler with fluffy white streamers on the handlebars and little training wheels.

Daddy was boasting to me just last night after we tucked you in that you will be riding without any training wheels in no time because you are so smart. I agree but also know it will be because he will race up and down the street by your side until you both are happily exhausted.

But alas my sweet child, Mommy's imagination is stronger than her heart. It breaks a little everyday that we are apart. Not just on birthdays and holidays but every single day. I miss the ordinary things we never were lucky enough to share. You would have started school this year and I wonder how hard it would have been to put you on the bus that first day. No matter how many tears I would have shed sending you off to school, it would be better than never getting to do it at all.

Whatever you see from heaven little one know...you live in my heart as surely you live in your daddy's. One day we will be together again...dancing and laughing and then Mommy's heart will be whole again.

Until that day...love and kisses,
We can never share too many,
Mommy

Luke stared down at the paper in his hand before glancing up. He heard several women sniffing but his eyes only sought out one. Her eyes were riveted on his face. They stood staring with a little white coffin and a heart wreath of pink sweetheart roses between them. He felt closer to Natalie in this moment than he had in eleven years.

Kathleen quietly made her way toward him and pressed a sisterly kiss to his cheek. He handed her the other paper he held and stepped to one side.

"Luke asked me to read this next letter. Most of us here today know that very sadly my sister and Reg lost their daughter together, Lily, last year. This letter is particularly touching because Sidney not only talks to Natalie in it but says something about the incredible man who she has shared the past decade with."

Dearest Natalie,
My sweet daughter, I wrote to you recently about my sadness that the baby I was expecting would not know you. My sadness has flip flopped since then, Nat, but of course you already know that. My second beautiful baby girl has left the earth for heaven. My little girls are together but without me. My heart can barely force my hand to write this painful truth.

Natalie, I know you will have found our Lily right away and given her a big hug. Mommy needs you to do something more. Please tell your sister a little bit about me. Tell her how I will miss sharing my bath with her, nursing her at night in bed and dancing cheek to cheek while she giggled the way you used to.

Lily's Daddy is a big strong man who held your tiny sister so gently in his big hands. Maybe you heard his beautiful deep voice singing to her as he rocked her for the first and last time. Natalie, your sister has a different Daddy than you did but he is a man your Daddy would like. He has a good heart and an incredible soul.

One day when your Mommy gets a little braver and a lot stronger, I am going to tell my precious Lily's Daddy about my first baby girl. About you. I know he will feel the same comfort I do that you are there with Lily to hold her tiny hand in yours and let her know how loved she is. I know you would be the kind of big sister to Lily that your Aunt Kathleen has been to me. The only thing I would like more than knowing my girls have each other is to think they have me.

Natalie, when you cuddle with your baby sister, you will know one of the greatest truths of all. Love knows no color.

Kiss your sister for me, Sweetheart,

Love Mommy

Sidney felt herself tugged backward into strong dark arms. Her eyes finally opened and saw Luke watching her in the embrace of another man. She felt closer to him in that instant than since the disastrous night she had asked him to agree to their daughter's autopsy. No matter what rifts remained between them, she knew one thing, he still loved her. He loved her enough to help her mend some burnt bridges with another man.

The minister was about to say a final prayer when Reg interrupted.

"Pastor, before little Natalie's memorial concludes, there is something I would like to add on behalf of her mother. Sidney has said that Natalie loved butterflies. Today we would like to celebrate her being committed to the earth by giving her something to look at all the way from heaven."

Luke studied the larger man as he spoke in a quiet expressive voice. His parents and Don and Sherry were handing out small waxed paper envelopes. He could tell from the expectant look on Sidney's face she knew exactly what they were doing. Suddenly Reg appeared before him, tugging Sidney by his side.

"This is something the two of you must do together," Reg declared.

Luke's brows knit together and immediately noted that Sidney stiffened.

"Reg, Luke can release one on his own. He doesn't want…"

The black man caught her chin. "Together, Mrs. Ryan. You had this child together. Natalie will expect it just as Lily had every right to expect us to do the same."

Luke glanced around at everyone gingerly holding their envelopes expectantly. He pinned Reg down with his inquiring gaze. "Just what is it we are supposed to do?"

Reg smiled gently. "Luke, I was late because I had to find a very special kind of farm."

Luke cocked an eyebrow at him. Maybe it was the stress of the day but he was growing more confused not less so.

"Natalie loved butterflies. Correct?"

"She was crazy about them."

Reg nudged Sidney. "Tell him."

"The envelopes contain butterflies from a conservatory. We are going to open the envelopes together so that a cloud of them are released. It will help us feel like we are celebrating our daughter, not just grieving her."

Awe lit his face as he eagerly reached for an envelope. A huge hand stopped him. "No, Luke. That one is mine. You and Sidney share this one. You made your daughter together. Say good bye to her the same way." Reg dragged Sidney's listless hand to her husband's.

Luke stared into her uncertain eyes and sensed sadly that she expected to be rejected by him again. "Sidney, would you grant me the honor..."

"Yes," she breathed as tears flooded her eyes. Together their fingers gently held the crinkly envelop.

"All right everyone...on three..." Reg directed. Envelopes opened, gingerly releasing their captives. Wings spread and slowly fluttered open. The summer sky was suddenly filled with a gorgeous suspended cloud of brilliant shimmering colors. The velvety wings of many butterflies quivered and flapped in a silent floating ballet in the air that drifted upward. The creatures fluttered gingerly about on wings that had been immobile for some time so they milled about, often coming to rest on the shoulder of the person that had released them.

Sidney felt infused with peace as she spontaneously reached for two hands. One was lean and tanned; the other dark and powerful. Her grip was tenacious and her composure slipped as she allowed herself to be tugged into one man's hold. Her face damp from falling tears was pressed against his shirt and suit jacket. A low rumbling voice whispered in her ear as his fingers gently disentangled themselves from hers. "Let go, Babe. Luke needs you as much as you need him. Let your daughter see her parents together."

She turned her face so large uncertain eyes could search out his while her fingers slid from Reg to twine around her husband's neck. Instantly Luke's hold tightened as he buried his face into the hollow between her neck and shoulders. Soft sobs shook his shoulders and she felt their bodies gently sway as one. She murmured sounds of comfort that were barely words merely endearments. Her eyes strayed to the butterflies that continued to mill about in this shady spot full of flowers. Natalie would have loved this. Virginia

Ryan would have hated it. With Reg's help, she and Luke had finally gotten it right.

It was important to stroll down the walk, Sidney knew, even as her stomach started the greasy climb into her throat. You never knew who might be watching. Lately it seemed like there were eyes everywhere. Who knew this condition also brought with it a healthy dose of paranoia? So calling up her most disciplined control, Sidney slowed her pace to a casual saunter and made her way down the shady back lane. It wasn't until her hand hit the back gate and the bitter bile bubbled into her throat that she broke into a run.

Her eyes barely took in the homey kitchen she typically rooted around in like it was her own. Instead her feet flew into the hall, skidding to a stop in the small room as she flung up the toilet lid, fell to her knees and let the shudder overtake her.

Her whole body trembled and convulsed in rhythmic heaves. Vile fluids left her splashing into the water just below her face as her bare arms wrapped around the cold porcelain base for support.

Sidney relaxed slightly as gentle hands smoothed her hair away from her face and gathered it to fall in waves over her back. She heard the water running in the nearby sink and sagged a little as her retching subsided into ragged little gulping heaves. Her vision was blurred and watery paths from her eyes to her chin marred her drawn pale face. She took her first decent breath and anticipated the comforting sound of her friend's melodic voice.

She froze as the hand that had been stroking lightly up and down her back came into her eye shot with an offering of cool water. Her breath strangled in her throat and another wave of reactionary nausea crashed ruthlessly through her.

"Take a sip, Sid. It will help," his kind deep tones implored her gently.

She shuttered as she complied and very slowly lifted panicky eyes to his. "I… I have the flu."

Sympathetic eyes bore into hers as two strong warm hands eased her to stand before him. He led her slowly to the nearby kitchen table and gently seated her at it. He pulled another chair away from the same table to face hers and sat down so their knees almost touched.

"As it happens, Sid, I know all about this flu. Rebecca had it twice," Carl told her softly without a trace of malice.

Tears stood in her huge eyes that seemed to overpower the rest of her oval face in intensity. She had no words. Two strong arms snaked around her and pulled her forward as she burst into tears. Carl stroked her hair until her she was able to curtail her sobbing into little sniffs. He eased her back so he could see her face as he spoke.

"Becca had to take the kids to the dentist. I had some personal time coming so thought I would hang around home for a bit..."

Her eyes became saucers. "Rebecca told you!"

He shook his head. "No. I guessed and she remained mute."

Sidney glanced downward and frowned. "Who made those dentist appointments, Carl?"

"I did," he said with a sly look.

She sighed and studied the floor tiles once more.

"He doesn't know," Carl declared bluntly.

Sidney lifted her shuttered gaze. "Maybe I don't know who *he* is."

Carl's eyes never wavered from hers and relentlessly bore into the depths of her brown eyes. "*You know.*"

"Why would he believe that? He has every reason not to."

Carl shrugged and idly tapped his hand on the nearby table. "You know, Sidney, maybe the real problem here, is not the man who is the father, but the man who isn't."

She shut her eyes in mute misery. A hand cupped her cheek just as a tear squeezed past closed eyes.

"Sidney, when two men are in love with the same woman, it is inevitable that one of them is going to get hurt. Badly. Both your men know that. One will have to endure it, just as you will. This was bound to happen. It just took more years to occur than I would have guessed and a pretty drastic..." Carl aborted his train of thought abruptly as he realized what he was about to blurt out.

"What?" Sidney narrowed her eyes suspiciously. "What were you about to say, Carl?"

He shook his head in a definitive gesture. "It's not mine to say."

Panic shook her to the marrow of her bones. "Carl..." she urged in a purposely menacing tone.

His gaze was brittle. "Forget it, Sid. I am the keeper of secrets, not the teller and it seems I just acquired one more."

She gulped. "I won't be able to keep this one much longer..."

"How far along..."

She cast him an incredulous glance. "Carl, do you really want further complicity in this?"

He gave her a thoughtful look. "Good point."

She saw her opening and seized it immediately. She was on her feet and moving toward the door in light speed. Her hand was just reaching for the latch.

"Sidney, you haven't said whether you are happy."

She turned with a blank expression to face him once again wholly intending to evade his question. The sincere warm light in his eyes prevented that. She gave him a beguiling smile. "Lord help me, Carl, but I am beyond happy."

The hard line of his mouth softened as his lips curved upward seeing joy sweep over her. "I can't think of any woman who deserves it more."

"This woman could likely end up alone…"

He was standing over her with stunning speed gripping her shoulders. "Sidney Ryan, get that foolish notion out of your head because regardless of those two men who love you….you are not alone. Not by one hell of a long shot! That was the greatest error in judgment you made when you left town all those years ago. You are loved by a wonderful family and many friends who couldn't be closer to you if we were blood. *You will never be alone.*"

She gave him a tearful smile and laid her head on his broad chest for a moment hugging him close. "Thanks for setting me straight, Carl."

"Yeah well, I wish I had done it about a dozen years ago."

"I think you tried. I wasn't in a place where I could hear it and besides then I wouldn't have met Reg. He changed the course of my life."

Carl gave her a small nod. There was no denying her words but he didn't feel inclined to embellish them either. He watched her leave his home to return to the house of her childhood. That woman definitely wasn't going to end up alone but his heart went out to the man who would.

Sidney opened the door of her bedroom and relief washed over her like a cleansing rain. She had managed to slip back into the house and upstairs without a single member of the household being any the wiser. She jumped as she turned to see her sister stretched out on the bed following her every move intently.

"At Becca and Carl's again, Sid?" Kathleen asked starkly.

She settled a plastic smile on her lips. "Yes, I needed to have a coffee in peace…"

"Funny, Delta says you haven't touched coffee in weeks. Doesn't agree with you apparently."

"Did I say coffee… I meant tea…"

"With Becca?"

Tension infused her. This was a trap. "Did I say Becca? She wasn't home. I had a drink with Carl."

"A drink?"

Her mouth opened. For a simple topic, this conversation was tricky as hell. "Juice."

"Not tea?"

Her heart rate quickened. "And tea. I was thirsty and Carl is congenial."

"And I'm not."

"Not this instant. No. Listen, I want to take a shower."

"Fine. I'll wait. We could stand a long chat."

Sidney headed to the bathroom.

"You are going to undress in there?"

She stilled. "Yeah…"

"Interesting."

Her heart was drumming out of her chest. "Not really, just habit. Reg seems to want more privacy these days."

Her sister nodded and then pursed her lips pensively. "I'm not Reg. Undress here and we can chat."

Suddenly a shockingly good cover struck her. "Kat, I'm on the rag."

Kathleen stared enigmatically into her eyes for a moment and then quickly got off the bed. "Sorry, Sid. I'll get out of here and give you some privacy. I wasn't thinking."

Sidney sighed partly in guilt for lying but mostly in enormous relief that her sister was leaving. In the past few weeks, her body had changed drastically. It was getting increasingly harder to conceal beneath the thin cover of summer clothes but impossible naked in the light of day. The last thing she needed was Kathleen privy to her dilemma while she was on a drug holiday.

Kathleen stood in the hall for a second as she listened to her sister's movements in the next room and exhaled slowly. The game was getting tedious and the stakes were higher than she ever counted on. Kathleen shook her head sadly and her blond hair grazed her shoulders. It was unfortunate Natalie died in her infancy. If she had lived, her mother would have known better than to use that ridiculous pretense about having her period. No one who has ever raised a child to puberty would buy that lame line but poor Sidney didn't have the necessary motherhood experience to know better. God help to have better discretion around others or she may pay dearly.

CHAPTER TWENTY-EIGHT

"She isn't here, Lucas," Vera stated flatly without looking up.

"Where is she?" a deep voice asked with obvious concern.

Vera took off her half glasses and looked up at the broad shouldered man with a gentle smile. "She left you a note."

"And the car," Luke added irritably. Vera was openly hostile toward him and that hurt as much as having it acknowledged Sidney only cared to explain her whereabouts to Reg.

Reg glanced up from the short letter Sidney had left him. "Sidney has gone to New York…"

Luke's jaw dropped. In the short space of time it took to have a beer with Reg to personally thank him for his help making Natalie's service memorable, she was gone. Again. "On foot?"

Reg didn't even crack a smile. "No. David McCreedy was here. She went with him."

"At least we don't have to worry about her driving," Charlie muttered from his chair near Vera's. Leaving was bad enough but what she left for his son was going to break his heart. Again.

Luke frowned at the page in Reg's hands. He certainly couldn't make out the words but the script was lengthy. "Isn't David McCreedy…"

Reg was already nodding while still scanning her note. "The Chief of Staff at St. Mark's. Kevin Salenger's little boy, Connor, has been admitted."

Luke's face fell. Sidney's worse prediction seemed to be coming true.

"Cynthia was poisoning the baby's formula with undetermined amounts of household cleaners. Small amounts at first but apparently, she was growing agitated and desperate because she couldn't seek a lot of medical attention without creating suspicion. She began poisoning the baby just prior to Kevin's arrival from work so that he could see the symptoms and take the baby to Emergency with her. What she didn't count on was Kevin really does have a great respect for both Sidney's professional opinions as well as her personal convictions. He began to scrutinize Connor's health and pattern of illness closely, while the hospital was hesitant to do so. Once a law suit is launched, care givers are extremely cautious. Kevin arrived home early and caught Cynthia doctoring the formula."

"Christ!" Luke cursed repulsed at this mother's repugnant actions. "The baby…Connor? How is he now?"

Reg sighed heavily. "Sidney writes that is unknown right now. He is stable but they are doing liver and kidney function tests to determine the amount of damage he might have sustained."

"The poor little fellow is barely a year and a half old," Vera lamented sadly shaking her head. How could a mother not protect her own child?

Reg suddenly turned toward the woman who for all intent and purposes was Sidney's mother. "How was she when she left? She says not to worry in her letter..."

Vera smiled warmly at the powerfully built man's concern. "She was upset of course but mostly eager to get to Kevin and see if she could help."

Reg gave one definitive nod of his head and strode out of the room toward the back staircase. Luke's voice stopped him.

"Where are you going?"

"To New York where I belong," Reg called as he took the steps two and three at a time.

Luke slumped into a nearby wing back chair dejectedly. He lifted his gaze when Vera thrust a packet into his hand.

"Sidney signed the divorce papers before she left. She said she didn't want to leave you hanging a second time and clearly your mind was made up as your signature was already on the documents." Subtle disapproval invaded her placid tone.

His head snapped up to stare at the calm serene woman sitting at the round parlor table pouring a fresh cup of tea.

"Reginald, is there anything I can get you for the drive?" Vera asked as the man came barreling down the stairs once more.

Reg gazed down at her sincere expression and felt warmed by it. Other than with his own family, he rarely experienced this kind of warm genuine acceptance. "No, I'll be fine but there is something I'd like before I go."

"Name it Reginald," her lilting voice implored.

"I'll claim it instead," he told her silkily and folded her slight frame within his massive arms kissing her lavishly on the lips.

Vera blushed and lowered her eyes demurely. "I'm glad you spent your convalescence with us."

He smiled into her eyes. "So am I."

"Sidney hated to leave without seeing you but she..."

"Was in a hurry to get to Kevin..."

"And didn't feel up to going into Smitty's."

Reg nodded with new understanding. She didn't want to chance seeing Luke. "I'll take care of her."

"You always have. When I have been most worried, I have felt comforted by knowing you were with her."

"Speaking of which I need to go," he commented with resolve.

"I'll see you there," a low voice said from behind him and Reg swung around slowly with a hard look in his eyes.

"Sheriff, I can take care of her. I've been doing it for years."

"I'm well aware of that. You tell me often enough," Luke ground out. Gone was the easy camaraderie of only an hour ago.

"Well maybe you should consider that your place is here, not in New York. You did just divorce her. Perhaps your timing is a little off," Reg asserted coolly.

"Let me worry about my timing," Luke retorted, dangerously close to losing his temper.

"We'll all worry about it," Vera reiterated in a light airy tone decisively standing between the two men. "Reginald, why don't you get on your way so that you won't be driving in the dark the entire journey."

Reg made an agreeable reply and strode out of the house with a bag slung over his shoulder. Luke's eyes followed him but was aware that two sets of eyes fell upon his back. He turned back toward Vera and Charlie as they heard the car leaving the drive.

Surprise flickered across his fiercely handsome face when he saw the white envelope Vera held out to him. He took it without comment to open it.

"She says she will be back in a day or two and needs to speak with me then," he reported in an expressionless tone. The note was brief and totally lacking any kind of sentiment.

"And…" prodded Charlie.

Luke eyed him with annoyance. "And she asks me not to follow her. She says she and Reg need this time alone." He made a disgruntled snort. "They have had a whole decade and better alone."

"And you just divorced her," Charlie reminded him in disapproving tones. "Serves you right if she comes back with a second ring on her finger."

Vera gave the man who owned her heart a communicative glance and he grunted an answer. Luke sighed and slumped into a chair once again. "I'm an idiot."

Charlie couldn't resist. "There's a claim no one will dispute but the million dollar question now is what are you going to do about it?"

Luke shrugged lamely as his mind drifted wildly to the other man in the equation who was speeding to her and likely sleeping by her side in their bed tonight. He was indeed an idiot.

"Again?" Luke groaned in disbelief.

"Apparently," Carl reaffirmed.

"Well, ignore it"

"Ignore it?" Carl echoed, eyes narrowing.

Luke tipped back his chair. "With the vacation schedule, we don't have the manpower to go chasing down possible intruders in a dwelling no one gives a rat's ass about."

"I didn't know Sidney was back," Carl stated evenly.

Luke made a dismissive motion with his hand. "She isn't. She's due sometime tomorrow…"

Carl gaze was implacable. "Funny, the description fits."

Luke lifted his head, laid down his pen and grabbed his keys. It had been two long days, in which he had only received information second and third hand. Apparently, the Salenger baby was doing well, the suit against Sidney had been dropped, a formal apology and compensatory settlement from her employer had been offered and for all Luke was informed, she was going to be reinstated. That was sobering. She would have plenty of reason to return to New York and little enough to stay here.

Carl smiled as he watched him depart. For a man who had just divorced his wife, he sure went charging after her in a damned hurry. If Sidney was back a day earlier than scheduled, perhaps she was suffering from a similar affliction.

Jack chuckled to himself. He was driving toward the prestigious hill neighborhood just as he received word from Carl to ignore the possible B & E at Virginia Ryan's former house. Luke was apparently seeing to it personally. That only meant one thing. It was his wife. Again.

His eyes suddenly narrowed in surprise and he glanced again in his rearview mirror. Jack slammed on the brakes and reversed until he was upon her. The woman in question was strolling down the sidewalk so lost in her thoughts she didn't notice him until his third call.

"Thanks for the offer, Jack, but my car is just ahead," Sidney told him feeling foolish. The man's expression was entirely too smug.

"So, Sidney Ryan, where have you been?"

"New York." Sidney rolled her shoulders, wary and prepared to play the situation coolly. It would be humiliating to admit that she had broken into Virginia Ryan's house…again, and even harder to fess up to what she had been searching for. On the drive back from New York, she had suddenly remembered the pair of baby shoes Virginia had wrangled out of her insisting they needed to be bronzed according to an idiotic family tradition. Perhaps it was hormones but the idea of getting them back had taken on an absurd level of importance. Her search had proven fruitless and she had left that foreboding place horribly deflated.

"After that."

"Ahhh…" She frowned pensively and then narrowed her gaze sullenly. "Shit! Is there surveillance up on that damned hill?" Maybe Virginia was calling in APB's from hell.

He laughed loudly. "I'll drop you off and maybe you can straighten this out before the Sheriff books you. He was checking it out personally."

"Figures." Sidney rolled her eyes but complied. Given the current status of their relationship, arrest might be a possibility.

Jack didn't bother to hide his amusement. "From what Carl said, I think he was a little anxious he might find you there."

She snorted. "He's likely more anxious to see me in cuffs." The words were barely out when she leaned forward in her seat. "Jack, there's smoke. Up ahead." Panic slid into her voice until it rose in pitch. "Oh God, *Jack*! It's coming from Virginia's."

Sidney voice was quivering on the edge of full blown hysteria as her eyes caught sight of the Sheriff's cruiser parked with the driver's door flung wide open. Smoke billowed from the front door of the house, leaving no doubt where Luke was.

The car screeched to a halt and Jack was flying out of the car as frantically as she was. They ran toward the front door as a neighbor came charging forward. "Luke thinks you are in there!"

Her eyes were wild as she surged toward the doorway but two strong arms held her back while she flailed desperate to resist his hold.

"No! You can't go in there!" Jack shouted over the roar of the fire.

"My *husband* is in there!" she screamed.

Jack stood nose to nose with her. "I'll get him. Promise me that you will stay here!" he yelled, his voice roughened by emotion.

"Jack…" she pleaded.

"Promise me!" he bellowed.

Time was too crucial to waste. "I promise! Go!" Shoving him away.

Jack turned to the house that was rapidly becoming engulfed like a tinderbox. Flames licked eagerly at the structure. Her hand made a desperate grab at his sleeve once more as she shouted over the inferno. "Our bedroom. Upstairs. That's where he'd go."

Jack ran through the door and up the stairs with his arm flung over his face. Sirens were suddenly wailing as a large fire engine came roaring up. A crowd was gathering quickly when Sidney ran back to the cruiser and frantically called the station. Carl's voice came across the static and she rapidly apprised him of the situation through her burgeoning hysteria. Her heart slammed against her ribs in drenching relief as two men tumbled out of the thick blanket of smoke.

"He's out. Carl… Jack has him…" She dropped the radio to fly back out of the cruiser to where Jack had stumbled with the burden of Luke across his shoulders. Rescue workers had descended upon them in a rush and were busily attending them both as she stood pale and terrified a few feet away. Luke's arms were flailing wildly as he fought the men who were trying to attend him. He was shouting something incoherently as they attempted to put an oxygen mask over his face. She scrambled to his side as she realized it was her name he was yelling. He was still obviously terrified she was inside the house that was steadily being destroyed.

"Right here!" she sobbed grabbing his face in her hands holding it still. "I'm right here Luke. I'm safe. You're safe. Jack is fine. Let them put the mask on. Please," she implored him beseechingly.

His panicked eyes were glued to her but he relaxed slightly. His fingers wrapped around her wrist in a steely bracelet as if to guarantee her presence. He finally allowed the men to place the mask that would deliver oxygen to him over his face but his eyes never left hers.

Shouts could be heard as windows blew out and walls began collapsing in the interior of the house. Any fire fighters near the structure were pulled back to a safe distance as it was clear now that there was no chance of salvaging the house.

Sidney stared in roiling disbelief at the sight of her mother-in-law's prize possession crumbling before them. She turned back to Luke and saw his eyes were still riveted to her. She peered into their hazel depths that were visible just over the mask. "Luke, I need you to know…I didn't do this. I wouldn't do this. I didn't like the place but…"

His mask was wrenched off in one swift jerk as he tugged her down so that he could speak directly into her ear. His voice was hoarse and barely audible. "I don't care if you did. I don't give a tinker's damn about that place. I just can't bear to think of losing you in it."

Her eyes welled with tears and she collapsed onto his chest crying, when Charlie came charging across the lawn with Vera following close behind. Fear was stark on both of their faces. Relief coursed through them to see the couple, who were clinging to each other a safe distance from the raging fire with rescue workers hovering near by.

"He's going to be fine," Jack told them and they jerked around toward his husky voice. One glance verified who was responsible for getting Luke out of the house. Jack's hair and clothing were black and singed. He was coughing and irritably batting away the attentions of an ambulance attendant.

"I don't need anything but a stiff drink and a shower."

"You'll get that at our house," Vera declared and Charlie's expression was concurrent.

Jack blinked. He hadn't heard them ever openly admit to living together even though they had been doing so for years.

"Some of my clothes ought to fit and Vera pours a mean drink," Charlie added as he stepped forward to lend his long time colleague and friend some support. "Thank you for saving my son."

Jack gladly accepted his pro-offered arm that wrapped around his back. "Consider it a thank you for sharing him with me all these years."

Charlie glanced over at where Luke was still being embraced by a weeping Sidney and then beyond them to the house that was crumbling under the strain of the relentless flames. He had always hated the place, only living there because of his son. It would have been cruel beyond belief, if its destruction had claimed his boy.

A young woman stood a calculated distance away well shrouded by shrubbery, her eyes brittle. How could her plan have gone so wrong? It was a fluke that she had stumbled upon the possibility of disposing of her problem this afternoon. It was by far not her preferable choice but it had seemed plausible. Now a huge sacrifice had been made for nothing and a tragedy of untold dimensions had barely been averted. Her planning had to be meticulous next time, she privately berated herself and crept off into the denser cover of the brush. It was time to slip away before anyone noticed her.

Luke came awake slowly. The first thing that struck him was the acrid scent of smoke cloying to what seemed everything. It clung to his skin, hair, thickly layered the very air around him voraciously, threatening to clog his throat, again, and renewed the clawing terror that some harm had come to Sidney. As he drew in a laborious breath that seemed absurdly fatiguing, blissfully the sweet scent of her lay beneath. It brought reassurance she was near and that alone had him relaxing back into the soft linens that were also miraculously perfumed with her.

He heard vague murmurs of activity. Water running, hushed movements, preparations of some kind. Quiet footsteps coming near had him trying to edge open leaden eyes but his vision merely wavered and faded out despite his best effort. He cursed thoroughly and vividly though his lips never moved, not a sound came from his throat, raw and sore. God dammit, he needed to see her. Now. To quell the dread that had a stranglehold on his heart. She was in danger. Every instinct warned him. He had always thought of his mother's house as a tomb, certainly for Sidney during the dismal months they had lived there after Natalie's death, but never had that seemed more true than today.

He moaned when the wash cloth touched him, moving in long soothing strokes. The pleasant fragrance of soap, fresh and welcome, rapidly replacing the offensive scent of cinder and ashes. The cloth was soft and delightfully warm, still he wished it were her hands gliding over him.

He must have dozed but came languidly awake to find his wish being granted. The groan sounded low in the back of his throat when nimble fingers threaded through his hair gently kneading his scalp, supporting his neck, and lifting his head off the bed. Tepid water flowed from a pitcher bathing his hair. His sigh was lost as the water splashed into a basin and her hands vigorously rubbed a thick towel over his damp head.

Luke felt her hands linger on his shoulders, kneading there as he expelled a long shaky sigh. The image of the flames shooting out of the second story windows and the abhorrent thought that she could be trapped within was, he suspected, one he wouldn't shake anytime soon.

He couldn't remember being taken home. In fact, something didn't quite fit. His bed didn't face this way. Yet, it was familiar. Right. Welcoming. Sidney permeated everything here.

She was so close now her breath tickled his cheek teasing his lips to a smile. The comb she held fell away as her hands fisted in his thick hair that now felt mercifully scrubbed. "Luke." Her voice fretful, breath hitching. "You're awake?"

He wanted to clutch her against him, whisper endearments, promises and hear them returned. His gravely voice was barely recognizable to himself as he croaked out, "Thirsty."

Her hands scurried in efficient response yet the glass pressed to his lips seconds later trembled. "Slow. Just a sip." His swallow was audible and hurt like a bitch.

· "Better," he murmured hoarsely as she eased him back upon the pillow. His eyes opened to slits needing to see her. She seemed ethereal in the moonlight and while her eyes were dry, silvery paths told him tears had barely dried.

Luke lifted his hand to cup her cheek and his heart broke open wide when she turned her lips to his palm and pressed a kiss there.

"I'm so sorry," she whispered brokenly, her impossibly huge eyes glistening with a fresh sheen of tears. "The house is gone."

His laugh was short and bitter before ending in a cough. "Good riddance."

Her eyes squeezed shut, her head bowed as shoulders that seemed too slight began to shake with silent sobs. God, she had almost lost him a second time.

Shaken he hauled her down to cradle her against his chest. "Shhh Sweetheart."

"I just wanted the shoes."

"The shoes."

Her words were teary, breath broken. "Natalie's. Your Mother took them. She wanted to have them bronzed." Yes, he knew that though he hadn't thought of it in years. "I didn't want to give them to her. Nat took her first steps in those shoes. Remember the little white ones that never stayed done up so you would tie them in double knots I could never untie." The memory of her grumbling under her breath as Nat tried to squirm a getaway made his lips curve. "But Virginia insisted she needed the shoes. Family tradition, she said." A very stupid one, Luke thought, as Sidney swiped at her nose, fumbled for a tissue and knocked the box flying.

"Dammit!" She knelt to pick up the box and found herself on her knees. "Dammit. Dammit. Dammit."

"Sweetheart..." Biting back an oath at the aches that were screaming, Luke levered himself up on an elbow.

She rushed to her feet. "No! Lay back!" She perched on the bed and pushed on his shoulders.

Luke complied swiftly because she was near again and stole the advantage to catch her hands in his. "Stay." Her eyes easily conveyed she might jackrabbit the second he released her. He easily circled both wrists in one hand and cupped her cheek with the other. "Sweetheart, when you were in the house..."

"I shouldn't have been. I'm sorry."

He waved that away. "Did you hear anything?"

"Anything?"

"Someone else."

Huge doe eyes widened. "No. No. I was alone. I was rifling through things, going from room to room..." She shook her head before looking him straight in the eye. "No one was there but me." She paused swallowing back her unease. "I don't know how the fire started. Nothing seemed out of the ordinary to me."

The cold ball in his gut froze. Whoever was there knew how to stay invisible though if she were rushing about distracted by her search that would have made it easier on them. She was so pale in the moonlight, he instinctively sought to soothe. "You are very observant Sid so I must just be paranoid. The fire marshal will likely find some problem with the wiring."

She desperately wanted to believe that as his hand trailed over her hair, toying with the ends. "Sid, I wished you had asked me about the shoes."

She shrugged with a twinge of embarrassment. "It seemed so silly."

He shook his head and kept his eyes locked on hers. "Not silly. I have the shoes, Sweetheart."

Her lips formed a silent O. "Virginia gave them to you?"

"No. Ed Tanner gave them to me after Mother took them to him to send away for bronzing. His affections were for you though Mother's business contributed heavily to keeping his dry cleaning business fluent. He called me to say if you wanted them bronzed, he would bronze them. For free. If not he wanted them returned to you and told my Mother they were lost during shipping." Luke almost chuckled as he watched her mind whirl, imagining the scene. "Ed offered to reimburse her and lost her business for keeps." The shouting match had spilled onto the sidewalk, ended up involving several other loyal customers and had taken both Charlie and Jack to break it up. "I kept them for you. Thought I could give them to you during one of our meetings with the lawyers but you never came. So, I held onto them. They're yours." The same way, Luke thought, he was hers. "You just have to claim them."

How could she take them from him? Her hand crept to her abdomen. How did you divide something so precious? "Why don't you put them with Natalie's letters and keep them in a safe place for us?"

God, she turned him to putty with a mere gesture. He threaded his fingers through hers and watched the storm in her eyes. Before he could comment on it, soft lips were on his, caressing, lingering, savoring, tasting…

A low noise of pleasure was born in his throat. It turned to a growl as her kiss deepened and the tip of her tongue invaded his mouth to explore the warmth there. His hand wove through the tumbling hair that fell in a silken curtain over him. The sheer rapture of the solace she was offering him overwhelmed his weakened senses. The rightness of it consuming him. She was where she had always belonged. With him. Beside him. Sharing his bed.

His breath caught as it finally penetrated the fog of his mind what was different. This wasn't his bed. It was hers. The bed they had shared during the first two blissful years of their marriage. She had brought him *home.*

He felt her easing away from him though their mouths were still locked in the consuming kiss. His one arm snaked around her slender back to haul her against him in the bed. Her mouth whispered against his. "You need rest…"

"*I need you,*" Luke protested with teeming emotion.

Huge eyes searched his wondrously and he glimpsed the sorrow there.

"You want your wife. I'm not her anymore. You said so yourself..."

"I'm an idiot. You are all I ever need."

Her eyes seemed to darken and held to his as her mouth curved sadly. "You may not think so in the light of day..."

"I will think so until my dying day, Sidney Ryan. You are my wife. Stay in this bed we shared so many years ago. Make love with me. I want to make another...."

Her mouth descended upon his with startling speed, swallowing the words about to tumble from his lips. She couldn't hear them out loud. Not yet. Tonight was too sweet. Too wonderful. Too much of what she needed after today.

So, she let herself give, let herself take and welcomed his hands on her. The love spun out as if time had no place in this room. Indeed it seemed to naturally warp as they came together in the same bed where that had once been the norm. If she let her mind wander foolishly, she could almost imagine a child, beyond beauty, sleeping in the corner.

The aftershocks of loving well were still shocking her system, when she buried her face in the warm hollow between his neck and shoulder and held him fiercely to her. His hands were tenderly stroking her back in long fluid movements as he whispered endearments near her ear.

One strong hand cupped her face and felt the wetness there. "You're crying?" Luke acknowledged in concern.

Sidney smiled up at him through her tears, knowing she had just experienced more beauty than she had a right to and prepared to lie. "It's been a long day."

Perhaps but there was more, he knew, watching her in the moonlight. Being less than battle ready tonight, he let it pass because this was one fight he intended to win. "I've always loved this room. Thanks for bringing me here."

Sidney ran her tongue over her lips. "Charlie needed you close." God, it was so hard to skirt the truth when those eyes seemed to see everything. "I needed you close."

His smile warmed as his heart loosened and he took a risk. "I loved this room most when there was a crib in the corner." He knew she wanted to curl against him, keep him close without the intimacy of eye contact. Luke eased her beside him and levered up on an elbow to gaze into those wary brown eyes.

Her fingers lifted to lay over his lips. "No more talking. Not tonight. I want more."

"So do I, Sidney." She distracted him when her hand scooted under the bed covers. "Sweetheart, I'm older now..."

Her knee nudged his groin as one slender hand fondled him. She smiled beguilingly into the shadows. "It appears tonight we have found the elixir of youth..." she teased.

He swallowed realizing the truth of her words. He had forgotten response like this was possible. His lips found hers once more and they melded together in searing heat. "A life time, Sidney," he muttered as he let the elemental magic between them take over. "That's what I want. A life time." Sensations rippled through them and exploded around them once again and afterward she wept quietly, tremendously relieved that he had fallen into an exhausted sleep, his mouth curved into a smile.

Sidney curled up in a cozy armchair in her aunt's study by the light of only one small lamp. She discovered quickly that she couldn't bear to remain in the room with her husband any longer as he slept. Her mind couldn't shut out the ecstasy of the past hours with her heart knowing it was likely the last she would know of it. In a matter of hours, certainly less than a day, she would have to make revelations known that would likely shatter the future he felt so certain about. Her eyes fluttered miserably closed. His faith in her would have to be unshakable for anything else. She knew too much of fate to believe.

Tears blurred her eyes as her fingers idly flipped through the pages of the manuscript her aunt had recently been leaving anywhere she might inadvertently stumble over it. It had been years since she had read...really read...one of her aunt's novels. They both knew it and glossed over the hurt.

Tonight she was determined to try in the quiet of the room she had loved in her youth. This space always made her feel wonderfully close to her aunt. The many nights she spent here reading the chapters her aunt had finessed during the day flashed in her memory. There was a time Sidney might have taken a stab at writing herself but those days had passed.

Her eyes studied the first typed page of text and she began to read. Slowly at first; grudgingly willing herself to enjoy it. By the end of the first chapter, no prodding was needed. By the third chapter, she was hooked beyond redemption, her heart beat thundering in the silent room. When she glanced up again, the clock had moved time considerably.

Her head snapped up when Vera burst through the door slightly ahead of her companion. The rare expression of impatience she wore was telling as Carlene nattered on behind her.

Sidney blinked at the sun streaming across them. Where had the night gone?

"Sidney!" Vera exclaimed in the shock of finding the young woman curled up in a night gown years old with part of a manuscript in her hands. It was like traveling in time. A time she had never been able to retrieve. Vera's alert eyes darted from the tracks of tears on Sidney's wan face to the manuscript she held. It was mostly read. Only a thin sheath of pages remained.

Sidney swallowed and stared up at the woman, who had raised her, struggling for composure and losing. "How could you?" she asked in choked tremulous voice.

"Sidney..." Vera repeated only in pleading tones now as she moved toward her.

Sidney pursed her lips as tears brimmed again and thrust out the pages she held in a blanched grip. "This is not a book..."

"Of course it is. The one we have been working on," Carlene piped up cheerfully, outwardly unaffected by the nerves vibrating in the room.

Vera stilled, remembering they were not alone. "Carlene, why don't you go look up those references?"

"The references?" the young woman stammered wide eyed.

"The ones we discussed earlier." Vera glanced meaningfully at her assistant. "Now please, Carlene."

Carlene realigned her gaze from Sidney to her employer. "All right... yes. Of course. I can return those periodicals..."

"Fine. Go," Vera bit out in a clipped manner she seldom used and was too distracted to notice that Carlene's eyes hardened in response. "Luke woke up an hour ago. He just left for home because he was convinced that you weren't in the house. We looked everywhere." She shook red curls in disbelief. "It didn't occur to me to look here. I never dreamt you would be here. There was a time, years ago, that it would have been the first place I checked." Hurt teemed in her eyes as she met the younger woman's gaze straight on. "But you and I both know those days have long since been over. This is the first book of mine you have really read in over a decade, isn't it?" her aunt asked bluntly.

Sidney held her steadfast gaze. "You know it is. I knew my calculated questions and comments didn't really fool you but I no longer believed in the kind of emotion you wrote about..."

Delicate penciled brows lifted. "It is interesting that now since returning home for the first substantial period of time in years you have picked up one of my books again."

Sidney's brown eyes flashed cold and defiant. "This isn't your book, Auntie. It isn't one of the stories that spring into your head from beginning to end that drive you to distraction until you can tell them. *This is my life! And you wrote it down!*" she shouted making the small panes of decorative glass shudder.

"Sidney…"

She shot to her feet and slammed the loose papers onto the carpet at her feet. "Don't you dare deny it! The names are different and some of the scenarios are altered, but essentially the story is mine. Mine, Luke's and Reg's. My babies'." Hot tears poured down her cheeks unheeded as she accused her aunt. "Why? Why would you invade my privacy…my life…"

Vera's eyes rivaled saucers. "Why? *Why!?* Sidney, a year ago, I walked into an Intensive Care Unit to hear a physician tell me the person I hold dearest in my heart might not survive. That you had tried to take your own life…"

"I'm sorry," she sobbed hoarsely. They stood two feet apart but the gulf was miles wide. "I've told you that over and over. I was so despondent after losing Lily. Losing both of my babies just seemed too unbearable."

Finally, Vera thought, the fight she had waited for, craved. "And you couldn't talk to Reg….really talk, because you had too many secrets he didn't know about. Too many you didn't think he would understand because you can't understand them yourself."

Sidney gulped knowing it would do little good to deny that fact. It was all too true. "But regardless Auntie, I got better again…"

Vera's eyes narrowed. "*You functioned again.* Beyond that, I could never be sure. You cover so well. I know all about it. Sidney, I live it. People always think Kathleen and I are similar. Outrageous, flamboyant, a little zany bordering on nuts…." She easily took in the shuttered expression overtaking the younger woman. "Sidney I hear all the whispers…the gossip…I choose to ignore it. I was once very much like you. Taking on all the responsibility in the world. Trying to meet everyone's needs while ignoring my own. Ask Charlie, he knows."

Sidney frowned lightly. She did recall Charlie referring to how her Vera was different when they were a young couple. She shook her head in outright confusion. "But you have always been the same since Kat and I came here…"

Vera softened at the memories. Her girls so small, so alone. "I had to be, Darling. I had to do a great many things."

Sidney made a soft scoffing sound. "Like what?"

"I married Jackson McCorkidale for one."

"You loved him…"

"Like a brother."

Sidney didn't looked the least bit surprised. "Of course you did. Auntie, your husband was gay."

Vera's jaw went slack. "How did you know that? Heavens, you were still a girl when he died."

"Jackson told me around the time he realized he was really sick and was going to die. He seemed to think I would need to know someday." Sidney paused considering. "Jackson had AIDS, didn't he? No one ever said."

Vera couldn't hide her keen sense of sadness the mere mention of Jackson's name provoked. "No one would have. We kept that a secret too, and truthfully, little was known about the disease then. It certainly wasn't the fashionable cause it is now."

Sidney looked her straight in the eye. "You give a lot to that cause."

Vera nodded. "I do. My novels have done well and I owe Jackson considerably for that. He encouraged me constantly during my first attempts at becoming published. He was my best friend."

"Charlie hated him."

Vera sighed forlornly thinking of the two men she had loved very differently. "Charlie never knew him. Not really. And he would have hated anyone who lived here with us when he couldn't."

A new thought occurred to Sidney suddenly as old memories surged forward. "Wasn't your hair brown like mine when you visited us in Carringville when Mom and Dad were alive?"

"I was bored with my appearance." Vera glanced away, shrugged. "It was too plain."

"Am I plain?"

Vera's head whipped up, aghast. "Sidney, you are beautiful."

"In the few pictures I can find of you and my mother as girls, you looked a lot like me."

Vera's expression softened and she reached out to touch the younger woman's hair. "You are prettier than I ever was."

"Have you run out of stories that you needed mine?" Sidney asked poignantly.

Vera walked over to an old oak filing cabinet and pulled out several folders. "These are outlines for three books and two short stories."

Sidney's eyes narrowed. "Then why?" she asked beseechingly gesturing to the manuscript scattered on the floor, fluttering in the breeze.

"I was desperate to reach you. I thought perhaps if you saw your story written down it might help you sort it out...."

"So I would come home and resume the marriage you knew wasn't legally over, live a few convenient blocks away, give you grandchildren..."

Vera gasped and seemed to pale under her generous coat of foundation. "Grandchildren?" she weakly repeated.

Sidney threw her an agitated glance. "Of course my children would be your grandchildren. I barely remember my mother after all these years. I may call you Auntie but everyone who knows you and I, knows *you* are my mother," she finished with both of them painfully aware there was little pleasure in her declaration.

Vera studied her with an odd look. "Then you should understand having been a devoted mother yourself, why I couldn't stand by and allow you not to come to terms with your past any longer."

Sidney shook her head wearily. "All I can see is that once again you have likely turned out another best seller Lara Lovelorn. Congratulations," she commended bitterly while rising to head toward the door. She paused to turn back briefly. "Although you likely should write an ending before sending it off to your agent."

Vera's brown eyes were dark and misty. She longed to reach out to her but knew she would only be pushed away. "Don't you see Sidney? I can't finish it. Only you can do that."

"That'll be a problem then."

Alarm shook the older woman. "Why?" she asked uneasy.

Sidney sighed. "Because to be a commercial success in the romance line, you require a happy ending. I can pretty much guarantee that is unlikely in my situation."

"Sidney, what do you…"

The younger woman held up one hand. "I have an appointment to keep. If I'm late, there is no telling what could happen. With my luck, someone might just fancy themselves a writer and come up with an ending of their own," she finished sardonically and walked out.

Vera watched her go feeling weak and shaken. She glanced down at the jumble of typed pages on the floor with disdain. Sidney was wrong. Her story promised to be a huge commercial success not that she ever intended on offering it to a publisher. The purpose behind putting pen to paper in this instance was far more noble. Unfortunately, her best laid plans had gone awry. Tears smeared makeup that was applied far too liberally and for the first time in decades she truly longed to wash it off and be done with it. For all intents and purposes, her charade was over and that knowledge was bittersweet to accept. After all, it hadn't saved Sidney anyway.

Sidney stiffened as the needle went into her vein and hurriedly turned aside from the sight of several vials being filled with her dark red blood by the efficient lab nurse who was chattering nonstop.

She waited with tried patience while applying pressure to the spot where the needle had been withdrawn until the nurse dutifully stuck a bandage in place. Sidney rose and scooped her purse from the floor thinking only of her haste to be gone. She blindly clutched the edge of the door to steady herself as her vision grayed.

"Oh you poor dear! You got up too fast. You need to think slow for the next months. Easy does it. Sit right here," a solicitous voice regaled her as she was eased back into the same chair she had eagerly sprang from. "I'll just give your sister a call to pick you up...."

"No!" Sidney burst out in sudden panic. The last thing she needed today was more family.

The RN was shocked by the severity of her reaction. "Kathleen would be glad to pick you up. Why just last week when she was in..."

Sidney came to full alert and straightened ram rod stiff. "For blood work?"

The RN waved away her question like it was a foregone conclusion. "Just the usual...lithium levels..."

Sidney blinked astounded but she recovered fast enough to ask the seemingly innocent question. "Are they therapeutic?"

"Oh of course. Why she and Dr. Dixon practically have things down to a science..."

Sidney stood up slowly and stumbled toward the door despite the woman's protest. She waved away her concern knowing the red haze in front of her eyes was from fury. "I'm fine. I'm merely doing what women in my family have been doing for generations."

"Having babies?" the woman responded with cheerful confidence.

"No... being manipulative, underhanded and deceitful," she ground out and left without a backward glance.

The typically talkative lab technician was momentarily speechless. Finally, she gave her head a little shake. And people always thought Kathleen was the sister with the dramatic flair.

CHAPTER TWENTY-NINE

Charlie swore savagely under his breath as his pencil tip broke off with only a couple of spaces to go. The unfinished crossword puzzle seemed to be mocking him. Number 12 across: a six letter word for *nefarious event.* He grunted. That clue should be a cinch for a former cop, but it wasn't. Not today anyway. He sighed trying to shake off the unsettled feeling he had felt creeping over him all day.

With burgeoning consternation, Charlie narrowed his eyes on the page. Number 3 down: *What some couples do after divorce.* That was easy. *Celebrate!* He certainly did after he was finally rid of Virginia. He grimaced. Too many letters. *Make endless love to the woman you dreamt of during your hellish marriage.* He rolled his eyes. Too many words.

Regardless his mind wandered to the woman of his life's affections. Her hair had been chestnut brown once. Years ago. He actually preferred that to the red rinse Vera favored for the last couple of decades, but he could persevere. After all, he could summon up her image in his mind easily enough and did occasionally in the darkness together. A serene, elegant, sedate beauty. Her appearance and her mannerisms had altered some might say drastically over the years but he had always taken most of the responsibility for that in his tortured conscience. An unthinkable one night affair, he couldn't even recall clearly, had altered the course of their life irrefutably. What they had planned. What they had dreamed. The townspeople may see a flighty eccentric novelist who jarred every fashion trend imaginable with her own eclectic style but he only saw her. The dark haired vision with the glorious smile and warm laughing eyes who taught him the true meaning of happiness.

That alone had helped keep him sane during the frigid years of wedlock he had endured for Luke's sake. Charlie smiled secretly. That and some stolen nights at his fishing cabin. Even years afterward when things looked their bleakest. First, when Vera left Barren's Creek for well over a year refusing to divulge her destination and then returning married to another man. Charlie snorted. If one could actually call Jackson McCorkidale that. Maddeningly, Vera still turned wistful to this day at the mention of the deceased man. Her best friend, she called him. Charlie's insides clenched fiercely at the mere suggestion.

Her voice shattered his revelry in a blinding instant. "Charlie, we need to talk. *Privately.*"

His entire body tensed as his blood grew sluggish in his veins. He recognized that tone. He could count on one hand how many times he had heard it and none of those conversations had ever turned out well. He held his breath, and painstakingly raised his eyes to hers waiting for the other shoe to drop. His chin fell to his chest with a thud.

"In my study, Charlie," Vera directed tonelessly.

"Is there a calendar in there?"

She went blank. "Whatever for?"

"I need to check the year. I think I have just lapsed twenty years or so."

Vera stood stock still staring at him staring back at her.

"Your hair isn't red."

"It was time for a change."

"You are barely wearing any face paint. No rouge at all."

"That needed to change too."

His eyes swept her head to toe. "Your clothes are different."

"Yes."

"Less frills." He angled his head studying her breasts. "I can't see through your blouse and your separates match."

"I borrowed a couple of Sidney's things. We are about the same size."

"Your tastes used to run very similar to Sidney's," he remarked absently. Something was falling so neatly into place he almost heard it click.

"Yes," she agreed haltingly still frozen to the spot where she stood. Their eyes had yet to stray from one another. Perhaps she should just say it here and get it over with.

"You're trembling."

"I'm scared," she admitted in a bare whisper.

He jolted aghast. *"Of me?!"*

"Of losing you."

He smiled faintly. "Darlin that'll never happen. Never again. You know that."

· She shook her head slowly with glistening eyes as tears leapt forward. "No I don't and neither do you until you know the truth."

Charlie shoved his chair back from the table in growing alarm and was facing her with ground covering steps in seconds. "I know every truth about you I ever need to know...."

"Sidney is my child."

The hands that were reaching for her fell to his sides.

"I am her mother, not her aunt."

His eyes bore into hers with cutting intensity.

"I went away for a year to carry her, give birth to her and nurse her at my breast before I had to leave for her own safety."

His teeth clicked together but he took one more step forward. "Because she is mine."

Vera stared at him pale and small. Her eyes confirmed his declaration more eloquently than any words could have.

Footsteps pounded on the porch steps and into the parlor. *"Where is my wife?"*

Vera and Charlie swung around at the crashing interruption of Luke's shout. Charlie whirled back with militant precision and accusatory eyes. "You let my children marry each other!" he yelled incensed and incredulous.

Luke gaped stunned. Charlie was quaking with rage and Vera....He did a quick double take. The woman in the front room was the lady of his childhood. The woman his mother would turn his face from if they met by chance in the street as if she was something grotesque. He vividly recalled the rare occasion when they did see one another without Virginia present. The pretty, chestnut haired lady was kind and warm. Her tinkling laughter and sunny smile still hid in the recesses of his memory until today.

"You were the woman from the cabin. I always wondered what became of her."

Two bodies spun back toward him flabbergasted.

"It is one of my earliest memories. Mother took me there. To the cabin. I was just over four." Luke indicated Charlie with a tip of his head. "You were there for several days and had just spoken on the phone. She said you sounded happy and made it clear she wasn't pleased. I remember thinking even as a small child, isn't being happy a good thing? I knew better than to say so to Mother. Even then." Luke's eyes clouded as he summoned up long forgotten images. "I was excited to go to the cabin but surprised she was taking me there. Mother, of course, hated the place. We parked a distance away on the main road and walked in. I didn't understand why at the time and she was angry at my curious questions. In retrospect, she was furious period. We were just coming in sight of the cabin when I heard you laughing. A full bodied unrestrained laugh that I never heard at home. The kind I only heard when you and I were alone. I heard it that day and was so excited. I was just about to run to you eager to join the fun when Mother yanked me back. It hurt. Even now, I can feel her long manicured nails biting into my arm but I didn't dare cry. And then I heard the Pretty Lady voice."

Vera swallowed uncomfortably. "The what?"

Luke lifted reminiscent eyes to hers. "That's what I called the pretty woman with the dark eyes and hair with the soft smile." His eyes narrowed as he looked closely at Vera's mouth. "Sidney has that smile."

A tear that had been clinging to her lashes fell to her cheek.

"Mother stiffened and said words you used to yell at her for saying in front of me. I was so lonely. I was stuck by my mother in her iron grip, but I desperately wanted to be with my Dad and his Pretty Lady. You were laughing and chasing each other. You weren't wearing very much." Two pairs of eyes shared a communicative glance that held for a long emotion strained moment. "At the time I thought you were playing tag. I know better now."

Charlie closed his eyes. "We conceived Sidney during those few stolen days."

Vera choked off a sob. "Yes."

"Natalie was conceived there too. I took Sidney there the night Kathleen threatened to kill her on the bridge because to me after that day it was a place where people found happiness... peace," Luke added, awestruck by the startling coincidence.

Vera pursed her lips to keep a precarious grip on her burgeoning sentiment as she observed Charlie's rigid stance and brittle expression.

"My children had a child together," he ground out between set teeth looming over her with barely leashed wrath.

Her dark eyes darted to Luke's. Charlie's followed and was slightly taken aback to see the calm in his son's expression. "I apologize Luke for my cantankerous attitude about your divorce. Obviously it is necessary."

Luke deftly cut him off. "I don't want a divorce. That's why I'm here. To beg her to take me back. She said in the night there was something that might keep us apart but she's wrong..."

"Don't be so sure," a low rumbling voice said from behind him.

Dread permeated Luke's every pore as Reg's presence registered. He turned around slowly to face the larger man who rivaled him for his wife's love. "Is there something more you would like to share, Reg? Like what the hell you are doing back here so..."

"Sidney phoned late last night and asked me to come a day early," he returned rapidly. "Something's wrong."

Luke's foreboding feeling magnified. "What did she say?"

"Nothing in particular. It was the quality of her voice..."

The lean muscle in Luke's cheek ticked with jealousy. She left his bed to call this man. "Of course, and you have had years of practice knowing when something is wrong. Well shove it, Buckman. She's my wife."

"In three months after the final decree, she will be whoever's wife she chooses," Reg reminded him tauntingly. "She's never divorced me before."

"She's never married you either."

"You'll make my daughter a good husband," a deep solemn voice acknowledged in grave tones.

"Your who?" Reg expounded slack jawed at Charlie.

"My daughter. Mine and Vera's. She should be with you. Her marriage to my son was clearly a grim error in judgment." Charlie threw a cringing Vera a brittle glance.

Vera turned helplessly to face the man who had been her universe even in the years they had been apart. "Charlie, you don't understand. This situation is not nearly as simple as you presume it to be."

"My son slept with my daughter and made her pregnant. Maybe there is a reason little Natalie…"

"Don't!" Luke snarled advancing toward him. His features rigid with latent violence.

Vera saw the building tension and grew desperate. "Charlie, my sister and I agreed that it was best for her and George to raise Sidney. I spent my pregnancy with them. They had decided after having Kathleen not to have more children for Violet's sake," she saw annoyed understanding in the older man's face and bewilderment on both of the younger ones. "My sister Vie was bipolar like Kathleen only not as well managed. It was called manic depressive disorder then. Vie's husband was incredible, thank God. We agreed as a group that it would be best to raise the girls together as sisters in a different town."

"Without me. The child's father," Charlie ground out bitterly.

Her eyes were pleading. "Charlie, if you knew you would have left Virginia…"

"In a frigging New York minute and then Woman, do you know what would have happened!" Tears brimmed in her eyes as he yelled scant inches from her face. "I would have divorced the shrew and we would have been the happy loving family we were always meant to be instead of spending half of our lives apart!" His voice had quickly escalated to a shout bringing two startled faces from the kitchen to stand awkwardly in the living room gaping at them.

"What about Luke?" Vera asked in small choked voice.

Charlie stared openly at her as if she were demented. "Good Lord Woman! What do you think? He would be with us of course. Part of a family with the Pretty Lady of his childhood dreams as his mother. Being a big brother to his sister instead of taking her to bed years later unbeknown to anyone but you!"

"Charlie, Luke was a big brother to Sidney for a number of years. I was so thrilled to see it happen. It brought me great joy to see them together. I had no idea anything else was between them until the fateful day of Sidney's high school graduation."

"What stopped you from saying something then? Before they were married!" he exploded.

Vera's eyes darted helplessly to Luke again who was watching them with rapt attention. "Natalie had already been conceived and Sidney came to my room that very night Luke proposed so publicly. Charlie, she was radiant and gushing over the prospect of being Luke's wife and a mother. She was not a trapped pregnant teenager. She was a young woman who had found the love of her life. I saw myself in her. I knew the kind of joy she felt. The kind I have always felt for you."

"It's still inexcusable. In fact, it is illegal for siblings to marry and you knew it," he charged vehemently spurning her overtures of love. "You also knew that in all likelihood they would have more children after the one that was already on its way..."

"I thought..." She hesitated a second with a fleeting look in Luke's direction once more. "I thought that maybe I could sort out a few things before that happened."

Charlie snorted with blatant disgust. "*Like what?* How exactly do you solve a problem of two people who share the same father?"

Vera clamped her mouth resolutely shut unwilling to elaborate further but she went limp with relief when another voice spoke. "We don't."

Charlie spun slack jawed toward his son's solemn voice. "Whatever Vera's faults are Son and at this precise moment, I had better not list them, she is an honorable woman. If she says Sidney is her child and mine, she is. What's more, I know it. In fact, I am a colossal idiot that I didn't figure it out long before today," he berated himself soundly.

Luke maintained stoic eye contact. "Vera is an honorable woman. Sidney *is* your daughter. My mother however is the least honorable woman we both knew." His voice was tight as he continued with Charlie's gaze intensely fixed on him. "I am not your son." He turned his eyes to the woman whose resemblance to his wife was now uncanny. "You knew," he accused softly.

"I suspected," Vera admitted. "Virginia couldn't resist throwing out a few hints."

Charlie's eyes bugged out of his head, thoroughly baffled, as he jabbed a finger at the lean muscularly built man who stood before him. "I don't believe either of you! You are mine!"

"In every way that matters but not in biology," Luke reiterated in regretful tones and regarded Vera again with enormous interest. "Why didn't you say something? You could have had everything you wanted."

"No. I couldn't." She smiled sadly. "Even though I grew to suspect heavily you weren't Charlie's son by blood, you adored one another. If his marriage to your mother ended and you weren't his, we would have no claim to you." She spun to Charlie now. "We couldn't be happy at the expense of a child. The cost was too great. What would have become of Luke alone in Virginia's hands?"

Luke shuttered as overwhelming emotion crashed through him at Vera's profound generosity. He watched as the man, he called Dad, sank into a nearby chair. Charlie finally lifted a bleak face to him. "How do you know I'm not your father?"

"Mother told me gleefully the day she died. She and I began to argue over Sidney. It was loud and bitter and as I was about to go, she pulled out her trump card. I was livid and accused her of lying of course. I couldn't believe you weren't my father and then she proceeded to tell me how she had launched her plan years ago to end your engagement to Vera. The saddest part was it was never really about love for Mother. It was about getting the best trophy piece and somehow she decided in all of Barren's Creek that was you, but Vera had your heart unequivocally. She doctored your drink after luring you over as a rookie answering a routine call. Nothing happened in fact she slunk out while you were sleeping it off and seduced the man who is my father."

Charlie closed his eyes in anguish and shook his head. "How can you be certain?"

"I confirmed it with blood tests once I became Sheriff by bending a few rules. I was pivotal in getting the annual physical requirement passed, remember."

Charlie's head shot up. "That's right. You were like a dog with a bone and I couldn't understand why the hell it mattered so much. You were new on the job and ruffling quite a few feathers."

Luke nodded grimly. "It took me years to verify what she had told me that day but by then it was merely confirmation. I had really accepted it as truth. Once I knew, some things started to jump out at me, seeing the man everyday…" he groaned suddenly realizing he had given away too much.

Charlie and Vera's gazes jerked toward each other. "Jack." They breathed together and their eyes flew to Luke's for confirmation.

"He needs to be told first before I can say one way or the other."

Vera laid a hand on Luke's arm. "You mustn't blame yourself for anything Virginia did. You endured a parent no child deserved."

One of his eyebrows rose wryly. "She knew that too by the end of our shouting match. I told her I used to fantasize as a little boy that I could go live with the Pretty Lady and my Dad in your cabin instead of her huge cold house; we would be happy and maybe they would give me a brother or sister. She went ballistic. As she ranted and raved incoherently, I turned to leave and she collapsed on the floor. At first, I accused her of faking something, it was a few minutes before I realized she wasn't pretending. I had a lot of guilt over that but Frank Barrett has assured me the time wouldn't have made a difference," he shrugged. "Maybe he was just trying to alleviate my guilt though. He disliked my mother as much as most people."

"What does Sidney say?" Reg asked quietly.

Luke was shocked at Reg's accurate assumption that he had confided in Sidney. "She said that my mother's hate caused her death. That she didn't know love when she was staring it in the face."

Reg smiled faintly. "Believe her Luke. Sidney is very smart about love. A decade ago absorbed in grief, she just forgot to follow her instincts." He looked from side to side. "Where is she anyway? We three have something to settle."

Vera began to cry softly and three men turned toward her in concern. "We had a fight. Charlie, she read my book during the night in the study. She was furious with me…"

Luke was astounded. "Over one of your books? A story?"

Vera sighed through her tears and Charlie moved to her side to gather her in his arms. She sagged in the cradle of his embrace with tears pouring down her face now. "It's not one of my stories. It is hers…and yours…" She gestured to Luke. "And yours." She gestured to Reg. "I thought if she read it she may be able to finally sort through it."

Reg grunted. "How does it end Vera?"

Vera smiled pleadingly knowing exactly what he was asking. "There is no ending. It's not mine to write."

"Is that why Aunt Sidney was so mad today?" a small voice timidly asked from the shadows of the living room just beyond the front parlor.

Vera regarded the prepubescent girl tenderly. "Did you hear us arguing honey?"

Her pale aqua eyes were huge and woeful as she shook her head dreadfully close to tears. Luke moved forward a few steps. "What did you hear Nic?"

She drew a gulping breath and her eyes ricocheted from one person to another with uncertainty. "She was fighting with Mom."

Luke smiled kindly at her. "Your Mom probably just said something off color and Sidney has a lot on her mind..."

"No," the young girl staunchly protested. "Aunt Sidney was furious with her." Tears streamed from her eyes now as she struggled to speak. "She was yelling. Telling Mom she was irresponsible, deceitful and manipulative. Mom was begging her to understand..."

Luke's face was set in a frown. "Understand what, Nicole?"

Her voice was almost inaudible with her distress. Reg had moved forward and reached out to stroke her hair. He was shocked when she hurled her slim frame into his burly one. She peeked out from the shelter of his chest. "I couldn't listen anymore. I just know Aunt Sidney will go to New York and never come back."

The adults in the room shared uneasy glances. Charlie gave Vera a communicative look. "I wonder how Sidney found out."

"Found out what?" Luke and Reg said in timely unison.

Vera looked pained as she glanced between the two men. "Kids why don't you go up and play on Zach's computer. We'll sort this all out. We always do," she attempted to reassure them and they reluctantly obliged her going toward the back staircase. Vera raised her faint eyebrows knowing it was a favored place to eavesdrop. "The front way please," she told them pointedly and followed them out to ensure they went all the way up. She returned to the front room and spoke softly. "Kathleen deliberately went off her lithium to bring Sidney back home. Obviously Sidney has found out."

Luke put a hand to his forehead in shock as Reg groaned and sat down. Just as Luke opened his mouth to speak, the front door burst open. Reg's huge frame tensed at the sight of his partner charging through the door. "Don? What the hell..."

"Where's Sidney?" he demanded urgently searching the room.

"We aren't entirely sure. Why?" Reg asked with caution.

Don ignored everyone else in the room and turned singularly to Reg. "Did you tell her about Rauja yet?"

"No I didn't want to say anything over the phone. Something was wrong as it was."

Tension emanated from the other man's shorter stockier build. "There's a lot more wrong than either you or I suspected."

"What the hell are you two talking about?" Luke demanded furiously.

Don glanced over at Reg and then back to Luke. "I had an autopsy done on Rauja. Mostly out of curiosity and to give Sidney some peace of mind over why he died."

Something gripped Luke's insides. "And?"

"He had ingested a common poison for killing rodents."

Luke frowned in puzzlement. "So? Isn't that possible?"

"Not in our apartment. Sid doesn't keep anything like that since she got pregnant with Lily. Our place is completely child proofed." Reg contended.

"What about Mrs. Gilpen though, the old lady…"

Don held up a finger of agreement. "That's what I thought and dismissed the whole thing. I didn't say anything to Sid thinking it would only upset her but then Reg reminded me that it was highly unlikely that Mrs. Gilpen had anything like that either."

Luke made a scoffing sound. "You would be surprised what some gentle old ladies have under their sinks!"

Reg shook his head with certainty. "Not this one. Sidney checked her out thoroughly as a potential care giver for our baby when she arrived. She had a whole list. Mrs. Gilpen passed with flying colors."

"But the coffee cinched it," Don added grimly.

Reg's eyes snapped to his partner. "There was something in that disgusting cup other than mold."

Don nodded. "Enough poison to kill a woman Sidney's height and weight before she could get to hospital."

Reg blanched. "Fuck."

"A regular Charlie Foxtrot," Don agreed and Charlie snorted.

Vera's eyes snagged his. "What's that?"

Charlie looked slightly disconcerted. "Ahhh…I'll tell you later Darlin."

"You'll tell me now if it has anything to do with our daughter," she implored emphatically.

Confusion claimed Don's features. "You two have a kid?"

"Sidney!" four voices said together.

"Oh!" Don replied bewildered.

"Long story, Don. We'll cover it later. First, Luke, what do you know about a full mug of coffee that was sitting on the hall shelf. Stuck at the back."

Luke frowned for a second before his eyes sharpened. "I poured it for Sid one of the mornings you were in the hospital."

Reg let out an agonized breath. "She didn't drink much…"

The moment came flooding back. "She didn't drink any. The phone rang when she put it to her lips and she set it down. I followed her with it so she could drink it while it was still hot but she had gone into the bedroom and was lying on the bed."

"So?"

Luke looked at Reg meaningfully. "I took one glance at her lying on your bed chatting with Vera and I couldn't stand to set foot in there. I shoved the mug on the shelf and forgot about it."

"Where did you get the cream?" Don questioned sharply.

Reg frowned. "I hadn't been shopping…"

"We brought from here. It was packed in a cooler along with a few other things."

Don shot a suspicious glance about the room. "Who packed it?"

"I did," Delta volleyed defensively from the kitchen doorway.

Vera shook her head. "No, Delta. We all did."

"Who's *we*, Vera?" Don asked urgently.

"The women of the house. Remember, Luke… Charlie… Sidney was distraught…" Vera gasped at what she was revealing but it was too late.

"About me?" Reg asked.

Charlie and Luke stalled momentarily, regarding one another hesitantly.

"Answer me, Sheriff," Reg bit out irritably.

"Sidney had misplaced her engagement ring and was frantic to find it," Luke ultimately informed him regretfully.

Reg shelved the blow to his ego with an effort. "You didn't drink any of the cream?"

Luke shook his head. "I take my coffee black."

Don's eyes were sharp. "Who knows that?"

Luke shrugged. "A lot of people."

"Everyone in this house?" he prodded meaningfully.

Luke's expression was a mixture of offense and gnawing fear. "Yes. But…"

Charlie's head jerked to Luke's. "The cause of yesterday's fire hasn't been determined…"

"What fire?" Reg asked, feeling a horrible uneasiness.

"My mother's house burned to the ground. Sidney had just been there."

Vera's chin trembled as she grasped Luke's shirt like a life line. "And we almost lost you because you thought she was inside."

Charlie swallowed hard as he recalled Jack, singed, his lungs clogged by smoke. He had saved his own son without a clue.

Don spun toward Reg. "This smells worse than a floater from the fall who's found in the spring. We have to find Sidney now!"

Luke stared at their concurrent concern. "You really believe someone who has access to this house…"

Don raised skeptical brows. "Someone who lives here even," he asserted coolly.

Vera wailed horrified. "No! No! That can't be!"

"Mrs. McCorkidale, it can be!" Don insisted adamantly. He turned swiftly to face Sidney's husband. "Your daughter died in this house…"

"She did," a grim voice repeated from the front hall. The entire group lurched about to see Frank Barrett standing disconcerted just inside the front door.

Luke strode forward. His gaze fixed on a sheaf of papers clutched in the coroner's grip. "Natalie's autopsy?" he demanded curtly yanking them from the other man's grip. His face hardened with a mixture of horror and rage.

"It can't be entirely conclusive after all this time…" Frank Barrett began to warn.

"Sounds pretty fucking conclusive to me!" Luke shouted goggling at the report that detailed fiber matches and clinical findings substantiating the cause of death.

"What!" Reg yelled as terror vaulted through his large body.

"Someone suffocated our daughter with that bloody teddy bear my mother insisted she be buried with!" Luke ground out through his clenched jaw. *"Where the hell is Sidney?"*

"Looking for me!" Zachary shouted out waving a piece of paper. "Or at least that's what this says. Nic and I found it on my computer and printed it off."

Reg grabbed the paper from the boy's hands and quickly scanned before thrusting it toward Luke. "You didn't write that, Zach?"

Zach vehemently shook his head. "I don't know what that note is talking about. I'm not mad at Aunt Sid…"

"Nicole, did you…" Luke called loudly.

"No," Nicole confirmed edging in from the front foyer. "We just found it on Zach's computer now. Whoever wrote it must not know he has autosave."

Several cops shared charged glances. "Or maybe they do," Don asserted quietly. "Where the hell is this *thinking place*?" he asked roughly but two men were already running down the front steps. They knew.

Charlie was hot on their heels knowing Vera was frantic by his side as a peculiar thought flew into his head. A seven letter word for what some couples do after divorce: *remarry.* The corresponding word in the puzzle was a six letter word for a nefarious event: **murder.**

"Sidney! Move out farther onto the bridge!" Kathleen hissed in a low voice.

Sidney's lower jaw trembled violently. "I can't!" she sobbed weakly clutching either side of the rope bridge in a white knuckled grip. Her eyes were transfixed on the menacing barrel of the gun that gleamed with deceptive brilliance in the midday sun.

"Do it, Sid! Now!" she shouted urgently.

Sidney shuttered and glanced downward through the slats of the swing bridge. The creek's current was gentle and almost cruelly soothing. It vaguely occurred to her that it had been moving much faster the last time she had been on this bridge looking for her nephew. It was spring then and the water was high...

"Move back!" the shrill female voice implored menacingly. The glittering barrel jerked indicating the desired direction of movement.

"I can't!" she stammered brokenly as her entire body quaked. "I hate bridges. *This* bridge in particular. You know that. Let's just go somewhere else so we can talk...."

"I'm done talking!" her furiously deranged voice spewed. "You should have stayed in New York. That was the plan! You were supposed to stay in fucking New York!"

Sidney felt terror assail her senses as she stood horrified by the woman before her. They had known one another most of their lives. Now it was abundantly clear, she had never known her at all. "There was a plan?" she stammered in confusion.

The other woman's features contorted as she tipped her head back in hysterical laughter. "Of course! Virginia concocted her plan methodically from the moment she learned of your freaking pregnancy with her son's child. Right down to when it would happen. She wanted you to have a good year to really get to know who you would lose."

Sidney's trembling increased drastically as horror swept through her unmercifully. This woman who had always appeared so harmless...so benign...suddenly exuded a dangerous aura. Her forehead furrowed as hypotheses flitted recklessly through her mind. Her head shot up to skewer her assailant with her eyes. The gun had instantaneously become inconsequential. Her mouth opened wide in profuse horror as the sickening reality hit her like a bolder. "Natalie...didn't die of crib death," she stated in carefully spaced words.

A vicious smile illuminated Carlene's otherwise plain features. Her free hand patted the hand that kept the gun trained on her intended victim. "Bravo Sidney! It only took you almost a dozen years to figure it out. Virginia planned it brilliantly but insisting on sealing Natalie in a crypt instead of burying her turned out to be a real glitch. She didn't really like mausoleums either but she went through with buying those tombs just to punish you further for stealing her son. She knew that it broke your heart just a little bit more to think of your baby there for eternity. She certainly never counted on you exhuming her. God knows, you can talk Luke into anything, he is so fucking bewitched by you!" she sneered in disgust. "But Virginia would like today! She would positively love that this is Charlie's gun. The one that is kept locked in Vera's bedroom closet where she indulges in sin. The handcuffs on Kathleen are his too." She laughed diabolically pointing to where Sidney's sister yanked helplessly against the end rail of the bridge she was attached to.

"Sidney! Get out farther onto the bridge!" Kathleen shouted frantically.

"Shut up!" Carlene spat waving the gun dramatically in her sister's general direction. "Dammit, you are impatient to die! First, I have to take care of this bitch. One at a time, ladies. Too bad your *Auntie* isn't around. This would make a terrific climax for one of her trashy books. One deranged sister murdering the other over unrequited love and then tragically turning the gun on herself."

Sidney listened intently to the exchange between the two women. One crazy and lethal before her; one frantic and protective behind her. Gingerly she inched backward farther onto the bridge. She was starting to see the desperate need to formulate an immediate plan. It was unlikely anyone else would be appearing to save them. No one knew she was coming here so she likely wouldn't be missed for some time. Reg still wasn't due for hours. Her heart clenched to think that his worst nightmare would see fruition. He would finally be too late to save her.

Sidney swallowed hard as the bridge swayed slightly under her feet but regardless she edged farther onto it. She was beginning to appreciate her sister's dictate. The deepest water was in the center if she were to fall in the creek this time of year. Self preservation and dormant vestiges of motherhood suddenly directed her strategy.

She forced her features into a calm passive expression. "Carlene, you can have what you want without hurting either of us. We're *old* friends. We can sit down and sort this out. Let's go over to the bank and Kathleen can wait across the bridge until we figure this out."

· A purely evil light gleamed in Carlene's eyes as she laughed heartily at Sidney's suggestion. "You stole what I want. You did years ago and just when things began to look promising you came back to do it again. God, you would think the death of your baby would have been enough but now I will have to kill another child and your sister. I honestly regret that. You however, it will be a pleasure to shoot. I've hated you thoroughly since your wedding night."

Sidney went whey-faced. "My wedding night?"

"'You don't think anyone heard, do you?' You simpering twit! *I heard it all.* I was listening from the little room that you eventually made into little

Natalie's bedroom." She thrust out a rigid accusatory digit. "That finally convinced me to go along with Virginia's plan. You moving the baby out of your bedroom so she wouldn't interrupt your carnal pleasures. You spent too much time reading that smut your stupid *aunt* cranks out."

Sidney was temporarily stunned. "Virginia killed her own granddaughter?"

Carlene gave her an inane look and snorted in disbelief at her stupidity. "She would have liked to but she couldn't enter that den of perversity for obvious reasons. Vera destroyed the sanctity of Virginia's marriage to the love of her life. She honored me by asking that I act in her stead."

Sidney stumbled backward in sheer unadulterated shock. She vaguely heard Kathleen encouraging her to keep going... to move farther... faster. "You? How?" she squeaked out.

A demonic smile curved her thin lips. "The large white teddy bear that Virginia gave Natalie when she was born. It was a very special gift with a very specific purpose. Natalie was sound asleep on her back clutching that stupid blanky. I watched her for a moment almost regretting what had to be done but Luke's mother was right. I was merely ending her miserable life before she followed in her mother's footsteps of ruining good men with uncontrollable lust. Natalie was amazingly strong for a one year old..." she sneered contemptuously. "Oh that's right! She never lived to see that special birthday party you were planning for her." Carlene smiled wickedly and began humming the theme from Winnie the Pooh.

Sidney felt herself go numb with pain at the cruel recitation of her baby's murder. She struggled outwardly to show nothing knowing it would only further endanger them. The three precious lives she knew she must protect or die trying.

"Virginia Ryan was a very conniving woman, Carlene. I'm sure she had you convinced you were acting properly under the circumstances. I hate what happened but sadly none of us can alter the past," she lied nervously. "Let's fix things now," she entreated softly. "I will go back to New York with Reg. The divorce is final in only a short time. Luke has told me many times how much he admires you. He hasn't approached you simply out of respect."

Carlene regarded her warily but Sidney could see some faint hope inflect her demented gaze.

"Yes, really. Luke, of course, was still legally married to me and didn't know how to get out of it without looking utterly ridiculous because we hadn't spoken in years. You know men never want to look less than absolutely capable, especially the town sheriff. The two of you can rebuild the house on the hill. The blue prints are still on file in the town hall." Sidney could feel the panic bubbling up and prayed it didn't show.

A brittle look claimed Carlene's eyes sending a chill dancing down Sidney's spine. It was compounded a thousand fold when two male figures soundlessly appeared on the bank behind Carlene. Both held drawn guns trained on the back of the young woman, who was oblivious to them. Their combined gaze found hers and held, imploring her to act with utmost caution. She thought her heart might thud out of her chest and bit down on the inside of her bottom lip to keep from crying out. Tears shimmered in her large brown eyes as her heart took a picture of the two men she loved most in the world and neither of whose arms she could ever dare hope would hold her close again.

"Sounds delightful," was Carlene's biting reply. "I would love nothing better than to rebuild that glorious mansion on the hill that overlooks the rift raft of this town, which of course as the Sheriff's wife I would insist he clean out the worst offenders and make them live elsewhere. Starting with your whorish mother and those two brats of Kathleen's she will be stuck with after today."

Sidney stared. "My mother is dead," she said quietly, realizing with growing trepidation just how insane Carlene was.

Carlene laughed satanically, thoroughly enjoying the control she wielded over this bitch. "She'll likely want to be once her precious Sidney is gone. If I have to spend one more afternoon listening to her lament your absence..."

Sidney was shaking her head in frantic confusion. "You'll be too busy as Luke's wife. He's very attentive..."

Carlene's face froze. "You would know, wouldn't you? That's why none of this can ever happen. You *slut!*" she jeered thrusting Sidney another step further out on the swaying bridge.

Sidney felt sweat drip from her neck to trickle between the valley of her breasts that were heaving with fear and ragged breathing. She summoned her best poker face in desperation. "Nothing's happened between Luke and I for years...."

"*Liar!*" Carlen shouted uncontrollably as she bore down on her intended prey. The gun was directed at her heart and then lowered to her belly. "You are pregnant with his baby! *Again!*"

Sidney blanched and instinctively put a protective hand to the slight rounding of her womb. "No! The baby isn't Luke's! It's Reg's child! I swear it, Carlene! The baby is Reg's! I conceived at the Inn," she cried brokenly. In her fear for her unborn infant, Sidney's hands left the rope bridge altogether. One hand remained solidly covering her lower abdomen while the other made a frantic appeal to a woman who was beyond reason. Her eyes flickered briefly to the two men, who stood ram rod stiff on the bank facing her. Their shell shocked expressions were more terrifying than the insane woman confronting her.

Carlene jeered contemptibly. "It's *his* all right."

"Reg will take me back to New York. We'll never come back to Barren's Creek again. I swear it! In fact, I can convince Vera and Kathleen to do the same. You'll have Luke all to yourself. You can have babies of your own," Sidney promised emphatically in desperate tones.

Carlene began to bear down on her ominously. "It's too late! You and this baby must die…"

Sidney rapidly cast a glance at the slow moving water beneath her and the savage face of her foe. A woman so evil as to murder a sleeping baby in her crib. *Her baby.* She took another step backward in an attempt to look cowed before her assailant. "Natalie said a few words. Did she say anything before you killed her?" she asked loudly and purposefully so that if she were silenced forever Luke would finally know the truth about their baby's death.

Carlene was momentarily taken aback by her question, but put her victim's bizarre query down to hormones. She deigned to answer anyway in the same spirit that someone who is about to be put to death is given an obliging last meal as well as for the sheer malicious pleasure. "Natalie fought the stuffed bear I pressed against her face. Once she almost knocked it out of my grasp. Fucking strong little bitch! In the second the plush toy was off her face, she cried for her mama." Carlene made a little sound of disgust. "I smothered her cry of course."

Hot bitter tears poured down her cheeks as she listened to the horrendous last moments of her baby's life. Sidney felt her heart splinter but she forced herself to follow through with her chancy plan rather than rip out the throat of her baby's killer as she longed to do, knowing she would die trying. Chanting a silent prayer, she sprang over the side of the rope bridge with stunning self preserving agility to plunge into the water below. The ringing in her ears was as shocking as the burning in her shoulder as she fell. In what Sidney presumed would be her last conscious thought, she pledged her undying love to a man who would never hear it now and perhaps not believe it anyway.

Two shots rang out as a distraught man hoarsely screamed her name. His voice was the last thing she heard thing she heard before she plunged into the water with pain ripping unmercifully through her. Blackness swallowed her up and Sidney prayed she would awaken to see her daughters that would never grow up.

Another splash made wide reaching ripples in the water. One woman fell to her knees and sobbed hysterically on one side of the foot bridge while another fought the cuffs that held her to it. Two men skidded recklessly down the steep bank that ended at the wide creek where Carl and Jack were already in the water.

Frank Barrett made a cursory examination of the first woman hauled from the water. "She's gone. There's just nothing I can do. The water was too shallow. Her neck's broken."

Luke's brain was numb with fear as he heard the words. He stared past where the coroner stood. Carl was surging out of the water with her still figure in his arms. She was chalk white except for the blood that dripped from her, coloring the water. His heart shriveled as he waded in powerful strides to take her. If she was going to die, she would do it in his arms.

CHAPTER THIRTY

Her eyes were so heavy. The lids seemed impossible to open. Stabbing pain made her grimace. A gentle hand was stroking her cheek. Brown eyes finally fluttered open to see him gazing down at him with untold concern. She tried to smile but a tear leaked out instead and he wiped it away with the pad of his thumb.

"I'm so sorry," she whispered despondently.

"Shhh. Don't try and talk. It's too soon," his voice murmured soothingly. "You are barely out of surgery. You took a bullet in your shoulder."

Her breath caught as her hand automatically flew to her womb. "My… my baby!" she wailed brokenly as tears brimmed in enormous fearful eyes.

A larger stronger hand covered hers over the curve of her lower belly holding it there. "Is fine, Sidney," he promised yet he could see the doubt linger. "I promise you, Sidney. An obstetrician examined you. The baby is in no danger. They did an ultrasound before and after surgery." He gave her a deliberately admonishing glance and stabbed a finger out authoritatively. "Have I ever broken a promise to you?"

She glanced away in shame. "No, but I have to you. You know that now. I'm so sorry. I never… never meant to hurt you… I *do* love you. *Please believe that.* I just love him…"

"More," he finished for her in sad resigned tones.

She closed her eyes in anguish for a second before speaking. "Differently. I love you both in different ways. It took a long time for me to see that… to accept it and what it meant. Knowing how badly it would hurt you," she lamented softly.

"Yes," he admitted in stark tones. "But watching that insane bitch hold a gun on you on that damned bridge, I learned I would rather have you alive and bearing another man's child than dead pledged to me."

Her composure slipped completely and he leaned down to gently gather her against him for what would likely be the last time. His own tears made tracks down his cheeks as they clung to each other for all that they had shared, for what was ending, and for what was beginning.

After a long time, he eased her back down onto the bed and tried to bestow a reassuring smile on her with only partial success. "Don't be sad, Sidney, when you think of me. Of us. No matter what else happens in my life I will always cherish the moments and memories we made together."

She tried to return his brave smile but it flip flopped in the making.

"Where will you go?" she whispered.

"To work." He held up a conciliatory hand at the instant panic he saw inflect her eyes. "I'll be careful," he pledged.

She sniffed back her tears knowing they wouldn't help lessen his pain. "We have some things..."

He nodded. "To work out. Kathleen has offered to assist with that. It'll be fine. You'll see," he tried to reassure her but his tone barely sounded convincing to his own ears. He bent over her to kiss her lips and dwelled there for a long moment as if trying to memorize every inch of her. He finally traced her trembling lips with his finger. "I have to go. I'm not the only one who has been waiting for you to wake up." His hand fell away from her face and traveled the length of her as he moved toward the door.

She stared at his back as he left the room and her life knowing there were no longer any other options for either of them. Silent tears slid down her pale face as another man slipped in the door.

"We have to talk," one grim faced man said staring intently into the face of an equally grave man. "Down there." He jerked his thumb to the stairwell.

The other man held his gaze with some difficulty. He knew the tremendous pain this man was tackling. Guilt shot through him. He now had what every lucky man dreams of and this man was hopelessly alone.

Sidney glanced up at the man who stood in the door of her hospital room. Tears welled as she glanced away in disgrace. "You must hate me."

He sighed and sat down on the edge of the bed. "How could I hate you? You have been my friend for years..."

"I've hurt him so incredibly..."

"You also loved him the same way. He won't forget that or regret it."

Tears fell unchecked onto cheeks that were still terribly pale. She laughed sarcastically through her soft crying. "Don't be too sure! Give him some time to reflect on my actions..."

"You are wrong, Sidney. You showed him parts of himself he never would have found otherwise," the man stubbornly contended. "Don't forget I knew him before you."

"And you'll know him after me," she stated with great remorse. "I know it sounds stupid maybe even callous, but I will miss him so..." she broke off, folded her lips together and struggled for control.

The man gingerly pulled her against him, wondering which wound hurt her more. The one requiring surgery or the crack in her heart. "This isn't easy for anyone."

She swiped at her wet cheeks with her good arm trying to get a hold of herself. She stared into his kind gaze with teeming emotion. "Take care of him for me. I'm so worried he won't be thinking straight and something…"

"I'll be vigilant, Sidney. I care about the big lug too."

She nodded as her crying renewed itself. "I know."

He held her at arm's length for a second battling his own emotions. "It may be a long while before we see each other again…"

Maybe forever, she thought dismally.

"You take good care of yourself and this baby…" he told her sternly.

"I will. I'll have help."

He smiled ruefully. "I know. I've seen your help. He's been pacing for hours."

She stared wide eyed not knowing what to reply.

With a last squeeze to her hand, he got up and went to the door. "I'm going to go tell him he can come in. He has waited long enough," he declared oddly stressing his last few words. "Damn, I'm going to miss having you around. No one makes brownies like you do."

Sidney pursed her lips in a tight smile. As the door closed behind him, she covered her face in her hands and wept. She wasn't sure she could ever stop. That she would even know how. This entire day had turned her inside out. She had fought with just about everyone who loved her during the course of it. Went to search for a little boy that she feared she had disillusioned and found her daughter's murderer instead. She could still feel the gentle swaying of the swing bridge beneath her feet unbalancing her. Still see the stunned faces of the two men she loved as they learned of the baby she was carrying…

"In the words of a great man, my arms are empty but I think if you'd let me I could help you with those tears."

She froze at the sound of his deep voice. It sounded so stark in the sterile hospital room. Her sobs caught in her throat and hung there suspended. His voice was so close. She hadn't even heard the door. Slowly she lowered her hands from her face and stared into his intent unsmiling face. His mouth was set in a grim line and his whole body vibrated with barely leashed emotion. Their gaze held in absolute silence for a long minute before she realized he wanted permission to come any closer.

Her tongue flicked over her lips uncertainly. Her stomach was jumping like an entire pond of frogs. She had no illusions about her situation. It would take a tremendous amount of faith for him to believe that she actually knew the parentage of this baby. That it was his.

She finally said the only words she could. "I love you."

He reached her with stunning speed then and crushed her against his chest with incredible care for her bandaged shoulder. "Oh God, Sid…" he moaned into her neck where his face was buried. "When I saw you jump from that bridge…"

Her hands abruptly pushed him away so that she could see his face. Her eyes were wide with panic as she stared into his startled ones. "Carlene? What happened…"

He nodded as he spoke thinking she would need to see his answer as well as hear it to really believe. "She's dead."

Her eyes flickered with concentration. "You shot her?"

"Yes. Unfortunately, not before she shot you. The wound from the bullet wasn't fatal but her fall was. She wasn't far enough out on the bridge. The water was too shallow." Thank God. The mere thought of enduring a murder trial was excruciating. "I'm so sorry I couldn't protect you… protect Natalie…"

Sidney's eyes narrowed as she tried to grapple the meaning of his words. "Who could have ever guessed that Virginia was so evil or Carlene so demented…"

"Natalie paid an incredible price," he choked out in a tight agonized voice.

Sidney searched his eyes and saw the shattering sorrow overflowing there. It mirrored her own. She reached for his hand that rested on the edge of the bed and threaded her fingers through his. He seemed lost in her eyes and she wondered what he saw there. If it helped his pain. Slowly she leaned toward him and ever so gently pressed her lips to his chest over his heart. She could almost hear his pulse quicken and felt his breath still above her.

"What are you doing?" he asked quietly; knowing but needing to hear it.

She slanted her eyes upward without moving her head. "Kissing it better."

He closed his eyes and groaned as a great deal of his tension left him in a rush. His eyes were still closed when she brushed her lips against his in a feather light caress. His upper lip quirked upward as he spoke into her mouth. "I wasn't hurt there," he told her softly enjoying her method of comfort.

She laid a hand against his cheek and waited until his eyes fluttered open to meet hers. "Referral pain. Any time you are willing, you might return the favor…"

A growl of satisfaction came from his throat. She was asking for comfort. From him. Lean hands gently framed her oval face as his mouth captured hers in a tender kiss that searched and found what he had waited years to reclaim.

One of his hands fell away to drop to her lower abdomen and splayed over the slight curve there. "Our child is beautiful."

Awe glazed her dark brown eyes. "*You saw the baby?*" she breathed begging for more.

"The doctor let me watch the ultrasound." Though he hadn't given the man many options. "The baby didn't stay still a single second…"

She laughed breathlessly in roiling relief. "This baby moves quite a lot," Sidney acknowledged dreamily.

His lips parted in surprise. "You have felt the baby move already?"

She nodded guiltily and suddenly laid her hand over his pressing it down. "Feel that."

His mouth opened wide in astonishment and his eyes closed as his lips formed a wistful smile in awe of the miracle stirring in her womb beneath his hand. "God… I love you."

She gave him a tremulous smile. "I've kind of been counting on that," she admitted almost shyly.

His eyes narrowed meaningfully and his hand caught her chin so their eyes collided. "Count on it forever, Sweetheart. I plan on making you my wife…."

"I am…"

He shook his head before she could finish. "I want the ceremony. The whole thing… the church… before our friends and family…" His voice lowered huskily. "The honeymoon."

"That too?" she asked starry eyed.

"That too," he promised with a sensual smile and sealed the resolution with a mind numbing kiss. She shuddered in his arms and he withdrew hastily. "Are you in pain?"

She shook her head silently. "My shoulder hurts but as for the pain that really matters….no. For the first time in a long time. No. Even learning the truth about Natalie….it will take a long time to accept but at least it is finally closure of some kind. I felt closure with Lily's loss but never with Natalie's. It never made sense to me until today."

He sobered as his eyes became shrouded with sorrow. "I'm not sure it will ever make sense to me. I was thinking while you were in surgery maybe it is time to talk to someone…"

"A professional?"

He tipped his head. "Yes."

She knew just the person. "Can I come along?"

He smiled and rubbed his knuckles lightly across her soft cheek. "I was kind of counting on that."

She smiled as their heads tipped until foreheads touched.

"As much as I hate to share you, I think we should let your parents come in. They have been waiting a long time."

She interrupted him in rampant confusion. "I don't have parents. You know that."

He smiled broadly. "Oh yes you do, Sweetheart," he contended staunchly and went to the door. He made a wordless gesture and moved to one side.

Vera appeared in the doorway immediately. Her eyes were wide, red rimmed and searching. Her gaze locked on the young woman in the bed and she let out a glad cry.

Sidney's eyes narrowed seeing an older version of her reflection before her and then jolted wide as the dawning came. Some of Carlene's statements that had seemed demented at the time came rushing back. "*You are my mother?*" she asked stunned. Her mouth remained open in shock as Vera nodded teary eyed. "Kathleen?"

"Is your cousin, my sister's child. We decided to raise you as sisters. It was the only solution that made sense under the circumstances to keep you safe." Vera's lips quivered. "But I didn't keep you safe..." she continued brokenly. "Virginia still found a way to hurt you and your precious baby..."

Sidney was shaking her head in her profound conundrum. "Why would Virginia hate me so much that you feared for me even as an infant..."

A tall broad shouldered man suddenly materialized to stand directly behind her mother. The earth shaking revelation hit her like a tidal wave. She leaned forward in the bed despite the pain it caused as if the movement might help her make sense out of all of this. "You are *my* Dad... not Luke's."

"I am your father," Charlie confirmed solemnly with pride. He laid a possessive hand on Vera's shoulder. "We're your parents."

"And we love you," Vera croaked through her sobs.

"And we love you," a deeper voice roughened with emotion confirmed from behind her shoulder.

Sidney blinked up at them in subduing shock. Her eyes flickered over to the man who leaned against the wall a few feet away. He smiled warmly at her. His happiness at her new found parents was her undoing. She burst into abrupt tears and three bodies surged toward her. One man held back with an effort. He watched her clutched in the arms of her parents for a long overdue embrace and felt his heart swell at her discovery. Her joy. Some of today's revelations were wonderful.

"Come here."

His eyes refocused as she repeated her request and he saw Vera and Charlie lift their faces to him. "You belong here as much as I do. Join us."

"Yes, Son. Join us," Charlie confirmed.

"I'm not your…" he began thinking it needed to be acknowledged.

"Oh Poppycock," Vera asserted.

"Yeah, poppycock. You are going to marry my daughter, aren't you?" he retorted gruffly. Why bother mentioning that he would bloody well insist upon it if it came to that. He owned a shotgun.

An almost leering smile spread across his face. "I am."

"Get over here then," Charlie commanded roughly.

Arms clutched one another in a reconfiguration of an embrace that felt so wonderfully right. Sidney almost hated to break the moment by speaking but decided this fact they would appreciate beyond all else. "*Mom, Dad*, the baby is moving. Do you want to…"

Two hands eagerly reached out and her eyes glowed as she watched the wonder spread across their faces. Her eyes shifted to his and saw the love in them. Her heart soared knowing at last, she had found home.

The multitude of candles flickered casting shadows against the taupe walls. Clothes were strewn across the thick carpet marking a trail from the door to the large columns of the bed. A silky gown lay in a careless heap on the floor attesting to the haste with which she had been wrestled out of it. Ivory shimmering stockings lay atop men's black dress socks.

A slew of giggles rippled from her as his heated gaze locked on hers. "This is supposed to be very sexy," he confided to her huskily glancing up from her thigh.

"Is it?" The fit of melodious giggles renewed itself. Her dark brown luminous eyes shone with adoration as she locked her eyes on him. "You're tickling me."

His teeth sank into the edge of the frilly blue garter and tugged as he growled low in his throat. He pulled the objectionable ornament down a well muscled curvy thigh and then continued on to her slender calf that his fingers ached to stroke. His actions took on more urgency as his eyes flickered over her enticing body. She was well rounded with his child now and never more lovely. Once he rid them of this last bit of bridal decoration she would be completely nude only bathed in candlelight. His breath grew ragged. It had been a long three months of self imposed celibacy. With dire need impressing upon his willpower, he ripped the garter the last few inches from her delicate barefoot intent on flinging it across the room.

It flew out of his fingers deftly snatched by his exquisite bride. "Oh no you don't! I have a use for that," she declared impishly.

"Do you?" One eyebrow jutted upward suggestively.

"Oh yes," she promised silkily. "Come to bed and I'll show you."

He groaned dramatically as he swung her in his arms to stride directly to the large bed. "Now that's an invitation!"

She framed his lean fiercely handsome face in gentle hands. "And one that has been issued a number of times over the past few months with no positive replies."

His breath caught in his throat as he laid her tenderly on the snowy sheets. "I wanted to court you properly. Charlie approved."

"Perhaps but my mother constantly offered her sympathies," she teased lightly.

Amazement flashed in his eyes.

"You're shocked."

"Well…"

"Just because my mother has tamed her fashion trends and cosmetic use doesn't mean she has forgotten what truly pleases a woman. And besides she is a new bride herself," Sidney reminded her bridegroom smoothly.

He leaned over her with a provocative gleam in his eyes and braced himself with an arm on either side of her, exuding a powerful mixture of masculine vitality and sensuality. "Did she pass along any secrets?"

Sidney burst into another brief fit of giggles before quieting to give him a sultry smile. "Do I need any?"

His eyes deliberately raked over her unclothed body in a slow heated perusal. "Not a one. You are all I will ever need. I have known that forever," he vowed.

She pursed her lips suddenly to stem the onslaught of emotion she wanted to put down to hormones but knew better. "Don't make me wait any longer…" Sidney told him in a choked voice.

He inhaled deeply and lowered his head to kiss her lips with tender thoroughness. The garter slipped from her hand as she gripped the back of his corded neck to hold him against her. A small sound of pleasure escaped her before his attentions became all consuming and two sets of hands were busily make bold passes.

"Now," she pleaded.

"Not yet. I want to make this last…"

"We'll do it again…."

"Sweetheart, I'm older now…"

"I'll prove you're not…"

"I'll hold you to it…"

A sigh escaped her as the world began to slide away into an incredible splintering of light where speaking was impossible and utterly unnecessary. Love was doing all the talking.

She sighed contentedly as she nestled closer to his warm frame and his arm tightened about her. "You should be tired," he murmured in her ear huskily.

"One more time ought to do it," she returned silkily.

His delighted chuckle tickled the tendrils of hair near her ear as his teeth lightly nibbled the edge. "I think marriage agrees with my wife."

"I know marriage agrees with your wife."

An easy silence passed and he wondered whether he ought to reluctantly rise to douse the candles before one of them drifted off. He rose over her first with a thoughtful expression. Candlelight would be advantageous when she answered. "You missed him today."

She blinked up at him in surprise at his direct statement. "That wasn't a question. Am I required to answer?"

"I don't want there to be any secrets between us, even painful ones. No, especially painful ones," he lamented.

Deep brown eyes reflected her astute perception of his need and she took a deep breath. "I think we can end our therapy sessions. You have taken over the role of counselor," she teased faintly.

He cupped her cheek lovingly. "Sidney, I understand why you would miss him. I only knew him for a number of months…"

"He was my best friend and one I have no right to anymore."

"Maybe someday."

She shook her head sadly. "How could that ever be possible?"

"I could deal with it. I know where you are going to park your bathrobe for the next seventy years or so and whose child was making your belly dance a few minutes ago."

Her eyes narrowed and she swallowed hard, reluctant to say what was on her mind and had been for months. "Do you?" she asked bluntly peering into his eyes.

"Yes," he stated flatly. "I knew the second Carlene said there *was* a baby while holding that damned gun on you that it was ours. *Mine.*"

Her eyes welled with tears. "How could you be sure?"

"*Because I know you.*"

She stared up at him and saw the sincerity in his face and smiled.

"Say you believe me, Sidney. I need to hear it," he asked her gravely. Their gaze was riveted to each other and the charge between them electric.

"I believe you, Luke."

"Good, but now I need to tell you that before Reg left, he gallantly took me aside and told me unequivocally that the baby was mine." Sidney gasped. "I didn't need to hear it but he needed to say it. He didn't want there to be anything further marring your happiness."

A tear trickled down her cheek. "I never deserved him."

He regarded her with a consoling smile. "Sidney, I rarely discuss my bank account. I really don't like to put a lot of emphasis on it for reasons you well understand but for all my wealth, I owe that man a debt I simply can never repay."

Silent tears traced down her beautiful oval face. "He wouldn't expect you to."

Her husband stroked away the tears with the pads of his thumbs. "Anymore than he would want you to say that you didn't deserve him. Perhaps someday the two of you can sort…"

Her brown eyes shone. "It would be dreadfully unfair…"

"Wouldn't that be for him to decide?" Luke interrupted to counter her point.

She frowned now and her eyes took on a glimmer of defiance. "Would it be enough for you if the situation were reversed?"

He maintained her intense gaze steadfastly. "You and I were friends long before we were anything else. If it were all I could have, I think I would want to try."

She raised her elegant brows unconvinced. "I don't want to argue with you tonight of all nights and over the past few months we have certainly proven we are good at it."

A slow smile graced his sensual lips. "Are we?"

She growled softly. "We are both strong willed and stubborn. Just consider the fight we had over setting today's date."

He chuckled with agreement. "There was that. A number of people thought I needed to have my head examined." Sidney had been undeniably furious when he proposed they wait three months to marry. Her animosity had piqued when he declared he wanted to refrain from being intimate until their wedding night so that they could have a more typical courting. He smothered a smile recalling the small object she had hurled at him just grazing his ear when he insisted on his plans.

"What they thought was that you were crazier than Kathleen off her meds!" she scoffed mildly. "And that garden shed of yours that you have painstakingly repainted in all colors of the rainbow hasn't helped convince anyone otherwise either."

"It still makes you smile," Luke contended twirling a lock of her hair around his finger. "As to the other issue at hand, I wanted there to be a clean break from the divorce so that today would be a fresh beginning and we would have some time to date without the intense circumstances of the past months when you first came home."

"It was a good idea," she said in a bare whisper.

His mouth formed a silent O as his shoulders shook with amused satisfaction. "What was that, Sweetheart?" he asked cupping a hand cockily behind his ear.

She laughed softly. "You heard me and incidentally if I haven't made it crystal clear in this room tonight and I have reason to believe I have…."

"Yes…" he rasped.

"You make me beyond happy."

Hazel eyes teemed with heartfelt emotion. "Just what is beyond happy exactly?"

"Everything!" she vowed with a spell binding intensity that made him tremble.

"I *love* everything," he breathed and swooped down to capture her mouth in a lazy exploration of her lips that promised to go on until neither of them could stand more. Desire poured through him with shocking speed that he tried to purposely dampen. Being seven months pregnant on their wedding day had to be exhausting. His eyes bulged out of their sockets when her cool hand boldly gripped a part of his anatomy that was searing hot. Her other hand soon joined the intimate exploration. He glanced between their bodies with an effort to see past the bulge that was their child and his eyes widened to see her fingers deftly twirling the long forgotten garter. "Sidney Ryan, what are you up to?" he asked warily.

She ran her tongue over her lips provocatively. "You'll see but incidentally, I prefer *Mrs.* Ryan."

His hips bucked slightly in reaction to her fondling and his mouth was incredibly dry. "So do I, *Mrs.* Ryan," he groaned. "More, Sweetheart. Whatever your intentions are… more."

"More is definitely on the menu. It's part of *everything*," she promised and then much to her husband's delight, delivered.

* * *